Peter Chapman was born in London in 1971. He was educated at Coopers' Coborn School and is a graduate of Exeter University. He attended Sandhurst and was subsequently commissioned into the Royal Artillery, in which he served operational tours in Cyprus and Kosovo. He left the Army in 2001, and now lives and teaches in Devon.

Peter Chapman

The 65th

Peter Chapman
Blundell's Road
Tiverton
Devon
EX16 4DP

ISBN 978 0956139 412

British Library Cataloguing in Publication Data.
A catalogue record for this book is available from the British Library.

Typeset in 12pt Bembo by Troubador Publishing Ltd, Leicester, UK
Production management by Matador
Printed by TJ International Ltd, Padstow, Cornwall

For my father, Ian Chapman

ONE

The waves would hit the coast at first light. The waves would be clean and powerful. The best waves of the year.

In the Badlands of North Devon, in the early hours, Charlie Taverner, a blond surfer of thirty-three, sat slouched in front of an old computer monitor. A few taps on a touchpad and he was soon browsing the websites that forecast surfing conditions. Taverner had been frustrated by the lack of decent waves in recent months, but now it looked as if his luck had changed. He had to make sure it was not a false alarm however, because the repercussions, if he did go surfing at sunrise, would be severe. The waves would have to be good enough to compensate for the trouble he would cause.

The Internet was now starting to show its age, and in a bizarre attempt to maintain the flagging interest of web-users, most sites had a ludicrous and unrelated theme to accompany their main purpose. The first site Taverner checked was Big Eddie's Pornstar Wave Modeller, in which Big Eddie suggested there would be 'six feet waves of pure love, baby.' Pancho Grigg's Surf Clichés came up next: 'Check this out, dude! Eight feet of radical stoke! Hang ten, man!' Even the League of Jewish Surfers

(*'Brought to you by Norman Steinberg's Kosher Deli'*) forecast an orthodox five feet and gave it a rating of five Stars of David.

All three websites had a reputation for accuracy, but it was the Lizard's forecast that sealed it for Taverner. The Lizard was another North Devon surfer and a specialist in disinformation and intimidation who hated city-dwellers turning up on good days to crowd his waves with drop-ins and urban competitiveness. In his usual attempt to deter these kooks from making the journey, the Lizard had produced a wholly inaccurate forecast for the day ahead: 'A very flat, very calm sea with barely a ripple, so if you're not local don't bother turning up unless you want your windscreen waxed and your tyres slashed.' Sometimes the Lizard would entice these pretenders from the cities with promises of epic waves when the ocean was genuinely flat, and only the dangerous transit through the lively suburbs from the safety of the Central Zones would offer anything in the way of an adrenaline rush. In earlier times, the Lizard may have faced prosecution under the law of Trade Descriptions; these days, in the Badlands, where the rule of law no longer existed, it didn't matter.

Six feet and clean! It had been a long time since Taverner could remember the surf being that good in North Devon. Surfers were the masters of understatement – 'six feet' was simply a vague adjective that had little connection to the actual height of the waves. Six feet, in reality, meant twelve feet or more in height, or *double-overhead* in surf-speak. He clapped his hands and clenched his fists as he pictured the waves that would soon be his, and on his sofa Flint, his black Labrador, casually opened one eye to see what the fuss was about before going back to sleep.

Taverner dialled a number on his telephone and peered out of the window as he waited for the answer, out into the darkness to the west where the waves would be advancing towards the coast at that very moment.

Two weeks earlier, a monstrous hurricane had developed in the Caribbean and had been christened *Hurricane Chloe* by the people who decided those sorts of things. Like all local surfers, Taverner had followed the progress of Hurricane Chloe to see if it would radiate any swell across the North Atlantic towards Europe. Hurricanes have all the predictability of an out-of-control Dalek, and Chloe had been no exception. She had screamed up the Eastern Seaboard of the United States, veered to the east off the coast of North Carolina, deepened, pottered about in the Atlantic for a while, feigned an uppercut on Massachusetts, roared in towards Newfoundland instead, and then bounced back out to sea to retire exhausted and weakening to the higher Northern Latitudes. It was the swell from Chloe that was about to hit the North Devon coast.

The phone was answered by a voice engravelled by the hour and by years of heavy smoking.

'I might have known it was you.'

'Good morning, Chalky. We're on. Chloe's about to deliver the goods.'

'Chalky' White was a work colleague of Taverner's; an older, laconic man. A sage among the local surfers.

'What exactly?' said Chalky.

Taverner heard a click at the other end, probably a Zippo snapping shut. 'Way better than expected,' he said. 'Six feet at least, and very clean with a light offshore wind.' He let the image linger. 'Tempted?'

Chalky had surfed all the epic swells over the years and

could be forgiven for lacking Taverner's enthusiasm, but it would have been such a waste to miss out on this. However jaded the old boys became, the spark never really went away.

'What the hell, let's go for it. Do the others know?'

'No,' said Taverner. 'I haven't told them, though I'm sure they'll be up for it.'

'I'll give them a call. How are you going to get past the guards?'

'A little plan I've had up my sleeve for a while. It's not particularly subtle, I'll admit.'

'There will be hell to pay.'

'I couldn't care less. You know it'll be worth it. I'll see you at quarter to five.'

Taverner's problem was the presence of the Army's coastal base at Windcheater Island. Or to be more specific, the problem was those who guarded it. To get access to the very best surfing beaches, he and the others would have to get past an extensive security system of armed sentries, CCTV cameras, rolls of razor wire and an electrified fence. The weak spot was the Sentry Post, located on a single road that was the only means of access onto the island. The guards were only human after all, and at five o'clock in the morning they would be tired, lacking in judgement and looking forward to a fry-up and bed. If Taverner could somehow get past the guards, race to the sea and paddle out, he would get a good fill of waves before they captured him.

He lay on his bed opposite a poster showing a surfer tucked inside a perfect tube of the clearest blue water. The expression on the surfer's face was one of immense joy from having every single pleasure zone in his brain stimulated by the experience. Taverner knew that feeling well, and the more he experienced it, the more he craved it.

He catnapped for several hours – too excited to sleep properly – and at half past four he made one further phone call before he went to collect Chalky and the others.

Windcheater Island Sentry Post   4.30 am

Night-time duty in the Armed Forces is known as the 'graveyard shift'. The phrase is said to have originated among wartime munitions workers on the night-shift, and there is an apocryphal story that the phrase was also coined because the night-shift tended to have more fatal accidents compared with their more alert daytime colleagues, either through lack of concentration or the fact that many workers rolled into the armament factories straight from the pub.

Several hours into his graveyard shift, Gunner Moffat of the 65th Regiment Royal Horse Artillery was manning the barrier across the road at the entrance to Windcheater Island. Moffat was from Merseyside, like most soldiers in the 65th. He was tired. Fatigue had crept up on him during his shift, and now there was lethargy in his muscles and a dull ache behind his eyes. By day he was a cheerful and extroverted young soldier; a motormouth who was always chatting away in a rapid-fire Scouse dialect, but the tiredness now rendered him much quieter.

It was mid-September and the air was cool and windless. To the east, the dark sky was already starting to turn a deep blue. At five minutes to six the daytime shift would take over, and Moffat would grab a quick scoff in the NAAFI and return to his room, where he intended to sleep until his beloved Tranmere Rovers won the double.

Nearby, Bombardier Podsnap sat in the Sentry Post, warmed by his tea and by the banks of CCTV screens. One of the screens was showing a vintage episode of *The Magic Roundabout*, a copy of which was doing the rounds. The telephone rang in the Sentry Post and Podsnap answered it.

The 65th was not a happy regiment. As a punishment it had been confined to camp for the past eight weeks by its hated Commanding Officer, Lieutenant Colonel Sandford, a man exasperated with the level of insubordination he encountered from the regiment. Even the soldiers' families were only able to leave the base after submitting the relevant clearance-chit applications one week in advance to civilian authorities who could always be relied upon to efficiently lose the paperwork in a pile of mislaid clearance-chit applications. In its enforced isolation the 65th was turning Windcheater Island into a violent place. Fighting was common in the NAAFI, and the Junior Ranks' Club was disassembled on a weekly basis, which was par for the course at the best of times. Regular ruckus ensued in the Sergeants' Mess, and the ever-trusty grapevine reported that even the residents of the Officers' Mess indulged in a little pugilism from time to time.

The window of the Sentry Post slid open and Bombardier Podsnap called out to Gunner Moffat.

'The Adjutant's just been on the phone,' said Podsnap. 'Operation Safe Haven has just been called. Apparently Colonel Sandford is coming back in. I didn't know he'd been out.'

'Nor did I,' said Moffat. 'I'm sure I saw him in camp last night. Is he signed out on the Movements Log?'

'No. The Adjutant said it was all hush-hush. ETA is about five o'clock.'

Just before five o'clock, Operation 'Safe Haven' swung into action. Gunner Moffat took up position in a fortified sangar next to the road, pressed a button to raise the barrier, and through a small slit observed the road that led towards the town of Holberton. Bombardier Podsnap turned on the floodlights, illuminating the area beyond the Sentry Post. They waited for the Commanding Officer to return.

Terrorist attacks on military vehicles were quite common and nearly always happened at night. The roads in and out of bases were popular ambush spots with the numerous enemies of the Federal British Republic, especially if the vehicle had to stop for any reason. Operation 'Safe Haven' was a night-time procedure to ensure all military vehicles kept moving as they approached and entered their base.

At five o'clock exactly, Moffat heard the vehicle approaching the Sentry Post. It was making a hell of a racket, a sort of vintage whine. He couldn't see any headlights coming down the road towards him, yet still the noise got louder, filling the interior of the sangar. He thought for a moment it might be coming from the sky above. Something wasn't quite right. He was about to reach for the switch to lower the barrier, then realised that the noise was coming from behind him, from *inside* the base, and he scrambled out of the sangar in a hurry.

'Bloody ... fookin' ... 'ell!'

Moffat recognised the Kubelwagen from Second World War films. It was the car the German officers were driven around in, but he had not expected to see one tearing out of the base past the Sentry Post. In the front were two helmeted German soldiers in period uniform. Sitting in the back were two stone-faced officers, and in between them a black Labrador raised a paw in salute as they passed by. Surfboards were strapped precariously to the side of the vehicle, which wailed into the floodlit area and beetled off down the road towards Holberton with a rattling *diminuendo*, leaving a cloud of oily smoke in its wake. Moffat lowered the barrier to seal the base. Podsnap killed the floodlights and was immediately on the phone.

Under their very noses, Captain Charlie Taverner had just escaped from Windcheater Island, along with Staff Sergeant 'Chalky' White and two Bombardiers.

The incident had to be reported up the chain of command, and across the base increasingly important telephones woke their owners. After Bombardier Podsnap had alerted the Guard Commander, he woke the Regimental Orderly Sergeant, who then woke the Regimental Orderly Officer who decided the Adjutant – the CO's personal staff officer – needed to be informed. Due to a combination of fatigue, the hour and the nature of Captain Taverner's escape, the report, by the time it reached the Adjutant, had become rather muddled.

'Sorry to wake you, sir. Orderly Officer here.'

The Adjutant was unable to recall from the Orderly Officer roster who was on duty that night.

'Any chance of a name?' he said.

'Reynolds, sir.'

The Adjutant sighed. Second Lieutenant Reynolds. Posted to the 65th two months ago. Naïve and eager to please, the Adjutant's first impression on meeting him was that Reynolds was not terribly over-burdened with much between his ears, and he had done a great deal in the last two months to reinforce the Adjutant's original opinion.

'There's been an incident, sir,' said Reynolds.

'What kind of incident?' said the Adjutant.

'A breakout. An escape, sir.'

Although a breakout was a serious incident, the Adjutant knew it could have been worse, like an out-of-hours suicide or murder, for which the resulting paperwork would have been horrendous.

'Who, why, when, where, how?' he said.

'Just bear with me a second, sir, I've written down all the details. It was … four Nazis, sir.'

'I beg your pardon?'

'Four Nazis, sir. You know, like the Jerries, whoops, I mean the Germans, during World War Two,' said Reynolds, suddenly remembering the Adjutant's wife was German.

'Thank you, Reynolds. I read Modern History at Oxford. I know what a Nazi is. What were they doing on the base in the first place?'

'I, ah, couldn't really say, sir. Bombardier Podsnap was on duty at the Sentry Post and says there were definitely four of them. But he says no Nazis have been recorded in the Movements Log.'

'Really?'

'Really, sir. Oh, and apparently Podsnap thinks one of them was impersonating you.'

'Me?'

'Yes, sir.'

'Who?'

'One of the Nazis, sir.'

'I don't quite follow.'

'Podsnap said someone phoned him pretending to be

9

the Adjutant. He said he thought it was probably one of the Nazis.'

In the manner of every new Second Lieutenant, bristling with righteousness and integrity, Reynolds was now quickly passing the buck.

'The caller, the one pretending to be you, sir, said the Colonel was returning to base after having been out on an operation.'

'What fucking operation?' said the Adjutant, now completely lost.

'An operation to get a shaven haven.'

'A shaven haven?'

'That's correct, sir. Bombardier Podsnap said it was all supposed to be very hush-hush, and speculated that the Nazis were in fact in disguise because it was all supposed to be hush-hush, sir.'

The Adjutant pulled the phone away from his ear and wondered if Charlie Taverner was playing another one of his practical jokes on him.

'Let me get this straight,' said the Adjutant. 'The Sentry Post thinks that someone pretending to be me phoned them to let them know that the Commanding Officer was returning to camp after a secret operation to get his nether regions shaved, and in order to maintain secrecy he and his escorts were disguised in full Nazi regalia.'

'That's about the long and the short of it, sir.'

'But in fact the Colonel did not return to base, and four Nazis somehow manage to escape instead, although they were never actually here in the first place. Is that what you're telling me?'

'Yes, sir.'

'Young Reynolds, I am fairly confident that the

Colonel is fast asleep in his quarters. If he had to go anywhere he would have let me know. The Colonel is certainly a progressive and enlightened man, but I very much doubt he intended to venture outside for the purpose of visiting a nocturnal intimate depilatory agency while dressed as Heinrich fucking Himmler!'

'Hmm, I'm beginning to see your point, sir.'

'You bloody idiot! Why the hell don't you try getting your facts right before waking me up?' said the Adjutant. 'You know, Reynolds, if your brain was made of cotton wool, there wouldn't be enough to make a sparrow's Tampax.'

'Thank you, sir,' said Reynolds.

The Adjutant groaned. The idiot seemed genuinely thankful for the comment. He couldn't even land an insult on this young buck.

'Tell me one more thing, Reynolds. Precisely how did they get out?'

'They opened the barrier for them, sir.'

'They opened the barrier?'

'Yes, sir. They, being the guard, opened the barrier for them,' said Reynolds, in a disapproving voice.

'So, exactly how did they get out?'

Reynolds cleared his throat and spoke slowly and deliberately, as if to an elderly relative. 'They ... opened ... the ... barrier ... for ... them ... sir.'

'Jesus H Christ! I mean, did they just walk out? Were they driving? I suppose they were fucking goose-stepping out the base!'

'No, sir, they were driving a German car.'

'A German car. Four Nazis in a German car. Oh splendid! That narrows it down a bit. What do you mean, a *German car*?'

'Something called a Cueball Farting, sir,' said Reynolds, reading from his hastily-written notes.

Everything then fell into place for the Adjutant.

'You mean a Kubelwagen,' he said. The Adjutant knew that Charlie Taverner owned a Kubelwagen. Only he would own such an eccentric vehicle, as well as having the nerve to pull a stunt like this. He'd probably gone surfing again with Staff Sergeant 'Chalky' White and those two Bombardiers whose names the Adjutant couldn't recall.

'Oh yes, sir, now I know what a Kubelwagen is,' said Reynolds. 'It's what the Krauts, whoops, the Germans drove during World War Two. Have you seen *Where Eagles Dare*, sir? Richard Burton blows one up on a bridge as he's trying to escape to the airfield. Come to think of it he was dressed up as a Nazi, sir. And then there's ...'

'Shut up, man. For God's sake, shut up. Send out the Provost staff to look for the vehicle, and tell them to try the beach first. And do not disturb me again unless it's very important, like murder or suicide. Preferably your own. Is that clear?'

'Perfectly, sir.'

'Jesus, how the hell did you beat six million other sperm, Reynolds?'

'To get into Cambridge, you mean?' said Reynolds, missing the point, but the Adjutant had already put the phone down.

Back at the Sentry Post, Bombardier Podsnap realised that, in his haste, he had not passed one vital piece of information up the chain of command; that one of the escapees was Captain Taverner. He stopped filling in the Incident Report and got back on the phone.

The Adjutant had just started to drift off to sleep and

was not impressed when Second Lieutenant Reynolds phoned him again, now very excited.

'We've got a name, sir, we've got a name! It's Captain Taverner! I've just checked his room and he's not there!' Reynolds sounded like he had just accomplished a great military feat.

The Adjutant hung up on him again and made a mental note to punish Reynolds with three weeks of extra Orderly Officer duties in the morning.

The breakout from Windcheater Island had been fun, and Charlie Taverner and the others had barely been able to keep a straight face as they roared past Moffat and Podsnap. They were at the beach at Saunton Sands within ten minutes and checked out the waves from the small slope that led from the car park to the beach, still dressed in their historic regalia and attracting some incredulous looks from the local surfers.

Two miles of beach and sand dunes lay to their left and sandstone cliffs formed a headland extending out to sea just to their right. In front of them was the reason why they were here; a sea as beautiful as anything they'd seen before. Heaving lines of swell advanced from the horizon like vast ripples of glassy corduroy – the echoes of Hurricane Chloe. The waves were massive and perfectly formed, breaking from a single peak and peeling gradually along the wave's length with tremendous power. Double-overhead.

They changed into their wetsuits and grabbed their surfboards. Taverner and Chalky rode bigger, heavier longboards, whereas the two Bombardiers preferred snappier, more manoeuvrable shortboards. They headed down the beach together; their senses and emotions now coming together in delicious overload; the sight and thunder of the waves, the coconut aroma of surfboard wax, the smell of the neoprene wetsuits and coffee on nearby Calor gas stoves. And the nervous ache in the pit of their stomachs at the thought of a long hold-down, or drowning.

Flint was content to be left behind to wander around the car park, where he'd always been able to scrounge some titbits from even the most hardened dog-fearer, with his floppy ears and pleading eyes.

The surfers reached the water and looked out. It was at least a three-hundred metre paddle to get out to the take-off spot and the waves looked even bigger at sea level than they had from the car park. A strong rip current ran alongside the rocks, where the water driven up onto the beach by the waves would flow back out to sea. Taverner tied the surfboard's leash to his ankle and waded into the sea. At waist depth he felt the pull of the rip, lay prone on his board and began the long paddle, with the others following on. The rip was like a conveyor-belt running out to sea – lethal to an unwary swimmer, but a useful ride out to the take-off spot when the waves were big. As he paddled, Taverner was wary of the jagged rocks to his right and the crashing peaks to his left, although waves rarely broke into the deeper waters of the rip. This was not the time to get intimate with the rocks. He paddled beyond the impact zone to the take-off spot where the water was calmer and the waves were just starting to break, and sat astride his board. Chalky and the two Bombardiers paddled up behind him. Enormous volumes of water were pitching around them. Just minutes earlier they had been perfectly safe on land, and now they were among such unpredictable energy. They scanned the sea to the west for the darkening of the horizon that would signal the arrival of the 'set' waves; occasional groups of bigger waves that would break further out. Taverner felt the fight–or–flight syndrome that he had become so addicted to; the feeling that he had bitten off more than he could chew and had no right to be there. Mother Nature's playground was an unforgiving place to be when she was in such a majestic mood.

The horizon darkened and a set approached. Taverner fought the urge to quit and make for the beach. He let the first two waves pass underneath him and went for the last and steepest.

He spun his board round and started paddling hard back towards the beach, looking over his shoulder at the twelve-footer rearing up behind him. It lifted him up high as he paddled, he felt the tipping point as the board picked up speed and became part of the wave, and as he started to drop down the face he jumped to a crouching position, keeping his centre of gravity low. He came off the bottom at high speed, but as he started to turn down the line, he knew he'd just made a very bad choice. The huge wave, instead of peeling gradually, closed out and broke along its entire length in a single movement. Several tonnes of water knocked Taverner off his board and instantly he was plunged into a tumbling cauldron, whiplashed and pummelled in the turbulent darkness under the wave. He had no idea which way was up and could sense from the pressure in his ears that he was quite deep. He could feel the pull on his ankle from the leash and hoped it wouldn't snap – it was a long way to swim in without his surfboard. He tried to relax. There was no point using energy fighting a wave like this. The turbulence gradually eased, he felt himself rising and he burst through the surface into the hissing foam left in the wake of the wave. He pulled on the leash, clambered onto his board and paddled back out to the take-off spot.

For the next twenty minutes he caught no more waves and just tried to survive; scanning the horizon for the big sets, paddling left and right to avoid the breaking peaks, and out to sea if the set was particularly big.

The horizon started to darken again and the other surfers started to hoot. Another set was on its way in. This one was the biggest yet. Furiously Taverner paddled out to sea, his arms wind-milling like mad, desperately trying to get beyond the waves before they broke. The first wave bore down on him — a massive, blackening face of fifteen feet. This was ridiculous, thought Taverner. He was way out of his depth in these conditions and wished he'd stayed on the beach. The wave's top was crackling — warning him that it was about to break. He paddled towards it, reached it just in time and went up the steep face, pivoted over the top and dropped down the back of the wave. In front of him the second wave was rearing up. He kept paddling hard. Again, the wave started to crackle. He found himself shouting at the wave, willing it not to break on top of him.

Not yet! Not yet! NOT YET!

He rode up the face and again dropped down the other side. He was then faced with the final and by far the biggest wave of the set, and was convinced that he was looking at his own watery grave. It was the most terrifying thing he had ever seen. This wave was still way out in front of him and on the verge of breaking. He felt utterly helpless and was overwhelmed by a sense of doom.

The conscious part of his psyche was resigned to his fate, but a primitive survival mechanism took over and he found himself turning his board back round towards the beach and paddling hard. He felt the wave pick him up and he was carried very, very high. He snapped to his feet and plummeted down a face so big it felt more like he was snowboarding down a steep mountain. As he came flying off the bottom with tremendous speed, he carved the board round to the right and tore along the wave.

He was actually riding the beast!

He drove up the face of the wave to the top, stalled, accelerated again on the drop and again went back up the face of this, the biggest wave he had ever ridden. Behind, the breaking lip pursued him and the wave started to close out. Taverner kept the board straight and raced the lip as it started to overtake him high above his head. Now there was only one place to go. He shot up the face of the wave and used it as a ramp, jumping high into the air, clearing the lip in a huge arc to land in the calmer water behind the wave.

When he surfaced, Taverner couldn't help himself. He hooted and screamed and punched the air in overwhelming euphoria.

TWO

Captain Charlie Taverner of the 65th Regiment Royal Horse Artillery stood outside the Colonel's office in Regimental Headquarters, in a narrow institutional corridor that smelt of furniture polish, Brasso and ozone from a nearby photocopier. Telephones rang softly behind closed doors. Taverner had swapped his German officer's outfit for the service uniform of the British Army – a khaki-green uniform with a highly polished crossbelt, brown shoes, forage cap, and seven medals pinned across his chest, including the Military Cross and the Federal Gallantry Medal. At his side, Flint sat to attention, looking rather more worried than his unconcerned owner.

Taverner cut a tall, tanned, athletic figure in the corridor, with blond hair that was just a little too long and a little too unkempt for the rest of the military, but *de rigueur* for an officer of the 65th. He was slim and extremely fit at an age when some of his slacker contemporaries were well on their way to middle-age spread. Below the peak of Taverner's forage cap, below a few wisps of his uncontained fringe, a very sharp pair of blue eyes scanned the regimental photographs on the opposite wall. People often found his stare a little too penetrating for comfort, while others found it almost hypnotic. Taverner's eyes were a most useful gift and he could barely remember the last time he had raised his voice to any miscreant under his command. It was enough simply to fix them with his stare. There were other advantages too. The opposite sex found his gaze complimentary and wonderfully expressive, and he'd had no problem charming his way into the beds of some very beautiful women.

Yet Taverner lived in remarkable ignorance of this particular talent. Leadership had always come so easily to him, though he never knew why; he just found it easy to impose his will on others. In his presence the decisive would hesitate, the recalcitrant promised to mend their ways, and the girls simply melted. The Army had been his natural calling.

He was the offspring of a successful merchant banker and a newspaper columnist whose notorious bed-hopping antics prior to his birth were well-documented and had made him wonder who his natural father actually was. There were a number of possible paternal candidates; a famous rock star, a business rival of his (official) father, a celebrated but alcoholic writer, even a minor Royal. Taverner hoped it was the wild rock star – blond, unusually clean-living for all his maniacal behaviour, dead at the age of twenty-six; his Lamborghini wrapped neatly round a tree on London's Embankment opposite the Ministry of Defence.

Taverner had been educated at Blundell's School in Devon and went on to complete his officer training at Sandhurst, the Royal Military Academy, where he developed a penchant for corduroy trousers in primary colours, demolishing sports cars and – in the opinion of his instructors – idleness on the drill square. His parents lived comfortably in tax exile and ensured Taverner's allowance enabled him to join an exclusive regiment like the 65th and indulge his passion for dangerous sports – surfing and windsurfing, scuba-diving and off-piste snowboarding – activities he was able to pursue in the very best locations across the world, and that his army salary on its own might have otherwise prohibited. The most expensive and definitely the most dangerous of his indulgences had always been the stunning, high-maintenance girlfriends. Lithe, wholesome English roses – bored, horny and usually insecure – and he changed his models every three to six months.

Now in his early thirties, people wondered if he was mellowing. He had got rid of the fast cars and had been going steady with Hannah for four years. He had his black Labrador and an old Land Rover – very much the up-and-coming career officer, suggested a few senior officers of the Artillery Board, who cautiously ear-marked his file. And if he popped the question to Hannah in the near-future, as he was expected to, then that would seal their approval. *Steady family man in the making. Shows the correct form. Just the sort of chap we want in charge higher up.*

Then again, others thought Taverner had simply transferred his energies elsewhere. He was still like an engine running continuously at full-throttle, they pointed out; constantly restless, always being distracted by something or another, and never really ready to embrace military life to the extent needed to impress the Board. He always volunteered for the dangerous deployments and frequently managed to arrange temporary attachments to other regiments if the nature of their tour might give him the thrill he was looking for, but it all seemed rather futile.

Such an unusual affliction, they so commented. Seeks out the thrill, but never seems to really *enjoy* it.

The simple fact was that Taverner was thoroughly bored with his job, and had been for some time. In the last few months, under the regime of the new Commanding Officer, his feelings for the Army had gone from resentment to hatred as the gap grew wider between what his superiors expected of him, and what he actually chose to do. He could no longer cope with the suffocating existence of life in barracks and the endless and numbing cycle of paperwork and petty legislation that it involved. Operational tours were what Taverner lived for and, years ago, they had offered the danger and excitement he craved. Nowadays, with the cretins in the government determined to seize the moral high ground on the international stage, he could only look forward to an endless cycle of ethical peacekeeping tours and, more recently, environmental protection duty. The element of danger was still there, but the rules of engagement under new Human Rights legislation were so restrictive that soldiers on peacekeeping duty were barely allowed to use a paint-ball gun to defend themselves. Of course, the politicians still wept and spoke of their regret and looked on solemnly each time the bodies were carried off at the Air Force base at Brize Norton to the accompaniment of Elgar's *Nimrod*, but they'd happily unleash their own army of lawyers whenever their country's soldiers overstepped the mark. After all, the communities had to be kept onside.

Taverner had cursed and ducked and sweated through the recent tours and vowed to leave the Army each time he got back. He'd type his letter of resignation – *'Sir, I have the honour to request leave to resign my commission blah blah blah ...'* – and he'd fold it neatly and seal the envelope, but could never actually post it. The letter would lie on his desk until he threw it in the bin. He could never leave the Army. He could not face up to the fact that he was in fear of Civvy Street and its associated unknowns. However much it frustrated him, he instinctively sought the institutional security of Army life and the continuity and camaraderie of the Officers' Mess. There was something about the 65th too; an invisible force that had drawn him in, as it had many others, and kept him there through good times and bad. Perhaps if Taverner had been in a lesser regiment he would have found it easier to leave, but the 65th was like no other regiment in the Army. Right now, however, he badly needed a decent mission.

Taverner had never taken soldiering seriously in the 65th and had never expected his soldiers to do so either. He had risen through various appointments and now commanded the regiment's small Air Defence Battery (motto: *It flies, it dies)*, known derisively by the rest of the regiment – all traditional artillery gunners by trade – as the *Cloud Punchers*. The technical side of Air Defence did not concern Taverner. During his time in command of the Battery his knowledge of its complexities had only ever progressed from a level of sluggish indifference to one of perpetual ignorance. He concerned himself with more important things in life. His soldiers knew their job perfectly well, whereas the officers of the 65th were simply fun-loving figureheads who were only needed to give the right order at the right time. There was no need to interfere. Professionalism was for other regiments.

Never the grey man, Taverner was only ever black or white, often both at once, and he could be breathtakingly hypocritical in command. He would demand staunch adherence to the rulebook, which made his constant rule-breaking all the more fun. He was a most rigorous defendant of the old-fashioned structured society, which had now been largely engineered away by the State. Without such structure to his life and to the world at large, his low-level anarchy had no meaning.

The man whom Taverner was about to see regarding the delicate matter of the events earlier that morning could not have been more different. He was waiting to see Lieutenant Colonel Sandford – the 'Colonel' – the ambitious Commanding Officer of the 65th, who had now kept Taverner waiting for fifteen minutes.

Probably quite deliberately, thought Taverner.

Probably just wanted to try and impose his scant authority.

Probably read about it in some Harvard management guru's bestselling guide to corporate leadership and motivation or some other bollocks that seemed to flick Sandford's switch. *Keep them waiting – they must all dance to **your** tune!* Bullet-point number three in *Ten Effective Habits of the Leading Alpha-Male Executive*. Sandford probably recited the lot to himself in front of his shaving mirror each morning.

You're a tiger. A Tiger!

Further down the corridor, the Regimental Sergeant Major had already started on Taverner's partners-in-crime and it sounded like he was tearing a strip off Staff Sergeant 'Chalky' White, as the two Bombardiers waited outside for their turn. The two were both combat veterans and blasé about coming under fire. There were bullets and there were bombs, but then there was the Regimental Sergeant Major, and the two Bombardiers looked very uncomfortable waiting to be dealt with. Protocol demanded that Taverner would have his misdemeanours dealt with by a fellow officer, albeit a more senior one like the Colonel. Not that anyone in the 65th thought Colonel Sandford cared much for protocol – he probably found the whole concept of protocol an unnecessary anachronism.

In the short time he had been imposed on the 65th Colonel Sandford had gained a truly appalling reputation. The regiment wondered what it had done to offend the senior officers of the Artillery Board to such an extent that they had posted Sandford to command the 65th. For a start, the man had never before served in the 65th. Indeed, there were doubts that he had ever gone through Sandhurst. The regiment was awash with rumours about his background, and legend had it that he was a former Administration Officer in the Territorial Army; a bean-counting desk-jockey who'd made the switch to the Regulars at some point in his murky past; a fantasist with ideas above his station who'd got lucky.

The Colonel's door opened and the Adjutant peered out.

'You may go in now.'

'At last,' said Taverner. He left Flint sitting in the corridor looking anxious and allowed the Adjutant to exit before he walked in smartly, shut the door and saluted.

The interior of the Colonel's office was in marked contrast to the service atmosphere that one found elsewhere in RHQ. Gone were the trappings of institution; the bright overhead strip lights, the grey lino, the regulation magnolia paint and the bland, functional furniture. In here it was minimalist, achingly cool, and the furniture had been arranged with little regard for right angles. On the walls hung a number of abstract works of art along with a single large photograph of Colonel

Sandford shaking hands with the British President. A 'grip-and-grin'. All in all, the office seemed at odds with the military nature of the business that was supposed to take place there.

Taverner marched awkwardly from the door in an elongated S-shape, avoided the huge Yucca plant in the middle of the floor and halted at the Colonel's desk. The Colonel, who disliked military uniform, wore his usual civilian suit and sat looking through some paperwork, refusing to acknowledge Taverner's presence. He was only about five or six years older than Taverner, but the two of them seemed to be a generation apart. The Colonel was a greying middle-manager, unremarkable in appearance except for a strikingly trendy pair of spectacles. Taverner noticed his slight paunch and wondered how long it had been since the Colonel had passed a fitness test, since he was never seen to do any PT with the regiment. As an expert in sartorial matters, Taverner thought the Colonel's shirt looked to be of fairly good quality, but his tie was not easy on the eye. The suit jacket was clearly High Street off-the-peg and almost certainly lacking in vents. Tasteless and shapeless. How very appropriate for the Colonel. Why the hell couldn't the man get himself a decent tailor?

Eventually Colonel Sandford spoke, still looking down at the papers on his desk.

'So, young man, I gather you know why you're here?'

'Absolutely, Colonel. Thank you for inviting me.' Taverner couldn't help himself, couldn't resist causing the inevitable carnage in the same way one is sometimes tempted to veer into oncoming traffic. 'It's an honour to be asked for my opinion,' he said, patting his pocket, 'I have his business card here. I'm sure you'll find his prices very reasonable.'

'I beg your pardon?' said the Colonel, suddenly looking up.

'My tailor, Colonel. He's coming down to the Mess next month to do a fitting for me. I'm sure he could make you a decent suit to replace your current ...'

'How dare you! How *dare* you be so insulting, young man! Don't you *ever* take that tone with me, *Captain*!'

That, thought Taverner, was the first sign of spark anyone had seen in Colonel Sandford. He stared back hard at the Colonel, forcing him to look down submissively, and the rest of the reprimand was delivered without much conviction.

'You are treading a very fine line,' said the Colonel. 'I was warned about you before I took over command here. If you ever take that tone with me again I'll have you posted to the Outer Hebrides.' He exhaled deeply and steadied himself. 'I will give you one more chance. I would like you to explain why you so flagrantly broke out of barracks this morning when the whole regiment is confined to base.'

'Colonel, I cannot offer any excuse.'

'Am I to understand you went surfing again?'

'Yes, Colonel.'

'You know the rules, and you bloody well break them! And you, a bloody officer too!' The Colonel looked at the paperwork on his desk. 'Looking at your records I see that this is the third time you have now disobeyed my orders. That disturbs me. That disturbs me very deeply indeed.' He recited the details. 'Two weeks ago you were absent from a regimental parade, then turned up two hours later at the Sentry Post on the flat bed of a tractor with your windsurfing equipment.'

'I miscalculated the tide, Colonel. I ended up on the far side of the estuary and had to hitch a lift back ...'

'And five weeks ago you filed release forms pertaining

to the fact that you were visiting *Major Buntfuttock* at Brigade, and Brigade said they'd never heard of you or a Major Buntfuttock. And now this! Now you are leading soldiers astray too!' The Colonel tried looking up again at Taverner, but still had to look away while he spoke. 'Such actions are entirely unacceptable, especially from an officer. Am I to understand that you also think it's funny to drive around dressed in the uniform of the Waffen SS, in some sort of Nazi Staff Officer's car? Would you care to explain?'

'Actually, the uniform was Afrika Korps, not the Waffen SS, Colonel,' corrected Taverner, with the air of a slightly-despairing schoolmaster. 'Rommel was *never* a Nazi. And my car is a Kubelwagen. My brother worked for a film production company that specialised in war movies. He was made redundant and they gave him a replica as a pay-off. I'm looking after it for him.'

'Captain Taverner! Silly, *Hooray Henry* behaviour is one thing, but this ...' Sandford searched for the right word, '... tribute to a very dark period in modern history is indeed sinister. May I remind you that we defeated fascism nearly eighty years ago? What you think is *good, old-fashioned British humour* most people now actually find inappropriate, not to say offensive. I was *so* angry this morning I had to be calmed down by the Adjutant. As an *officer* in this regiment, Captain Taverner, you are a vital link in the chain of command through which my orders are carried out. This regiment is a bloody disgrace and I am here to put it right. You may not like my medicine, but you are going to take it all the same. It is precisely at times like these when you should be leading your men effectively and setting an example to them. Instead, you offend me by doing this. Am I to understand you're quite a popular young officer with your Battery?'

'I wouldn't know, Colonel.'

'I think you *do* know. Don't try to pretend you don't, young man. Tell me, do you think it's a good thing to court popularity with your soldiers?'

'I don't set out to be popular, Colonel. The boys either like me or they don't. I couldn't care less.'

'What did they teach you about leadership at that confounded Academy they call Sandhurst? How are you to take difficult decisions if all you're concerned about is your bloody vanity and popularity with your men? Commanding men is not a popularity contest.'

'As well you seem to know, Colonel,' said Taverner, making it sound like flattery.

The Colonel missed the insult and pondered for a moment, steepling his hands and touching his fingertips to his lips, appearing to consider before passing sentence, but it was for effect only. He had clearly made his decision some time before.

'I wholly believe in the concept of collective responsibility and therefore in the concept of holistic sanctions, or what you unenlightened types might call *Collective Punishment*. So, for this outrage this morning, all your soldiers will make themselves vastly more productive by doing daily Regimental Fatigues for the next four weeks under the direction of the Regimental Sergeant Major. They will do all the guard duties for a similar time. I am not punishing *you* directly for this. I am punishing *them*. I'm sure your soldiers will thank you in their own special way. And if you or any one of them screws up again just *that* much, I will have your surfboard, your stinking dog, and you, on my bonfire! Do you understand?'

'Yes, Colonel.'

'Good. Now, *get out!*'

Taverner saluted, pivoted round and marched out,

smiling to himself. Carrying out full drill movements in the CO's office, as an officer, was strictly *infra dig* and Taverner guessed the Colonel wouldn't understand the insult. Retrieving his bicycle he set off back to the Officers' Mess to get changed into his normal working uniform.

How different it would have been under old Colonel Fairbairn, he thought. Fairbairn had been a proper Commanding Officer. He would have settled this matter by listening to one's squirming explanation while his face turned redder and redder. At the very moment one expected to see the pulsating blood vessel on his forehead burst, Fairbairn would suddenly smack his hand on the back of his head causing his glass eye to drop out onto his lap, then his monocle would fall from his good eye, and while you stood there speechless in horror he would reach over the desk and launch a haymaker of a punch onto your conk with unnerving accuracy for one so blind. He'd bawl you out, then call you back in again for a quick snort of scotch, all kiss-cuddle-and-make-up-so-we're-friends-again, and you would bloody well enjoy the scotch if you could stop the blood from ruining it when you raised it to your lips.

And what about *his* predecessor, the permanently-pissed Colonel Edgar, who would have bypassed any punishment and immediately broken out the scotch in celebration, such was his stated opinion that:

A. *All rulebooks, be they those of the Officers' Mess, King's Regulations or Common Law, were inherently subversive and any contraventions thereof were to be actively encouraged.*

B. *There was no place for boring officers in the 65th.*

C. *Boring officers should all be shot.*

Fairbairn and Edgar were part of the Old Guard. Like most former Commanding Officers of the 65th, they had been wonderful leaders of men – if also a few rounds short of a full magazine. Soldiers, especially high-calibre soldiers like the Scousers of the 65th, would only ever trust their well-being to such maniacs who had absolutely no compunction about putting anyone's life on the line – usually their own – in circumstances that rarely warranted such terrible risk. Reckless tactics in the field and a disregard for the sanctity of life always inspired confidence in the ranks. It elicited fear in the enemy in war and bewilderment in other nations on peacekeeping tours. Such a savagely mindless approach to operations was part of the tradition of the 65th, through which it aspired to the very highest achievement on the battlefield; the complete annihilation of the regiment.

In the 65th's eyes there was something particularly noble about the obliteration of an entire regiment, especially an artillery regiment which, although relatively close to the enemy, was not exactly cheek-by-jowl like the infantry or the cavalry, yet in spite of this handicap the 65th was proud to have achieved the honour several times in its long and bloody history.

If you were staring defeat in the face, so the reasoning went, there could be no half-measures. You bowed out in style and took everyone with you.

Back in his office, Colonel Sandford gathered up the papers on Captain Taverner and called for the Duty Clerk to take them away for filing. He got up from his desk and looked out of his office window at his wretched regiment and watched Taverner disappearing down the road on his bike, with his dog cantering behind.

Colonel Sandford had only been in command of the 65th for ten weeks and he was having a very rough ride. He knew the 65th had something of a difficult reputation, but he had not envisaged it would be this bad. Everyone in the regiment seemed to be utterly indifferent to him. As Sanford saw it, the 65th regarded itself as languishing in an elegant imperial past, as if fighting a stylish action on a frontier somewhere, even to the extent of the officers addressing waiters in pidgin Hindustani on formal dinner nights.

What hope was there for a regiment like that? The 65th clung to the past with a fervency that made Sandford wonder if the regiment was beyond recovery. It was like an old rubber band found lurking at the back of a drawer, one that had had its uses, but had since been stretched beyond its elastic limit; brittle, not fit for purpose, and perhaps best discarded.

Nevertheless, the 65th was now his regiment and he intended to run it according to his own modernist principles, although his methods were not going down well and he knew he was not liked. Just that morning, on his way into the office, he'd got upset because two soldiers had walked past and failed to salute him, and at morning coffee-break he always seemed to be standing around on his own while the other officers rudely carried on their conversations, seemingly oblivious to his presence.

Dammit, why couldn't the bastards respect his rank? He was the Colonel, for Christ's sake! The rank demanded the very highest respect within the regiment and when it failed to materialise he became frustrated and angered.

The other officers knew why. Though he was a Lieutenant Colonel, Sandford was not sufficiently acquainted with the Army – the *real* Army, that did the fighting and the dying – to know that the respect of these soldiers, combat veterans all, needed to be earned over time the hard way, sometimes the very hardest way of all. Sandford was an office man; conventional in thought and managerial in style, lacking the flair the 65th expected in its Commanding Officers, constrained by the rule-book and by adherence to policy, and too career-orientated. Now he was in command of a proper regiment he might find the opportunity to prove himself, but until then the regiment would reserve the right to be a little indifferent. Sandford wanted everything handed to him on a plate simply because of his rank and position. That was not the 65th's way.

Throughout his military career, Sandford had been careful to avoid any sort of position where he might have had to command soldiers or deploy to a war-zone, and had opted for the career-proof office job. A little dull perhaps, but much safer, in every sense of the word. A progressive education at a minor public school that no-one had ever heard of had left him with a sizeable chip on his shoulder that was never more in evidence than when he was put in command of the 65th. He was used to dealing with civil servants and low-ranking government ministers, the managerial classes and the think-tanks, and he was quite happy drawing up far-reaching policies to modernise the Army and updating legislation to keep everyone in line. Recently he had been part of the team tasked with introducing into the Armed Services the government's flagship policy of the CODE – *Community, Opportunity, Diversity and Equality*.

But it had been a shock to come face-to-face with real soldiers and officers whose lives he'd been influencing from a distant office in London for so long. He envied the easy, relaxed manner of the officers, the way they all seemed to know each other from school or university or through some family connection, and their smooth demeanor at social functions where he, in contrast, always seemed to be anxious and edgy. They talked of places he'd never been to and of people he didn't know. Nor did he know the *form*. One evening, shortly after taking command of the 65th, he'd gone to the NAAFI to share a matey beer or two with some of the soldiers – an astonishing *faux pas* that had raised eyebrows and provoked much laughter across the regiment. Officers *never* drank in the NAAFI with the ranks, but how was he to have known?

Sandford mostly resented the other officers because he was not one of *them*, and could never be. Of course, Sandford thought it was simply a matter of class. He could never accept that one's class was largely academic – the Army was far too meritocratic to get bogged down in class – but the simplicity of his argument comforted him. Class was, after all, the default explanation of the Correct. Yet he simply couldn't understand why these upper-middle class twits were so liked by their soldiers; the cheeky working class Scousers. It went against everything he knew to be true. The Colonel considered himself to be something of an expert in social anthropology, but the 65th didn't make any sense to him. So, the more confused and out of his depth he got, the more he lashed out. Commanding a regiment was not a popularity contest (this had become one of his favourite sayings) and he took this belief to new extremes. He punished the soldiers and he punished the officers, yet they all took it in their stride as if such sanctions were normal. They even seemed to enjoy it – he had even overheard one subaltern commenting that it was just like being back at his old school.

In a perfect world, Sandford would have had Taverner and his ilk posted onto another regiment, or sacked. However, there were barriers to that. The Army was so heavily committed to putting the world to rights that soldiers and officers now had to give (or be given) two years' notice to resign. Sandford couldn't just throw them out as and when it suited him. And then there was the whole bizarre business of the Officers' Mess. Unlike most messes, the Officers' Mess on Windcheater Island did not belong to the Ministry of Defence. The building belonged instead to a former Commanding Officer of the 65th, who interviewed prospective officers to ensure they were the type of individual he wanted living in his property. By admitting only the right people to the Mess, he had near-total control of the recruitment of officers to the 65th.

The Mess was nothing short of a private gentlemen's club – just the sort of divisive elitism that Sandford hated. And although he was now the Commanding Officer of the 65th, astonishingly he was *not* a member of the Officers' Mess. Sandford had been horrified to learn on his arrival that, having never before served in the 65th, he'd have to be interviewed by the owner of the Mess, and he would be damned if he, a bloody Lieutenant Colonel, was going to jump through the hoops and subject himself to a patronising social interrogation by some florid old buffer in order to be accepted! However, no interview – no place in the Mess. He lived in a house on the base and had to be entertained in the Mess on formal dinner nights as a bloody *Invited Guest*! In his own damned regiment!

All of this might have driven Sandford to impose ever-greater sanctions on a regiment that seemed to care little for his authority. But Sandford had one hell of an ace hidden up his sleeve, and when on the receiving end of these nasty little slights he took comfort in the knowledge of what he called *The Great Plan*; something only he knew about.

Sandford's posting to the 65th was not simply the regimental command appointment that eventually came round for most Lieutenant Colonels. There was a lot more behind it. His aim to try to convert an obstinate regiment to his modernist principles was actually of little importance in the overall scheme of things. He'd give it a go, and more importantly, be *seen* to give it a go, but whether the 65th ever changed its ways was inconsequential.

Shortly before he had been appointed to command the 65th, Sandford had been called to a very private meeting at the Ministry of Defence in London with some senior civil servants in charge of long-term planning. He had listened with great interest to what they had to say and was flattered when they asked him to be involved. He understood what he was going to have to do, as well as the need for absolute discretion. Sandford had done most of the listening at the meeting, but he'd made one particularly good suggestion that impressed the mandarins, who were always conscious of the need to save the pennies and keep costs down. They knew they had the right man for the job.

And so Colonel Sandford looked out of the window of his office, out on the base, watching the 65th go about its business, and he smiled.

Bless them, he thought. They had no idea what was coming.

There was much to accomplish in the meantime though, and as much as Sandford detested them he would need the whole regiment to pull all the stops out if he was to realise The Great Plan. The mandarins had been adamant. *On time and under budget.* His future career would depend on it.

Sandford believed that with any other regiment it would have been easy to whip everyone into shape. But the officers and soldiers of the 65th were just too truculent, too set in their ways to follow his orders to the extent he would soon be demanding.

He would need a deputy. A Second-in-Command. Someone to whom he could delegate command of The Great Plan while he busied himself with other matters concerning *his* future. There were certain criteria that the deputy would need to fulfil. He would certainly need to be ex-65th, someone the regiment would respect, someone who Sandford could boss around, someone lacking in ambition; a hen-pecked fool who could be kept in the dark, but good enough to get the job done, for which Sandford would then rightfully claim the glory.

He had sent his request up to the Ministry of Defence and they had responded quickly. Out of four possible candidates one stood out by a mile. Sandford pulled a few strings – years of working in the MoD had taught him which ones to pull – and began to make the arrangements to have this particular man posted to the 65th. He needed him in position by the end of the month. The man would be perfect.

THREE

Taverner cycled back to the Officers' Mess. He was still exhilarated by the morning's surf and chuckled to himself as he recalled Colonel Sandford's attempt to give him a bollocking. The sea shimmered in the distance, the trees were full and green after a good summer and a salty coolness in the air hinted at the autumnal weather to come. Out in the estuary the curlews sang and the sandpipers were preparing for their journey south. Windcheater Island had never looked prettier, thought Taverner.

The island was a former Royal Air Force base, located on the northern shore of a wide estuary just to the south of the town of Holberton, although it was not really an island in the traditional sense of the word. At high tide it was surrounded by seawater on three sides. A narrow dyke, which ran along the northern edge of the base, with sluice gates at either end, separated it from the mainland. The seawater dispersed rapidly on the ebbing tide to reveal extensive and treacherous mud-flats. Sailing was a popular sport in the 65th and yachts in various states of seaworthiness were moored, and often sunk, just off the island.

Windcheater Island was one of the most secure bases in the British Army and it was unlikely that the new wave of terrorists would ever try to attack the base. If one believed the government and their lackeys in the media, it seemed that every group with a gripe was now resorting to violence. Not a week went by without an attack by some outfit, real or imaginary. Continuity Animal Liberation Front; The North London Academy of Peace Studies and Martyrdom; The paramilitary wing of Help the Aged. Not even the threat of detention without trial or rumours of a Special Measures Programme seemed to deter them.

Being a former RAF base, there were three runways on the island that overlapped each other, now cracked and gravelly through disuse. In the middle of the triangle formed by the three runways was an old control tower. Influenced by the Telecom Tower in London, some genius had decided to turn the control tower into a rotating NAAFI Function Room. It was still used as such, but it had lost its ability to rotate after it was hired out for a military wedding reception, during which a pissed artificer had found and removed the protective buffer circuits, causing the room to spin at a speed its designers had never intended, and pinning a number of jiving grannies to the windows in the process. The cost of repairing the burnt-out clutch was too great, and the tower had since stood mercifully still.

Grouse were kept in a coop in a small wood on the southern tip of the island and, given that they were bred for the sole purpose of being shot, the 65th was careful to ensure the authorities stayed blissfully ignorant of their presence on the base. In observing the traditional opening of the Season, a visitor to the base would find increased levels of security during the *65th RHA Invitational Clay Pigeon Shoot*, which always took place on August 12th, since shooting grouse was now a serious crime. Shooting game was a serious crime. In fact, shooting any living creature was a criminal activity that incurred the full wrath of the authorities. Except humans, of course, the shooting of whom was generally tolerated by the State, especially if done in the furtherance of terrorism or crime.

Most of the regiment's buildings were located on the western side of Windcheater Island. In contrast, the eastern side of the island was very sparse; just a small chapel, the Sailing Club and a few houses where the married officers lived. Dominating this area, set a few hundred metres from the water's edge, was a large red-brick Edwardian manor house – the Officers' Mess of the 65th.

The base was not in a good condition. Nearly all buildings suffered from damp, and paint flaked from every surface as mould burrowed underneath. Water pressure was intermittent and the hot water supply in buildings was, at best, inconsistent, as tired boilers were pushed way beyond their working life. In the winter, frozen pipes would burst every day. Every six months, inspectors from the Defence Estates Agency visited the base to assess the cost of repair. Noting how the mould had advanced since their previous visit, and seeing the dandruff of flaked paint at the base of walls, they would tut in disapproval and promise to act, as long as there was money in the system, which there never was. Windcheater Island was beyond economic repair.

Yet the soldiers of the 65th did not actually mind living in such squalid conditions, for a very simple reason. Every soldier in the British Army paid an accommodation charge, deducted automatically from their pay; the amount according to a sliding scale of the accommodation's quality. As the 65th's accommodation was graded *Unfit for human habitation*, they paid absolutely nothing to live there, all the happier to have more beer tokens to spend each night in the NAAFI.

Taverner left his bicycle propped up against the front wall of the Officers' Mess and went inside through the revolving doors. The cleaners were hoovering further down the corridor and from the dining room he could hear the sound of the breakfast table being cleared. The Mess Manager, Staff Sergeant Lomas, was in the foyer.

'Morning, Staff!' said Taverner, cheerfully.

'Good morning, sir. Did you have a pleasant chat with the Commanding Officer? I've put out some coffee in the anteroom in case you needed a little refreshment.'

Taverner threw his gloves and forage cap on a table and ran a hand through his hair.

'Thank you, that's very kind. No, Staff, it wasn't too bad. Getting a rocket from this CO is like being savaged by an angry lettuce,' he said unprofessionally, and not caring a damn.

'By the way, sir, Regimental Headquarters has been on the phone asking for you. They're still waiting for your Battery's ethnic-monitoring forms.'

Theatrically Taverner threw his hands in the air. 'Christ! Are we all destined to be slaves to the bureaucrats? Is there no escape from the CODE? Please give me strength!' He stormed off into the anteroom.

Ethnic-monitoring forms! Did RHQ not have anything better to do? Nobody in the 65th gave two hoots about one's ethnic background. Why did the Colonel have to make it an issue? There was no racism in the 65th – they were soldiers and everyone was equally worthless. Anyone would think the Army only existed so idiots like the Colonel could constantly evaluate it. Well, screw the Colonel. Screw the CODE and the whole blasted system!

Taverner had just started to sip his coffee when he had an idea, and went into the Mess Manager's office and phoned his Battery Sergeant Major.

'Hallo BSM, it's Captain Taverner. That bloody Diversity Return thingy. RHQ are on my back. Did we get round to distributing those ethnic-monitoring forms to the boys yesterday?'

'No, sir, they're still on my desk. I'll get onto it now.'

'No, don't. Just fill them in yourself and run them up to RHQ.'

'Sir, the boys have to do it themselves. It's supposed to be confidential.'

'What? Oh bollocks to all that. We haven't got time, BSM.'

'As you wish, sir. It shouldn't take too long. There're the Khan twins, Dixon, Dharni and Henderson. I think the rest are all White.'

'No, no, no, BSM, that's far too boring. Tick the box that says Chinese-Welsh.'

'For who, sir?'

'For the entire Battery, BSM.'

'I'm not sure, sir. The CO won't be a happy bunny.'

'Condemned out of your own mouth, BSM, the forms are supposed to be confidential. The CO won't see them, well, not until the information is collated by Brigade and they send him a hard copy. He won't even know it's us. Data Protection Act, you see. Still, it should raise a few eyebrows at Brigade.'

'Chinese ... Welsh,' said the Battery Sergeant Major, slowly, as he wrote it down. 'Ah-so, boyo.'

'Thank you, BSM. I'll be in later this morning.'

Back in the anteroom, Taverner's coffee tasted a little better.

FOUR

In a desolate café within a neglected motorway service station, a lone and rather rumpled gentleman sat working his way through the miserable fare that passed for a fried breakfast. He was short, stocky and had clearly lost the battle with his waistline some time ago, and his sports jacket and comb-over gave him a comical, archaic air. The gentleman was jet-lagged and on his first visit to England for several years. Though he was English and a fervent patriot, he had no desire whatsoever to be back in his homeland and, spearing a morsel of sausage with unnecessary vigour, he silently damned the system that had posted him back to the country he had never wanted to see again; a country that, according to his first impressions that morning, had changed beyond recognition.

Major Tom Hesketh's posting had come as a complete surprise to him. He had been a contented British Liaison Officer with the Canadian Armed Forces in Edmonton, Alberta, with a year of his commission left to run before he retired. His wife was a senior nurse and their children were doing well at college. With no intention of ever returning to England, they had applied for, and been granted, Canadian citizenship, effective on his retirement.

Then, ten days ago, out of the blue, he had received a posting order back to England. It was most unusual that an officer would be moved around in the twilight of his career, especially one such as himself, who had long since been passed-over for further promotion. Almost as much of a shock was the news that he was going back to his old regiment, the 65th RHA, as the Second-in-Command. His family would remain in Canada and put up with his absence for one year, rather than move yet again.

He had landed at Brize Norton military airport in Oxfordshire just before dawn and had drawn a car from the military motor pool; an asthmatic, speed-restricted excuse of a vehicle that made him long for his powerful Buick back home in Canada. He didn't like right-hand drive and his gear-changing had become rusty. He thrashed the wretched car through its limited rev range without a care, in the manner of those who drive cars that do not belong to them, and headed west towards Devon. The motorways, he knew, were always crowded at morning rush hour, so he chose a minor road. He was hungry and had hoped to take breakfast in a pleasant little tea-room in a quiet village somewhere.

The early morning mist lifted to reveal a landscape that was not the picture-postcard Oxfordshire countryside that Hesketh remembered. Gone was the rich foliage of hedgerows and copses and the deep corn-coloured fields after the harvest that should have prevailed at this time of year. Instead, the landscape looked overgrown and untended, with weedy patches of vegetation poking up through chalky earth. It reminded him of certain parts of Cyprus. He drove through several villages, which all seemed utterly deserted. There was nowhere open for breakfast; as far as he could tell there were no businesses open anywhere. In one village the only welcoming thing he saw was a large billboard featuring the grinning British President above a slogan:

State Partnerships. Working for the Rural Community!

As Hesketh threaded his way through the Mediterranean panorama, he occasionally passed through huge areas of tended, borderless fields. Either side of the road, neat rows of prefabricated accommodation formed a corridor, and groups of labourers stared at him as he drove by. These must be the State Collective farms, he thought, the result of a government initiative to nationalise agriculture. It was their idea of a rescue package for farming.

He gave up on the idea of a scenic drive to Devon and found the M4 motorway, stopping at the service station near Swindon.

Hesketh was in no hurry to get to Windcheater Island. He let his breakfast settle and bought a copy of the *Daily Telegraph*. On the front page was the President again, above an accompanying article about the fulfilment of the Urban Crime Reduction Pledge, with a gushing editorial praising the President for his drive and clarity of vision. There was no irreverent cartoon to accompany the headlines, nor could he find the crossword, and he turned instead to the obituaries. If he had been expecting a précis of the life of some eccentric old soak who'd recently dropped off his perch, he was disappointed. The current crop of recent deaths was rather stale in comparison – celebrating dull but earnest citizens who had seemingly devoted their lives to the cause of social justice.

The coffee was as foul as it was strong. Hesketh forced down another cup and set off down the motorway towards

Bristol. The M4 was surprisingly bereft of traffic, but the car's speed was electronically-limited and he couldn't take advantage of the empty road. Flat out at sixty miles per hour, the engine sounded as though it was trying to strangle itself.

Major Hesketh had served twice before in the 65th. He had been posted there many years earlier as a young subaltern straight out of Artillery School, and although his career had then taken him outside the regiment, he had later returned to take command of a Battery.

Hesketh had been held in very high esteem by those he had commanded and soldiers always recalled his name in a revered tone. As a Battery Commander his primary concern had always been the welfare and morale of those under his command. He imparted a sense of style to his Battery and he got the best out of his soldiers, fending off unnecessary work and fighting their corner tenaciously, with a wonderful talent for doing so without causing offence.

He was not an ambitious officer and took little interest in the thrusting and networking necessary to get noticed by his seniors, knowing that the mosquito that buzzed the loudest was usually the first to get squashed. Perversely, he had enjoyed watching the less-capable officers get promoted ahead of him, and took considerable delight in observing their Machiavellian manoeuvring, their bitchy posturing and inky-pellet flicking. In time, as it dawned on him that he had been well and truly passed-over, and as his last appointment in command of soldiers had neared its end, some of the spark had gone out of Hesketh and he resigned himself to the inevitable round of dead-end staff jobs that would take him up to retirement. Though he would never command a regiment, at least the school fees would be covered and his pension secured. Battery Command in the 65th had been his peak; thereafter he had been landed with Staff Officer (Grade Two) with responsibility for the provision of Portaloos on Salisbury Plain, after which he had served two years as Officer-in-Charge of Historical Re-enactment and Military Museums (North East), where his most notable achievement had been a superbly-choreographed recreation of Bloody Sunday for the benefit of some schoolchildren studying GCSE History, who were profoundly disturbed by its brutal realism and subsequently had to be offered counselling. Soon after, he was offered the post of Liaison Officer in Canada and he had spent the past eight years living in Edmonton, working with the Princess Patricia's Canadian Light Infantry, far from a home he cared less and less for, as he watched it sink into the abyss.

Hesketh passed Bristol, followed the M5 motorway as far as Tiverton and took the North Devon Link Road towards Holberton. Unlike Oxfordshire and Wiltshire, the North Devon landscape was much greener in an overgrown, untended sort of way. Near the town of South Molton, he passed another vast State Collective farm, which somehow looked different to the others he'd seen that morning, but for a reason he couldn't immediately put his finger on.

As he entered Holberton, Hesketh remembered why. Somewhere within the fields he had seen a herd of cows grazing; some black-and-white Holsteins, he recalled, and some chunkier beef cattle that might have been Herefords or Limousins. There had been a few sheep, too. They were the only livestock he had seen that day, in over a hundred miles of rural motoring.

Holberton had always been a forgettable little town and Hesketh could see that little had changed. He drove down the High Street, turned left by the Ship and Shovel – the soldiers' local pub – and followed the winding lane south out of the town. Another mile along this lane brought him to the Sentry Post at Windcheater Island. He drove over the dyke and stopped his car by the sentry; the first British soldier he had seen for years.

The sentry only looked about seventeen, but his boots shone like black glass, his uniform was clean and pressed, and he carried his rifle in the relaxed and confident manner of the well-trained.

'Good morning, sir. Could you please open the boot and the bonnet, and sign in over there, sir.'

The shiny boots, the calm confidence and that wonderful Liverpudlian accent, thought Hesketh, reassured. England might have changed, but the 65th was just as he remembered it.

While the sentry checked the car, Major Hesketh walked into the Sentry Post where Bombardier Podsnap was on duty again. Podsnap braced up when he recognised Hesketh.

'Sir! Good to see you again, sir!'

'Goodness me, as I live and breathe. Young Podsnap. You'd only just joined up when I last saw you. Bombardier now, eh? The 65th must really be desperate.'

Podsnap filled out a car pass for Hesketh. 'Did you have a good journey from Canada, sir?'

'Very long and very boring.' Hesketh felt the tiredness start to wash over him, now that his long journey was nearly at an end. He had been travelling for about eighteen hours. 'I take it the Officers' Mess is still where it used to be.'

'Of course, sir. Welcome back, sir.'

At the Officers' Mess, Hesketh was shown to his room by Westlake, the deferential Mess Bombardier.

'I'll have your bags brought up, sir,' said Westlake. 'Shall I inform RHQ of your arrival?'

'No, thank you.'

'Not even the Adjutant, sir? He does like to be informed of new arrivals.'

'Especially the bloody Adjutant!' growled Hesketh. 'I intend to stay incognito until I've caught up on some sleep.'

Westlake departed. Hesketh removed his jacket and shoes, and lay on his bed. He had many unanswered questions and tomorrow perhaps he would discover why he, a passed-over Major at the end of his career, had suddenly been parachuted into the number-two spot in a famous regiment, prior to a discreet and anonymous retirement. He did not dwell on this for long, and quickly drifted off into a welcome sleep.

That evening, Charlie Taverner was in the bar long before the other officers, and took his pre-dinner gin and tonic out into the garden behind the Mess to watch the setting sun, drawing to a close another crushingly boring day in the 65th.

His Battery had just finished its month of regimental fatigues, by way of Colonel Sandford's punishment, yet his soldiers had cracked on without complaint. Taverner didn't want to cause any more trouble for them for the time being, and had decided to toe the line.

The 65th was still confined to barracks by the Colonel and would remain so for the foreseeable future. Soon the winter months and the ski season would be upon them; a period when the Officers' Mess traditionally decamped *en masse* to Méribel or Verbier, but Sandford was now threatening to cancel everyones' leave over Christmas. Taverner wondered how much more of it he could take.

Civvy Street was not an attractive proposition for Taverner. Ex-Army officers could rarely find suitable employment once they'd left – they were deemed to have been tainted by their military service. He knew of acquaintances that had left and drifted around for a bit, then joined back up again. As someone who was addicted to excitement and heart-stopping situations, there were few options open to him. Perhaps he would become a mercenary in Eastern Europe or Africa. Or he could photograph surfers riding the huge reef breaks off the coast of Chile. Maybe he would find contentment as a recluse on a small island in the Outer Hebrides.

He was interrupted in his reverie by a portly, balding older man with a round face.

'Goodness me, and I thought I was early for dinner. Mind if I join you?' said the man.

'Not at all. Glad of the company,' lied Taverner. He shook the man's hand. 'Charlie Taverner. And you must be the new Second-in-Command. Won't you sit down?'

'Tom Hesketh. How do you do.'

Hesketh took in the younger officer. Taverner was dressed in a beautifully cut dark-grey suit, a pink shirt and muted silk tie. A Sea Dweller on his wrist and a whiff of Penhaligon's *Blenheim*. He spoke in a lazy and well-modulated tone. A standard-issue officer of the 65th, thought Hesketh. *Nothing has changed.*

On cue, Bombardier Westlake appeared.

'A pint of foaming ale please,' said Hesketh, enthusiastically.

'Certainly, sir.' Westlake assumed the manner of a head waiter announcing the specials. 'This evening I can offer you *Witches' Cauldron Hocus-Pocus Special* or *Old Bugger Me Sideways*, sir.'

'Hmmm, and what would you recommend?'

'Quite frankly, sir, I'd recommend a gin and tonic,' said Westlake, speaking as someone who had to clear up the results when officers had dared to quaff even a modest quantity of the two ales.

'Then a g. and t. it will be, and the same again for Mr Taverner,' said Hesketh.

Westlake bowed slightly and departed.

'A very wise choice,' said Taverner. 'You'd be bloody mad to try those ales. They'll go through you like crap through a goose, if you can keep them down. The only people who sample them are the new warts. And that's not by choice either. Mess initiation.'

'What an awful shame. I was rather looking forward to a decent pint,' said Hesketh. 'Perhaps I'd better have a word with the Wines Member and get some proper ales in.'

Presently the rest of the officers started to congregate in the bar, and Taverner and Hesketh went through to join them.

If the 65th's base at Windcheater Island was a place where a young soldier could escape from the casual violence of life on the council estates, then the Officers' Mess was a place where young Army officers could escape from the wholly violent business of soldiering. The officers were an eclectic bunch, and although Colonel Sandford had instinctively categorised them solely on the basis of class, he was some way off the mark. It would be true to say that the unique qualities that the 65th sought in its officers tended to suit the idle-rich, but for each one with an entry in Debrett's, for each one with no real idea of his vast personal wealth, there would be another officer who'd been educated at a sink-estate comprehensive, or had come up through the ranks. They had been selected for the 65th for a number of reasons; style and substance over military ability, a devil-may-care attitude to risk and a clear determination to enjoy life as it came to them. They'd come straight from Sandhurst and Artillery School, and from this raw material the 65th had smoothed out any rough edges and moulded them to the required specification. There was no place in the 65th for thrusters and backstabbers, or those who might use the regiment as a stepping stone to higher things. The regiment was everything. To be ambitious was very bad form.

Taverner introduced some of the officers to Major Hesketh.

There was Lieutenant Fraser; a floppy-haired Troop Commander in Taverner's Battery, and Captain Entwistle, in a dark three-piece suit with a fob watch, who was known as *The Teamster*, for reasons no-one knew, not even Entwistle himself. Captain Mellor, a former soldier in the Royal Tank Regiment, recently married to a beautiful doctor and just back from his honeymoon, and Captain MacNeish from Easterhouse in Glasgow, offering a round of cigarettes to two aristocrats, Lieutenant Chief Mbotu and Lieutenant The Honourable Skeffington. Skeffington was the ugly little rich boy, wealthy beyond comprehension and cadaverous in looks and build. An Army cross-country skiing champion, Skeffington possessed a phenomenal level of fitness that was not remotely affected by a forty-a-day habit, and whatever he chose to spend his money on, it was not clothes, as Skeffington's threadbare suit suggested.

Zsa Zsa Gabor supposedly once said, "There is no such thing as an ugly rich man". She was wrong. She had never met Lieutenant Skeffington. He was simply hideous to look at, and even his vast wealth seemed unable to compensate for his ugliness. Everything he'd learnt about the opposite sex had been down to the very expensive high-class whores who were chauffeured discreetly to the Mess at weekends for his pleasure.

Across the other side of the room, and cutting the most dapper figure of all, was the Camp Quartermaster; a simpering officer in his late fifties, and another former soldier who had worked his way up through the ranks before being commissioned as a Late-Entry officer. He stood with his left foot turned outwards like a ballet dancer and held his cigarette in the air with straight, rigid fingers as if halfway through a karate-chop. His hair was an unlikely nut-brown colour and in his lapel he wore an outrageous carnation that he selected from the Mess greenhouse each morning.

'He's as straight as a right angle,' Taverner told Hesketh. 'Has his godson to stay some weekends. Seems to have an awful lot of godsons, if you know what I mean.'

'I know. When I first arrived in the 65th as a young subaltern, he was my Troop Sergeant. He hasn't changed a bit.' Hesketh went over to make the introduction.

At the dinner table, Hesketh remembered the custom of never occupying the seat at the far end of the table. No-one present that evening was allowed to sit there. Not Hesketh, not the Commanding Officer – not even Royalty, had they dropped in for dinner. The place was permanently reserved for Colonel Cobbaton-Farr, the owner of the Officers' Mess. Behind his empty seat hung his portrait, dominating one end of the dining room.

The building had been erected on Windcheater Island by Cobbaton-Farr's ancestors, who had made a fortune from importing guano – fertile bird droppings – from South America for the Victorian garden. Windcheater Island had been requisitioned by the Royal Air Force in the 1930s, although the family had continued to live there (the RAF officers had been accommodated elsewhere) and it was by a little luck and a lot of string-pulling that Colonel Cobbaton-Farr had eventually realised his vision, taken command of the 65th and got the RAF kicked out. His ancestral home had become the Officers' Mess soon after.

Major Hesketh recalled Colonel Cobbaton-Farr as a diminutive, rather distant man with a fixation for honey, which he added to his tea and coffee, to his toast, to his breakfast sausages and his Sunday roast, in fact to every single thing that passed his lips, being not remotely concerned if he offended the good tastes of those he so often entertained. Cobbaton-Farr's young Filipino wife, seldom at ease in her husband's sumptuous surroundings, eventually eloped with a young officer, who consequently eloped to Civvy Street where such behaviour was not frowned upon. Cobbaton-Farr, having been in a state of shock for weeks afterwards, rocked up to coffee-break one memorable morning, just in time to see the Adjutant's spaniel brazenly snag the last of his honey-biscuits from the plate and dash gleefully from the room to devour the snack in private. For Cobbaton-Farr, it was the last straw. The World and the Adjutant's dog were against him, and without another word he walked outside, drove off in his Bentley, and pranged it a mile outside Holberton.

Cobbaton-Farr now lived in a caravan somewhere on the Dorset-Somerset border, where he had become a bee-keeper. He was fiercely loyal to the 65th and he insisted that the officers still live in his Mess. He paid for its upkeep, he paid for the servants and he paid them well. He still interviewed young officers who wished to join the 65th, but was quite content to pass his days tending to his beloved bees. He would always expect to receive invitations to official functions from the Mess Secretary so he could politely decline them, and a place was always set for him at the dinner table, in the house built on birdshit.

'How is the old dog?' said Hesketh, nodding towards the portrait of Cobbaton-Farr.

'Still barking mad,' said Taverner, peering round a large silver centrepiece of a bee. 'He still selects all young officers for the regiment. He's difficult to get in touch with. I'm doing my stint as the Mess Secretary and I have to send all correspondence via his local pub.'

Next morning, Major Hesketh was still feeling rather jet-lagged, but rose early to prepare for his first full day back in the 65th, and after breakfast he started the usual round of courtesy visits to the different branches of the regiment.

At morning coffee-break, a tray of champagne was produced by one of the subalterns on his promotion to full Lieutenant. Hesketh declined any more glasses after the first two and carried on with his tour of the regiment. At every stop he encountered familiar faces and began to get a little tired of the whole how-are-you-how-was-Canada-how's-the-wife-and-kids-delighted-to-see-you-back-old-chap routine. Much to his increasing dismay, nearly everyone produced a bottle of single malt and two glasses from a drawer, each thinking they were unique in doing so, and Hesketh was far too polite to refuse the offer. Colonel Sandford was too busy to see Hesketh that morning when he called by, so Hesketh went to see the Regimental Sergeant Major instead. The RSM produced some port (of which he normally took a slug before drill to oil his larynx), which didn't mix at all well with the champagne and the scotch.

Hesketh drove his car unsteadily down the main runway to get to the Mess for lunch, grateful for the runway's exceptional width, of which he used a fair proportion, all the time grinning inanely at the wheel. He left the car parked at a rakish angle in front of the Mess and, as he staggered towards the revolving door, he narrowly avoided being run over by another officer who was inebriated from the champagne at coffee-break.

Afterwards, Hesketh returned on foot to walk off the effects of the alcohol. Back in Regimental Headquarters, with a good lunch inside him and still pleasantly drunk from the morning's tour, he went to the 65th's History Room, where he let the story of one of the Army's finest regiments soak back into him.

Hesketh worked his way slowly along the cases of silver and medals, carefully reading the captions and citations, reacquainting himself with the heroes and campaigns of years gone by. There had been some towering personalities commanding the 65th in the past, and perhaps the two most revered gentlemen in the regiment's history were commemorated with particularly lavish displays.

There was Colonel Kirby who, in 1833, had laid siege to the huge fortress at Meghinstala, with the desperate aim of clearing his large gambling debt with the Mullah of Meghinstala by killing the Mullah. Kirby had failed spectacularly and the Mullah's army had wiped out the 65th for its pains.

And at Talavera there had been Major Fotheringham,

an over-sensitive commander who, still smarting from a remark made by a cavalry officer of the 23rd Light Dragoons at a ball a few weeks earlier, ordered the 65th to fire into the Dragoons as they formed up nearby prior to charging the French infantry − the first ever recorded blue-on-blue. The surviving cavalry had ignored the enemy and cut down their own artillerymen like scythes through corn.

There had been other attempts throughout the 65th's history to emulate these wonderful endeavours, but they had never achieved the same degree of sheer futility. Kirby's and Fotheringham's actions had been in the finest traditions of the 65th and all serving officers were expected to be familiar with their example.

How times had changed, thought Hesketh. Nowadays, the title *65th Royal Horse Artillery* was a misnomer. The Royal prefix was clearly inappropriate in the fledgling Federal British Republic, horses were associated with hunting and steeplechase racing − both long since outlawed − and the regiment's Howitzers had been mothballed and put into storage where they were tended to minimally by uncaring civilian contractors. In fact, the *65th RHA* was no longer the official title of the regiment. When the British Armed Forces had been placed under the full command of EuroCorps, Brussels had re-designated the 65th as the *8th Battalion of the 34th Artillery Regiment (Southwest England) EuroCorps, Former United Kingdom.*

The new title hadn't caught on − the *8th Battalion of the 34th ARSEEFUK* did little to suggest even a modicum of military professionalism.

The door to the History Room was opened by a man in a suit.

'Major Hesketh?' he asked.

'Yes?'

'So here you are. No-one can seem to find you. I'm Colonel Sandford.'

'My apologies, Colonel. Tom Hesketh. How do you do.'

Hesketh offered his outstretched hand and was surprised when, instead of shaking his hand, Colonel Sandford merely thrust a file into it, smiling as he did – a smile, Hesketh noted, that did not extend to his eyes.

'Settling in?' said Sandford. 'Good, good. We've got a lot to discuss and no doubt we'll do so in the future. There's a Command Community Conference on Monday morning and we'll be discussing that,' he said, pointing at the file, on the cover of which was written *8th of the 34th – The Way Forward*. Sandford started backing away to the door as he talked. 'You'll need to be up to speed on it for Monday, but you should find it quite straightforward. I'll be in my quarters tonight if you have any questions about it. Perhaps after that we can meet up and have a chat.'

And with that he was gone.

Hesketh stayed in the History Room for another hour, following the 65th's adventures up to the present day, then walked back to the Mess for the evening, wondering about Colonel Sandford.

If Hesketh had been expecting the Commanding Officer of the 65th, as one might, to be the epitome of élan and smooth urbanity, he had been most disappointed.

FIVE

After dinner that evening, Major Hesketh and the Camp Quartermaster took their coffee through to the anteroom, as the younger officers headed back to the bar. Years earlier, when Hesketh had joined the 65th as a young Second Lieutenant, the now Quartermaster had been his Troop Sergeant. He had tried to cover up his inclinations at that time and, though they were always suspected, he took the gibes well and was good enough at his job to get himself promoted to the rank of Sergeant Major. A few years ago he had been given a Late-Entry commission as the Quartermaster, and the Officers' Mess had allowed him to relax into his natural campness in surroundings rather more genteel than the rough and tumble of the Sergeants' Mess. In the anteroom the Quartermaster gently reminded Major Hesketh of the mistakes he had made as a subaltern in the 65th, and the fact that Hesketh had evolved into such a highly respected officer was proof enough to the Quartermaster that his mentorship of the young officer so many years ago had been successful.

'I must confess,' said the Quartermaster, 'I'm very surprised to see you back here. A cushy little number out in Canada. All nice and settled. Why have they sent you back? Whole bloody country's gone to the dogs. Couldn't ever imagine you wanting to come back. Did you not plead with the Postings Board?'

'No. You know what they're like,' said Hesketh. 'They would never change their minds and I'm not going to grovel to them. It's only for one year, although I have absolutely no idea why I've been sent here. Maybe the CO can shed some light on it. Quartermaster, tell me about Colonel Sandford. I met him today very briefly, but thought him a very strange individual.'

'Charming, isn't he. No personality whatsoever. If he appeared on colour television he'd still come out in black and white.'

'Is it just lack of confidence?'

'No, I think being rude just comes naturally to him.'

'So he's not ex-65th. A gentleman is never rude unintentionally. I'd never heard of him before.'

'No, well, you wouldn't have done.' The Quartermaster dropped his voice and tapped the side of his nose. 'We're not supposed to let on about this. Not only has he never been in the 65th – he has never actually served in the Artillery,' he said, letting the failing hang in the air like a bad smell. 'I know a bit more about him than I really should let on, but you must keep it schtum. He started his career in Personnel. The only thing he's ever commanded is a desk.'

'So why in God's name is he now commanding the 65th?' said Hesketh. 'I could think of several people far more suited to the job.'

'So could I. The Old Guard, Tom. They're no more. They've all emigrated. Funds. Family. Fido. The lot. All gone.'

'Curzon?'

'Bermuda.'

'Andersen?'

'Northern Cyprus.'

'Marlow?'

'Lincoln Prison. Life sentence. When his estate was repurchased, he took on the chaps from the Interior Ministry. Single-handedly. Mortared them when they came through the gates – with some accuracy, so I understand. Then tried to blow his own head off with his shotgun. Silly bugger missed his brain altogether and took off most of his face. Still, always was an ugly bugger.' The Quartermaster chuckled at the recollection and became serious again.

'No, Tom, I'm afraid I get the impression the 65th is heading for a bit of a dark period. You see, the 65th has never been flavour of the month with some of our more progressive leaders. As our penance for adhering to tradition and custom, they withhold budgets, overstretch us operationally and let the boys live in squalor. I suspect the Ministry of Defence hoped that so many of them would leave that they'd have no choice but to disband the regiment. But when all is said and done, it's our standards that have held the regiment together and ensured it has survived where others haven't. They try to force their silly ideas on us – we tell them to sod off.'

The Quartermaster sipped his coffee and continued.

'The 65th has always had top cover from some bugger somewhere who went for the stars, against his better judgement. They kept a look out for us, kept the wolves from the door when the mandarins were sniffing around for sacrificial lambs at each round of cutbacks. They're all gone, Tom. We're more exposed than ever – which is why we get landed with an arse like Sandford.'

'He's a very unusual choice for the 65th,' said Hesketh, 'and I agree, it does not bode well for the future. And while we're on the subject of change, what the hell has happened to our green and pleasant land? When I drove down from Brize Norton yesterday I barely recognised it. The whole countryside looked parched and abandoned. I was quite shocked.'

'What is it, seven or eight years since you left?' said the Quartermaster. 'This is no longer the England you'd remember. The rot started to set in about the time you left for Canada. Yes, it's been going on for years, but recently it started to get out of control. In the last five years the State has done more damage to this country than our worst enemies could have envisaged in their wildest dreams. Take the Monarchy, for example. Gone. Swatted aside like a fly. Very subtly, of course, we barely noticed. Loophole in the European Constitution. Some rubbish about Heads of State and legal incompatibility. Allowed to stay on in some sort of elegant caretaker way like the Belgian or Dutch royal families, but quite impotent. Can't imagine that went down well in Canada.'

'We were aghast, Quartermaster.'

'Elsewhere, everything has been "modernised". The Judiciary, the Church, the Health Service, the Police Service – who are no longer called the *Police* – they are *Regional Crime Reduction Partnerships* and about as useful as a chocolate fireplace. Parliament exists only to rubber-stamp decisions taken in private by a government that can no longer be held to account. The Home Office was re-branded as the Ministry of the Interior and, overnight, gained a considerable portfolio. It's a huge bugger. Law, transport, culture, health, education, immigration, national security, even the media. It runs the whole show. A very tight ship and very *very* sinister, so the word is. And everything is driven by the CODE.'

'Ah yes, the CODE. I remember reading about this,' said Hesketh. 'The government's blueprint for "a fairer society". Community, Opportunity, Diversity, Equality. How very catchy.'

'You can't get away from it,' said the Quartermaster. 'A glossy, persuasive motto that permeates almost every aspect of modern life. A very slick mandate for massive State interference.'

'How long has the CODE been around?'

'It must be in its fourth year now. There are even separate ministries for it – a Ministry of Community, a Ministry of Opportunity and so on. The CODE was first piloted in the Civil Service, as it was called back then, and as it developed it was introduced into other areas such as education, the Health Service and the police. It's a system to make everyone rather more socially aware, as they put it; to get people to "understand their social responsibilities". Then it becomes law, and now private businesses also have to comply with the CODE, just like Health and Safety. In the Army, we were safe at first. We watched all this going on out there and couldn't stop laughing at the pointlessness of it. It would have taken a brave bugger to try to impose the CODE on us, so they left us alone. Sadly, it was only a matter of time before they got round to it. Chesterford handed it to them on a plate.'

Hesketh knew what the Quartermaster meant. The name Chesterford was up there with Warrenpoint, Hyde Park and Bloody Sunday; all of them dark days in the history of the British Army.

Chesterford – a suburb in a northern town. A stifling summer and the simmering tension in bored youths had spilled over into a riot. The police were overwhelmed and in desperation had called in soldiers from a nearby training depot. Just three weeks into their Basic Training, these sixteen-year old recruits had found themselves on a baseline, with petrol bombs raining down from above and roofing slates skimming into their shins. Exactly how they had been issued, mistakenly, with live ammunition had never been adequately established by the subsequent inquiry, but the result had been eight dead and many injured.

'The soldiers were arrested,' said the Quartermaster, 'then most of the Generals too. Culpable homicide, you see. Needed to be made an example of. The Army was castigated in the media and a task force from the Interior Ministry was sent in, found severe failings at every level and ordered the whole Army to be re-educated in the doctrine of the CODE. Now, we've got no top brass to tell them to wind their necks in. They've all just been given the sack. And who have the government put in their place? Senior Civil Servants. Chief Executives. Managing Directors. Captains of bloody Industry! None of them have ever served, but they've all been given rank of Major General or Vice Admiral or whatever, and brought in a whole raft of very unpleasant measures to modernise the Armed Forces. And needless to say, all these buggers are very "in" with the government.

'Anyway, this is where our new Colonel comes into play,' said the Quartermaster, coming full circle. 'He's a head-office man to his boots and has read the changing atmosphere like a book. A clever bugger, he managed to avoid the purges and carried on fart-arsing around Whitehall, then he wrote a paper about recruiting, arguing that the recruiting of soldiers to certain regiments on a purely geographical basis was expensive and divisive, and that other more important factors should be considered. So the silly bugger suggested they form a regiment of homosexual soldiers. Ridiculous really, but the new Generals loved it. And bugger me if they didn't actually put it into practice! Anything to show how committed they were to modernising the Army. My dear, just think about it – an entire regiment of queers! What a splendid idea!' The Quartermaster became quite animated. 'Such lovely, healthy young boys. Damned if I can remember their official name, but they became known as *The First Battalion The King's Own Queens.* Resources galore poured into the project. An entire regiment cobbled together in three months. You should have seen them. Quite exquisite specimens! Damn near applied for a transfer the very next day!'

Hesketh shook his head in disbelief as the Quartermaster continued.

'So these poor buggers got sent to the Balkans in a blaze of publicity, and then it all went a bit pear-shaped. Got themselves into a firefight with some pissed-up policemen and got a right bloody hiding. They should have been covering each others' arses, not watching them! Ha! Returned to Catterick after a month to lick their wounds, so to speak. All in all, a bit of a farce, but it got Sandford noticed and he was ear-marked for better things, just as the Generals started to turf out the Colonels lower down. They wanted weedy "enlightened line-manager" types to replace them, and started putting these new buggers in charge of a regiment here, a battalion there, even a Brigade or two – very few of them with any operational experience whatsoever and all of them such piss-poor leaders that the boys wouldn't even follow them to the thunderbox if they were stricken with amoebic dysentery. In their eyes, Sandford was perfect.'

'So why the hell do the soldiers stay?' said Hesketh. 'Surely they'd all be leaving in their thousands.'

'It's not that simple, Tom. As a *civilian* employee, whatever your job, you are required to attend in-service training in the CODE twice a year, and over time you build up CODE credits. Company directors love the idea because with their employees having a solid grounding in the CODE, they are able to avoid expensive lawsuits where some disgruntled employee or customer sues the company for wrongful dismissal or discrimination. The responsibility has been shifted onto the lower orders, who are deemed to have been trained and are therefore personally responsible if they "offend" or "act inappropriately". These days, companies simply won't employ anyone who hasn't got a good smattering of CODE credits. They simply can't afford to take the risk. In any case, insurance companies and the unions won't allow it. Academic qualifications or years of experience are becoming worthless in comparison. But, as thankful as we were for not having the CODE forced on us in the military, it was a bit of a double-edged sword. While everyone else has been getting themselves indoctrinated, we've been fighting their wars and got left behind. Most firms won't touch an ex-soldier with a sterilized bargepole and would rather take on a pimply sixteen-year old with Level Three Citizenship than a switched-on thirty-year old ex-Sergeant. He can't afford to get trained up because it's too expensive to go private, but he can't get a job because he's not accredited. He'll only get work on the black market.'

'It all sounds a bit far-fetched, Quartermaster,' said Hesketh. 'You mean to tell me, for example, that the local newsagent in Holberton has to send its paperboy on a CODE training course?'

'No, Tom, it doesn't apply everywhere, certainly not in these parts. Only in the big cities, in the Central Zones, where the work is. They are the only places that matter to the government.'

'I hear London is a very different place these days,' said Hesketh.

'That's putting it mildly. A few years back, when the level of crime was astronomical and the police so hamstrung, certain areas of London started to be patrolled by private security companies employed by the big insurance firms. At first it consisted of just a few blocks in the more affluent areas like Kensington and Belgravia. Then the areas grew bigger, and in time they were sealed off. Kept the scum out, you see, and in no time the idea had spread like wildfire. They were called Secure Areas and they started cropping up all over the place. CCTV everywhere and Biometric and Vehicle Check Points to get in and out. Inevitably, crime plummeted and everyone was very happy. Then the government started to interfere, as usual, and linked the Secure Areas into one enormous Central Zone. They reckoned there were too many targets in Central London for Johnny Terrorist, so a Ring of Steel would be the answer, running from Twickenham to Islington, to Bethnal Green and down to Clapham.'

Bombardier Westlake appeared at the door.

'Two Taliskers, please. Doubles,' said the Quartermaster.

'So what about the areas outside this Central Zone?' asked Hesketh.

'Tatty, neglected, violent. Vast, sprawling estates, crime levels through the roof, no effective police and rampant narcotic addiction. Fast food take-aways and discount shops everywhere. Graveyards of ambition, Tom. Ghastly places.'

'And this just in London?'

'Good God, no. Every city has a Central Zone and squalid suburbs of decay surrounding it.'

'So what about the countryside?'

'Very different.'

Westlake brought the malt whiskies.

'Rural England is quite unimportant to the government,' said the Quartermaster. 'They have just left it to fend for itself, hoping that it would just go to ruin. Some places have indeed gone that way and are largely abandoned, but there are many pockets that seem to thrive. They're poorer than a church mouse and there's no law and order, no economy – no *legal* economy – yet these places somehow look after themselves. If the Government is a benign dictatorship, and I think it's fair to call it that, then what has evolved in the countryside is a benign anarchy. The funny thing is, it works. Take teenage yobs, for example. In the suburbs they're hauled up in their thousands in front of the beak and given their weekly slap on the wrist. Down here there's no need. The locals are judge, jury and executioner. In Holberton a few months back, some idiot of a boy-racer came screaming down the High Street doing the ton, as I believe it's called. The following evening he was sitting in the stocks outside the Ship and Shovel being pelted with rotten fruit at closing time, then the little scumbag was tarred and feathered and run out of town for good. No need for the police. Not that anyone's seen a policeman for years. The rural life is good as long as you don't mind living in poverty, but most people can't take it. They'd much rather live in the Central Zones where there's full employment and a very high standard of living. But to live there you have to sell your soul and conform to the CODE. You may have a good job and a good salary, but you do need to be *very* guarded in your opinions. Make a remark that someone might interpret as offensive, or against the *spirit* of the CODE, and you're putting your job on the line. If it's a minor transgression then your employers will suggest a little bit of re-education as your penance. With a mortgage and a family to support, you're not going to decline, are you? But if you were to get fired for *really* overstepping the mark, then you wouldn't ever find work again anywhere in a Central Zone. You'd be an outcast. *Persona non grata*, old chap; no job, mounting debt and you'd have no choice but to sell up and move out. The partner usually stays behind with the kids. Divorce courts always find in their favour.

'Needless to say the Central Zones are rather ambiguous places. I've been there on several occasions. With their high culture and clean streets, everyone's a picture of smug good health. But look a little deeper. Their lives are not quite so perfect. They have to conform and they live in constant fear. It's the threat of being sent beyond the wire. People do what is required of them in order to stay. So, you see, we must be grateful for the 65th. If it wasn't for this regiment I would not know what to do. I'd have nowhere to go. Canadian citizenship? Tom, you don't know how lucky you are. I think we should drink to that. Long live the 65th.'

'Long live the 65th,' repeated Hesketh.

SIX

Taverner's mood became increasingly despondent over the following week as Colonel Sandford continued his relentless shake-up of the 65th. There had also been a noticeable increase in the number of meaningless forms to be completed and returned to Regimental Headquarters: *'In no less than four pages, summarise how your Battery has implemented the latest Regimental Anti-bullying Policy'; 'Outline your proposals for increasing the diversity of your Battery'; 'State your Battery's* **Objectives***'; 'Send in all details of every soldier's training in Health and Safety for the previous five years, including rank, number, date and location of training attended, and results if applicable (these will be verified against regimental records)'*. The Colonel would then chair numerous meetings to follow up and discuss the data with his officers, and Taverner wondered where it would all end. He was not an organised person – he thrived in chaos and disorder – and when he missed the Colonel's deadlines or failed to complete the forms to the required standard, or resorted to flippant answers, the Colonel only had to threaten his Battery's soldiers with more punishment to force him to pull his weight. Major Hesketh, the new Second-in-Command, seemed to be a good egg, but whether he could do anything about the tyrannical reign of Colonel Sandford remained to be seen. Taverner was almost at the end of his tether with the 65th. He resolved to give it another three months, and if things hadn't changed dramatically by then, he'd quietly slip away one night, and to hell with the formalities of resignation. By the weekend, his mood had improved considerably, as it did each weekend Hannah came to stay.

The officers' girlfriends usually spent the weekend at the Mess, and Hannah had surprised Taverner by arriving a day early on Thursday evening – the throaty rumble of her sports car pulling up outside announcing her arrival to the Mess. For the rest of the weekend, Taverner could forget about Colonel Sandford and the 65th, and indulge the love of his life; the girl who was, in so many respects, more than a match for him.

They had met at a local point-to-point, and Taverner had been smitten not only with her physical appearance – she was tall and curvaceous – but also her inner confidence and the pleasure she clearly got out of life. She was a few years younger than Taverner, raised and educated in Switzerland, but British by birth. Her father had been an aristocratic racing driver; a gregarious and charismatic individual who had perished when thrown from his vintage Bugatti. Her mother, a second-generation supermodel, also passed-on soon after – of a broken heart, some said.

Hannah had inherited the best features of her parents. She had long fair hair and an angelic face with high cheekbones and dark brown eyes that could be extremely innocent one minute, highly seductive the next, and she radiated sensuality. At the time of their first meeting, Hannah had another boyfriend, much to Taverner's disappointment, and he'd had to be patient. But he gently persisted, sending her flowers on her birthday and twelve red roses on Valentine's Day, and Hannah, who was used to being flattered, hitched up with him in due course. They had now been together for four years and were still as happy as they'd always been. She was a hugely popular visitor to the Mess, captivating everyone she met and, despite the parental tragedy of her teenage years, Hannah was remarkably content with life, which made her so much more attractive than the insecure and needy girls who'd once plagued Taverner. She lived on her own in Gloucester and travelled down to Windcheater Island most weekends. Following in her father's footsteps she had also done some motor racing for a few years, with some success, and it was a rare occasion that Taverner had not been petrified as a passenger in her little sports car, as she had the talent and lack of fear to make the vehicle – a Caterham Seven – do things way beyond the abilities of mere mortals, on country roads unencumbered by speed cameras and State surveillance technology.

The weather had been good that weekend and the whole Mess spent most of Saturday on the small beach at the south of the island, rounding off the day with a large volleyball match, with the Mess staff barbequing in the background.

Sunday morning meant the Church Service, which was a three-line whip for all officers. They paraded in their smart Service Uniform, and if the officers didn't exactly look forward to the service, their girlfriends certainly did. It was a rare chance to dress up and try to out-do each other in the fashion stakes.

As they filed into the chapel, they couldn't help but notice the Padre's face was a picture of ecclesiastical delight. The Padre had seldom seen so many in attendance and was grinning in a quite ungodly way from a cheeky draught of the communion wine. He was also taking a considerable interest in the young officers' girlfriends, all of whom the Good Lord had seen fit to bless in all the right ways. God, he believed, was clearly smiling on Windcheater Island that weekend.

Church Service was an onerous duty for the officers, even for those who were faintly grateful for the chance to repent for another sinful and over-indulgent week. The chapel was musty and chilly, and the Padre could bore a congregation to death at fifty paces. However, the girlfriends did provide a degree of visual interest, and on that criterion alone, the girl who Lieutenant Skeffington escorted trounced the others by a mile. She was quite stunning, but she did not come cheap. It was common knowledge that Skeffington had parted with several thousand Euros to buy her company for the weekend. A number of elderly civilians from Holberton were in attendance too, denied the chance to worship elsewhere when their local church had closed. The Commanding Officer was not present, but no-one was surprised.

The service started and everyone stood for the first hymn, *Glorious things to thee are spoken*. Elsie, the dear old organist, launched into the introduction and a congregation largely familiar with her musical inabilities tensed collectively in anticipation. Playing the organ in the chapel every Sunday was the highlight of Elsie's week, but she was savagely arthritic in both hands and her sense of tempo varied with whatever medication she was on at the time. Her fingers took an agonisingly long time to feel for each chord and she was always a steady half-bar behind the congregation, who

73

were forced to put in plenty of *rubato* at the end of each stanza in the hope that she would catch up. A quick glance at her, engrossed in the moment, rocking back and forth in front of the keyboard, wearing a pained and serious expression, suggested that it would be unlikely. And although only four verses were ever written for that particular hymn, Elsie played a fifth bonus verse at no extra cost, quite unable to register the polite silence coming from the pews.

The Padre said a short prayer before embarking on a very long reading.

At the back, Taverner, Skeffington and the Regimental Doctor, Captain Joseph Meckie – known to all as *Mengele* – were deep in hushed conversation.

'He's arriving tomorrow evening and he's been booked in for dinner,' whispered Taverner. 'Everyone must be ready to move as soon as we hear he's got to the Sentry Post. I'll take care of the Mess. Skeffington, get the Battery parade sorted out for Tuesday morning. He's got C-Troop.'

'Ouch,' said Skeffington, his face puckered in genuine concern.

'The Battery Sergeant Major will help you out,' said Taverner, 'he knows what to do.'

They stood for another hymn, which was comprehensively annihilated by Elsie, after which Taverner turned to the Doctor.

'He's going to report to you on Tuesday afternoon for his medical.'

'How, er, comprehensive a medical?' said the Doc.

'I don't know. I'm not a bloody doctor. Nothing invasive. Just make sure he has to do you know what with the whatsit in the thingimijig.'

'Okay.'

'And don't tell a soul!' hissed Taverner.

'Absolutely! Mum's the word,' said the Doc. 'By the way, what's the new officer's name?'

'Second Lieutenant James Cavendish.'

The third, and thankfully final, hymn didn't really stand a chance in the circumstances. As they made their way back to the Officers' Mess after the service, Taverner and Skeffington continued with the subject of Second Lieutenant Cavendish.

'This is important, so listen carefully,' said Taverner. 'After our bit of fun, he is to be treated like a brother officer of old. Make sure everyone knows that.'

'That's a bit unfair,' said Skeffington. 'It's at least six months before anyone is even supposed to acknowledge the mere presence of a wart.'

'Accepted. This one though, I want him to think he's got off lightly. Initiated tomorrow night, gets C-Troop the day after, and some other business with Mengele the same afternoon. That's all.'

Skeffington lit a cigarette and dragged greedily on it. 'You know, Tav,' he said, blowing smoke upwards, 'unless you're going soft in middle-age, I get the distinct impression that you have other plans for this new chap.'

'Would I do a thing like that?'

'Of course you would. Any chance of letting me in on it?'

'Don't be ridiculous. All good things to those who wait.'

A curry lunch was served in the bar. The Korma and Jalfrezi were cooked to perfection and did much to subdue the aroma of stale nicotine that hung in the room. Taverner and Skeffington left their partners in the company of some older officers, and went back for seconds.

'I've rather come to enjoy our enforced Sundays here,' said Skeffington. 'Funny, isn't it? Spiritual invigoration. Penitence and Prayers. Curry lunch. Afternoon shagging. It's a fine way to round off the week.'

Taverner nodded towards Skeffington's partner.

'Delightful girl, by the way. Is it true love this time?' he asked, with heavy sarcasm.

'Helena? She's Lebanese. Trained at the finest boudoir in Paris. She's managed to slot me in this weekend, for want of a better word, but I had to gazump a Westphalian heart surgeon. She only has a few clients. Not cheap, but worth every penny.'

'And pray what do you get for your money?' asked Taverner, intrigued.

'Everything. The works. Tav, she's *phenomenal*. She's made me realise how unimaginative I am.'

Taverner found that rather worrying, considering the rumours surrounding Skeffington's exotic tastes. They both looked over to her. Helena was very much the centre of attention in a pack of slavering middle-aged officers.

'It's fascinating, the depraved depths to which the female mind extends,' said Skeffington, dreamily.

'I'm sure it is.'

'Why, are you interested?' asked Skeffington. 'She takes bookings several months in advance.'

'Good God, no! I'll never pay for it!'

'Well, always treat yourself to the best, I say. Oh, shit! What's the time?'

'One fifteen.'

'Bollocks! Her chauffeur's picking her up at half past two. Sorry Tav, please excuse me. I must get my money's worth. This curry's given me one *hell* of an appetite.'

'What will it be today?' said Taverner. 'Spiderman and

Wonderwoman?' Skeffington's taste for role-playing in his private life was public knowledge in the Officers' Mess.

'What? No way!' said Skeffington, indignantly. 'That was a long time ago, Tav. I've moved on from that.' He rescued Helena from the drooling throng. 'Now we're doing Batman and Lara Croft! Tally Ho!'

The poor girl smiled weakly at Taverner as she was dragged hurriedly out of the bar.

Major Hesketh also sloped away early from the curry lunch, for rather more professional reasons. No doubt the afternoon would descend into one of collective inebriation and he'd had the good sense to leave well before the point of no return. The following day, Colonel Sandford was due to hold a commanders' meeting, or, as he liked to put it in his management-speak, a Command Community Conference. Hesketh had to digest the contents of the folder given to him by Sandford in the History Room, and changed out of his military uniform into some civilian clothes before he settled down to read.

8th Battalion of the 34th Artillery Regiment
(formerly the 65th Royal Horse Artillery)

'THE WAY FORWARD'
Lieutenant Colonel H R Sandford RHA

Contents

1. Community
2. Opportunity
3. Diversity
4. Equality

An interesting title, though Hesketh. Colonel Sandford was clearly very keen on the CODE and it would be fascinating to see how he intended to link the CODE with the rather different business of running a regiment. Not being someone who ever read a document through from the beginning, Hesketh thought he'd start with a gentle perusal of Chapter Three: *Diversity.*

Diversity

The mandatory requirement for every State and State-licensed institution to reflect the diversity of our national community is the main effort behind 'The Way Forward'. I am keen to see the 8th of the 34th Artillery Regiment (formerly the 65th RHA) lead the way in showing the Army Community how best to adhere, rigorously and effectively, to the principals of Symmetry in Command Diversity (SCD). (Chapter 3 'Diversity' p. 154 para. 2 refers.)

Which was no doubt very true, thought Hesketh. He turned to paragraph two on page 154: *Symmetry in Command Diversity (SCD).*

The first stage in the establishment of SCD will be the submission of Diversity Balance Sheets (DBS, see Appendix A) in order to identify Diversity Balance Development Needs (DBDNs) in order to apply Diversity Cost-Benefit Analysis (DCBA) using Diversity Competencies. This will be used to provide an overview of regimental diversity so that the subsequent Diversity Action Plan (DAP), tied in with the Diversity Implementation Cycle (DIC) will enable benefits and

opportunities to be defined, optimised and harvested.
Primarily it will be essential to achieve a balance between
diversity and critique ...

And if Hesketh had to read the fucking word 'Diversity'
one more fucking time then he would slit his fucking wrists!
He wondered if the document was some sort of parody.
There were over two-hundred pages of this drivel, and
somehow he would have to make sense of it if he wasn't
going to make a complete idiot of himself at the Colonel's
meeting the following day. The thought of having to
assimilate it started to make him tetchy, and the noise coming
from the room above – where one of the Lieutenants lived
– wasn't helping either. Someone, or something, was being
kept against its will and broadcasting the fact quite openly.
The noise became more rhythmic and Hesketh twigged in
disgust that the grunting was vigorous coupling.

Bloody subalterns! On a Sunday afternoon! Did they
have no shame?

He turned to Chapter Two: *Opportunity*.

Opportunity

The Command Community must modernise and actively
seek to orchestrate vertical networks. This requires all
commissioned and non-commissioned ranks to embrace
innovative open-source metrics while disintermediating the
traditional non-essential paradigms. Performance
optimisation can only be achieved through local regeneration
and the systematic, sustained and sustainable programme of
efficiency and measures for improved micro-empowerment,
thus achieving more centrally-derived targets.

There was no way Hesketh felt he could go on reading without losing the will to live. He scanned through some more pages and it was clear from where his eyes settled on a few words that there was no let-up.

Textured Management Command Functions …
Demand management process …
Vibrancy of a well-balanced workforce …

He turned to the final paragraph in the vain hope that it contained something in the way of a straightforward summary, and was met with a literary *coup de grâce*.

Polyvariate morphogenesis … Time-Space Dendritic portals … the strategic and ergonomic distribution of Geopathic Stress Eliminators will make a most positive contribution to communal energy and vitality.

The document told him less about the *Way Forward* for the 65th, and a lot more about Colonel Sandford's state of mind. Hesketh became aware that the grunting from the room above had ceased for a moment. By the sound of it, someone was climbing over furniture, and a girl's voice cried out in heavily-accented English.

'Raid me! Raid me! Raid my tomb, you caped studmuffin!'

There was a momentary silence, then a squeal and a colossal crash of bedsprings. The grunting started up again with even more vigour than before.

Hesketh threw the document on the floor. It was a waste of time. He went out for a long walk round the perimeter of the island and didn't return until after sunset.

SEVEN

Major Hesketh need not have worried about his inability to understand Colonel Sandford's document. At next day's Command Community Conference, it was apparent that not a single person present could understand it either, nor did they seem too concerned about their ignorance. Colonel Sandford had taken his place at the head of the long table in the Conference Room and launched into a half-hour discourse, in which he simply read out his document to the assembled officers; head down and barely pausing for breath, deriving a perverse delight from being the modernist lecturing the out-dated. Taverner and the Quartermaster spent the conference discreetly engaged in a game of Bullshit Bingo, furiously ticking their cards as the Colonel's jargon poured forth, and elsewhere, the doodling eventually gave way to nodding heads, as people fell asleep.

It was embarrassing. Hesketh even found himself feeling a little sorry for the Colonel, and occasionally asked for some clarification, regurgitating a few of his phrases.

'Could you take a moment to clarify the Modes of Application Diversity, Colonel,' said Hesketh, looking remarkably sincere.

'Well, the principal of achieving performance optimisation, as it relates to the regimental overview of diversity and emotional intelligence, and its related implementation life-cycle, will, in the medium and long term, lead to improvements in the vibrancy of a fulfilled and well-balanced workforce ...'

Hesketh let the Colonel continue, nodding several times to show that he was clarifying very well indeed, which he wasn't. The Colonel's invitation for any questions drew a blank response from the audience and he drew the conference to a close.

Colonel Sandford was relatively unconcerned what the officers thought of his document, or even if they understood it. It was sufficient that they know of its existence and general outline. The document was destined for distribution outside the regiment; it had very little to do with the future of the 65th and everything to do with showing off his impeccably progressive credentials to the people that really mattered.

At a quarter to six that evening, the new officer, Second Lieutenant James Cavendish, arrived at Windcheater Island.

Cavendish was not long out of Sandhurst and looking forward to taking up his first command appointment. He was also a little apprehensive of what lay ahead. The interview with Colonel Cobbaton-Farr had taken place in a pub a month earlier and he was delighted to learn that he had been accepted into the 65th. Cavendish couldn't wait to meet his Troop of soldiers and get stuck into the life of this most famous regiment. The joining instructions had clearly stated that he should arrive between half past five and six o'clock, as his room in the Officers' Mess would not be ready before then. He had followed the instructions to the letter, arriving in Holberton early and waiting in his car until it was time. It was important to make a good first impression.

However, the officers of the 65th had other plans for Cavendish.

There was seldom an occasion quite as daunting for a new subaltern than his first day in his new regiment, and these 'warts' were given a hard time by all. For the first few weeks they resembled the new schoolboy who arrives halfway through the term – unfamiliar with his surroundings and always in the wrong place at the right time. They reacted with hesitation to the first few salutes thrown in their direction – as new officers they were not used to them, and forgetting that they were no longer at Sandhurst they irritated Sergeant Majors by constantly addressing them as 'sir'. Perhaps the worst part of this rite of passage was what he could look forward to in his new home – the Officers' Mess.

It was not necessarily outright hostility that was shown by his brother officers; it was the way the wart was generally ignored except when he was required to be the butt of dubious pranks. Of course, he was expected to endure this purgatory with the sufferance and resigned good humour of the officer class. Every officer in the 65th had gone through it.

The only people who would be nice to him at first were the wives of the more senior officers. He would mistake their smiles for genuine warmth, failing to realise they were, in fact, ruthlessly exploiting his loneliness to rope him into all manner of unpleasant tasks; from baby-sitting to pouring the Earl Grey at their flower-arranging evenings.

New subalterns were always initiated into the Mess in some ghastly manner and the Army's Top Brass had become very sensitive to criticism as some of the exploits found their way into the tabloids. The combat regiments were notorious in this respect and, as the CODE had started to permeate through the Army, they had been ordered to calm things down. The mavericks of the 65th considered themselves above such petty legislation and had simply doubled their efforts to elevate the art of initiation to an unspeakable level. Of late, it had been particularly coarse, and Taverner, in his capacity as Secretary to the Officers' Mess Committee, was keen to inject rather more style into the general humiliation.

At the Sentry Post, Second Lieutenant Cavendish signed in while the sentry checked the boot and engine compartment of his car. He had been booked in for dinner at half past seven in the Officers' Mess and had plenty of time to spare. He got back in his car, put the car pass on display and turned the ignition key.

Nothing.

He tried again. Still nothing.

'Oh, for God's sake,' he muttered.

He kept turning the key, but it was no use. He got out, opened the bonnet and peered over his glasses. It was beginning to get dark and he couldn't see very much.

'Is everything alright, sir?' asked the sentry.

'No, the bloody thing won't start.'

The soldier shone a torch at the engine. 'Battery okay, sir? I'm not very good with cars.'

'I'm sure you're far more knowledgeable than myself,' said Cavendish, who had read Theology at university, and for whom the intricacies of the internal combustion engine were akin to the Occult.

The sentry looked at the engine. He ran his fingers along various wires and tugged at the connections at each end. 'Try it again, sir.'

There was an incessant clicking, but the engine was not going to start.

'I reckon your starter motor's fucked, sir.' said the sentry.

'Bloody hell.'

The Bombardier who had issued the car pass poked his head out of the Sentry Post.

'Sir, are you booked in for dinner in the Officers' Mess?'

'Yes.'

'It's just that it's nearly six o'clock, sir.'

'Dinner is at seven-thirty.'

'No, sir, on Mondays it's at six. The Mess staff finish early.'

'You're joking. That's in ten minutes. How far away is the Mess?'

'About a mile. Follow this road to the end of the island. You can't miss it, sir. If you end up in the sea, you've gone past it.'

Cavendish was reluctant to abandon his car and belongings at the Sentry Post, but he had no choice. One could get away with many things in the Army. Suicidal tactical decisions? Quite acceptable. Shelling your own soldiers? Apparently a speciality of the 65th. Drilling the Brigadier's wife? Of course, especially if she was pulling rank. But being late for dinner was quite out of the question, and he started running along the road into the base. The sentry stopped him in his tracks.

'Sir! Where're you going? On Mondays they wear Regimental Mess Uniform to dinner. You can't go like that,' he said to Cavendish, who was wearing a blazer and tie.

'Heck! Why didn't they tell me?'

Cavendish opened his boot and scattered the contents of his suitcases everywhere in a desperate attempt to find his Mess Uniform. It took a long time to locate the various components, all of which were dreadfully creased, but they would have to do. Small, black jacket faced in red, black waistcoat, white shirt and high-waisted trousers strapped over black boots with silver riding-spurs. After some more frantic searching he found a bow tie. With five minutes to go, and a good mile ahead of him, he sprinted off.

However dashing the uniform might have looked, it was certainly not made for any sort of physical activity. It chafed him painfully in vital areas and pounding the road in his boots was pure torture.

In camp, a few soldiers were ambling towards the NAAFI. They barely registered interest when they heard the metallic clanging of spurs and saw a panicking young officer sprinting through camp in his Mess Uniform. It was a fairly common sight.

Cavendish just kept running through the unfamiliar base, hoping that the sentry had given him the right directions. The road led to a vast open area, and in the distance he could see what he hoped was the Officers' Mess. He was certainly going to be late, and he imagined the senior officers complaining loudly; hungry, unable to eat because they were all waiting for him. His military career was rapidly going downhill in a world of burning lungs and blistered feet.

He reached the Officers' Mess just after six o'clock, headed through the revolving doors and caught his breath in the foyer. Beads of sweat had formed on his forehead and his shirt was uncomfortably damp. In the warm atmosphere of the Mess his glasses started to steam up.

Cavendish followed the noise to the bar, where the other officers were also dressed in Mess Uniform. His was the only uniform bereft of medals and he felt very conspicuous because of it. A tall, blond-haired Captain wandered over.

'You must be Cavendish,' said the Captain. 'I'm Taverner, your Battery Commander.'

'James Cavendish.'

Taverner did not shake his hand, but fixed him with a glare instead.

'You're late.'

'My car broke down.'

'And?'

'I'm sorry.'

'Don't apologise. It's a sign of weakness. I'm afraid we don't take kindly to members turning up late to dinner, and you've also embarrassed *me* because you're going to be an officer in my Battery.'

'I'm sorry.'

'Stop apologising!' Taverner kept his eyes on Cavendish and yelled out to the Mess Bombardier. 'Bom' Westlake! The Yard, please.'

'Certainly, sir. Bugger Me Sideways?'

'Of course.' Taverner addressed Cavendish again. 'Officers who are late to dinner must do the Yard of Ale. The slowest time ever recorded is six minutes and thirty-four seconds. Do not exceed it.'

By now, the other officers had gathered around and a bucket had been placed at Cavendish's feet. Cavendish could smell the ale before he saw it. Westlake handed him the brimmed Yard and before he was ready someone with a stopwatch shouted 'Go!'

The liquid was a cloudy, sulphurous, vinegary

nightmare, and in less intimidating circumstances he would not have gone near the stuff. But to refuse in these surroundings was unthinkable, and somehow he managed to drink it all down, gagging all the time, his eyes watering, trying not to imagine what it would be doing to his insides.

His time of four minutes and five seconds was quite respectable and formally recorded in the Book of the Yard, along with the rare observation that the contents of the Yard did not make too swift a reappearance.

Dinner that night was a vague blur that would stay locked up somewhere deep within Cavendish's memory banks, beyond the limit of significant recall. The next thing he remembered with any lucidity was a gradual awareness of a harsh overhead strip light and the deep glow of pain in his back and his right shoulder. He could feel nothing of his right arm, having cut off all circulation in it. The floor he was lying on felt wet and his face was pressed up against some pleasantly-cool porcelain. He felt incredibly weak and for a few moments he stayed put, becoming aware now that he was in a cubicle of some sort, wrapped round the back of a toilet. When he tried to push himself up, he found he couldn't; his paralysed right arm was not responding. He rolled onto his side and pushed up with his left hand. At the instant his head came vertical, it hit him. Firstly the dizziness, then the smell. Rancid, pervading, acidic and terribly familiar, and he was covered in it. He was hit by a wave of nausea and retched into the toilet, pausing only to rest his chin on the rim. He was irrationally struck by the fear that his right arm would become gangrenous if he didn't stimulate some circulation into it. He crawled out of the cubicle and, once outside, he twisted his torso sharply to the left to shake the useless limb into life, succeeding only in swinging it round in an arc and punching himself hard on the nose. He managed to get to his feet by a wash basin and drank from the tap before the water became too hot to swallow. His right arm was beginning to tingle as the circulation returned. The reflection in the mirror was not a pleasant sight. His expensive uniform was covered in vomit, his bloodshot eyes peered out from a very pale face and his nose had started to bleed from where he had struck it seconds earlier.

Events started to come back to him. His car breaking down. Running to dinner. The hideous Yard of Ale.

Outside in the corridor, he bumped into the Mess Manager, Staff Sergeant Lomas.

'Good morning, Mr Cavendish.'

'Morning. What time is it?'

'Coming up to six o'clock, sir. The chef's just arrived. Breakfast doesn't start until half past seven, although I'm sure he'd do you something earlier if you'd like. Bacon and eggs?'

Cavendish felt the urge to rush back into the gents' lavatory, but closed his eyes and took a breath.

'Thank you, but I'm not sure I could face it this morning.'

'No problem, sir. Your cases are in your room. Room 208. It's on the second floor at this end of the building.'

Cavendish somehow found his way to his room, threw his uniform on the floor and climbed into bed. His new room hadn't been spinning around him for more than fifteen minutes before there was a knock at the door. It was the Mess Manager again.

'Sir? Sorry to trouble you, but Sergeant Major Ferguson from the gym is here for your Basic Fitness Test.'

Cavendish groaned and pulled the sheets up a little higher.

'Are you awake, sir?' said the Mess Manager. 'He asks that you be outside in your PT kit in the next five minutes. Thank you, sir.'

Cavendish had not long finished his course at Sandhurst and was still in awe of Sergeant Majors. One never questioned their orders, no matter how untimely. Every cell in his weakened body protested vehemently against his doing so, but somehow he forced himself out of bed and found some sports kit in a suitcase.

A Land Rover was waiting outside the Mess to take him to the gymnasium.

'Heavy night, sir?' said the muscular PT Instructor at the wheel.

Inside the gym, there were about twenty soldiers lined up for the Basic Fitness Test. Cavendish could barely stand up straight as the PT Instructor outlined the test; press-ups, sit-ups, and a 1.5 mile run. The press-ups weren't too bad and he achieved sixty in two minutes, a pass. The sit-ups were not pleasant, both on his delicate stomach and his spinning head. The run, to be completed within ten minutes, was sheer hell. He puked his way round the course; along the road, back up the runway, then weaving through the buildings with no idea of where he was supposed to be going, content just to follow the others. There was no relief in finishing, but at least he passed. The other officers had come to watch him in his misery as he finished the run, and they were kind enough to drive him back to the Mess, where he was still unwilling to take breakfast.

EIGHT

Colonel Sandford finally managed to find some time in his schedule later that morning to meet Major Hesketh, his new Second-in-Command. Sandford tried some small talk at first, but it was clearly not his forte and he gave the impression that he was rather pressed for time. He quickly steered the subject round to the 65th.

'So you've been here a few days now,' said Sandford. 'Glad to be back?'

'It's a change from Canada,' said Hesketh. 'Colonel, you are aware that I'm retiring in nine months? If I was being honest, I am a little surprised I've been posted here.'

'We'll come to that in a minute. How do you think the regiment is at the moment, Tom?'

'It's just as I remember it. The boys are perhaps more battle-hardened than when I was last here, but that can only be a good thing. A good war always brings the best NCOs into the limelight. The officers are as erratic as ever. Colonel, the regiment's in fine fettle.'

Sandford shook his head in disagreement.

'I'm pleased you see it so, but I can't agree with you. Tom, this regiment is living in the past. The 65th is so out of touch with the modern world it's in real danger of being left behind. Times are changing, and the sooner we appreciate that, the better. For example, look at that conference yesterday morning. I don't think many of the officers had the slightest idea what I was talking about.'

'The same thought had occurred to me,' said Hesketh, ambiguously.

'Well, as tricky as some of the jargon is, we've simply got to face up to the fact that this is the language of the future. We need to bring the 65th bang up to date. It won't happen overnight, Tom. We must start with the basics. Rome wasn't built in a day, after all. We must start with the environment.'

Here it comes, thought Hesketh, a lecture on climate change.

'What do you think of the base?' said Sandford.

'It's certainly not in a good condition. But it never has been.'

'I'm so glad you think so, Tom. So do I. When I took over here a few months back, I was struck by how squalid it was. It's virtually uninhabitable. I don't know how the men put up with it.'

'And I imagine it'll stay that way, Colonel. There's never been enough money in the system to sort it out.'

'Up until now,' said Sandford, triumphantly.

Hesketh narrowed his gaze inquisitively as Sandford continued.

'After weeks of negotiating, I have finally persuaded the Ministry of Defence to release funds to restore the whole base to the very highest standard. Here, have a look at the plans.'

Hesketh flicked through the glossy brochure.

'This is remarkable,' he said, after a few minutes. 'New accommodation blocks, new housing, offices modernised, a new sports hall, a state-of-the-art gym, even a swimming pool. Wow.'

'I thought you'd be impressed.'

'I am.' Hesketh carried on reading for a moment. 'This is not going to be cheap, Colonel. It's going to cost millions. If you've persuaded the bean-counters to loosen their purse strings to that extent, then congratulations are in order.'

'Thanks. It took a lot of work, but spending so many years in the MoD does have it advantages. It's simply a case of knowing who to talk to and knowing how the system works. However, as you say, the cost is going to be very high and with all these things there is inevitably a degree of compromise. What you're looking at there is the favoured option, but it can't be achieved without a bit of give-and-take.'

Hesketh's warning antennae went to full alert.

'You see, the MoD,' explained Sandford, 'must be seen to offer the taxpayer real value for money. There will be the cost of materials, plant hire, consultancy fees, surveyors' fees, architects' fees, and goodness knows what else, but the biggest cost of such a massive project will be the wages of the workforce. The minimum wage is astronomical, and in this case possibly prohibitive.'

'Meaning what, Colonel?'

'Instead of hiring professional builders, it has been suggested the soldiers do all the building work themselves. The skills needed are diverse, but they can be trained up as required.'

'That sounds like free labour.'

'Not free, Tom. These soldiers are being paid to sit around on their backsides all day until they get called up for their next operational tour. This would be a wonderful application of resources, and it genuinely empowers them because, at the end of the day, it's their own base they're restoring. The Roman legionnaires did the same thing in their day, too.'

'I wouldn't have been surprised to find they originally built this place, judging by the state of it. You say this idea has been suggested, Colonel. When will the final decision be taken?'

'It already has. The 65th are going to be trained up and we will do the work ourselves. It will save the taxpayer *millions*. The MoD has taken us off the Arms Plot for the next year. No operational tours, no external training exercises, no peacekeeping duties. We will be untouchable. Everything can be focused on the restoration of Windcheater Island. Now then, Tom, this is where you come in.'

Hesketh put down the brochure and listened carefully.

'This is going to be a massive undertaking,' said Sandford, 'and the reason you have been brought back to the 65th is because you are going to be in charge of it. You are going to be the Project Manager.'

'Me? But I know nothing about Civil Engineering or Construction.'

'You don't have to. I've seen your reports, Tom. You can turn your hand to just about anything and make it a success. In the MoD they think you've got the Midas Touch.' Sandford looked as sincere as he could. 'The soldiers here need strong leadership and, as ashamed as I am to admit it, the 65th are having a few problems accepting me as their Commanding Officer. So I'm delegating the task to you. You'll have professional help from outside consultants of course, but the whole thing will be driven by you. As your Commanding Officer I will give you my full support in this operation. Anything you want you will get. If there are any problems with plans, contractors, manpower or the MoD, then I will fight for you one-hundred percent. Think of me as your top cover. You can get on with the task in hand without any outside interference. I can deal with Whitehall and keep them off your back – that's my area of expertise. What I need to know, Tom, is do you accept the challenge?'

'Colonel, I really don't know ...'

'Tom. The MoD specifically asked for you.'

Hesketh thought for a long time.

'I guess I don't have much choice.'

'Good.' The Colonel got up to show that the meeting was over.

'Can I keep the brochure?' said Hesketh.

'No. This has to be confidential for the time being. I will announce the plans to the whole regiment just before lunch on Friday. Until then our conversation is not to go any further.'

As one very experienced officer of the 65th left the Colonel's office pondering this unexpected swansong to his military career, elsewhere, another was taking his first fledgling steps, and it was not going well.

A hangover of staggering proportions had kicked in and Second Lieutenant Cavendish felt hideously sick and very weak. He looked terminally-ill and his insides rumbled alarmingly as Lieutenant Skeffington briefed him on the sequence of the Battery parade, where Cavendish would meet his soldiers for the first time. He wondered if he would ever actually make it onto the parade in the first place.

'I've got A-Troop, Fraser has B-Troop and you've got

C-Troop,' explained Skeffington. 'They'll be lined up in three ranks. We march on from the right, halt in front of our Troops, turn to the right and wait for the Battery Commander.'

As Cavendish marched out in front of the soldiers, he hoped to God he wouldn't faint in front of them. Captain Taverner marched out in front of the Battery and barked his orders.

'C-Troop stand fast. A-Troop and B-Troop, under your Troop Commanders, carry on.'

Taverner marched up to Cavendish and stopped short in front of him, his blue eyes boring into him, willing him to do something, but Cavendish did not know what he was supposed to do.

'Try saluting me!' said Taverner, eventually.

Cavendish saluted and Taverner returned it.

'C-Troop has twenty-three soldiers ...' prompted Taverner.

Cavendish repeated sheepishly.

'C-Troop has twenty-three soldiers ...'

'... and one officer ...'

'... and one officer ...'

'... on parade, awaiting your disposal, sir.'

'... on parade, awaiting your disposal, sir.'

'Good. Fall out and inspect your Troop,' said Taverner. 'I will follow you around.'

C-Troop was arranged in three ranks and Cavendish started moving along the front. This was the first inspection he had ever done. He felt utterly drained by the nausea and the physical exertions of the morning, and the knowledge that his intimidating Battery Commander was next to him didn't help. The first three soldiers seemed to be reasonably turned out, as was the fourth, until Cavendish saw the state of his boots. He decided to say something to the soldier with the dirty boots.

'Your name is Gunner …'

'Moffat, sir.'

'I, ah, think you might have put a little more effort into your boots, Gunner Moffat. They're a bit dirty.' Cavendish's words sounded weak.

Gunner Moffat was indignant. 'Eh? Fook off, sir. They're better than 'is!' he said, pointing to the sparkling toe-caps of the soldier next to him. 'Fookin'ell, sir, you need to get down to Specsavers. You need new fookin' glasses, sir.'

Cavendish was shocked by his insubordination and looked round to Taverner for support. Taverner just glared back at him. The rest of the soldiers started to snigger and Taverner snapped at them to be quiet. As Cavendish started on the second rank, a mobile phone rang somewhere in the Troop. Its owner even had the temerity to answer it.

'Hiya sweetheart. No, not now, I'm a bit busy. Catch you later! Hey, babe, last night you were fan-fookin-tastic!'

The soldier put his phone away and struck up a conversation with the man next to him.

'Fook me, that bird was fit,' he said.

'The fit one in the NAAFI?'

'Yes.'

'Shot over?'

'Shot out! Fookin' right!'

'All rounds complete on target?'

'All rounds complete on target!'

'Report guns empty?'

'Report guns empty!'

'You lucky bastard.'

Cavendish's depleted reserves of moral courage simply dried up. It was better just to ignore this blatant disrespect; he couldn't have soldiers answering back to him again. Clearly he had got the wrong impression of the 65th. It was an elite regiment, he had believed, but nothing could have been further from the truth. And if he thought it couldn't get any worse, a quick glance at the soldiers in the rear rank suggested otherwise.

They were dressed in a mish-mash of military clothing and their boots varied between roughly black and seriously muddy. All were unshaven and some, like Cavendish himself, reeked of alcohol. The very last soldier in the rank looked like something out of his worst nightmare.

'This is Bombardier Longmoor,' said Taverner.

Cavendish looked up at the giant and actually felt some pity for him.

'Bombardier Longmoor is the cause of most of the problems in the Battery,' said Taverner. 'He has been thrown out of the SAS for the attempted murder of three NCOs. He'll be court martialled shortly, but will stay with us until his trial comes up.'

Cavendish was quite tall, but the behemoth in front of him must have been well over six feet ten and heavily-built with not a sign of fat on him. Longmoor's neck seemed as wide as a tree-trunk and his grey eyes were devoid of any emotion. Above a face like a well-used grenade range was perched, inexplicably, a fluorescent yellow beret.

'Be *very* careful of Bombardier Longmoor,' said Taverner. 'He is an extreme psychopath. Oh, don't worry, he can't hear us. He's schizophrenic. A sort of sleeping sickness, say the doctors.'

Longmoor stared into the distance.

'Until his Court Martial comes up, you'll need to keep

your eye on him,' said Taverner, who led Cavendish off to the side.

Once they were out of earshot of the soldiers, Taverner launched into him.

'Have you not been taught how to carry out an inspection?' said Taverner. 'That lot are a *disgrace*. And what did you do about it? Nothing! If you are lacking in moral courage then this regiment is not for you. Do you understand? I suggest you get that lot in your office straight after parade and rip their heads off. You're their officer now. Get a grip of yourself and fuck off out of my sight!'

It was a very glum Cavendish who was shown into his new office and he sat down behind his desk. This was proving to be a dreadful start to his military career and he wondered whether it was too late to apply for an immediate transfer out of the 65th. The bulk of C-Troop had been ordered to line up outside the office to await his reprimand, and without invitation the gargantuan Longmoor marched in and came to attention in front of his desk, stamping his feet with such force that a picture fell off the wall and smashed on the floor. They were the only two in the office.

Cavendish tried the friendly approach and smiled at the creature, who looked as if he could break the young officer in half without too much effort, should he have decided to do so.

'I'm Second Lieutenant Cavendish, your new Troop Commander. That's a very interesting coloured beret you have, Bombardier Longmoor. Not sure that it's right for the 65th!'

In response, Longmoor reached down to one side of the heavy desk and flipped it over with a huge crash, as easily as turning the pages of a book. Cavendish recoiled backwards in his chair. Now there was nothing between him and the monster.

'There was no need for that, was there?' said Cavendish, thinking that his life expectancy might be down to mere seconds.

Longmoor then pulled over a filing cabinet with another mighty crash, at which point six soldiers came rushing into the office in an attempt to overpower him, and an almighty ruckus ensued. Fearsome punches were thrown and, as they connected, teeth flew out, blood started to flow and people lay out cold on the floor. One brave soldier picked up a desk lamp from the floor, climbed up Longmoor's mountainous back, managed to loop the cable round his huge neck and pulled as hard as he could. As Longmoor's arms began to flail harmlessly, he dropped to the floor and the remaining soldiers piled in with a flurry of kicks and punches, relenting only as it became clear that the giant was on the verge of losing consciousness.

The soldiers climbed off and let Longmoor get up. The giant was in quite a bad way and no longer such a threat. Longmoor staggered over the debris of the office, stepping over the two soldiers out cold on the floor, towards the ashen-faced Cavendish, this time with his hand outstretched and a wry smile on his bloody face.

'Come on, sir, where's your sense of humour? The name's Longmoor, sir, but I'm actually the Battery Sergeant Major. How do you do. Welcome to the Battery, sir. Hope you didn't mind our little introduction.'

He turned round to the soldiers who'd just 'subdued' him.

'Nice one, lads. Get those two down to the Medical Centre and the rest can clear up.'

Longmoor shadow-boxed towards the door on his way out.

'Still the fucking daddy!'

In the afternoon, Second Lieutenant Cavendish had his mandatory medical examination with the Doctor, Captain Meckie. All the usual tests were carried out; pulse, blood pressure, urine and blood samples, and an ECG. It was a very comprehensive medical. So comprehensive, in fact, that he was even required to produce a sperm sample. The Doctor explained that some of the soldiers in the regiment had been exposed to depleted uranium rounds in certain operational theatres and were being monitored for possible reduced fertility. The SMF – Sperm Motility Factor – of soldiers in the 65th, was regularly tested against a control of younger, unaffected soldiers – into which category Cavendish now fell. The Doctor showed him into a cubicle, handed him a container and pulled down a screen over the window.

'Take your time. Awkward business I know, but it has to be done,' he explained. 'There are some publications in the drawer you may find useful.'

Cavendish locked the door of the cubicle and checked the screen to see if anyone could see through. Satisfied that he was alone, he took out the magazines and perused them. They ranged from the tasteful images of *Penthouse* to the rather more graphic *Sex Sluts in the Slammer*, and he went ahead and did what he had to do.

He had been in the 65th for less than twenty-four hours and in that time he had not exactly excelled himself. Clearly he was destined for a very brief military career, and he wondered if the climax of it had just occurred in the Doctor's surgery.

NINE

Being unable to project his voice to the required extent, Colonel Sandford had to resort to using a loudhailer when he proudly announced to the assembled regiment that the base was to undergo a substantial restoration. The Regimental Sergeant Major, whose parade-ground shriek could be heard far beyond the perimeter of the base, looked on in a mixture of sympathy and disdain as the Colonel's attempt at a rousing, eve-of-battle-style speech was thwarted by his flat voice and ear-splitting feedback.

Sandford's announcement was well received by the assembled ranks, but it was his closing remark – to the effect that from lunchtime that day the 65th was no longer confined to barracks – that really got them cheering. He made it sound as if it was his personal gift to the regiment and, as they cheered, for a split second he thought perhaps they might have loved him.

That night, determined to enjoy their new freedom, the regiment poured into Holberton on a wave of aftershave and attitude. The Ship and Shovel had little warning and its locals left early, leaving the soldiers to drink the place dry by ten o'clock, before staggering back to their base.

Life also improved for Second Lieutenant Cavendish after the horror of his first day in the 65th. His brother officers became friendlier and welcomed him into their fold. His soldiers – far from being the squaddies from hell that he had first encountered – were in fact a group of battle-hardened young men who took great pride in their professionalism, and each had the sick sense of humour that comes with years of tough operational tours. Cavendish was delighted to discover that his soldiers already had a nickname for him – *Harry Potter* – on the basis that he wore glasses and both his parents were dead. Initially he had been disappointed to learn there would be no operational tours in the offing, but he looked forward to playing his part in the refurbishment of Windcheater Island. In fact, he did so with a little too much exuberance, and one afternoon his Troop Sergeant quietly took him to one side to let him know that it was bad form to be too keen as a young officer in the 65th. The Senior NCOs ran everything, the Sergeant explained, and as an officer Cavendish was not expected to return to work after lunch.

The Indian summer held out until the final week of October. With the tree leaves saturated with starch after a good summer, the lustrous green foliage of the North Devon landscape changed to an intense yellow as autumn arrived late. Copses on the tops of distant hills caught the light of the rising and setting sun so well they looked as though they were on fire.

Around this time, a team of building consultants arrived at Windcheater Island. Their main task was to educate Major Hesketh in the art of construction management. They spent a week with him, at the end of which he had a much clearer idea of what he would have to do. There had been a last-minute change to the operational Arms Plot from the Ministry of Defence – the 65th would now be eligible for an operational tour from the beginning of the following July, and the project *had* to be completed by then. Work would have to start the first week back in January after the Christmas holiday.

Hesketh had an empty house turned into his Project Headquarters, and was given a team of clerks to deal with the inevitable administrative burden. His first task was to send the regiment back to school. In less than two months, four-hundred soldiers had to be trained up as bricklayers, carpenters, plumbers, surveyors, plasterers, electricians, fitters, roofers, digger-drivers and crane operators, and each soldier needed to be proficient in two separate trades, so that no-one need be sitting around if there was a drop in demand for one of their skills at any particular time. The training courses were booked and, a week after the Colonel's announcement, Windcheater Island was practically deserted as the soldiers went away to learn their new skills.

In the peace and quiet that followed, Hesketh knuckled down to six weeks of intensive planning. There was a phenomenal amount of work to do before the soldiers returned and he put in punishing hours, arriving at work before first light and rarely making it back to the Mess in time for dinner. He was in his element overseeing this vast project. He planned with great attention to detail and, despite his inexperience in the field of construction, he had quickly got it figured out. Advice from the consultants was only a phone-call away, and as the plan started to take shape, an outside observer might have thought Hesketh had done it for a living. His ability to foresee problems and plan for the unexpected was uncanny, and he ensured the plan was flexible enough to cope with such eventualities. However, the new deadline was tight and the only way he could achieve it would be to have the regiment working continuously round the clock on a two-shift system, with each shift working for twelve hours. That way, he reckoned, he could have the whole project finished by the beginning of May, ahead of schedule.

The workload would have taxed someone half his age and Hesketh was out of condition, eating sporadically and sleeping only for a couple of hours each night, nor did he take a single day off. It was a transformation from the gentleman of leisure he had become in recent years and it had been a very long time since he had felt such a sense of purpose. He was out of his comfort-zone, and loving every minute of it. The soldiers of the 65th deserved something much better than the godforsaken place they currently inhabited, and the success of the restoration ultimately depended on him. Though he would have never worked so hard in any other circumstances, for the 65th he would make an exception and, despite the long hours and lack of sleep, he woke each morning refreshed and raring to go.

It was as though Hesketh had fallen in love. He had only been back in the regiment a few weeks and yet he wondered why he had ever left the 65th. This unique regiment, standing out as one of the last beacons of worth in a country of vulgar mediocrity and vindictive rulers; a regiment now a little rough around the edges, a little vulnerable too, and in need of his close attention; a regiment that had always occupied a special place in his heart and that many years ago had turned him into the man he'd become; he more the fool for having ever walked away from it.

It did not worry him that his home and family back in Canada began to feature less and less in his thoughts.

By the time the newly-trained soldiers returned to Windcheater Island in the middle of December, Hesketh's plan was ready to be put into action. The soldiers were moved into some temporary demountables that had been built while they had been away on their courses.

The 65th then departed on two weeks' leave over Christmas. The soldiers headed back to Merseyside, Colonel Sandford went back home to North London, Hesketh flew back to Alberta, and the rest of the officers headed to Verbier to catch the first snow of the season.

The refurbishment of Windcheater Island started on the first day back in January. The soldiers, wearing hi-visibility vests and hard hats, watched from a safe distance as Colonel Sandford ceremoniously started the demolition.

In the cab of the crane, Sandford pressed a button and there was a sharp clang from above as the steel hawser holding the heavy iron ball in place was released. The inertia of the ball was tremendous and it was not travelling particularly fast by the time it connected with the side of the accommodation block, but with a mass in excess of a ton its momentum was more than sufficient. The wall sagged inwards from the blow then fell to the ground in a swirling dust cloud as some timber and tiles fell from the unsupported roof above.

Within an hour, all three of the old accommodation blocks lay in a mound of rubble and the excavation vehicles moved in to remove it onto the waiting dumper trucks. By the end of the day it had all been cleared and only the original foundations of the blocks remained.

Over on the married patch, a few houses that were

beyond salvation were also demolished, while soldiers swarmed through others, gutting and stripping them bare in preparation for re-decoration.

The day-shift finished their work at eight o'clock, ate their evening meal in the cookhouse and retired to the NAAFI for a few beers. The night-shift would work through until eight o'clock next morning, under the glare of floodlights and the drone of generators.

By the middle of February, the new buildings had started to take shape. Once the soldiers' new accommodation blocks had been completed, they were able to move out of their temporary demountables into their new rooms. Elsewhere, the first batch of houses had been fully renovated with new roofs, windows and a fresh coat of paint on the outside, while the fitted kitchens and bathrooms got the soldiers' wives cooing in approval, and the expensive new entertainment systems similarly impressed their husbands.

The month brought some bitterly cold weather to the whole country. A freezing northerly wind whipped across the base, making life a misery for those working outside. The main road through the base had been resurfaced, and attention now turned to tarmacing the runways. The soldiers who'd been given this particular task were also exposed to the weather and were grateful for the heat from the bitumen holder, around which they gathered intermittently to grumble about the pointlessness of resurfacing the old worn-out runways, even though, as Major Hesketh had explained to them, they were classed as roads and would therefore need to be repaired as well.

The regiment had warmed to Hesketh. He had been a much-needed injection of old 65th-style into its hierarchy and, hiding an astonishingly intelligent mind behind the exterior of a genial old buffer, he worked with everyone's interests at heart. A hearty laugh would herald his arrival as he visited the building sites each morning and he made a point of speaking to every soldier. He knew all their names and made each of them feel as though they were playing a part in a very important project. In comparison, Colonel Sandford was rarely seen around the base, either being shut away in his office pushing electronic paper around, or absent on some supposedly essential business. Some began to wonder if he was actually still in command of the 65th.

Everything was running to plan. The soldiers had been well trained – the quality of their work was outstanding and the speed with which the new buildings were going up was remarkable. Inevitably there were always a few problems for Major Hesketh to sort out; one or two daily hiccups, but nothing that couldn't be taken care of with a couple of phone calls or a quick five-minute conference.

It was not long after this that people began to notice a distinct change in Major Hesketh. During the day he was normally a professional, jovial and humorous character, and out of working hours he was capable of being as outrageous as any young subaltern when the situation demanded it.

So when he stopped touring the building sites each morning, and no longer came to dinner in the evening, everyone noticed. The Quartermaster asked him if he was okay, to which Hesketh had replied that he had been feeling a bit under the weather these past few weeks, but that normal service would resume soon. It never was, however, and with each day Hesketh seemed to become more introverted and more withdrawn from life in the 65th.

TEN

The younger officers of the 65th were not in the least bit concerned about the building project and the rest of the regiment, quite frankly, wanted them to stay out of the way. The officers were happy to oblige. They popped into the office each day, tried to look interested, took an extended coffee-break and were usually back in the Mess well before lunch. Afternoons usually saw them sailing or windsurfing out in the estuary, propping up the bar if the weather was bad, or indulging in any other activity devoted to the pursuit of pleasure.

As the weeks wore on, they had something new to distract them. Although few of the officers ever watched television – most of what was broadcast was quite unwatchable – they had become hopelessly addicted to a daily soap opera on BBC1. Lunch, which had always been a leisurely affair in the Mess, quickly descended into a messy display of force-feeding in case anyone missed the start of the programme.

The Quartermaster, who was as addicted as the rest of them, watched the repeated episode in the relative quiet of the television room each evening after dinner. One evening he invited Major Hesketh to join him. Hesketh had been trying hard in the last week, but his heart no longer seemed to be in it, and whatever the trouble was, he was unwilling to discuss it with anyone. He seemed to spend his day locked up in his office, just like Colonel Sandford. The Quartermaster thought that maybe a bottle of scotch and the provocative nature of the programme they were about to watch, might open him up a bit.

'It must be at least fifteen years since I last watched television,' said Major Hesketh. 'My wife and I have never had one.' He reached round the back of the old set, plugged it into the socket, then fiddled about with the remote control in the manner of most people over the age of fifty, optimistically pressing lots of buttons in the vain hope that one might operate the desired function. As the auto-tune function started scanning for the umpteenth time, the Quartermaster began to reminisce.

'I used to have a television of my own, some years back, when I was stationed at Larkhill. Ancient piece of crap. There I was, settling down to an episode of *The Simpsons* when the screen went blank and smoke started rising from the back. I remember the date very well. 7th June 2008. The Mess Bombardier died that day. Died because of my television. Hughes was his name. Geek. Consumptive bugger. Ended up working in the Mess because the Medical Officer felt that all that drill, PT and track-bashing on the vehicle park would finish him off. Anyway, that evening, when the old cathode ray threw a track, I summoned Lance Bombardier Hughes to help. The man was a nerd, you see, and he gave the impression that he was a dab hand with all things technical. Ha! Wrong, Quartermaster, quite, *quite* wrong! When he saw the smoke, the silly bugger dashed out, came back in with a jug of water, and poured the whole fucking lot into the back of the television. I didn't have time to tell him it was still plugged in. Still, I can't imagine he suffered much. Got an almighty fucking electric shock and broke his neck when he was launched into the far wall.'

Major Hesketh somehow stumbled across the correct channel. Still the Quartermaster wasn't done.

'I remember the boys gave Hughes a sobriquet. Posthumously, of course. *Sparky Hughes*. Now, what was it they used to say? I remember.'

'Heard the news?
Old Sparky Hughes
Blew his fuse
Now get his name off the fucking ration roll'

'What is this programme you're so keen for me to see, Quartermaster?' asked Hesketh.

'It's called *The Codes*.'

'The Codes? As in "The CODE"?'

'Correct.'

'You've got to be joking.'

'Not at all,' said the Quartermaster. 'Apparently it's the most popular programme in broadcasting history. I've watched quite a few episodes. I should snap out of it really, but it's so insidiously addictive. Ah, here we go. You might want to turn the volume down here.'

The catchy little theme tune dittied and bopped to its conclusion and the screen went black. A large gang of kids screamed out.

'THE CODES! YEEEAAAAAHHHH!'

'Jesus Christ,' said Hesketh, fumbling for the volume control. Still the gang roared.

'COMMUNITY! OPPORTUNITY! DIVERSITY! EQUALITY!'

For the next half hour, Major Hesketh was transfixed, his troubles forgotten as he became engrossed in *The Codes*. The programme was generated entirely by computer and written so as to appeal to both children and adults. The graphics were outstanding and the actors and environments were photo-realistic; their virtual origins betrayed only occasionally by a slight anomaly – a facial expression that was too symmetrical, a slightly awkward gait or the unlikely parabola of a thrown object. That was just nit-picking though. It might have been fake, but it was truly outstanding.

The stars of *The Codes* were the family of the same name. There was Sophie Code, the mother, struggling to bring up her three children – Emma, Abu and Felicity. They were a very modern family. The children addressed their mother by her first name, never 'Mum', and they lived in a block of flats in some anonymous metropolis with Jimmy – Sophie's live-in boyfriend, *über*chav and ne'er-do-well – and their three-legged dog, Tripod, who spoke to the children once the adults were out of the way. It was impossible to place the ethnic origins of the Code family, who resembled some exquisitely-engineered hybrid of several races; not predominantly from the Indian sub-continent or the Caribbean or Anglo Saxony or the Orient, but somewhere in-between. Their accent was a Home Counties twang; whiny, emanating from a point behind the nose with a fashionable layer of transatlantic drawl and ghetto-speak.

The characterisation amused Hesketh. The children were like mini-adults. They dressed like adults and spoke coarsely like adults, "getting well-stressed, right, about social justice and stuff." Their vocabulary — street and correct, of course — was extensive for ones so young and would have put the most precocious child to shame, except during the frequent arguments that erupted without warning and rapidly descended into loud slanging-matches, after which they all made-up with tears and hugs. The adults, with the exception of Sophie, were all thoroughly objectionable citizens. The local social worker was boring and rather creepy. The community policeman was a power-mad yob and also a pervert. The local shopkeeper was a pervert who aspired to be a policeman. The schoolteachers, who aspired to be shopkeepers, subtly hinted at private lives involving a level of depravity that was way beyond any healthy scale.

Hesketh and the Quartermaster watched for about twenty minutes before Hesketh spoke.

'And this is the programme that has the highest ratings ever?' he asked.

'Highest in history. About forty million, just over half the population'.

'It's … very clever, but it's the most appalling trash!'

The plot of tonight's episode was typically implausible. While her siblings went to school or played truant, Emma, the angelic little five-year old, managed to secure a voluntary post at a local soup kitchen, where she got into conversation with a struggling family who had been turfed out of their tenement flat. Apparently, an evil multi-national pharmaceutical company had bought the tenement land six months earlier and their sinister agents had been knocking on doors, looking for residents to assist with clinical drug trials, especially those with young children. Because the family had refused to cooperate, the suits had had them evicted. Emma was horrified to learn of their situation. In between her tantrums and primal screams, she managed to calm down sufficiently to consult Tripod, who offered a few wise homilies about large companies and how they exploit the poor and keep them in poverty.

But, wait a moment, what was that?

An unexpected knock at the door!

Please no, don't let it be them! Sophie opened the door and yes, there he was! The evil agent, slick and sincere, with the offer of a lifetime. Lots of lovely cash paid up front for assistance with their trials. Emma emerged from her room and the agent's eyes narrowed. She'd be just the right age! He upped his offer to Sophie. A free holiday? Lottery tickets for life? A new kitchen? Just take the pills and sign the disclaimer. Sophie took his pen and started to sign her name. And on that agonising cliffhanger, the episode ended.

What an absolute bastard, thought Hesketh, as the credits rolled and a concerned voice-over encouraged viewers to call an Interior Ministry helpline if they'd had any problems with pharmaceutical companies asking people to take part in unscrupulous drug trials. Despite the shocking bias and the wafer-thin plot, the producers and scriptwriters had done a wonderful job, weaving together the components of the story in a most compelling way. Hesketh could see the programme for what it was, but there was some part of him, some place deep within his mind over which he did not have full control, which now made him feel less than charitable towards large drug companies. He'd be damned if he'd ever buy Lemsip again. Unconsciously, he made a note to watch the next episode at the same time the following evening, before the Quartermaster brought him to his senses.

'What do you think?' he asked.

'Powerful stuff. Total crap of course,' said Hesketh.

'Quite, but it makes you think, eh? Actually, that was one of the milder episodes. There is nothing whatsoever that they will not tackle, no issue is off-limits, there is no standard of decency below which they will not stoop. Hard drugs? No problem. Incest? Bring it on! Get it out in the open. So much *healthier*! Felicity has so many boyfriends I wouldn't be surprised if they collectively refer to her as the Facility, and every so often Abu, the little lad, has a little crisis and keeps wondering if he's actually not a little bit queer. Yet the little bugger's only supposed to be ten years old. Jesus, I shouldn't like to be the bloody dog Tripod. Bound to get rogered to death in a future episode as some bestial sicko needs to express his individuality. Damned programme, it's so bloody watchable!'

'And how often do you watch *The Codes*, Quartermaster?'

The Quartermaster rose from his chair. 'More often than is good for me! Now, let us join the others in the bar and you can tell me what you've been up to these past few days. We hardly ever see you any more.'

ELEVEN

Although the 65th was busy with the building project and not concerned with anything military for the time being, Colonel Sandford still had a regiment to micro-manage, and every Monday morning he held his tedious Command Community Conference in Regimental Headquarters. Taverner, as one of his Battery Commanders, was required to attend and did so with the greatest reluctance. One morning he took his place at the conference table, quickly glanced through the agenda and saw that there was very little that concerned him or his Battery. Even the start of a new week had failed to ignite any motivation in him, and as the Colonel entered and sat down at the head of the table, Taverner's mind drifted away to more pleasant thoughts of clean waves and Hannah's curves.

Much of the conference was taken up with feedback from the Colonel's recent meeting at Brigade and concerned the usual trivial matters, but there was one item of note.

'Headquarters EuroCorps has announced the formation of a new unit called the European Rapid Deployment Force, or ERDF,' said Colonel Sandford. 'It will be a multi-national force, about Brigade-size, and you should note that it will probably involve personnel and units from the British Armed Services, attached on a rotating basis. It will be a tri-service force, comprising ground and air force units with some smaller naval and marine units as well. It will maintain a high state of readiness and be ready to deploy at short notice, hence its name. The bulk of the force will comprise airborne and airmobile troops, their supporting arms and aircraft, although it will retain the ability to support a variety of other assets too, from paramilitary police to a light tank squadron. The Headquarters of the ERDF is being formed at the moment and it is expected that deployable units will be attached as soon as June this year, with the Force becoming operational with immediate effect. This is going to be a very high profile organisation and it will be EuroCorps' main effort this year. Considerable resources and capital have been made available to get it up and running. As we have seen in the past with similar formations, there will be a need to justify the new Force as soon as possible to show that it means business, probably by sending it on an inaugural operation or peace-keeping tour in the weeks following its formation.'

The officers scribbled down the details, except Major Hesketh, who was still in his dark mood and staring menacingly into the table, and Taverner, who really couldn't have cared less.

'Onto regimental business. Major Hesketh, can you update us on recent progress?'

'Colonel, the accommodation blocks have now been completed and occupied, and the boys appear to be very happy in their new homes. The new houses on the married patch have now gone up, with all existing houses re-wired, re-plumbed and re-decorated. Now that work on the regiment's accommodation is almost finished, we will start later this week on the new garages and offices, which should be finished by the end of this month. The tarmacing of the runways continues, and the minor projects, the Sailing Club, the kindergarten and the new superstore, are progressing ahead of schedule.'

'Good. Quartermaster, how are you getting on disposing of the gate guardians?'

Colonel Sandford had decreed that the old decommissioned artillery pieces, known as *gate guardians*, found outside offices and Batteries, would not be in keeping with the newly-modernised base and they would have to go. Windcheater Island, he had pointed out, was not a meant to be a bloody museum.

'Colonel, the Thunderbird Missile and the Iraqi D30 gun have been sold to the National Museum of Modern Conflict, and the 17-Pounder will go into storage,' said the Quartermaster. 'We were going to put up the German 88mm gun for international auction, until I learnt of a man in North America, a rich armchair general if ever I saw one, who buys up vast quantities of old tanks and guns from across the world and recreates famous land battles on his ranch from the last hundred years. He's going to make us an offer on the gun and I think that ...'

'Thank you, Quartermaster,' interrupted the Colonel. 'Well done on finding a potential buyer. If he doesn't take it in the next few weeks, auction the bloody thing or scrap it. I find it a most inappropriate piece of history.'

Taverner doodled away on his copy of the agenda, sketching all the officers sitting round the table from his perspective. He drew Colonel Sandford strapped into an electric chair at the head of the table, with big levers in front of the other officers. *Power. On/Off.* If only.

Colonel Sandford started to draw the conference to a close.

'Right. On Friday, myself and the Adjutant did a snap inspection of all Battery offices and garages. As you know, I take Health and Safety very seriously indeed and you will all be familiar with my Health and Safety Directive and the numerous amendments since its original issue. It is incumbent on us that we are seen to provide a safe working environment for our soldiers, whether here in barracks or in a trench on the front line. The new Health and Safety notices have been issued to the Batteries, but there are far too many of *last* year's notices still up on the walls. They are now out of date and must be replaced with the new ones.'

The Colonel turned towards Taverner who was still doodling away, in a world of his own, putting the final touches to his masterpiece.

'When we looked round your Battery,' said the Colonel, 'we could not see any Health and Safety notices at all, not even those from previous years, Captain Taverner. Could you tell me why?'

Taverner jumped at the mention of his name, looking like a guilty schoolboy. He had not been paying attention.

'Er, could you repeat the question please, Colonel?'

There was a collective intake of breath round the table and the other officers stopped scribbling and looked up.

'*Captain* Taverner. Was I boring you, just then?'

Taverner couldn't miss this opportunity.

'Just at that moment, Colonel? Yes, you were.'

Having now put the knife in, thought Taverner, he might as well give it a twist.

'Immensely, in fact, Colonel.'

The room went silent and time seemed to slow down.

Taverner glared at the Colonel, who could say nothing and had to look away. The other officers looked back and forth between Sandford and Taverner.

It was Major Hesketh who spoke first and, when he did, it was with a sharpness of tongue that was quite out of character, and he slammed his hands down hard onto the table.

'Captain Taverner! Do not *ever* speak to the Commanding Officer like that! Get out at once!'

Everyone turned to Hesketh in astonishment, including Colonel Sandford. No-one had heard him raise his voice like that before. Taverner, who was largely impervious to insult or criticism, expected some fireworks for his honesty, but nevertheless felt a little stung because they had come, quite unexpectedly, from Major Hesketh. He pushed his chair in and left the Conference Room, wondering if, in career terms at least, he had passed the point of no return.

Later that morning at coffee-break, Hesketh sat on his own, flicking through the newspapers and clearly not wanting to be disturbed.

The Quartermaster was telling Taverner about the American buyer for the German 88mm gun.

'The man's an extraordinary bugger. Tried to join the Army in his youth, but failed to get into the military academy at Westpoint. Went into business instead and made billions out of junk food, but he'd never quite forgotten about his military ambitions. So the old bugger decided that if they won't give you an Army to play with, you build your own instead. He lives somewhere in Kansas on a huge ranch and likes nothing better at the weekend than recreating huge battles from the past. Apparently he's got a thing about the Second World War and the Eastern Front at the moment, and is looking to do Kursk, hence his interest in the 88mm gun. A pity we haven't got any old Russian tanks – he's snapping up T-34s all over the place. I dare say he'd make you a good offer on your Kubelwagen. Do you know the bugger even has his own workshop making the ammunition for these old pieces from the original templates?'

'Some people, eh? Too much time, too much money,' said Taverner. 'Anyway, changing the subject, what's got into Mr Grumpy recently?' he said, nodding in the direction of Major Hesketh.

'One might ask the same thing of you, dear Charlie. We all find the Colonel boring, but we have the good manners not to tell him to his face. You, on the other hand … you fool!'

'He asked me a direct question and I gave him a direct answer. I would never lie to a Commanding Officer.'

'You shouldn't do it, Charlie. He's a vindictive bugger and he will just make things even worse.'

'Quartermaster, I couldn't care less about the Colonel and have no wish to waste my precious coffee-break talking about him. I'm more concerned with Tom. Why is he in such a foul mood at the moment? Is he homesick?'

'Unlikely.'

'Has his wife left him?'

'Not as far as I'm aware. My guess is that it's finally dawned on the poor bugger that he's come to the end of the line. Seen it happen before for people like him, like me in fact, the Army is all they've ever known. You join up at eighteen, become completely institutionalised and suddenly you're fifty-five before you know it. Service no longer required, old chap, and off you toddle to Civvy

Street. Fear of the unknown, you see. Like an old blind dog. No idea what's out there. Makes a man *snappy.*'

'Don't talk such rot, Quartermaster. I'm sure he's looking forward to retirement. He could easily adjust to life in Civvy Street.'

'Not as his age. It's easy getting out when you're thirty, but stay in much longer than that and you'll have to stay the whole course. Too late to make the change. Charlie, take my advice. If you don't get out soon, at your age — that is, of course, if your career survives, which, on the basis of your bloody performance this morning I very much doubt — twenty years from now,' he said, looking towards Hesketh, 'that'll be you. Mr Grumpy.'

They were both wrong in their speculations about Major Hesketh's dark mood. Hesketh chain-scoffed his way through an entire plate of biscuits without realising and read the newspapers from cover to cover without taking in the words; he alone recently burdened with a terrible secret, with little idea whether he should share it with anyone, or even who that person should be.

TWELVE

Taverner was certain he was going to die and he prayed it would be quick and painless when they hit the tree.

Hannah was driving him in her little Caterham Seven, going like the clappers along a winding country road. Being so low to the ground in a sports car with no roof or doors, the roar of the freezing wind and howl from the exhaust amplified the sensation of speed. Taverner, clad in one of Hannah's flying jackets, felt like he was strapped into a rocket-powered coffin. At near-suicidal speed they approached a tight right-hand bend and Hannah couldn't resist taking it at the absolute limit of adhesion. She still had the throttle buried to the floor way past the point at which most sane drivers would have been stomping on the brakes out of a sense of self-preservation. As Taverner thought in horror she had perhaps failed to notice the bend, she trod violently hard on the brakes and rapidly flicked down two gears, heel-and-toeing so smoothly he could not even feel the gear changes. The little car's nose dipped under braking and Hannah used the extra grip from the front tyres to turn in towards the small bank on the inside. Even before she got to the apex of the bend she was hard on the power again, the back of the car breaking away into a lurid powerslide towards a tree on the outside, the engine screaming, the tyres scrabbling for grip, Hannah casually applying a touch of opposite lock, and Taverner instinctively trying to squeeze down inside his flying jacket. Just as a heavy 'goodnight' seemed imminent, the rear tyres bit, Hannah snapped the steering wheel straight and she accelerated hard away.

Conversation was impossible. When Hannah was driving fast – which was to say whenever she was at the wheel of any car – her concentration was total and she rarely spoke. Occasionally she gave a little commentary on the events in her rear-view mirror, as she enlightened yet another fool for whom the sight of a pretty girl at the wheel of a fast sports car was like a red rag to a bull. No matter what they were driving, her challengers could never keep up and would disappear out of sight after a few bends, often into the scenery.

She roared into the car park of a pub, turned off the engine, peeled off her driving gloves and hopped out over the hot, ticking exhaust. Taverner sat in the car for a little while, his ears ringing, briefly enjoying the simple pleasure of being alive. Even after four years together, he was still not sure if Hannah was genuinely crazy or whether she really was that good a driver, but he supposed that since she had once held the lap record for single-seater Formula Fords for the circuits at Silverstone *and* Brands Hatch she must have really known what she was doing.

A small river flowed next to the pub's beer garden and they sat down at a table. The sun was out, but the northerly wind was cold and they kept their flying jackets on, looking as though they had just arrived in a biplane.

'You don't think that we got a little bit close to that tree, darling?' he suggested.

'Which one?' said Hannah. 'Oh, you mean the bend where I had the back out. Nah, miles away.'

'You had the back out on every bloody corner.'

'I know. It's so naughty of me, the tyres are so terribly expensive to replace. Perhaps you should drive back, Charlie.'

'No thank you. I'm through with your Driving Miss Daisy jibes. I admit it, alright? I'm a slow bastard. I might as well be wearing a flat cap when I'm at the wheel.'

'Middle-age is clearly catching up with you, Charlie,' she teased.

'I guess so.'

'Is that also why I beat you down that black run in Verbier?' Hannah's smile widened.

'How many times do I have to explain?' said Taverner. 'Snowboards are slower than skis. They have a lot more surface area in contact with the ground. Anyway, I had to slow down when we got to the nursery slope. I'd have easily whipped your arse if that bloody snake-train of little kids hadn't cut me up. If I'd run them over at the speed I was going, I'd probably be on a multiple manslaughter charge.'

'Gave up, did we, because the nasty little kiddies got in the way? What a load of old cock, Charlie. You were still going fast enough for that man with the radar gun to confiscate your lift pass.'

'Miserable old git. Of course he was going to take mine away. I had disadvantages.'

'Such as?'

'I'm not fluent in French, and I didn't have lovely eyelashes to flutter and gorgeous hips to wiggle at that bloody jobsworth. That's the only reason you kept yours.'

Hannah beamed at his compliments.

'He was quite sweet really,' she said.

'Not when he was lecturing me. I couldn't understand a word, but he certainly made his point.'

A waitress brought them their lunch.

'Charlie, are you still thinking about buying a chalet out there?'

'Yes. I've been thinking about it a lot since we got back. We could run it for six months through the ski season, then rent it out in the summer when we go travelling. It's money for old rope. It's got to be more exciting than the bloody Army. Seriously, Hannah, if I bought a chalet, would you come with me?'

'Of course. You're not the only one who needs a change of scenery.'

'How is work? Is that pervert of a boss still infatuated with you?'

'Not since yesterday. Filthy swine!'

'He's only human, you can't blame him. Did you have to have words with him again?'

'No, better than that, darling. It was very bad of me really, but he's been getting worse of late, so I had to do *something* to put him off. He's taken to standing behind me when I'm sitting at my desk, so he can see right down into my blouse. The filthy swine doesn't realise that I can see his reflection in the window. So I decided that enough was enough. Instead of politely telling him to get lost, as I usually do, I flirted with him dreadfully all week, wore some awfully revealing clothes and matched his filthy innuendo. It was driving him mad! You always know when he's feeling racy because his upper lip gets damp. Anyway, pretending that I had simply given in, I promised him a big surprise at the end of the week. I said I was taking him somewhere special, but only on condition that he was a very good boy and brought a thick blanket to keep us warm and a bottle of something to get us in the mood. So, yesterday, the two of us jumped into my car at lunchtime and we went for a *very* fast blat ...'

'Oh Hannah, you didn't?' Taverner covered his face with his hands.

'Yes I did!' she squealed with delight. 'I couldn't resist it!'

'The poor man.'

'We did my usual twenty-mile loop and I beat my personal best by over two minutes. *And* there was other traffic on the road *and* I was two-up. Aren't you proud of me? I nearly lost it twice and I got all four wheels off the ground at one point.'

'How was your boss?'

'Speechless. He looked simply awful by the time we got back to the office. I left him in the car park, sitting on a wall with the blanket wrapped around him and told him to go back home to his wife. I think he got the message.'

Taverner smiled at her in appreciation. 'Well done, darling.'

'Thank you. I did have so much fun in Verbier, Charlie. Please can we go again before the season is over?'

'Just so you can beat me again?'

'Of course. When do you next get leave?'

'Not until April. The snow might be gone by then.'

'How very boring. Then why don't we both go AWOL,' she said, dreamily.

'I'd be surprised if I haven't gone AWOL by then, the way things are going. I've never been so bored. The Commanding Officer is the most incompetent tyrant ever to be thrust upon us, the Second-in-Command has turned into a manic depressive and isn't talking to anyone, and the regiment is working all round the clock on this bloody building project. I joined the Army to be a soldier, not Bob the bloody Builder, and no doubt as soon as that's finished we'll be sent on yet another wonderful humanitarian tour for six months where we can try, yet again, to persuade the local savages that genocide and mass-rape are not the way to going about winning hearts and minds, that is if they're not too busy trying to blow us up.'

'You seem so down, Charlie. Really, I've never seen you looking so glum. Why don't we just elope, hmmm? To a tropical island somewhere in the Indian Ocean? Just the two of us. No-one for miles and miles around,' she said, her big dark eyes starting to seduce him.

Taverner laughed gently, and he then spoke semi-seriously.

'If we did go, then it would be at very short notice. And I'd never be able to come back here, you understand?'

'Why stay? What's left here that's any good?'

'You're right.' He ran his hands back through his hair and sighed. 'My God, I can't believe I'm actually contemplating this. A deserter. Do you know, not so long ago they used to shoot people like me?'

They paid the bill and headed out into the car park.

'If you don't mind, could you slow down on the way back?' said Taverner.

'You're so pathetic.'

'Those clouds on the horizon look a bit heavy,' he said. 'Do you think we can make it back before it rains?'

'If we don't, we are going to get awfully wet!'

'You'll have to slow down then, Hannah.'

'Not bloody likely.'

Taverner slid himself down into the passenger seat and strapped himself into the four-point racing harness.

'Hannah, how soon could you be ready to go if we decided to clear off for good? In theory?'

'A week.'

'Only a week? I thought you would have needed at least a month.'

'You're forgetting, Charlie, when a girl like me gets the order to go,' she said, as the engine roared into life, 'I don't hang around!'

THIRTEEN

It was not long after that weekend with Hannah that Taverner finally snapped and resolved to leave the Army; not in the proper way, with a formal letter of resignation followed by two years of marking time and counting down the days, but on his own terms – as and when it suited him. The decisive moment came, not in the grip of frustration with the Colonel, nor with the belief that life was passing him by, nor because the sheer boredom of regimental life had finally broken him. He made the decision while sat astride his surfboard watching the setting sun on a beautiful and deliriously calm evening.

It was late March and Taverner was back at his favourite beach, Saunton Sands. The sea temperature was as low as it was going to get – so low that anyone foolhardy enough to enter the water without a wetsuit would have lasted a matter of minutes before hypothermia set in. In addition to the thick wetsuit designed for such conditions, he also wore neoprene boots and gloves. The kit was cumbersome and he wondered how much better it would be if he was somewhere else where the water was so warm he'd only need a pair of boardshorts. But this was North Devon, and though the water was cold the place had a magic all of its own. It would be hard to leave here, and he felt downcast at the thought of no more evenings like this, of all those waves unridden, but leave it he must.

Only rarely did the elements come together like this. The sky was clear, save for a long band of cirrus cloud extending across the horizon, and the sun gradually sank lower; a long, bright glare reflecting off the surface of the water smoothed to glass by the gentlest of offshore winds. This hour of the day, known as the 'evening glass-off', was a near-sacred time for surfers, and there were quite a few locals in the water at the north end by the rocks. Taverner acknowledged them, but needed solitude and paddled further down the beach.

The surf was not big that evening – even the biggest waves were not even head-high – nor was there the gut-wrenching fear that Taverner experienced on the bigger days. But these calmer, more contemplative sessions were just as important to him; a fix that he craved as much as any adrenaline-charged big-wave session.

The sun descended towards the horizon, changing colour from white through yellow to orange, and as the waves broke, the wind blew the spray back over the waves, lit up for a moment like a shower of orange sparks. There was no need to compete with other surfers for the waves, or to paddle around to get into the optimum position for a breaking set. Taverner could have surfed more waves if he had wanted to, but he chose to sit astride his board where he was, not far out to sea, soaking up the imagery around him; each element of the scenery blended together to create, like the most beautiful waves, something that was unique at that given moment and would never again be replicated exactly so. Just to be in the water that evening was pleasure enough. The deep, dark blue above his head merged with the orange sky on the horizon – an incredible intensity of colour that mere photographs or paint on canvas could never have done justice to. Then, just as the sun touched the horizon, slowly merging like a water drop with its reflection off the sea, the underside of the cirrus cloud was lit up in a fiery orange – a display as dramatic as it was short-lived.

A wave approached. Taverner snapped out of his reverie and caught it, paddling hard towards the beach, a moment of darkness as the peak blocked out the low sun, warning him that the wave was close, and then he popped up into orange sunlight again, dropping down into the shadow, building up speed then turning and riding up to the lip again; sunlight, darkness, and finally sunlight again as he kicked out over the back of the wave.

He stayed out beyond sunset until he could no longer see the waves. It was a long walk across the sand to the car park, with the faint smell of smoke from a distant cottage's coal fire wafting across the beach. Taverner's spirit was recharged and he had a wry smile on his face, because he knew by this time next week he would be out of the Army for good.

At work the next day, Colonel Sandford let it be known that Easter leave was being cancelled 'in order to maintain the momentum of the building programme, with leave to be taken *in lieu* after the building work has been completed.' There was no hint of regret in his voice as he made the announcement to the officers, who groaned quietly, having been looking forward to some skiing at the end of the season.

In contrast, Taverner seemed happily indifferent. Taking the decision to go AWOL was wonderfully liberating for him. He failed to attend an important meeting, let a stream of incoming paperwork pile up on his desk throughout the day and ignored summonses from the Colonel. Taverner was far too busy planning his exit strategy. He would have to leave the country, of course, but he had the means to ensure it would not be a hardship. Back in his room, he started to make discreet enquiries about shipping his belongings to his parents' home in the Bahamas. The contents of his room were packed into three large boxes, and the firm of accountants who had looked after the Taverner family's finances for generations started to move his funds abroad. He arranged for a lorry to take his possessions away at night later on in the week, to be stored and shipped at a future date. All he would need in the interim period would be his trusty Land Rover and his dog.

By Thursday of that week, he was almost ready to slip away into the night. The final thing he needed to do was to tell Hannah.

At lunch the following day, Major Hesketh sat down next to Taverner. Hesketh had stopped talking to anyone recently, and Taverner was a little surprised by his approach. Hesketh now appeared to be back to his old self, cheerful and gregarious, and Taverner wondered briefly if it was because he too was about to do a runner from the 65th in the dead of night.

'I wonder if you'd join me and the Quartermaster in my office after work today,' said Hesketh. 'The three of us need to have a little chat.'

'Certainly. Can't we do so here?' asked Taverner, wondering if Hesketh had somehow rumbled his plan to go AWOL.

'Not here,' he said. 'I'd prefer somewhere a little more discreet.'

'Of course,' said Taverner, suitably intrigued.

'Let's say five-thirty. Oh, and not my office in Regimental Headquarters. Meet us in the one next to the building site.'

'Anything I should be worried about?'

'Not in your case.'

Taverner went back to his office later that afternoon to phone Hannah, locking himself in to avoid interruption, but then decided he had better wait until he'd had his meeting with Major Hesketh and the Quartermaster. Whatever it was they wanted to see him about, it was very unlikely to interfere with his plans. It would need to be something very spectacular to sway him from his intended course.

At half past five, he met Major Hesketh and the Quartermaster in the Project Headquarters. All the clerks had left, there was no-one else in the building, and the two older officers looked very grave.

'Charlie,' said Hesketh, 'for reasons that will shortly become apparent, I need your word that none of what you are about to hear or see must be spoken of outside of these four walls, or in any company except the three of us here.'

Taverner thought for a moment, trying to second-guess what Hesketh might be about to tell him. Then he nodded slowly.

'You have my word.'

Satisfied, Major Hesketh then started to tell him about events three weeks earlier, when someone in the Ministry of Defence had got their wires crossed, and he found himself party to some information that was certainly not meant for him.

FOURTEEN

Three weeks earlier

Colonel Sandford was absent yet again, attending a seminar important enough for him to be away for the whole week, though not so important that people needed to know what it was about or where it was being held. In his absence Major Hesketh, as Second-in-Command, automatically took over the 65th. The delegation of command was a mere formality in most regiments, but Colonel Sandford found it very difficult to trust anyone, believing that too much delegation was a recipe for a career-annihilating disaster. While he was content to let Hesketh run the building project, he was certainly not going to let him run the regiment as well. Before leaving on his sojourn, the Colonel summoned Hesketh and the Adjutant to his office, as he did before every absence, and read out a long list of things they were not to do, people to whom they were not to speak, actions they were not to take and orders they were not to give. If they were in any doubt, said the Colonel, don't.

With no way of getting in touch with the Colonel – he had not left any contact details – most outside enquiries had to be politely rebuffed by Hesketh or the Adjutant until, they explained to the caller, the Colonel got back.

Hesketh had returned to the office after a wet and windy tour of the base to find a message from the Duty Clerk asking him to contact the Ministry of Defence as a matter of urgency. On returning the call he found himself speaking to a young bureaucrat; a brusque, abrupt little upstart who introduced himself as:

'... the Executive Assistant Controller, Housing Services Division. Is that the Commanding Officer I'm speaking to?'

Hesketh lied.

'Yes, this is the Commanding Officer.' He was becoming mildly annoyed at constantly having to explain to outsiders that he was only the *Acting* Commanding Officer.

The bureaucrat spoke rapidly.

'We haven't received confirmation that Phase Three of the Domestic Euro-orientation Plan is complete,' he said.

'The what?' said Hesketh.

'The Domestic Euro-orientation Plan. Phase Three.'

Hesketh wondered if the man had got the wrong number.

'I'm sorry, say again?'

'Jesus Christ! The Domestic Euro-orientation Plan? The new living quarters on Windcheater Island? We've had no confirmation that Phase Three is complete. We can't sanction the next phase until we've had confirmation.' The civil servant worked for a very senior military officer – an irate Major General – and was therefore under the misapprehension that, despite being a civilian, he was entitled to speak to any military officer below the rank of Major General in the same rude and sarcastic manner as his boss.

Hesketh kept his calm.

'Living quarters? On Windcheater Island? I don't know what you're on about. All I can tell you is that they are being refurbished at the moment,' he said.

'Yes, thank you for that. I *know* they're being refurbished, everyone *knows* they're being refurbished, Jesus Christ, but is ... Phase ... Three ... complete?'

'What the hell are you on about, young man? I'm not aware of any "phases" or any "orientation plan".'

'We spoke about it last week! Don't you remember? For Christ's sake, I sent you the forms electronically. Hello! HELLO!'

'Who did you speak to last week?'

'You! The Commanding Officer! Remember me?'

'You spoke to Colonel Sandford?'

'Yes!'

'This is not Colonel Sandford you're speaking to.'

'What do you mean? You just said you were.'

'No, I didn't say I was Colonel Sandford. I said I was the Commanding Officer. Colonel Sandford is out of the office all week. You are speaking to Major Tom Hesketh.'

'*Major* Hesketh. Christ Almighty!'

'That is correct. I am deputising for the Colonel in his absence.'

'Well, *Major*, you can start *deputising* for him right now. We need that confirmation today. Understood? Colonel Sandford is aware of the phases.'

'Then if Colonel Sandford is aware of it, might I suggest you actually try speaking to Colonel Sandford because I have no idea what you are talking about. Now, if you don't mind, I've had quite enough of your ...'

'I don't care,' interrupted the caller. 'I said I need it by close of play today, got it? You really need to get a grip of this, I'm afraid.'

Hesketh had had enough and put the man in his place, his voice still calm and controlled.

'You should be afraid, you stupid prick. I am a commissioned officer in the Royal Horse Artillery with thirty-five years' service and I was dodging bullets in South Armagh while you were still pissing in your fucking romper suit! How dare you speak to me in that manner.'

The bureaucrat hesitated for a second, but still did not give up.

'It is very important. You see ...'

'Excuse me? Didn't anyone teach you any manners? You asked me to do something and I've explained that I'm unable to furnish your request. The person who you need to speak to is Lieutenant Colonel Sandford. He is not here and will not be back until next week.'

'Yes, that's all very well, but you'll need to get in touch with him ASAP.'

'Please don't ever attempt to give an order to an Army officer, young man. You are a civilian.'

'But I work for a Major General, you know. Therefore you have to do what I say.'

Hesketh laughed heavily down the phone.

'Do I? And which Major General do you work for?'

'Major General Ogilvy.'

'Ogilvy? Major General Ogilvy? Ah, he's a very good friend of mine. We were at Sandhurst together many years ago as young officer cadets. Between us we deflowered many comely young ladies of Camberley. If you ever speak to me like that again, I will be speaking to him about the way you speak to his old buddy, and you may rest assured I will not be terribly complimentary. He holds your bureaucratic ilk in even more contempt than I do.'

'Fine. Fine!'

'And by God, you'd better be sitting to attention while you're on the phone to me. Now, kindly bugger off.'

Actually, Hesketh had never heard of any Major General Olgilvy, nor had he ever come across anyone in the military with that name. Nor, come to think of it, had he extensively deflowered the comely young ladies of Camberley while in training at Sandhurst. He had been too exhausted for that. And if he thought that his blustering story about a mutual friendship with Major General Ogilvy would get the bureaucrat off his back, he was quite wrong.

Five minutes later, after a distinctly one-way telephone conversation, Hesketh reckoned he knew a fair bit about Major General Ogilvy. The General did most of the talking, and his tone was by no means chatty, pointing out that if his employee's request was not answered by 1700hrs, he would personally come down to Windcheater Island with the aim of deflowering the comely Hesketh.

As tempting as it was to ignore it out of pure spite, a General's order was like a Papal bull. Hesketh had no option but to comply. Wearily, he set about looking through his paperwork for anything to do with 'Domestic Euro-orientation Phases', as the possibility that he had overlooked something important nagged away at him. And why did the imbeciles at the MoD seem to think that Colonel Sandford would know the answer? Hesketh was the Project Manager, after all. An extensive search of relevant files in Regimental Headquarters came up empty, although the Duty Clerk pointed out that Colonel Sandford may have stored the information electronically, and if so, only the Colonel could gain access to it.

Later that morning at coffee-break, Hesketh happened

to mention his difficulty to Taverner, who sent for Lance Bombardier Thacker.

Thacker was the Systems Manager for the Air Defence Computer in Taverner's Battery; a near-genius with computer systems, who had, before joining the Army, put his talents to rather more nefarious uses. Not for nothing was he known as 'Thacker the Hacker' by those elements of the Liverpool underworld involved in identity theft.

Hesketh felt uncomfortable at what he now asked Thacker to do. Colonel Sandford had a desktop computer in his office, protected by the latest security system, which allowed access to the machine only after it recognized the unique body odour of the registered user, however faint. Thacker was able to bypass it as easily as nicking a sweetie from a baby, and logged himself on as Colonel Sandford. After a few keywords were typed in – *European, orientation, domestication, phase* – the machine highlighted five separate files. Once he had printed them off, Thacker handed them to Hesketh, shut down the system and was careful to leave no trace that he had ever been there.

The hunch paid off. 'Domestic Euro-orientation' was an insignificant matter that in no way warranted the effort needed to find it in the first place, though it was typical of the Ministry of Defence to get their knickers in a twist over something so trivial. It concerned the requirement to ensure that all electrical fittings in the domestic accommodation on Windcheater Island were EU-compliant; so that any imported electrical appliances purchased on the European Continent would be able to work without the need of an adapter for the traditional three-pin plug socket. There was nothing particularly unusual about this – all homes in the Federal British Republic were required to be EU-compliant within five years, as the Continental two-pin socket was phased in, and all new homes on Windcheater Island had the new sockets as a matter of course. Hesketh did not know why Colonel Sandford had kept the information to himself, suspecting it was just an oversight, since there was no reason to hide it from anyone, and telephoned Major General Ogilvy at the MoD to confirm that 'Phase Three' had indeed been completed a fortnight earlier.

All military documents carried a security classification, graded according to the sensitivity of their content, with the classification printed in capital letters at the top and bottom of the page. Anything relating to housing would carry the lowest grade of security classification – UNCLASSIFIED – and of the five files printed off by Lance Bombardier Thacker, four of them were graded as such. Were they to fall into the wrong hands they would not put any lives at risk; the numerous enemies of the Federal British Republic were unlikely to gain much strategic benefit from a comprehensive insight into the Army's housing arrangements.

However, the fifth document that Hesketh now held in his hands was far more sensitive. It was a single sheet graded SECRET – FOR THE COMMANDING OFFICER'S EYES ONLY, and though Hesketh knew he should have immediately shredded it before he even looked at it, his curiosity got the better of him.

The document was dated one month earlier, and it did not make for pleasant reading.

INTERIM REPORT:
European Rapid Deployment Force

Proposed European Rapid Deployment Force (ERDF) confirmed operational by Headquarters EuroCorps. ERDF Headquarters and Spearhead Battalions

('Adler', 'Libertaire' and 'Goodwill' Battalions) to be located at Windcheater Island (South West Region; Federal British Republic/Former United Kingdom) no later than 1st July this year. The base is midway through an extensive phased refurbishment and extension programme, undertaken by current Unit-in-Residence (8th of the 34th ARSEEFUK, also known as 65th RHA). Initial orientation and occupation of Windcheater Island to be carried out by advance admin echelons of ERDF immediately following disbandment of the 65th RHA and its removal from the British Army's strength.

Hesketh felt a muted explosion of warmth in his abdomen as he tried to take in what he had just read. He had to read the passage several times to make sure he fully understood. There were further revelations in the next paragraph.

... confirmation that the ERDF Force Commander will be Lieutenant Colonel H R Sandford, at present the Commanding Officer of the 65th RHA and currently overseeing the refurbishment, to be promoted to Brigadier on taking up his new appointment, rank effective from the date of the formal handover of Windcheater Island to the ERDF ...

A little research on the Internet did not reveal much information to Hesketh about the ERDF, other than a few vague releases from official sources. Certainly there was no mention of where the organisation was going to be based. A lot of things started to become very clear to him, and each sudden realisation felt like a punch in the face until his head was spinning.

So, he thought, without anyone in the regiment yet

knowing, the 65th was going to be disbanded, but not before the soldiers had unwittingly upgraded Windcheater Island to the high standards demanded by the ERDF; the force in which Colonel Sandford had quietly secured his place as the Commander. No wonder the document was graded SECRET – the lying scumbag was taking them all for a ride. The runways on Windcheater Island would be needed by the ERDF's aircraft – so much for all that rubbish about them being classed as roads in need of resurfacing. Similarly, the lies about the 65th having to go back on the operational Arms Plot in the summer, bringing the deadline forward and forcing the soldiers to work round the clock. The real reason was because the ERDF wanted to be in its new home before the summer was out. The bean-counters at the Ministry of Defence would no doubt be congratulating themselves on the money saved by using squaddies as cheap building labour, while ensuring a high standard of work by having them believe that the refurbishment was for their own comfort. This was a conspiracy that went very high indeed.

Hesketh sat for a moment, dazed at the scale of the betrayal, then shredded the four UNCLASSIFIED documents, but retained the one marked SECRET. It was fortunate that Colonel Sandford was not present on the base at that moment, because Hesketh, in all likelihood, would have walked straight into his office and killed him. It was all he could do to resist the temptation to go outside and tell the soldiers to down-tools and stop work immediately.

Despite the atrocious weather that day, Hesketh took a long walk, traipsing the whole perimeter of the island. He needed to think. Donned in a long waxed jacket and a wide brimmed hat, off which the water dripped, he resembled a catholic priest of old, head down and deep in thought, immune to the wind and rain.

The shock of the discovery subsided in him and gave way to an astonishing anger. There had been very few occasions in his life when he had ever felt quite so livid, and whenever he had, the anger went hand-in-hand with a remarkable clarity of thought. It was at such moments as this that Hesketh, the bluff, bumbling stoic, was at his most dangerous as he ruthlessly considered the options open to him.

One. Confront Sandford with the evidence when he got back.

Two. Inform the soldiers and see how they'd respond to the news.

Three. Do nothing at all. Actually rather tempting. There were advantages in not rocking the boat. He was retiring in a few months and would probably be gone before the 65th even learnt it was going to be axed. A farewell dinner in the Mess, a little speech and some hollow words from Sandford – if he could be bothered to be there – and Hesketh would depart with his awful secret. He would return to Canada and his comfortable existence in Alberta, take his Canadian citizenship, become a gentleman of leisure again, fish for trout in the Rockies in the summer and ski at Jasper in the winter. But since he had come back to the 65th, Hesketh realised that his home and family were now so very distant, in every sense of the word. He had become disconnected from his old life and the 65th had filled the void. It was a common experience when posted overseas.

Soldiers far from home, especially those on operational tours, were preoccupied with their immediate existence, and their old life, whether they were descended from landed gentry or raised on the council estate from hell, no longer seemed relevant. The mundane day-to-day aspects of normal life back home – mortgage repayments, washing the car on a Sunday, waiting for your wife to put her face on to visit the garden centre – became meaningless, and when your old life caught up with you, in context it could seem absurd.

Take a moment, perhaps, lying on your cot at a Forward Operating Base. You're resting in between patrols and the temperature is well over a hundred degrees. You haven't slept properly for days, but the adrenaline is still pumping and keeping you sharp. A strong wind is blowing off the mountain and whipping sand through the tent. You're dusty and sweaty, you've finished cleaning your rifle and you've replaced the rounds in the magazine fired off when you came under contact earlier. In ten minutes you'll be out on the ground again, putting yourself back in harm's way, faced with the real possibility of burns, blindness or mutilation, and if Death is to come for you then you pray you won't suffer. Pour some water down your parched throat and quickly read those unopened letters from home.

A reminder from your bank that you are still exceeding your overdraft limit and are incurring penalty charges.

A Notice of Intended Prosecution from the local Safety Camera Partnership who detected you exceeding the speed limit – sixty-five in a sixty – that'll be two-hundred Euros and three points please.

A letter going into far too much detail about the expensive carpet ruined when so-and-so spilt red wine on it at the reception last week: 'absolutely *ruined* and it's going to cost a *fortune* to get cleaned, it's simply *ghastly*.'

Best of all is a 'Dear John' from your girlfriend: 'Look,

you can't just expect me to hang around while you're off playing soldiers for six months, sorry and all that, but I've met someone else who really understands my needs. He's always there for me. He's my best friend and my soul-mate. My rock and my shoulder to cry on. And anyway, the sex is *so* much better.'

Surrounded by death and fear, it was amusing to think that there were people out there who seriously believed that you actually gave a damn about overdrafts, speeding tickets and being dumped.

Admittedly, the surroundings of Windcheater Island were rather more genteel than some of the warzones Major Hesketh had served in, but the trappings of his life in Canada, as comfortable and secure as they were, now seemed just as banal and irrelevant to him. He simply couldn't bury his head in the sand and see the 65th disbanded; the regiment that had given him back his dignity and his sense of purpose, killed off at the stroke of an indifferent mandarin's biro. Hesketh would not have been able to live with the guilt that he had known, and had chosen to do nothing.

The burden of this knowledge was more than one man could bear and had caused him great torment until he eventually confided in the Quartermaster. After some lengthy discussions together, they decided that there might be another course of action, something that perhaps only the 65th would have ever dared to undertake.

Taverner was now reading the same secret document three weeks later in front of Hesketh and the Quartermaster, and felt a similar sense of shock and betrayal.

'Good God,' said Taverner. 'This isn't some sort of joke?'

For the time being he had forgotten about his intention to go AWOL. This was serious.

'I've made some very discreet enquiries,' said Hesketh. 'It's for real.'

'It's outrageous. Is there anything we can do to stop it?'

'No. The decision has already been made.'

'When do you suppose they intend to tell us?'

'I strongly suspect after we have completed the building work. They'll have no need for us after that. Of course, they'll expect us to grovel and plead when they finally tell us we're for the chop, and no doubt they'll be an impressive outcry from former members of the regiment, yet it only ever gives these vindictive bastards more satisfaction when they see the old buffers enraged.'

'Does anyone else in the regiment know about this?'

'No-one. We're the only three that know. Not including Colonel Sandford, of course.'

'What a vicious, scheming bastard.' said Taverner. 'Why don't you make this document public knowledge and let the boys know? They would down-tools straight away and stop work, probably even wreck the place. That would certainly scupper the Colonel's ambition, if the ERDF and the MoD are relying on him to get the base ready on time.'

'I considered it.'

'Or perhaps Lance Bombardier Thacker could put something rather incriminating on his computer for the police to discover.'

'A possibility. But Charlie, it would be easy to discredit the Colonel and, as tempting as it is, it would be a Pyrrhic victory. It won't stop the 65th being disbanded and it won't stop the ERDF taking over Windcheater Island.'

'Do you propose to do anything?'

'No,' said Hesketh. He made it sound like a 'yes'.

'Well, at least give me half an hour with the Colonel in a locked room,' said Taverner, his anger building. 'Christ, what I'd do to him!'

'In the meantime the boys keep on working and the base gets finished on schedule,' said Hesketh. 'Life goes on as normal. The 65th will only find out when the news is made official, whenever they decide to tell us.'

Hesketh dropped his voice conspiratorially.

'But in the evenings, the three of us are quietly going to get together to thrash out a little idea that the Quartermaster and I have discussed in embryo. Charlie, we're going to make sure that the smooth, straightforward handover of the sparkling new Windcheater Island, that the ERDF is expecting, will be nothing of the sort. No-one will ever make fools out of the 65th.'

'I like your train of thought,' said Taverner. 'And where do I come into this?'

'When the time comes, it would be to our advantage to have someone on the outside. Away from the regiment, acting independently, sneaky-beaky and all that. Besides, I get the distinct impression you don't need the Army any more, and want out. Two years is a long time to wait, isn't it, Charlie? Would you be prepared to leave the Army rather sooner, and help us? This would be a lot of fun, a bit cheeky, and our outsider must be very flexible, able to think on his feet, survive on his own initiative, and show a Machiavellian level of cunning. It may also be very dangerous. You're the only one that fits the bill, Charlie. Yes or no?'

Taverner had been on the verge of walking out of the regiment, bored after several years of dull, unexciting deployments, now suffering under the intolerable regime of Colonel Sandford and recently cheered at the thought that in a matter of days he and Hannah would be on a plane out of Heathrow, popping open the champagne in First Class before the regiment had even noticed he was missing.

'I'm in,' he said. 'Tell me what you have in mind.'

Over the following few weeks, the triumvirate went about their daily regimental business – Hesketh oversaw the building project, the Quartermaster cut about the base looking more dapper than ever, while Taverner, as usual, was nowhere to be seen. Not a word of Hesketh's discovery was mentioned to anyone. But each night, in great secrecy, they drew up their plan. Hesketh had a goal, and it was up to them to achieve it. Lance Bombardier 'Hacker' Thacker was recruited as a sleeping partner and, though he was kept ignorant of Hesketh's true intentions, he taught Hesketh how to externally interrogate the Colonel's computer and intercept his e-mails. They built up a very extensive picture of what was going between the Colonel, the Ministry of Defence and the ERDF. This intelligence allowed them to add some shape to the first draft of their plan. Perhaps *plan* was too specific a word at that stage; rather, they had envisaged a series of likely possibilities and were trying to prepare as best they could for each one. It was then '*war-gamed*' – tested in theory – by playing it out against a number of scenarios, the variables and the what-ifs that might occur, after which the plan was adjusted accordingly. It was as sound as it was going to be for the time being. With Hesketh's eye for detail and ability to anticipate, the Quartermaster's common sense and Taverner's audacity and casual attitude to risk, they were confident they would achieve their aims.

There were some other tasks that needed to be carried out away from Windcheater Island. This was now Taverner's concern, and with no need for him to stay in the 65th he was ready to achieve his dream and leave the Army for good.

Well, *almost* ready to leave.

FIFTEEN

An officer leaving the Army was normally dined out of the Officers' Mess by way of a formal dinner night. The Ladies' Guest Night at the 65th, to which wives and girlfriends were invited, would on this occasion also quietly double-up as Taverner's dine-out, though only he, Major Hesketh and the Quartermaster knew anything at that stage of his intention to leave the Army.

Taverner was Secretary to the Officers' Mess Committee and in charge of organising the evening; sending out the invitations, liaising with the chefs about the menu, selecting the wines and drawing up the seating plan. As well as the wives and girlfriends, a group of single girls had also been invited, all of whom had connections to the 65th and were known to be predatory in nature. They would keep the unattached officers happy for the evening.

Black Tie was the form that night – that oft-misinterpreted dress code that simply requires gentlemen to provide an understated backdrop of black and white against which the ladies can stand out; ladies whose couture that evening ranged from the safely-elegant to a couple of daring numbers that might as well have been spray-painted onto the wearer.

Taverner welcomed the guests into the anteroom and, in between greetings, he took quiet pleasure in watching Hannah work the room. She floated from group to group, charmed and complimented, making everyone feel better for their interaction, and each time she excused herself from one slightly spellbound group and moved on to the next, she would catch Taverner staring at her. Across the room they would exchange the briefest of glances that only two people so close would ever understand. On occasions such as this, her aura was perhaps never brighter. Some of the ladies, especially the younger ones, evidently wished to flaunt and stand out, and ended up going a little over the top. Hannah had no need to. Her dress was simple and modish, tastefully suggesting the contours of the stunning figure beneath. Her jewellery was just as discreet and she wore only the lightest application of make-up. It was almost as though she was somehow aware of her presence and deliberately trying to suppress it. She was not loud or gesturing, she did not actively draw attention to herself, and yet she was the dominant presence in the room; a bright centre of radiance on everyone's subconscious radar.

It was the first time that any of the officers had met Colonel Sandford's wife. From the moment Taverner greeted her, it was abundantly clear that she did not want to be there. Fate had not been kind to her. Her face was just chubby enough to soften the tight lines of sourness from her permanent mask of constipation, and she quickly withdrew to a quieter corner with her husband – she hesitantly sipping her tomato juice, he self-conscious and trying to make small talk with her, silently hoping that someone would come over and rescue them. She wore something that looked like a nomad's carpet thrown strategically over her shoulder, with sandals probably from the same region. Her dress was long, though not long enough to hide her hairy ankles. Taverner even made an effort for a few minutes, but she did not converse easily and he gave up, repelled by her appearance, and went to the Mess Manager's office for some writing paper to take care of one last little matter.

In due course, the Mess Manager announced that dinner was about to be served, and the guests filed into the darkened dining room as a string quartet played '*Roast Beef of Old England*'; the candles on the long table forming an island of cosy intimacy within the vast room.

The Colonel called for silence.

'Padre, would you say grace, please.'

'Let us pray,' said the Padre.

'O Lord.

God of Power, God of Might,

Bless us as we meet this night,

Bless this food and all our guests,

And tomorrow, please, give us lots of rest. Amen.'

It was Second Lieutenant Cavendish's first formal dinner night and he was keen to impress his girlfriend, Madeleine, a university student. He was also Mr Vice for the evening; a role normally given to the most junior subaltern. He pulled out the chair for his girlfriend and sat her down, but when he pulled his own chair under him he found the underside had been coated in Marmite. With his palms covered in a thick, black mess, he picked up his starched napkin to wipe them, flicked it deftly to release the folds, and managed to shower the Adjutant's wife opposite with the flour and jellybeans that had been hidden inside, for all the world looking as though he had done it intentionally.

If Cavendish had thought the ritual of initiation had ended on his first day in the 65th, then he was quite mistaken. And the Marmite and jellybeans were only the start.

Taverner was sitting between Hannah and the Colonel's wife. The starter was a game terrine, and with Hannah busy enchanting the officer sitting on the other side of her, Taverner had to try again with the Colonel's wife. She was hard-going. All he could ascertain about her was that she worked as a schoolteacher. If Hannah had been speaking to her, she would have persisted, probably taken pity on her and turned on the charm, but Taverner had no such grit. Sensing her inverted snobbery he cranked up the swaggering, self-assured public schoolboy and spoke to her like a fellow member of his tribe, giving her the impression that, contrary to popular opinion, the aristocracy was far from dead and every bit as arrogant as she wanted to believe.

Further down the table, things were going from bad to worse for Cavendish. His hands smelt revolting, the Adjutant's wife now regarded him with some suspicion, and he'd only been able to eat his starter after the Mess Manager had provided a pair of scissors to cut the fishing line that had been looped through the finely-drilled holes in his cutlery. Now he found that he couldn't pronounce his words properly. His lips had gone numb from the Novocaine anaesthetic that had earlier been smeared round the rim of his wine glass. He was making no sense and starting to drool, and thinking he was drunk, his girlfriend simply told him to be quiet.

As the starter was cleared and a sorbet was served to clear the palate prior to the main course, the Mess Manager handed Cavendish an envelope.

'With the compliments of Captain Taverner, sir.'

The letter inside was written by hand and headed '*The Three Tasks of Second Lieutenant Cavendish*'. It specified three actions that Cavendish was to carry out before the main course was finished; three dangerous assignments to mark his first formal dinner night. As Cavendish read the letter he learnt that the penalty for failure or refusal was something he would not be able to bear. It seemed that Taverner had monstrous insurance to cover the possibility. Surely Taverner wouldn't do such a thing, not in such polite company?

A glass of wine later, Cavendish decided that Taverner *was* capable of such a terrible act and, fortified by the alcohol, he asked the Mess Manager for some tweezers, and slipped below the table.

'Now, the Mess is owned by Colonel Cobbaton-Farr who is a former Commanding Officer of the 65th,' Taverner said loudly to the Colonel's wife, boring for NATO. 'We're very lucky. He pays for the servants and the chefs. Life would simply be intolerable otherwise. Have you met Colonel Cobbaton-Farr?'

'No.'

'Oh, you simply *must*. He meets all the officers and their wives. As well as this building, he owns property in Switzerland and Aix-en-Provence, but at the moment he's living in Somerset, in a caravan. He's an eccentric, you see. Have you ever been to Aix?'

'No.'

'Oh, you simply *must*. My family has a vineyard down there. I used to fly there, but now it's far more fun to drive. If you've got a decent set of wheels you can be there in under six hours from Boulogne. Of course, the *gendarmes* on the *péages* are normally ruthless, but they don't seem to mind my Aston Martin. I never let my speed drop below one-hundred and forty. And of course, nothing else on the road makes you feel like such an international man of mystery! Now, a Porsche is a *very* different matter. Let me give you a very good piece of advice. Listen to me – never let the *flics* catch you speeding in a Porsche. I should know …'

Underneath the table, Cavendish crawled towards his target, trying to stay to the centreline where he was just out of range of a steady salvo of kicks from those officers who somehow knew he was there. He counted the legs and the place settings until he could hear Taverner above.

'Did you ski this year?' he was saying to Colonel Sandford's wife.

'No.'

'We went to Verbier at Christmas. My family has a chalet out there. It was simply marvellous. Two feet of powder on Boxing Day! Have you ever been to Verbier?'

'No.'

'Oh, you simply *must*.'

'OWW!' she yelped. Her husband turned round.

'Is everything alright, petal?'

'No it isn't! I've just caught my leg on a nail or something.' she said, reaching down to rub her leg. There was a sound of scurrying, then a thump, and she looked under the table suspiciously.

Moments later, Cavendish emerged by his seat, rubbing his head.

As the main course was cleared, the Mess Manager returned the letter in the envelope to Taverner. Cavendish's reply was written on the back:

Dear Captain Taverner,

Sir, You are an evil bastard. In response,

1. *The Colonel's shoe laces could not be enclosed. He's wearing slip-ons.*
2. *A single hair from his wife's shapely leg is enclosed in the envelope. That was not a pretty sight.*
3. *Nor was her underwear, which is blue, by the way.*

I trust this satisfies your demands.

Yours Aye,

Second Lieutenant James Cavendish.

'I trust this satisfies your demands,' repeated Taverner, to no-one in particular. 'Fat chance!'

'What did you say, darling?' asked Hannah.

'Oh, nothing.'

She leaned in towards his ear. 'How are you getting on with the Colonel's wife?'

'Not well. She's about as much fun as a road accident.'

'Hard work, is she? Never mind, not much longer, darling. I'll make it up to you. You've got me all to yourself later on and, you never know, I might have a little surprise for you. I hope you don't intend to do any sleeping tonight. I don't!'

Taverner sighed. 'You know, I wish you hadn't told me that, Hannah. The rest of this meal is really going to drag. Tell me more, give me a clue, anything.'

'Nope. It's a surprise,' she said.

Taverner gently touched the top of her leg, but went

no further. 'It look's like I'm not the only one getting a surprise tonight. Young Mr Cavendish will shortly be providing the entertainment. He thinks he's got out of it, but he hasn't. That's his surprise.'

The conversation in the room got louder and the laughter more raucous as the wine bottles kept coming, and after the final course, decanters of port, small port glasses and tumblers of water were placed on the table. Though the Loyal Toast to the Monarch seemed unnecessary – there was no longer a reigning monarch to toast – some habits died hard in the older regiments. It was normally initiated by the Commanding Officer, but as a committed republican Sandford was unwilling to do so and deferred to Taverner. Once everyone's glass had been filled with port, Taverner took a block and gavel, and rapped for silence.

'Mr Vice, the King.'

Cavendish stood up. 'Ladies and Gentleman.'

Everyone else stood up except the Colonel's wife.

'The King, our Captain General.'

The quartet played the first verse of the old National Anthem. The Colonel had decided to stand, probably out of politeness, but he was getting one hell of a look from his wife.

'The King,' they repeated, when the verse had finished. The officers passed their glasses of port over their tumblers of water before taking a sip.

When they sat down, the Colonel's wife turned towards Taverner.

'Why do you all swing your glass of port over a glass of water?'

'We are toasting the King,' he said. 'The exiled King, over the water.'

She let out a snort of contempt and did not speak to him again for the rest of the evening.

There was a second toast – this time to the ladies – after which the humidor was offered round; fat, stubby cigars for the gentlemen and Karelia Slim cigarettes for the ladies.

Second Lieutenant Cavendish received another letter from Taverner.

Dear Mr Cavendish,

Thank you for your prompt response. The tone of your letter was most arrogant and not the manner in which I would expect to be addressed by one of my Troop Commanders. You have therefore failed.

Actually, I hope you did not entertain any thoughts that I would not carry out my threat. It took an awful lot of planning, you see. The possibility of me backing down was about as likely as the crew of the Enola Gay being awarded the Freedom of the City of Hiroshima.

So sit back, Mr Vice, and enjoy.

Sincerely,
Charles Taverner

With most people happily puffing away, Taverner once more rapped the gavel and stood up to make his speech.

A good speech, he had once been told, should be like a bikini; containing enough material to cover the important bits, but small and short enough to grab the attention. He thanked the Mess staff and the chefs for the evening, gave his humorous observations on some recent events in the Mess, and indulged in some gentle leg-pulling of his fellow officers.

'The final thing I wish to do tonight, on behalf of the Commanding Officer and the President of the Mess Committee, is to formally welcome James Cavendish and Madeleine into the Officers' Mess. He has quickly settled into regimental life and is a good egg to have here in the Mess. I think he is very much an officer in the style of the 65th. For example, his monthly bar bill has yet again exceeded his monthly pay. He is already into his second week of extra punishment duties from the Adjutant. And perhaps his title this evening of Mr Vice has never been more appropriate, because we have discovered, ladies and gentlemen, that he does indeed have a substantial vice. A vice that marks him out as true 65th officer–material. You see, the man is a sexual deviant!'

The polite laughter turned to a raucous cheer. Cavendish looked terrified.

'Now, in this litigious day and age, what I've just said is potentially slanderous,' said Taverner. 'One simply cannot label someone as such without some hard evidence to back it up.'

At one end of the room, the Mess Manager had set up a projector, illuminating a bare part of the wall. Cavendish ran his hands nervously through his hair, desperately trying to smile. Taverner was really going to go through with it.

'So we set out to collect the evidence. Ladies and gentleman, if you should like to turn your chairs that way, I give you Second Lieutenant James Cavendish, sexual deviant! And please feel free to leave now if you are easily offended.'

Everyone turned to the large image projected onto the wall.

It showed the inside of a cubicle in the Doctor's surgery.

It was the same cubicle where Cavendish had produced the sperm sample on his very first day in the 65th – the cubicle in which he now knew a video camera had been hidden. When Cavendish appeared on the screen, the officers rapped on the table in anticipation.

At his seat, a mortified Cavendish buried his face in his hands and could only listen to the laughter and the volley of ribald comments. His girlfriend put her arm round him.

'What's he gone for? *Sex Sluts in the Slammer*! Good choice! Well done that man!'

'Have a good rummage round for Mr Wriggly. He's in there somewhere. Unleash the beast. Ah, there we go!'

'Where is it? Good God, is that it? I've seen bigger earplugs! The poor man! Pity his girlfriend!'

'Here we go, here we go, vinegar strokes! Woah, easy tiger!'

'Just under two minutes. He doesn't hang about, does he! My God, it took him longer to finish the Yard of Ale!'

Cavendish then made the best move of his life. Publicly humiliated beyond any limit of decency, and no longer feeling any shame whatsoever, he climbed onto the table, turned and faced his tormentors, and proudly took a deep bow. He received a huge round of applause and the second biggest cheer that night.

He knew, without any doubt, that he was now a fully-fledged officer of the 65th.

Seconds later, the Colonel and his wife stormed out in disgust, and the roar that followed was loud enough to wake the dead.

SIXTEEN

If Taverner had known that getting thrown out of the Army would be so much fun, he might have done it years ago. There were a number of ways in which he could quickly get his marching orders – gross financial misconduct, selling the regiment's rifles on the black market, even treason, for which there would all be unpleasant legal ramifications. He had originally planned simply to go AWOL; a military offence that would have resulted in his arrest had he not intended to emigrate immediately. Now he was required to stay in the country to help the 65th from outside, and he needed another way out. From a brief chat with the Doctor, Captain Meckie, he learnt that he might be able to effect his swift exit under the latest Amendment (Armed Forces) to the Revised Social Disorder (Mental Health) Act. So Taverner set about having a nervous breakdown.

At coffee-break on Monday morning, with all the other officers in their working uniform, Taverner sauntered in wearing a dress. It was one of Hannah's tighter outfits, and a red feather boa completed the look. The narrow shoulder straps cut painfully into his shoulders and he did not look particularly comfortable. The senior officers muttered and the junior officers found it all very amusing, but no-one was surprised. After all, this was Charlie Taverner.

On Tuesday morning he got into his full Afrika Korps regalia and drove his Kubelwagen as fast as he could round the base. He threw up a few Nazi salutes at soldiers on the building sites as he passed them, parked the vehicle outside the Colonel's window, and marched into the coffee room where he casually handed his forage cap, gloves, baton and long overcoat to a junior officer. Taverner ignored Colonel Sandford when he asked him to leave, and it fell to Major Hesketh to quietly escort him from the room.

Nonetheless, Taverner obeyed the Colonel's subsequent summons and found himself tapping the boards in Sandford's office a few minutes later, or rather, clicking the heels of his jackboots together. The Colonel, who felt, as ever, rather uncomfortable in Taverner's presence, started by telling him that he never wanted to see the outfit again. Taverner responded by undressing and stuffing the bulky uniform, with marginal success, into a waste paper bin. He did not stop when he got down to his boxer shorts.

'Perhaps this is to your satisfaction, Colonel?'

They faced each other across the desk. Taverner, standing to attention, was wearing nothing except a malevolent stare. Colonel Sandford did not know where to look.

'You're obviously a very sick man, Captain Taverner,' said the Colonel, as he reached for the phone. 'Provost Sergeant? This is Colonel Sandford. Get over to my office with an escort party.'

At the mention of the fearsome Provost Sergeant, Taverner's air of defiance dissolved in an instant.

'No, please!' whimpered Taverner, now leaning forward

over the desk. 'Anything but the Provost Sergeant! Please, Colonel! I beseech you!'

The Colonel instinctively pushed backwards in his chair, away from Taverner. 'And hurry!' he yelled into the phone.

'Don't be like this, Colonel.' Taverner was now shaking uncontrollably and started to urinate on the Colonel's desk. 'For pity's sake we can work it out. You and me together! The Provost – he's crazy. Do you hear? Crazy! Please God, no!'

Picking up an envelope opener, Taverner stepped back from the desk and pressed it into his own jugular vein, as the Colonel looked on aghast.

'Don't make me do it, Colonel. Call them off now. I'll bloody do it! I will! I'd rather end it all now!'

'Adjutant!' shouted the Colonel in an awful monotone towards the office next door. 'ADJUTANT! Now, please!'

But Taverner dropped the weapon. He streaked out the office, down the corridor, and turned on his heels as the Provost Sergeant and the escort party piled in through the front door of Regimental Headquarters. He dashed down another corridor and then collided with a paperwork-laden clerk who was refilling his cup at the water dispenser. Taverner and the clerk crashed down to the floor, the paperwork flew up in the air, and the water dispenser split and gushed out its contents. Taverner, now covered in soggy paper and crying loudly, tried in vain to crawl away. The Provost Sergeant's team picked him up and carried him kicking and screaming over to the Guardroom, where they locked the slavering lunatic away in a cell.

When the Doctor had finished his morning surgery, he accompanied Major Hesketh to see the casualty in the Guardroom.

'This is very serious,' said Captain Meckie, after having made his preliminary assessment. 'He has schizophrenic delusions that he is Erwin Rommel and wishes to launch an attack on Tobruk before first light. That's in addition to sporadic suicidal tendencies. He shouldn't be here on camp, certainly not in a place with access to weapons and ammunition. For the time being I've given him a mild sedative, but I'm going to have to have him Sectioned. He'll need to be transferred to the Home for the Socially-Challenged in Bridgewater.' Captain Meckie shook his head. 'Poor man. He's gone clean off his rocker. Provost Sergeant, would you arrange transport to take him there within the hour?'

'Certainly, sir.'

'I'll go with him,' said Hesketh.

Some of Taverner's clothes and personal effects were collected for him, as well as a large sum of money purloined from regimental funds by Major Hesketh.

Before lunch, they set off to the mental home in an Army Land Rover; a driver, two escorts, Hesketh, and Taverner who was handcuffed for everyone's safety. Several miles beyond Holberton, Hesketh told the driver to pull into a lay-by and ordered the soldiers to unlock Taverner's cuffs.

'Let me know where you're going to be and we'll have the rest of your kit brought out,' said Hesketh. 'I'll take care of Flint in the meantime.'

'Don't let him eat too much.'

They left Taverner by the side of the road and drove back to the base.

'If anyone asks,' said Hesketh to the others, 'we escorted Captain Taverner to the loony bin at Bridgewater where he currently resides. Understood?'

Taverner walked back into Holberton and found what he was looking for in the window of a newsagent. A faded yellow card with a phone number, written in an arthritic scrawl.

'*Well behaved pets welcome. No DHSS.*'

The house was in a quiet street at the back of the town and owned by an elderly couple; Mr and Mrs Hall. The basement flat was furnished simply, but clean and well-kept. Mr and Mrs Hall were happy to let Taverner have the flat. Not only was he a very nice, well-spoken young man, he paid three months' rent in advance. And when their beloved dog, a docile Alsatian called Duke, and a guard-dog from the time when Holberton had been a rather rougher place than it was today, took to him from the moment he saw him, it sealed their approval. You could always tell, they reckoned.

The following day, Taverner's Landrover was driven to his new address, with some more of his belongings, and most importantly he was reunited with his surfboard and with Flint. He allowed himself two days of R'n'R at the beach, then got down to some work.

It was well into April when winter finally gave way to spring, and with the emerging daffodils and the hint of warmer weather to come, the building project on Windcheater Island entered its final stages. Only the vast new Leisure Complex – the skeleton of which was already in place – remained unfinished, and now the entire regiment came together, swarming over the site like ants day and night, to complete it in just over three weeks. The massive hole in the ground was concreted, sealed, painted and turned into a swimming pool. Next door to it was a sports hall big enough to hold two basketball matches simultaneously. There was also a new gymnasium, a weights room, changing rooms, a reception area, and offices for the PT staff.

Eventually, all the equipment the regiment had used, from the diggers and the scaffolding down to the tools and hard hats, was taken back to the hire companies and storage depots, and a final sweep of the base was carried out.

The building project was finished a month ahead of schedule, just as Major Hesketh had planned.

Colonel Sandford carried out a formal inspection with Hesketh and the building consultants. The inspection took most of the morning and started at the Sailing Club over on the east coast. The building stood out brightly in new white paint and the boat park was much tidier, now that all the neglected boats and dinghies had been taken away. The inspection party then climbed into their vehicles and headed along the smooth new road to the west of the island. Inside the new kindergarten the walls were bare, but the kids would no doubt have a great deal of fun filling the space with their pictures and handicrafts. Over to the cookhouse next, where the chefs were preparing lunch in a huge state-of-the-art kitchen. Then onto the accommodation blocks for the single soldiers, which had been occupied now for several months. They were fully air-conditioned and each soldier had his own room, with six rooms forming a pod, in the centre of which were the ablutions, a fitted kitchen, a laundry and drying room, and a living room with a large, flat-screen television fixed to the wall. On the married patch, a beaming Bombardier and his wife were only too pleased to show the Colonel round their smart new home. Not far from the married patch was the new superstore. It would look more welcoming once the shelves were stacked.

With lunchtime approaching they finished their inspection at the Leisure Centre, following the smell of chlorine to the swimming pool where the water lay quite undisturbed. A few soldiers were sweeping up, and as the Colonel's party walked in they came to attention with their brooms. The consultants gave their verdict to Sandford; there were a few minor problems, but they could be easily rectified in due course. Overall, they were satisfied and seemed very impressed.

The Colonel turned to Hesketh.

'Congratulations are in order, Tom. Well done.'

'Thank you, but it's really the regiment you should be thanking, Colonel.'

Now that the base was finished, Colonel Sandford knew there were certain other people from London and Brussels who would want to come and have a look round, though rather more discreetly. Hesketh had just given him the opportunity to get the regiment out of the way for a while.

'I agree, Tom. I'd like to reward their hard work. The regiment can go on leave as from today.'

'That's very decent of you, Colonel. For how long?'

'For one week. You can tell the regiment yourself.'

'One week? Thank you, Colonel, I'm sure they'll be delighted. I'll tell the RSM to get the regiment on parade.'

As they left the swimming pool, there was a series of splashes behind them as the soldiers christened it, followed by loud swearing as they climbed out as fast as they could. No-one had told them the heating hadn't yet been turned on.

After their week's leave, the officers and soldiers of the 65th returned to Windcheater Island, glad to be back in their normal uniforms. They had done no military training for about six months and the regiment immediately embarked on several weeks of refresher training to re-acquaint them with their military skills.

The early morning physical training started up in earnest, and as impressive as the new sports hall might have been, it did not stop the PT instructors from making the circuit training as hard as ever. The building work had largely maintained the soldiers' upper-body strength, and it did not take long to get their speed and endurance back up to a high standard. In the afternoons, the soldiers were bussed down to the rifle ranges on Dartmoor to practice and improve their shooting skills. After two weeks they moved off the ranges and into the field, carrying out live-firing attacks in open ground.

Meanwhile, Major Hesketh put together a training exercise for the regiment that would consolidate everything they had learnt. With his retirement imminent, he explained to Colonel Sandford, the exercise would be his swansong.

SEVENTEEN

Taverner was revelling in his freedom and, three weeks on from his departure from the 65th, he was in the best physical shape of his life. Each morning he rose at five-thirty and drove to the car park at Saunton Sands, from where he pounded out a forty-minute run. Two miles along the beach to warm up, then a tortuous circuit in the sand dunes, his legs and lungs burning as he forced himself to successive peaks in the soft, yielding sand, then along a path back to the car park, finishing off with several circuits of press-ups, sit-ups, and pull-ups on the bar over the car-park entrance. He took the dogs, Flint and Duke, along for the exercise – they even kept up with him for a bit, but were happier after a while to head back to the car-park and play around until Taverner returned.

Then it was back to Holberton, to the house on the quiet street, to the welcoming smell of fresh linen and frying bacon. Mrs Hall would be up and happily cooking breakfast. Every morning she offered some to Taverner, but he always stuck to cereal and orange juice, and it perplexed her that such a strong and healthy young man could survive on so little.

Once he was showered and changed, and leaving Flint

to sleep off his morning exercise, Taverner set out on his particular task for the day. As he went out the front door, he would bid goodbye to Mrs Hall, who would be absorbed in the most important part of her daily routine; meticulously polishing her prized collection of tiny crystal cats displayed on top of an old sideboard, beyond the lethal arc of her dog's wagging tail.

Taverner's first priority had been to familiarise himself with the whole area. Though he had a good knowledge of the local geography, he did not yet have the necessary detail for what he might need, so he spent many days traipsing across the countryside and around the coast. He found old farm buildings, barns, silage tanks, woods, copses, footpaths, and he learnt where the impassable boundaries were, where the barbed wire fences lay and where there were gaps in between, where the streams ran and where the ground was flooded or waterlogged. He found vantage points across the estuary with excellent views of Windcheater Island. He learnt and memorised the layout of Holberton until he could have found his way around the town blindfolded.

Holberton had flourished in the Victorian era, as genteel folk flocked to the West Country in their droves over the summer months. It had gained a reputation as a pleasant, if not especially affluent place to spend a holiday. Business had always been seasonal and fluctuated with the state of the economy. The economic recession of the early 1990s had hit the hoteliers hard, bringing many to their knees, and it was the Department of Health and Social Security that had offered them a lifeline. There were people out there who needed housing, said the DHSS, people who had fallen on hard times and needed the chance to get back on their feet again. The hoteliers, facing imminent bankruptcy, responded like a drowning man to a straw.

The vast majority of those who moved to Holberton through the DHSS were perfectly respectable, but there was a small group of individuals who were not particularly healthy nor in any way sociable; people who were not in the midst of misfortune through illness or unemployment, let alone inclined to lift themselves out of their dependency on state handouts, and for whom it was very difficult to find accommodation in between their periodic incarcerations in prison. They were drug dealers, addicts, louts, thieves and troublemakers, and they came from towns and cities all over England, where the local DHSS offices were delighted to pass the problem onto the well-meaning but ignorant landlords of the West Country. In any case, among those responsible for this initiative was a strong element of *Schadenfreude* at seeing the peaceful inhabitants of quiet little rural towns putting up with the same misery inflicted on so many in urban areas.

Holberton had quickly found itself in the grip of a drug-fuelled crimewave. Tourists gave the place a wide berth as the charming fabric of the town disintegrated under a wave of litter and violence. Businesses started to move away, fed up with the break-ins and the indifference of the police. Shops that had lined the High Street for years closed down, to be replaced by squalid little enterprises where the locals could buy back their stolen televisions.

For years the problem persisted. Those residents who were able to do so moved out. The local police station was only manned during the day and, since night-time policing was covered from Exeter fifty miles away, the yobs had the run of the town; intimidating, doing and taking what they liked, pushing the limits with casual indifference and knowing they could get away with it.

But they went too far.

An old lady discovered a burglar in her front room, rifling through a cabinet. The burglar could have just taken what he wanted and left – the owner was hardly in a position to stop him. Instead, he snapped the head off her pet budgerigar before battering her unconscious for the sheer fun of it.

Everyone in the town knew the thug responsible, but with the victim too traumatised to point the finger, the police were powerless. Just to make sure she didn't talk, a few tins of gloss paint were emptied over the flowers in her front garden.

Something snapped.

Late one evening soon after, the thug left the Ship and Shovel after a skinful, and staggered and belched his way home along the High Street. He was too drunk to kick in any shop windows that night, as was his usual wont, and also too drunk to recognise any of the individuals who jumped out of a van he was passing, bundled him in and drove him out into the countryside. The beating he received was so savage that he ended up on a life support machine, and was not expected to live. His mates – fellow hooligans all – even laid flowers down in the High Street at the point he was abducted, in anticipation of his death. But their shrine was premature. He survived, though he would take food through a straw for the rest of his life.

In the days that followed, others who had become prominent in the town for the wrong reasons were on the receiving end of similar attacks, every bit as violent. Their assailants were the same on each occasion; about four or five in total, wearing boiler suits and balaclavas, and they spoke with local accents. Holberton, it seemed, had had enough.

Lesser troublemakers received death threats, and most of them had the good sense to pack up in the night and were never seen again. A few stupidly ignored the intimidation, though it did not take much to persuade them otherwise, and in due course they too were gone.

Crime plummeted. But the townsfolk found it rather puzzling that the police now chose this moment to descend on Holberton in numbers never seen before. However, they were not there to catch the hooligans, who had since been turfed out of town – they were there to find the vigilantes. The police were spurred on by their local political masters; the same people who had been callously indifferent to the brutal assault on the old lady, but who were now horrified that people were taking the law into their own hands. One local government officer was quoted in the *Holberton Gazette* as being 'shocked and saddened at the mindless attack on a vulnerable young man whose only crime had been to express his anger at the inequality of modern society.'

Although the operation to find the vigilantes was extensive, they had covered their tracks well and were also helped by the silence that gripped the town; the law of *Omerta* that would have impressed the most ruthless families of the Sicilian Mafia.

The police misjudged the atmosphere and, under increasing pressure to find the culprits, their posture became more confrontational. With people being randomly stopped and questioned in the street, and the endless and increasingly terse door-to-door enquiries, it was the innocent civilians who now felt like the criminals. As the police realised they were getting nowhere, they scaled down their operation and withdrew. Holberton had never forgotten the episode, and great hostility towards the police and the authorities persisted to this day, though the town had been untroubled by the presence of either in recent years.

The events had left a bitter aftertaste. Few businesses or shops ever returned. Younger people had moved away, much of the population was over sixty-years old, and the place was poorer than Job's turkey. The overwhelming urban focus of the government in the new Republic, and with it the diversion of funds and the mechanics of law and order, had effectively abandoned the countryside, reducing it to a state of local anarchy. Yet, paradoxically, Holberton had now become a far safer place to live. Crime was practically non-existent. People felt secure. Front doors could be left unlocked and car keys could be left in the ignition. The streets could be walked at night without fear of attack.

Of course, there were a few characters in the town who might have started to head down the wrong side of the track, but they were swiftly encouraged to change course by a group of individuals who looked after the town.

Whoever they were, Taverner was very keen to make contact with them, and with this in mind, each evening he visited the Ship and Shovel.

EIGHTEEN

With the 65th's refresher training completed, it was time to put the regiment to the test on an arduous ten-day exercise. The background scenario to the exercise centred on Devon's neighbouring county of Cornwall, from where the fictional 'Cornish Popular Front' had despatched a militia over the border into Devon, with the aim of capturing some alledgedly-disputed regions.

Fifty soldiers were selected to play the part of the 'enemy' and were issued sand-coloured desert uniforms to mark them out as such. They were separated from the rest of the regiment to much abuse and jokes about pasties and emmets.

The exercise started on Windcheater Island with a defensive phase. With the base under threat from the Cornish militia, four-man slit-trenches were dug all round the perimeter of the base, positioned to allow all possible land and sea approaches to be covered. The trenches had to be dug by hand, and it was back-breaking work. Sandbags were filled and piled up on the parapets, and sheets of corrugated iron were used to line the earth walls, held in place by iron pickets hammered into the ground. At either end of each trench a small sleeping dugout extended into the earth. Several miles of barbed wire were unrolled around much of the perimeter of the island.

The regiment settled into the routine of defence – sentry duties, communications, re-supply, eating and sleeping when time allowed, and waited for the enemy to appear.

When news came through that the enemy had been spotted in the middle of Dartmoor, the 65th received orders to move out and the soldiers were driven to the outskirts of the moor on the regiment's fleet of antiquated Bedford trucks. With another twenty miles still to cover, and the Bedfords unable to go any further on the moor, the soldiers 'tabbed' the rest of way on foot over the moor – each carrying a forty-kilogram Bergan in addition to his rifle and webbing. The weather on the moor was miserable and navigation was difficult. It made them long for even the worst days on the building site.

The enemy was located and a series of ambushes, skirmishes and set-piece attacks drove them out of the area. The regiment was nearly a week into the exercise and had been on the go for the entire time. Sleep was snatched whenever the opportunity arose, and rarely lasted for more than an hour.

With the Dartmoor phase completed, the 65th set off back to Windcheater Island on the Bedfords. On their way back, news reached them that Windcheater Island had been seized by the enemy in a desperate last stand.

On the last morning of the exercise, the regiment 'recaptured' their base in the manner one would have expected of the 65th. They stormed the island by sea, roaring up in a flotilla of small 'Rigid Raider' boats that had been loaned for the exercise. The final attack was about as untactical as it could have been – for a start, it took place in bright sunlight – but the emphasis that morning was definitely on style and elegant choreography.

Colonel Sandford, who had not taken part in the exercise, came out to watch the final attack. He was unable to get any work done in his office, what with the bangs of simulated grenades, the rattle of blank ammunition and the smoke drifting across the island. It all sounded very impressive and looked utterly chaotic.

Over the radio Major Hesketh called ENDEX. End of Exercise. The soldiers reported to their Batteries to clean and oil their rifles before returning them to the Armoury. They were utterly exhausted, and after a welcome lunch in the cookhouse they went back to their accommodation for a long shower and some shut-eye.

Later that afternoon, Colonel Sandford summoned Major Hesketh to his office. Maybe it was the look on Sandford's face or a series of unconscious gestures that betrayed him, but as Hesketh sat down he instinctively knew what Sandford was about to tell him.

In the months since he had been in command of the 65th and had known about the secret plans for its disbandment, Colonel Sandford had entertained detailed fantasies about the moment he would announce the terrible news to the assembled ranks lined up in front of him. Gleefully he visualised their collective shock. He would look into the eyes of a regiment that was long past its sell-by-date, and he wondered too, when it came to it, if he would be able to hide the sheer pleasure it would give him.

In the end, his nerve failed him. He chickened out of announcing the news directly to the soldiers and delegated the unenviable task to Major Hesketh. Sandford put up a good story about how he had fought the regiment's corner when he had been told, yet it had all been to no avail. The new European Rapid Deployment Force needed a home, he explained. It was unfortunate that their demands had coincided with the latest round of dynamic rightsizing, and under so much political pressure from the Europeans it was a *fait accompli* — sorry, no pun intended — but there really was nothing he could do.

Next morning, Major Hesketh broke the news to the 65th. It hit the regiment like a bombshell.

He started in the Sergeants' Mess, to which the officers had been invited that morning, and read out the relevant paragraphs of the official letter from Mr MacDonald, the Secretary of State for Defence, formally announcing the disbandment of the 65th. He didn't bother to read the insincere platitudes thanking the 65th for three-hundred years' service, and left them to drown their sorrows together. Hesketh then visited each of the Batteries in turn and read the same letter to the soldiers.

Whenever the Ministry of Defence announced that a regiment or battalion was to be disbanded or amalgamated, it normally allowed the unit a year's grace before the axe actually fell, and everyone in the 65th assumed it would be the same for them. Prudently, Hesketh delayed telling them that, in fact, they only had four weeks left. That news was given to them the day after, giving time for the clerks to set themselves up in the gymnasium to mass-process the soldiers of the 65th on to other regiments or Civvy Street.

Knowing how bad the employment situation was, most soldiers in the 65th wanted to stay in the Army and asked to be transferred to other regiments, but after the latest cutbacks very few vacancies remained and they were quickly snapped up. All Senior NCOs – those who held the rank of Sergeant or above – were offered the choice of leaving and qualifying for their full pension, even though they would not have served the full twenty-two years needed to qualify. Many of them took it.

Very little could be done for the rest of the soldiers. They were entitled to resettlement vouchers to help them retrain for jobs in civilian life – in this respect their new skills in construction might come in useful – but their association with the military and their lack of CODE training would count heavily against them. Most of them chose to go onto a new list called the Holding Reserves, where soldiers who'd been made redundant could hold down a civilian job and remain eligible for call-up as and when the Army needed them, though they would receive no pay. It sounded attractive and was slickly marketed, but it was a dreadful con. There were many thousands of soldiers on the Holding Reserves and less than twenty had ever been re-called, though the MoD was happy to include them when calculating the overall strength of the Army.

NINETEEN

With his charm and easy manner, it did not take long for Taverner to ingratiate himself with the locals in the Ship and Shovel. They quickly warmed to him, ribbing him for his accent and, by their standards, his intolerance to alcohol. His military background did him no harm either. The general disdain that society had for the military had not yet filtered down to this region; here, military service was still something to be respected and seldom did an old soldier, sailor or airman ever have to buy his own drinks.

Taverner had frequented the pub because he was very keen to meet and enlist the help of the tougher members of the town – the vigilante group of legend – and if the locals were content to reminisce proudly about their activities, they said very little about who *they* actually were. But it would hardly have needed Poirot to figure it out.

It was Friday evening, the busiest night of the week. Taverner was sharing a beer with Terry; a squat, shaven-headed man as wide as he was tall, who looked as if he could start a fight in an empty room. Local accent, with a faint layer of something else, thought Taverner. South London? Difficult to place, being a man of few words.

Terry was the owner of the Ship and Shovel and a few other pubs in the town, and was never seen working behind the bar, always choosing to sit out front as a convivial host might do, although a friendly greeting or a warm smile to welcome people into his pub was certainly not part of Terry's repertoire.

They were soon joined at the bar by Billy who, with his pipe and his beard, his thick Devonian accent and his woolly sweater, looked to be the epitome of geniality, were it not for the sheer size of him. He was a builder, and perhaps not the sharpest tool in the box, peppering his conversation with so many double-negatives it was easy to lose track of the point he was originally trying to make, and like Terry he was clearly not a person to get on the wrong side of.

The pub locals seemed to defer naturally to Billy and Terry. Where the rest of the punters might have had to thread their way across the busy floor of the pub, or squeeze themselves courteously between groups to get to the bar, the crowds simply parted before Billy and Terry as if by some unseen force. There was more to it than simply their physical presence.

'I was just tellin' yer man here about the time those tossers was turfed out of town,' said Terry to Billy.

'Right you are,' replied Billy. 'Back, when was it now ... ten years ago? Don't we remember it well! Those little scrotes got a right good hiding, eh? They didn't know what hadn't hit them, they never.'

Between them, Billy and Terry recollected the events of that pivotal night in Holberton some years earlier, when people decided they had suffered for long enough and the first thug had been taken out on the moor and crippled. With a glint in their eyes, the two of them strenuously denied any involvement, revealing far too many details to have been anything less than up to their necks in it.

'Course, after that the bleedin' police come down on us like a ton of bricks,' said Billy. 'No-one here ain't never seen no police for years, then cos we got rid of the scrotes they go and get all upset over it. Well, I tell you, no-one ain't never got no time for no police no more round 'ere. They leave us well alone now. If anyone steps out of line, it's simple. They get a good slap from us and they're told to behave themselves. Well, I say from *us*, but not really, from others, like, if you know what I mean.'

'Yeah. Others,' said Terry, in support.

'Cos they know that if people like us is going to be scared of the law they can do what they damn well please, cos the law only ever protects the criminals. Well, we wasn't never scared of the law, was we? Well, I say *we*, but you know, others, like, if you know what I mean.'

'Yeah. Others,' said Terry, who beckoned over the barmaid. 'Same again?'

'Please,' said Taverner. He was enjoying their indiscretions, but at the same time wondered whether or not they would actually be of any use to him in the coming weeks. They were not the most tactful of individuals.

'And these ... enforcers, whoever they are. Do you know them personally?' said Taverner.

There was a sharp intake of breath from Billy, as if Taverner had overstepped the mark.

'I wouldn't have no idea, Guv. Not a clue, I wouldn't,' said Billy.

'Not a clue,' repeated Terry.

'Not even a dicky bird,' said Billy.

'No way. Not even a dicky bird.'

'Profile lower than a snake's arse. Still, they reckon that a nod's as good as a blink to a deaf man,' said Billy, winking at Taverner. 'Ain't that what they say?'

For several evenings, Taverner shared a few beers with Terry and Billy, and some of their trusted friends. He regaled them with stories from his Army career, injecting humour into situations and events that had certainly not warranted it at the time, and slowly, as and when the opportunity arose, he steered the conversation round to the 65th and the future of Windcheater Island. Billy and Terry were aware that the 65th was being axed – most of the town knew about it – but what was not generally known was that the base was going to be taken over by the European Rapid Deployment Force. Taverner told them of the underhand way in which this was being carried out; how the soldiers of the 65th had been hoodwinked into building the ERDF a new base while being kept in the dark about their own regiment's imminent demise. He did not tell them of Major Hesketh's plan, nor his own smaller part in it. That would come later. For the time being, he prepared the way for their assistance by stoking their fears.

'Do you know what the government calls this part of the South West?' Taverner asked them later that week. 'The Badlands.'

His audience were proud of the accolade.

'They think it's entirely lawless,' he said. 'There's no police. No local authority. No system of law enforcement nor any sort of regulation that they'd recognise. It's a no-go area for them.'

'So who cares?' said Billy. 'Bloody good thing, I reckon. They couldn't give a damn about a place like this.'

'I wouldn't be so sure. You see, an awful lot of money

and effort has gone into putting this new European Rapid Deployment Force together. Some very powerful people have staked their reputation on it. It's the Cornerstone of European Defence Policy, and I use their words, not mine. Windcheater Island was always going to be the perfect location for the new force, but there were two little problems that needed to be sorted out beforehand. If you've ever been on the island you will know that the buildings on the base were so dilapidated that they were virtually uninhabitable. That's now been taken care of. The base has been entirely refurbished. You wouldn't recognise it. The second problem is that Windcheater Island is in the largest anarchist zone outside of Scotland. The authorities are not just going to put the ERDF here on Windcheater Island – slap bang in the middle of the Badlands – without the sort of safeguards and assurances that only they would understand.'

'Such as what?' asked Billy.

'Local government. Some means of accountability to London and Brussels. A new police service. And not just the politically-correct, paperwork-laden police of old, or the friendly beat-bobbies that your parents might recall. They would be like the police in the Central Zones, indoctrinated in the ways of the CODE, imposing their own version of law and order according to their own narrow interpretation, and utterly indifferent to the needs of the town.'

'But we don't need no police,' said Billy. 'The place is as safe as it's never been.'

'We know it's safe, but that doesn't concern them. They cannot comprehend that a peaceful place could exist unless they themselves have imposed that peace.'

'This is all just hearsay though, isn't it?' said Billy.

'I only wish it was, but I'm afraid it's a fact. I can show you documents to back up everything I've just said. They were leaked to the 65th.'

'Might it bring in some more money and jobs?' asked Kevin, one of Billy's foremen.

'I doubt it.' said Taverner. 'They don't want to create jobs, just a regulated environment where everyone has to live by their rules. Have you ever been to the Central Zones? The one in Bristol? No? Try the one in London. You'd be horrified. People live in fear – not of crime or unemployment, or not being able to get their kids into the right schools. It's the fear of being thrown *out* of the Zone. An inappropriate remark, a throwaway comment taken out of context, that's all it takes. Bye bye. Just for the privilege of staying in the Zone, people spend their lives kow-towing to the type of self-important jobsworths that are soon going to start bullying their way round this town. The Interior Ministry. The police. Armies of busy bodies and the enforcers from the CODE Directorate to oversee everything. Fear will once again return to Holberton.'

Taverner didn't say much more that evening. The hatred that the inhabitants of Holberton had for the authorities ran deep, such was the way they had, with the best of intentions, ruined this once-pleasant little town. As the evening wore on and more ale was drunk, the conversation became rather heated. It was having the desired effect.

The group left the pub that night in a sombre mood. Taverner stayed behind while Terry closed down the pub. A lone drunk perched on his stool by the bar.

'Aint it time you went home?' said Terry, to the drunk.

'Just one more, then I'll be on my way' said the drunk. 'Can I get you one?' he asked Taverner.

Taverner accepted his offer of another pint. The man was not part of their immediate circle, though he and Taverner had developed a nodding acquaintance. He was thin, unshaven, in his mid-forties and he wore the smart agricultural combo of a check shirt and moleskin trousers that suggested a moneyed-rural type, despite the clothes' threadbare appearance. He would chat away amiably to friends and strangers alike, buying drinks and offering cigarettes, but there was something deeply melancholy in him – a sadness that was barely suppressed by his effected cheeriness.

Taverner learnt that the man had once been a vet; in fact he still was, in an unusual kind of way. He told Taverner how he'd been a partner in a successful small-animal practice in North London dealing with the usual sort of stuff; neutering cats and dogs, wielding the needle of mercy to spare suffering, pleading with the owners of ever-ballooning Pomeranians to stop overfeeding them. He started to laugh at the memory of it, but couldn't quite let himself enjoy the moment to the extent he might, and took another deep draught of ale. As the vet's practice had been located in the Central Zone, he'd had to live under the CODE of course, though he was an intelligent man and it was easy for him to adapt and avoid doing the sort of things that would attract the attention of the infamous CODE Directorate. His work was varied and important, he enjoyed it and felt his comfortable income was well deserved after the years of impoverished academic slog at veterinary school. He and his elegant – if rather independent – wife lived in a large house with their three children; the smug, glossy-magazine ideal of happy and successful urban living.

He was never able to fully establish why he had lost his job. Some sort of CODE violation, he later learnt. An unspecified complaint had been apparently made about him, and the Initial Investigating Officer from the Directorate had suggested that there was some substance to it. Try as he might, he hadn't been able to recall any recent occasion where he might have transgressed.

Here in the pub, after another pint took effect, he revealed to Taverner that he suspected his bitch of a wife might have been having an affair with her handsome yoga teacher, who was also a local government officer by day, and they had figured the best way to get him out of the way was to tarnish him with a CODE violation, though one sufficiently minor to ensure his hearing would take months – even years – to come before the Appeals Board. Regrettably, in the meantime, he would remain unemployed and unemployable. Friends from veterinary school and colleagues in the same business were unable to help, indeed they now gave him quite a wide berth, although he did get a steer in the direction of the Ministry of Agriculture.

And that was how he had ended up in the West Country, on a farm collective about ten miles from Holberton near the town of South Molton, trying to reverse the effects of a cattle condition known as the Devereux-Denford Disease – DVD Disease – a highly infectious but otherwise non-descript condition that might have passed unnoticed were it not for the fact that it caused a massive loss of libido in bulls. The initial epidemic had occurred some years earlier and attempts to contain it by widespread slaughter had not kept up with the high rate of infection.

Still unable to reproduce, cattle, once widespread across the English countryside, were now a rare and novel sight. The vet oversaw a small programme on the collective which aimed to restore cattle to full reproductive health.

Until recently they had not been having much success.

'That's when we thought about trying pheromones,' he told Taverner.

'Pheromones?' said Taverner, in disbelief. 'Like the stuff you can buy on the Internet, supposedly making you smell more attractive to the opposite sex?'

'That's the idea. The chemicals we're currently synthesising are designed to mimic the female attractant secreted by the heifers. Although it's not a technically-correct comparison, think of it as an aromatic version of bovine Viagra.'

Taverner was intrigued. 'Are you having any success?'

'We're making progress. The trials have been fun, to say the least.'

'It sounds like a very interesting job.'

'Interesting? Are you fucking kidding?' said the vet, suddenly becoming rather aggressive. 'It's *shit*, mate. Complete and utter *shit*. We haven't been paid for the past three months. I live in a caravan that lists over to one side because the fucking supports have rusted away. My brain has so much trouble keeping up with the way everything's at an angle that I have a permanent fucking headache. It's level when I'm in bed, but as soon as I get up in the morning the whole fucking thing rocks over and comes crashing down again. Is it any wonder I come here and get pissed every night? You call that an interesting fucking life?'

'Oi! You! Cool it,' said Terry, who had been unplugging the fruit machines. 'Less of your fucking language. Get on your way home.'

'He's right. I best be getting back,' said the vet, now calm again. He used the bar for support as he climbed down off the stool. 'Sorry mate, I didn't mean to have a go. Thanks for listening.'

'Not at all,' replied Taverner. 'How are you getting back?'

'Like I always do. I walk. It's not far – only about ten miles. Maybe I'll be home by dawn!'

TWENTY

After learning of the regiment's demise, the soldiers of the 65th collectively went through an emotional process similar to bereavement in the short time they had left. After the shock of the announcement came the anger and frustration. The soldiers would eventually come to terms with what was going to happen and resign themselves to their fate, but for the time being the sense of betrayal bit into them as it had done to Major Hesketh months earlier. Their regiment, in which they took so much pride, was facing the chop from the sort of faceless accountants who, as they kept saying to each other, knew the cost of everything but the value of nothing. To add insult to injury, their shiny new base, into which they had put so much effort, was to be occupied by a foreign organisation.

The officers of the 65th were the main focus of the soldiers' anger. It was they who should have been fighting the regiment's corner, but they had been beaten, and for the time being the officers wisely stayed cooped up in their Mess. At night, the Provost staff took to patrolling the whole base as the drinking and fighting reached unprecedented levels. With little incentive to look after their new accommodation vandalism became common, and Colonel Sandford ordered that the cost of repairing any damage be automatically deducted from their wages.

A lot of the soldiers chose to leave of their own accord. They packed up their cars and drove back to Merseyside – officially AWOL – though no-one in the regiment was too worried. Others were in denial, determined to stay to the bitter end, seemingly unable to accept that the 65th's days were numbered. Regimental life carried on as normal with early morning PT, parades and sport in the afternoon, but the anger simmered away below the surface. Major Hesketh knew this would be useful when the time came.

It was assumed that there would be a formal regimental parade on the final day to mark the passing of the 65th, yet Colonel Sandford was quite unwilling to grant the regiment what it saw as its right. He just wanted the 65th out of the way with as little fuss as possible. Major Hesketh tried to persuade him otherwise, pointing out that the soldiers who were left were simply milling around the camp, playing sport and getting violently drunk in the evenings. Preparing for a Final Parade would give them something to do. Colonel Sandford eventually gave in, but he had conditions.

'Nothing over the top or sentimental,' he said, 'and no doddery old bores. No longer than half-an-hour. They're hardly Trooping the Colour.'

'As you wish, Colonel.'

'It's going to be a very busy day, Tom. Not only has the whole base got to be ready for the handover, we've got the Advance Party of the ERDF arriving late afternoon and I've got two VIPs to host at the evening function – Dr Ulrich Müller and the Right Honourable Geoffrey MacDonald.'

'The European Defence Minister and his British counterpart?' said Hesketh. 'What an honour.'

'They're very senior politicians, Tom. You can't expect them to pass up a photo-opportunity like this.'

'What, bidding farewell to the 65th?'

'No! Welcoming the first soldiers of the ERDF. This is very high profile stuff.'

'Clearly.'

'And they want to have a look round the new base. I'll tell you something else as well, Tom. This place had better be in perfect condition for the handover. If it isn't, I'll keep back some of the soldiers until it's up to standard. I don't care if they're unemployed. Better make it happen, Tom.'

'Colonel, rest assured the base will be left spick-and-span. On the subject of the Final Parade, since we're unlikely to get an Inspecting Officer at such late notice, perhaps Dr Müller and Mr MacDonald would like to inspect the ranks on the parade?'

'Out of the question!'

'The boys would really be chuffed, Colonel.'

'Ridiculous.'

'It would mean so much to them. It is their final day.'

'Not a chance, Tom.'

But Hesketh kept up the pressure and the Colonel once again relented. Dr Müller and Mr MacDonald would be the Inspecting Officers on the 65th's Final Parade.

Colonel Sandford would have been alarmed to find out that Hesketh had known about the visit of Dr Müller and Mr MacDonald for rather longer than he pretended to, and that their participation in the events of the final day was going to be rather livelier than they would have liked.

The soldiers now had something to do until their last day. The Regimental Sergeant Major busied himself putting together the Final Parade, and he would be damned if it was only going to last half-an-hour. The uniforms were dusted off and the soldiers put in many hours of bulling and starching to bring them up to perfection.

Each day the soldiers rehearsed the parade. They were rusty at first, out of step as they marched and their collective movements were not particularly sharp. The RSM – stalking the Parade Square, pace-stick at the ready and liable to explode into a hysterical fit of screaming at any second – soon brought them up to standard. With just one week to go before the Final Parade, the soldiers of the 65th knew the sequence of the parade so well they could have done it in their sleep.

Taverner received regular letters in the post from Major Hesketh. Some contained information and updates, others contained instructions to be carried out. One morning, Taverner received the personal details of several British soldiers who were due to join the European Rapid Deployment Force as soon as it had moved into Windcheater Island. Lance Bombardier 'Hacker' Thacker had provided the details courtesy of his extraordinary dexterity in cyberspace. After some consideration of the individuals listed, Taverner decided to head to Bournemouth, where he spent two days observing a man who worked as a supervisor in a large superstore. The man was also a part-time soldier in the Territorial Army. While he was at work on the second day, Taverner put an official-looking letter from the Army Postings Board through the front door of his flat. The store supervisor was not an intelligent-looking man and didn't look as if he would be troubling MENSA with a membership application in the future. Hopefully he would accept the instructions of the letter without verifying it with the Board. In the unlikely event that he did query them and dialled the telephone number of the Board printed at the top of the letter, he would find himself speaking to Major Hesketh, who, despite never having been employed by the Army Postings Board, felt he could easily pass himself off as such.

Taverner then headed to Liverpool, to meet a forger who came with Thacker's highest recommendations. There were a number of items that Taverner needed and it cost him double to get the items in forty-eight hours. He spent the weekend with Hannah in Gloucester, then returned to pick up the items. They were flawless.

That evening, Taverner was back in the Ship and Shovel with the usual crowd. The conversation inevitably turned to the future of Holberton after the ERDF had moved in. It was all they had talked about for the past few days, and the thought of State authorities moving into their town was playing heavily on their minds.

'Can't we do anything to stop them?' said Billy, late in the evening after the arguments had died down.

Now was the time, thought Taverner.

'Gentlemen, perhaps there is something we can do.'

'Like a petition?' said Kevin. The group all turned round to look at him in bewilderment. 'Sorry,' he said.

'I was thinking of something a little more lively than a petition,' said Taverner, quietly. 'A little more *direct*, shall we say?'

Taverner turned to look at a nearby group of drinkers who were in earshot, and narrowed his gaze. Terry caught sight of the gesture and immediately understood.

'You lot. Move over there, could you,' said Terry, pointing to the far side of the pub. When they were alone, Taverner spoke again, calmly yet so forcefully he had their attention like never before.

'Gentlemen, I am going to come straight with you. The reason I am now here in Holberton, as an ex-Army officer, is to stop the ERDF from occupying Windcheater Island, because my regiment, the 65th, is being axed to make way for them. I intend to persuade the ERDF that this is not as good a location as they might think. Precisely how I am going to do that I cannot reveal at this stage, but I, and others in the 65th, have been planning this for a long time. In a few days the 65th will be no more, the ERDF will want to move onto the base, and our fun will start. And I can promise you it's going to be spectacular.'

The group listened, some nodding in understanding, others just trying to take it all in.

'But my regiment could really do with some help,' he continued. 'We have a common interest here. You clearly wish to maintain the secure *status quo* of Holberton and do not wish to see it disturbed by a sudden influx of suits who think they know better than you. Perhaps you, we, could convince the government in London that this area is so lawless they could not ever hope to rein it back in, and it is best left alone.'

Taverner spoke persuasively, his piercing eyes sweeping back and forth across the group like a searchlight. He spoke as he had done in the past when briefing his junior commanders before a tricky operation, giving them faith in his intentions and infecting them with his confidence, addressing each of them in turn so they felt an integral part of whatever he was planning.

The group realised there was rather more to this

affable, well-spoken surf-bum than had been apparent. Taverner won them over with ease and they agreed to help. With their spirits lifted by the knowledge that they were now going to do something, they drank late into the night.

'One last thing,' said Taverner, before they departed, his voice cutting through the alcoholic haze while fixing each of them in turn with a stare so penetrating he might have made Medusa herself turn to stone. 'You do not talk about this to anyone else. I really mean it.'

The group departed, elated, but also a little unsettled. A distinct power shift had just occurred; a disturbance in the natural equilibrium of the pecking order.

Terry ordering the group of drinkers to move away out of earshot.

Billy subserviently offering Taverner his support.

It was unprecedented. Taverner had been quietly lurking in their midst for weeks, and now, in a little over a few hours, he seemed to have calmly taken his place at the top of the tree.

They were excited, too. There had not been much call for their particular brand of muscular utility for some years. These days it was just the odd teenager who needed to be straightened out. Whoever the government intended to send down to Holberton when it all kicked off – the police, the Interior Ministry, even the Armed Forces – they couldn't wait to pit themselves against adversaries worthy of their talents.

Taverner called in some favours that week. Firstly, he went with Billy to a vehicle breaker's yard, and after he found the car he was looking for, Billy persuaded the owner of the yard to modify it to Taverner's specification.

One night later on in the week, he was at a service station on the westbound carriageway of the M5 motorway near Taunton, waiting in the darkness. He had fixed a trailer to his Land Rover and was parked up between two articulated lorries which would shield him from any CCTV cameras.

The Pantechnicon lorry arrived not long after two o'clock. Inside the lorry were six large wooden crates, one of which the lorry driver manoeuvred out onto the hydraulic ramp with a pallet trolley. Each crate contained thousands of tins of hot-dog sausages from an American junk-food company based in the State of Kansas, which had been collected an hour earlier from the docks at Bristol. With the import duties paid, the crates were released from the bonded warehouse to the man who now helped Taverner secure this particular crate to the trailer. As a legitimate importer, wholesaler and distributor of food throughout the West Country, the man would not attract any undue attention with such a cargo. Through the pub trade he was also a friend of Terry's, and had been content to collect and deliver the crate for a very tidy sum of cash and no questions asked. He would have little trouble selling the contents of the other five crates.

Taverner motored back to Holberton. His was the only vehicle on the road at that hour and he felt very conspicuous, as anyone might, towing a trailer with a crate containing a few layers of tinned hot-dogs and twenty-five live rounds for a German 88mm anti-tank gun from the Second World War.

It had been a close call. With just days to go until the 65th was disbanded, the shells had arrived in the nick of time. There were other items in the regiment's Armoury that would have been better for the job they had in mind, but such an eccentric solution to the problem was typical of the 65th.

As tempting as it was, Taverner decided against delivering the crate and its murderous contents immediately to the Armoury on Windcheater Island. There would be no-one there at that hour, so he left the trailer secured in Terry's yard then went back to his house to catch up on some sleep. He would deliver the ammunition later that morning, when the 65th was due to hold the annual, the infamous, and probably its very last Officers versus Sergeants Cricket Match.

TWENTY-ONE

If the pioneers of the gentle game had been able to travel
forward in time to witness the ugly charade played out at
the Annual 65th RHA Officers versus Sergeants Cricket
Match, they would surely have held back and buried their
idea, not wishing to inflict such a brazen display of
corruption masquerading as sport on the far flung corners
of the British Empire.

The cricket match between the two Messes had been
played every year since anyone could remember, regardless
of where the 65th was stationed; on exercise on the plains
of North Germany, or the prairies of Canada, or on
operations in the Middle East. The match had even taken
place within the confines of a tiny mortar-proof base in
South Armagh.

With the refurbishment of the base and the regiment's
imminent disbandment, the 65th had had rather more
pressing matters on its mind and the cricket match was
almost overlooked, but the entertainment funds of each
Mess were full and the match presented a last opportunity
to spend them.

The two Messes competed for an unusual prize – an
old wooden toilet seat mounted on a small plinth, on

which little silver shields proclaimed each year's *Victor Ludorum*.

The Sergeants had won the match the previous year. They had also won the year before that. Indeed, the Sergeants had won the match every year since its inception, and it was a foregone conclusion they would win again this year. The result of the match was academic; the Sergeants would win; the only variable in the proceedings was the extent to which they would crush the Officers.

The success of the Sergeants had very little to do with their collective cricketing ability which, despite having a couple of useful all-rounders, was shockingly bad. Their yearly triumphs had rather more to do with taking one of Sun Tzu's maxims – *All battles are won before they are fought* – to extraordinary lengths. Umpires rigged, bribed or even blackmailed, sozzled scorers, an excessive level of intimidation of the Officers when at the crease, and a startling interpretation of MCC laws. It was all to be expected from the Sergeants.

The Officers faced their annual destruction in good spirits and certainly looked the part with their blazers, Panama hats and old school cricketing jumpers, now shrunken and faded with the years. As well as looking forward to a pleasant afternoon's cricket, with sun and Pimms, the crack of leather on willow and polite applause from the boundary, they were also eager to see what the Sergeants had dreamt up. The various ruses devised by the Sergeants to guarantee success had become remarkably elaborate in recent years, but with such little time to prepare on this occasion, they resorted to a fairly standard procedure that could be relied upon to produce the desired result, and quite innocently volunteered to take care of lunch, tea and general refreshments for the day.

The Sergeants won the toss and chose to bat first. Lieutenant Skeffington, as captain of the Officers, distributed his fielders around the ground with a confidence that belied the fact he had no idea what he was doing. The opening batsmen for the Sergeants were courteously welcomed at the wicket by the Officers, and it was left to Captain Mellor to deliver the first over. The batsmen were a little hesitant in the face of Mellor's medium-pacers and did well to score three runs off six balls.

For the first time in memory, the Sergeants appeared to be playing in the spirit of the game. The two umpires looked trustworthy and sober, and when the Officers took two quick wickets during the third over, they sensed that they might be in with a chance. They girded themselves, hunkered down in their fielding positions, senses now on full alert, the tantalising possibility of an unprecedented victory now dangling before them.

From the boundary, Major Hesketh was following the proceedings from his deck chair, binoculars in one hand and the first of many gin and tonics in the other, when a voice cut in.

'I'd be happy to make up the numbers, but they seem to be doing perfectly well without me. Please excuse my rig.'

Hesketh looked round.

'Charlie,' he said. 'Good God, I hardly recognised you.' It was the first time he had seen Taverner since he had left the 65th. With his scruffy blue hoodie, his straggly blond hair and an improving beard, Taverner looked somewhat Bohemian. He looked as though he had been hitting the weights and the treadmill in earnest – the shoulders might have been a little thicker and the hips were still narrow.

'Eight runs for two wickets?' said Taverner. 'Maybe we'll be in with a chance this year.'

'It looks like it. It's about time they let us win this bloody match.'

Their optimism was short-lived. At the end of the third over, Skeffington rearranged his fielders, as eleven white-jacketed stewards from the Sergeants' Mess took to the field, each carrying a silver salver with a pint of ale for each officer.

'Oh, that's below the belt!' said Hesketh, indignantly. 'And very unimaginative too. I dread to think what's in those pints. They'll be lucky if it's just ale.'

Any officer who refused to drain their pints came under a barrage of homophobic abuse from the boundary. The stewards returned to the hospitality tent, where some well-drilled members of the Sergeants' Mess prepared the next rounds like a Formula One pit-stop crew.

Three overs later, the stewards were back on the field again with another pint for each of the officers. All things considered, the Officers did well taking five wickets for only thirty-five runs by the eleventh over, as the pints kept coming. There were even a few nervous looking faces among the Sergeants, who wondered if they'd underestimated the Officers' capacity.

They needn't have worried. It all started to fall apart in the twelfth over. Captain MacNeish, the Glaswegian officer, who had never played cricket in his life, came on to bowl, and a combination of his inexperience, hatred for the Sassenach game, and the alcohol now streaming through his system, resulted in an over that included three wides, a surprisingly accurate beamer, and a ball that bounced three times before it reached the batsman, by which time it was rolling along the ground. From the boundary, the Sergeants struck up the theme tune to '*The Dambusters*', and MacNeish stuck two fingers up when someone loudly referred to him 'Captain MacBarnes-Wallis'.

Major Hesketh and Taverner watched the promising start from the Officers disintegrate in a flurry of sixes, fours and wides, and their interest waned.

'I wish they'd put as much effort into their fielding as they're doing into sinking their pints!' said Hesketh. 'How are things going, Charlie?'

Taverner looked round to ensure no-one else was in earshot.

'We've got the main players onside. I thought it would be harder to persuade them, but I've never known such hatred for the authorities. I'm glad they're on our side, these good ol' country boys. They're up for a fight and whatever the authorities send, they won't know what's hit them. Oh, bloody hell,' he exclaimed, as Captain Mellor staggered and tripped at the last minute, trying to prevent a ball heading for the boundary. The Sergeants roared in approval.

'How much do these friends of yours know?' asked Hesketh.

'Enough. Only what they need to know at this stage.'

'You've told them rather earlier than I had wanted, Charlie. They had better not talk.'

'They won't. I had to let them know something. I needed their help to get the ammunition for the 88mm gun.'

'You've brought it here?'

'Already secured in the Armoury.'

'Good. The ERDF have already had a quick look around. Some of their senior officers were here last week and Colonel Sandford was very careful to keep them away from the soldiers, as well he might.'

'How did they take the news?'

'Better than I thought, given the suddenness of it. Lots of them have already gone back to Merseyside. Only a few have been able to transfer.'

'When are you going to go public with your plan?'

'Tomorrow morning. Those that want no part in it will have forty-eight hours to clear off before the Handover Parade.'

'And you're still confident they'll want to stay?'

'I really hope so. It would be a shame if they all decided to bugger off. No, I think most of them will stay. The resentment that's simmering away is astonishing. My, how they hate us! They hold the officers entirely responsible for letting this happen. It will be the perfect outlet for their anger.'

At the end of their twenty overs, the Officers had taken just five wickets for one-hundred and seventy-three runs, and staggered off the field for lunch. With some content to simply lie on the ground, others stuffing their faces with food, and one or two being discreetly sick, the scene resembled a provincial town's kebab shop late on a Saturday night. They were too drunk even to recognise Taverner.

Captain Mellor and the very dim Lieutenant Reynolds opened the batting for the Officers. Once they had been helped into their pads, they weaved their way out onto the wicket, physically supporting each other. The Sergeants welcomed them at the crease with a loud chorus of quacking.

'Why are they making duck noishesh?' asked Reynolds.

'Think about it,' said Mellor.

'Can't think. Can't even shee shtraight. Any tipsh?'

'Yeah. Just twat the fucker.'

Lieutenant Reynolds did not disappoint the Sergeants and was clean bowled with the first ball.

Lieutenant Skeffington replaced Reynolds at the crease and batted fearlessly, taking huge sweeping swings at the ball. His appalling sense of timing let him down – by the time the bat had reached the lowest point of the swing, the ball was already in the wicket-keeper's hands. In frustration his swings became wilder, and when he finally connected to send the ball through gully he also launched his bat a similar distance towards mid-wicket. He took the run, only to be told by the umpire that he needed his bat for it to score, and that if he didn't hurry up and retrieve it he'd be given out. He ran after his bat, collected it, but was run out long before he returned to his crease. Skeffington did not protest. It was unofficer-like.

Unable to watch any more heroics, Taverner went off to collect some items from the Quartermaster's Store – two old PRC-351 radios and the brick-like batteries that went with them, as well as a few maps and some sheets for encoding messages. The Clothing Store issued him with four complete sets of uniform.

With everything stored in his Land Rover, Taverner returned to the cricket match to watch the final disintegration of the Officers. The score was now fourteen runs for eight wickets. Captain Mellor despatched the ball solidly to long-on, tried to take a single, but tripped over his bat halfway down the wicket and was run out.

The Adjutant had to be taken away on a stretcher after he took a ball in his unprotected testicles – a moment that saw both sides groaning and clutching their nether regions in male kinship and sympathy.

The Officers were all out by the eleventh over. Second Lieutenant Cavendish despatched one ball comfortably towards the boundary, though he and Captain MacNeish decided to run anyway to make sure. Halfway down the wicket they collided head–on and lay in a heap. Before they could pick themselves up, Cavendish was run out.

The Sergeants had triumphed again.

'How pleasing to see that some things never change,' said Taverner, getting up to leave. 'I must be on my way.'

'Good luck, Charlie. Unless you hear from me in the next two days, we're hot to trot. Have fun out there, won't you. Keep us informed as best you can, but don't get into any trouble.'

Taverner shook Hesketh's hand.

'Goodbye, Tom.'

TWENTY-TWO

'Stupid tart,' said Gunner Jones, 'why's she goin' into the fookin' wood? At dat time of night! Don't she know nut'in? She deserves to fookin' die!'

Jones tended to talk a lot when he was a little bit scared. An outsider would have found it difficult to understand his Scouse accent.

'I fookin' love dis bit,' said Gunner Moffat, with relish. 'What 'appens is dat psycho-boy follows 'er with 'is thermal camera, then when 'e's got 'er where 'e wants 'er, 'e's gonna fookin' tear 'er guts out, then stick 'is 'ead in the cavity. Dat's the only way 'e can fookin' get off cos 'e's such a sick fook.'

'Could you shut the fook up?' said Jones. 'Yer keep spoilin' it forrus, for fook's sake!'

They were sitting in their new room in the dark, watching a cheap gore-fest on the huge screen that took up much of the wall. A steady hum from the air conditioning unit kept the temperature low and the room smelt of pine and new paint.

'Fookin' 'ell.'

The sudden and messy evisceration of the girl in the film caused the large speakers to rattle.

'Jesus, 'dat is such a fookin' waste of a good body. Reminds me of a bird I 'ad, right, and I kid you fookin' not, she was the spittin' fookin' image of 'er.'

'Fook off you ever did,' said Jones. 'For fook's sake, why's 'e goin down there? You stupid prick she's dead, dat was 'er screamin', getting 'er fookin' guts ripped out. Don't you fookin' get it? Get the fook out of there now! And dat poxy fookin' potato gun aint gonna be no use against 'im.'

'She aint dead, though. Psycho-boy's using 'er to bait 'im.'

'Will you fookin' stoppit?' said Jones, who got two more beers from the fridge, as Moffat gave him a running commentary.

'Dat's fookin harsh. 'E can see 'er dangling from the tree across the swamp, but 'e knows she's alive. She aint so fit now, is she!' he said to the screen, 'Not like when you was bangin' 'er earlier. What're you gonna fookin' do?'

The sound of repeated gunshots filled the room.

'Dat's what! He's wasted 'er and put 'er out of 'er misery!' said Moffat. 'Fookin' perforated 'er! And dat is what I'm gonna do to the first fooker who tries to come in through the gate!'

'What, rip their fookin' guts out?'

'No! Fookin' perforate them.'

'What does dat mean?'

'Fill them with fookin' lead. They're gonna eat every fookin' round from my fookin' magazine! I can't fookin' wait!'

''Ow long do you reckon Major 'esketh 'ad dis idea, then?' said Jones. 'Dat is the best fookin' thing I've 'eard for ages. I reckon 'e must 'ave 'ad it up 'is sleeve for fookin' months.'

'Fook knows. Why didn't he tell us fookin' earlier, the

stupid fat wanker? 'E's as bad as the rest of 'em. I mean, 'ow long ago did 'e know dat we was getting chopped and if so why did 'e not tell anyone? I mean, we could've stopped work, downed-tools and all dat shit. No way would we 'ave done all dat work for them other fookers. Like …' Moffat put on a posh accent, '… well done, very well done indeed, young man, thank you so much for all your service over the years and now could you fark orf.'

'Podsnap 'eard dat Colonel Sandford knew we was being shafted even before 'e took over. The fookin' wanker, eh? Reckons also dat Major 'esketh only found out about it by accident.'

'Well 'e should have fookin' told us anyway. And I'm gonna fookin' tell 'im next time I see 'im.'

'Anyone else thin out today?'

'Walker's gone. So 'as Simmons and Ginge. Fookin' cowards.'

'Yeah, but they got family though.'

'So? Fletcher's staying. 'E's got family.'

'Yeah, but 'e fooked 'is wife off, didn't 'e. Loves the regiment more than 'er. Anyway, if I had a wife dat looked like dat, I'd tell 'er to fook off too. Face like a fookin' camel eating toast.'

'Thing is though, Major 'esketh is right,' said Moffat. 'Either way we're fooked. There's fook all forr'us to do and fook all work. And I aint goin' on the giro when I get out of 'ere. I'd rather do a stint in Bridewell.'

'If he goes through with dis, then dat is precisely where we're all goin'.'

'He said dat we can say we was actin' under duress, under 'is orders, like.'

'Dat aint gonna wash with the fookin' beak though.'

'So what? We'll only get a few years. I've taken enough

fookin' shit for dis country. Now they can give me a bit of flock and brecky.'

'What if they send the troops in?'

'They won't. They wouldn't dare. Still, I don't give a shit who they fookin' send, they're goin' down. They can send in the fookin' SAS if they want. I aint fookin' scared. If I'm cornered, like, I'm gonna take as many of the fookers with me as I can. They are *goin'* ... *fookin'* ... *down!*'

'You are so full of shit, Moff.'

When the horror movie had finished, they put on a war movie and drank some more beer. That they ever managed to get up next morning was something of a minor miracle, but they were both present for the RSM's full rehearsal of the Handover Parade.

In the afternoon there were a number of briefings to attend as Major Hesketh discreetly issued his operational orders to the regiment. The 65th had always been a very close regiment and now the sense of camaraderie was as strong as anyone had ever known. A few more soldiers departed guiltily during the day as the harsh reality of what they were about to do dawned on them, but the final strength of the 65th on its last day was sufficient; twelve officers, twenty-eight Warrant Officers and Senior NCOs, and one-hundred and thirteen other-ranks.

Colonel Sandford had been away for the last few days and arrived back on Windcheater Island late that afternoon. He immediately summoned Major Hesketh to run through the programme for the Final Day.

TWENTY-THREE

'By the left! Quick march!'

The Regimental Sergeant Major barked out his command, the drummer from the Band of the Artillery hammered out five beats for tempo, the first few notes of *Through Bolts and Bars* filled the air, and the 65th Regiment Royal Horse Artillery took to their Parade Square for the very last time. In earlier times, such a regiment would have been given a thoroughly lavish send-off into history. Not so today. The Handover Parade was taking place behind closed doors, as Colonel Sandford had insisted. He'd been adamant – no senior officers, no Blimpish types, no former members of the regiment in their blazers and berets and blankets and wheelchairs, bristling and boring with their patriotism and jingo. That day, the only audience for the parade consisted of a few families; their cars already packed up, the wives hoping they could get away soon after lunch. Their husbands out on the parade had no such intention of departing so early, and hoped to stay for the afternoon's regimental wake.

There was official representation at the parade from the European Defence Minister, Dr Ulrich Müller, and the Right Honourable Geoffrey MacDonald MP, Müller's equivalent in the British Government, although their main role that day was to formally welcome the Advance Party of the European Rapid Deployment Force onto Windcheater Island. The two senior politicians were accompanied by a Close Protection Team from the Interior Ministry; three dangerous slabs of muscle compressed into bad suits with the ubiquitous earpieces and lapel microphones. The team was nervous and jumpy despite being within the confines of a secure military base. This was North Devon – the Badlands – and they looked as though they were expecting some sort of trouble. A photographer was also present to record the moment when the base was formally handed over to the ERDF.

The weather that day was overcast; dry, but threatening and unpredictable. A saluting dais had been placed at the front of the Parade Square and, behind it, the flag of the 65th flew somewhat hopefully. Escorted by Colonel Sandford and Major Hesketh, Dr Müller and Mr MacDonald approached the dais, with the 65th formed up in front of them. The RSM barked out another command and the entire regiment 'presented arms' with a rhythmic double-crack as the soldiers slapped the sides of their rifles and stamped their cleated boots into the ground. The presentation of arms was a formal military way of paying respect to honoured and important guests on parade.

Privately, the two politicians found such a ludicrous display of military servility rather amusing, as a jungle explorer might do when a tribe welcomed him with an ancient and bizarre ritual, though they did as they had been asked and tried to look interested. Neither of them could have been considered to be the British Army's greatest fans, but they were not so inhumane as to deprive a condemned man of his last wish before his final walk to the gallows, and with a serious expression they were shown along the front rank of immaculately presented soldiers, each one ramrod straight, with their boots bulled to black glass, buttons Brasso'd, creases starched to razor-sharpness and, from under the peak of their forage caps, the eyes with their sinister stare of a thousand yards.

Once the politicians were back on the dais, the regiment marched past in both slow and quick time, giving a sharp 'eyes right' as they passed the dais, then formed up again in three ranks for the address from Dr Müller. He did not speak as if he had a regiment of soldiers in front of him, rather, as if it was the world's Press instead, and gave a vacuous political speech that was most notable for the clever way it managed to say nothing whatsoever. He mentioned 'World Peace' more times than his beauty should have warranted – he was certainly no *Miss World* contestant – and made only one passing reference to the 65th, managing to raise a few eyebrows when he described the assembled ranks as '… very lovely, really very gorgeous indeed.'

Once the wretched speech was over, when prompted, Dr Müller granted permission to the Adjutant for the 65th to leave the Parade Square. The regiment stepped off again, this time to the sound of *'British Grenadiers'*, and marched off the square and out of sight. Colonel Sandford could barely contain his pleasure as he watched the Provost Sergeant slowly lower the flag of the 65th.

With the parade over, the politicians and the officers headed to the Officers' Mess, where lunch awaited. The Mess was now the subject of a Compulsory Purchase Order and no longer the property of the eccentric bee-keeper Colonel Cobbaton-Farr. Colonel Sandford was now able to enter the Mess for the first time without the need for a formal invitation, and as he sat down to lunch in between Dr Müller and Mr MacDonald, he had never felt so successful.

The past ten months had been a tricky and sometimes murderously stressful time for Sandford. It had been difficult enough trying to balance the need to command the 65th with the requirement to discreetly head over to Brussels at regular intervals to oversee the formation of the ERDF, but he had achieved it. There had been the constant worry that someone, somewhere, would inadvertently leak the true agenda to the 65th, which would have created innumerable problems for him. Thank God it had never occurred. As expected, the 65th had been too wrapped up in itself to consider the bigger picture. Still, the men had done their job and were quietly being put out to pasture, and the ERDF was at that very moment on its way to Windcheater Island. He had arrived at this momentous day without a hitch and it felt like a great weight had lifted from his shoulders. For Sandford, there was a new appointment to look forward to, promotion to Brigadier, a new command and new soldiers. Proper soldiers this time. Compassionate and articulate, worldly and politically-sound. Receptive to his progressive framework of administration. Responsive to the doctrine of the CODE. Each soldier a willing stakeholder in the future of the European peacekeeping effort (he liked that last one and filed it away for future use). There would be no need for the punishments and sanctions he'd had to impose on the alcoholic savages of the 65th.

Seeing the 65th disbanded appealed deeply to a particularly vindictive streak in Sandford. It was delicious revenge for all the slights he'd endured, the comments behind his back, the indifference of the Sergeants' Mess, the open hostility of the Officers' Mess and the insolent Captain Taverner. In fact, *disbanded* was not the right word, thought Sandford. It was too mechanical, and implied that the 65th could be resurrected. *Dissolved* was more appropriate. Never again would this vile, swaggering monument to the past be allowed to inflict itself on others. From today it would only exist in the sort of obscure history books that no-one ever read. He would admit, in all honesty, that the way the 65th had been used during recent months was perhaps not terribly fair, but the overriding requirement for a new base worthy of the ERDF took precedence over any need to be entirely upfront with the 65th. Besides, they were soldiers and were paid to follow orders however unpalatable, without needing to know the real reasons behind them. They would not think well of him in the future, when they learnt of the depth of his involvement, but he was not seeking their approval. They were moving on, while he was moving up. In his head he kept repeating his new title to himself.

Brigadier Sandford. Commander, European Rapid Deployment Force.

It was almost too good to be true, even if he did say so himself. People would talk about this for years. Ten months ago, he had taken command on Windcheater Island and been plunged into the cesspit that was the 65th, and now he had come up smelling of roses.

Sandford looked down the table at the other officers. They were tucking into lunch without a care in the world, seemingly indifferent to their fate. Perhaps it was delayed shock or their inability to accept that change was inevitable. For far too long they had treated the 65th as their own private club; a cosy, elitist little establishment isolated from the real world. Well, they would all be unemployed at midnight, and tomorrow they were going to get a very harsh lesson in reality, and not before time either.

Hopefully, thought Sandford, they would be clearing off later without too much fuss. He felt a little uncomfortable having the rest of the officers present at today's lunch, given their propensity for hooliganism at any dinner table they sat down at. He feared they would seek to embarrass him in front of the politicians. In fact, their conduct was exemplary. They were well-behaved and polite to his guests, and not a single bread roll got airborne.

There were still things to do that day, and while the other officers could take their time over lunch, Sandford and his guests still had much to discuss. With Major Hesketh, the Adjutant and the Close Protection Team, they walked off their lunch with a tour of the new base.

Back in Sandford's office in Regimental Headquarters after the tour, coffee was served and the politicians continued to heap praise onto him.

'Excellent, Sandford. It's really very impressive,' said MacDonald. 'Ahead of schedule *and* under budget. You're gaining a hell of reputation in Whitehall. "Who *is* this man Sandford?" people keep asking me. I tell them. A man who can make things happen and get things done. Many congratulations on a first-rate job.'

'Thank you, sir,' replied Sandford, beaming.

'And what about you, Major Hesketh? Where do you go from here?'

'I'm retiring. My home's in Canada and I'm flying back next week. It's the quiet life for me from now on.'

'And what about the soldiers?' MacDonald did not sound like he was particularly interested.

'After the base is handed over, most of them will go back to civilian life,' said Hesketh.

'Of course, they have been resettled in any case, sir,' added Colonel Sandford. 'They all now have transferable skills in construction as a result of their involvement in the project. Building firms will snap them up. And the cost of the training courses they were sent on was more than they would have been entitled to through the normal resettlement procedure. It was a most generous package, for which they are extremely grateful.'

'Have any been able to transfer to other regiments?'

'Some,' said Hesketh. 'But with your government's latest round of cutbacks, vacancies in other regiments are rather limited.'

Sandford shot a look at Hesketh. That was going too far.

'Hmmm. Of course, I sympathise, but we're all being asked to make sacrifices at the moment,' said MacDonald. 'None of us will ever be beyond the range of the Treasury's ever-swinging axe! Now then, turning to the timetable for the handover to the ERDF, the Advance Party is arriving today, so when is the remainder of Headquarters due to get here?'

'A week's time.'

'Good. They need to be in place as soon as possible. With the situation in Burundi deteriorating every week, the ERDF will be the first to deploy if Brussels gives the go-ahead.'

Sandford and the two politicians wittered on in self-

218

congratulation as Hesketh sat back, listening and waiting. The Adjutant, who had earlier been called away by the Duty Clerk, now returned and let himself into the Colonel's office. For a split second the Adjutant caught Hesketh's eye and they exchanged a brief but knowing glance. The fun was about to begin.

'I'm very sorry to trouble you, gentlemen, but it seems we've got a bit of trouble at the Sentry Post,' said the Adjutant.

'What sort of trouble?' said Sandford, sharply.

'A small crowd has gathered. The guards say they're protesting about something. It's all very peaceful. Nothing we need to be too worried about.'

'Probably just peaceniks,' offered MacDonald. 'Bloody hippies! Don't worry, we're quite used to a bit of jeering and egg-pelting. There's no unofficial press among them?'

'Not that the sentry specifically reported. It sounds like they're locals from the town.'

'Then it's not a problem. How nice of them to turn out!'

The leader of the Close Protection Team did not seem quite so unconcerned when the Adjutant stepped outside to brief him.

'This is the Team Leader.' he said into his lapel. 'We've got a one-seventy-three-type situation at the entrance to the base. Am assessing now. Out.' He turned to the Adjutant. 'Get me up to the entrance.'

It was too far to walk, so the Adjutant drove him up the road and stopped about a hundred metres short of the Sentry Post. A crowd of about fifty civilians had gathered harmlessly on the road beyond. The gate was wide open, the barrier across the entrance was raised and there were clearly no soldiers on duty.

'Jesus Christ! They could just walk right in!' said the bodyguard. 'Where are the bloody guards? What sort of security is this?' he snapped at the Adjutant. He spoke into his lapel. 'Confirming we've got a one-seventy-three at the entrance, fifty strong. Area integrity breached, repeat area integrity breached. Secure and evacuate VIP party immediately. Be aware hostile third parties may be on the base. Acknowledge. Over.'

There was no response in his earpiece. He repeated the message. Still nothing came through.

'Bollocks! Get that bloody gate shut!' he ordered the Adjutant, furious at this appalling lapse in security.

The Adjutant leant on the bonnet of his vehicle and casually lit a cigarette. 'I beg your pardon?' he said, condescendingly. He did not take orders from a civilian.

The bodyguard did not hear him and was still fiddling with his lapel microphone.

'Hello? Hello? This is the Team Leader. Hello?'

'Are you listening to me?' said the Adjutant. 'You do not have any authority on this base.'

'Hello? Hello? What the …'

The bodyguard looked at the Adjutant, scarcely believing what he was seeing. The Adjutant was poised with his cigarette dangling from his mouth, his left leg forward, his left hand cupping his right hand in which he held a 9mm Browning pistol. It was pointing straight at the bodyguard's head.

'Get your hands up.'

The bodyguard was so shocked that he momentarily forgot his training and did exactly as he was told.

'Lie down on the ground with your hands out in front of you. Make any sudden movement and you will lose your head.'

A group of soldiers dashed out from the Sentry Post, handcuffed the bodyguard and removed his weapon.

'Good,' said the Adjutant, his pistol still trained on the bodyguard. 'Now perhaps you'll listen to me.'

The other members of the Close Protection Team had been similarly disarmed and escorted to the safety of the Guardroom, where Major Hesketh was waiting. The photographer was told that there had been a change of plan, and with his presence no longer required he was ordered off the base. When all the bodyguards had been locked up in the cells, Hesketh made his way back to the Colonel's office with the Provost Sergeant and four armed soldiers who waited outside in the corridor.

Inside, Hesketh calmly updated Colonel Sandford and the politicians on the situation at the Sentry Post.

'It's just as they reported,' he said. 'Nothing to worry about, just a small crowd of locals saying goodbye to the 65th.'

Hesketh then did a curious thing. Instead of taking one of the unoccupied chairs near the others, he walked round the Colonel's desk, sat in his chair and lit a cigar.

'Tom, could you not smoke in here,' hissed Sandford. This was embarrassing.

Hesketh ignored him and took a drag. 'Cohiba,' he said to the politicians, looking appreciatively at his cigar. 'Pre-Castro. Very rare, you know. Been saving it for a special occasion.'

'Tom!' snapped Sandford. 'What the *hell* do you think you're doing?'

Hesketh now put his feet up on the desk and blew smoke towards the ceiling. For some reason the politicians thought this was very funny.

'The protest at the gate,' said Hesketh, shaking his head. 'It's really nothing to worry about.'

Colonel Sandford sensed that something wasn't quite right.

'However, gentlemen, *this* is something you *should* be worried about.'

Hesketh removed his feet from the desk and sat up, and pulled out a 9mm pistol. He held it sideways in front of him, appearing to read the side of it. Slowly he pointed it at Sandford and stared very hard at him.

Sandford looked confused as he tried to comprehend. 'Tom? Tom?'

The door of the office then burst open with such violence that its handle became embedded in the wall behind it. The Provost Sergeant and his team crashed into the office and pointed their rifles at the Colonel and his guests.

'Strip,' ordered one of the soldiers, looking at the two politicians.

'I *beg* your pardon,' protested MacDonald.

'He said FUCKING STRIP!' screamed the Provost Sergeant in a voice that sounded like he gargled on razor blades each morning. Even Hesketh recoiled instinctively. Sandford seemed paralysed.

Still unable to comprehend what was going on, but not for an instant doubting the force behind the command, the politicians did as they were told and rapidly disrobed. They both had emergency transponders on them in the event of such an occurrence, but events had happened so quickly that neither had time to activate them. One of the soldiers located the transponders in their suit pockets and crushed them beneath his boot. The politicians were given blue coveralls to change into, and were escorted out of the office at gunpoint and driven to the Officers' Mess.

Colonel Sandford stayed behind in his office with Major Hesketh, shaking and fighting the urge to panic. Hesketh smiled at him, shook his head and quietly tutted, with his pistol still pointing at Sandford.

'I'm not going to make a long speech at this time,' said Hesketh, 'far too much of the James Bond villain about it. No white pussy cat or an underground monorail for a start, and my ego isn't really up to it. Suffice it to say, however, that you played a very merry game with us all along, didn't you? Got the boys to build you a new base for the ERDF, *your* ERDF, future '*Commander*', yet you knew all along what was going to happen to the 65th. The funny thing is, so did we! We've known for ages. Oh, I know we weren't supposed to, but we found out. You thought you'd played us for fools all along, didn't you. It looks like we've beaten you at your own game. You've been out-manoeuvred, Colonel.'

The colour had drained from Sandford's face and he had aged many years. He couldn't possibly begin to accept what was happening, and yet what Hesketh had just said seemed so plausible. Everything had just collapsed, and for the first time in his life, like the thousands of soldiers who'd served on operational tours that he'd been careful to avoid, he felt fear. *Real* fear. The racing pulse, the taste of metal, the ice in his stomach, the draining of strength from his muscles. He badly wanted to see his wife again and struggled to control himself, drawing shallow uncontrolled breaths like a sobbing child.

'Tom. I don't know what you're doing, but you'll not get away with it, whatever it is.'

'You'll find out soon enough.'

Hesketh called for the escorts, and Colonel Sandford was led away to be secured with the others in the Officers' Mess.

Later that afternoon, a young Lance Bombardier of the 65th was driving with his wife on the North Devon Link Road out of Holberton, towards the M5 motorway. Their baby was asleep in the back. The soldier had been made redundant from the 65th and had taken part in the earlier parade, but was now heading to his mother's house for a few weeks so he could get himself sorted out and start looking for work.

There was very little traffic on the road, and if it was going to be like that for the whole journey, they should be in Liverpool by late evening. Holberton was about ten miles behind them, when they came across the scene of a road accident.

An articulated lorry had somehow lost control and become jack-knifed across the entire width of the road, blocking traffic in both directions. No other vehicles were involved and the driver of the lorry was sitting by the side of the road clutching his head, being attended to by other drivers. A group of ramblers had gathered ghoulishly on the footbridge overlooking the scene of the accident. The young soldier was a practical man and looked around to see if there was any way in which he could help. In the queue of traffic that had built up in the opposite direction, he noticed a convoy of khaki vehicles from the European Rapid Deployment Force – the new unit taking over Windcheater Island.

A few ERDF soldiers were milling around on the road; smoking cigarettes, making telephone calls, tyre-kicking, waiting for the emergency services to arrive and open the road again.

There was a sudden tinkle of glass and the bonnet of one of the ERDF vehicles erupted in flames. The Lance Bombardier looked up to the bridge, where the ramblers were lighting petrol bombs and raining them down on the ERDF convoy. He ran back to his own car and got inside.

On the other side of the stricken lorry the ERDF soldiers did the same. The petrol bombs did little damage to their vehicles, and the flames quickly went out once the fuel had burnt off. The barrage of bricks and rocks that followed was rather more destructive, shattering windscreens and breaking side windows and wing mirrors. Still the ERDF soldiers stayed put inside their vehicles. But when a battery of shotguns started firing from the tree-line, the ERDF decided it was time to beat a hasty retreat. Neither knowing nor caring why they had been singled out for this treatment, they swung their vehicles round, side-swiping others in the process, and took off in the direction they had come.

They kept going until they were clear of the Badlands – the infamous region that had just lived up to its reputation.

TWENTY-FOUR

It was eleven o'clock on the morning of the next day and the Adjutant was in his office in Regimental Headquarters. Over in the accommodation blocks the soldiers were waiting to go to the cookhouse for an early lunch, and the officers were having a late breakfast in the Mess. Major Hesketh was in his new office next door to the Adjutant's.

For the first time ever, the Adjutant had nothing to do. As the Commanding Officer's personal Staff Officer, he would have normally been snowed under with the endless regimental administration that his job involved. Today was very different. Officially, the 65th had been sent to the chair at midnight; strapped in and despatched into history, but very few outside Windcheater Island knew that the regiment lived on.

The phone call came just after eleven. The display showed the call was coming from the Ministry of Defence in Whitehall. The Adjutant let the phone ring three times before he answered it, as he contemplated the fact that some very powerful people were about to learn something that was really going to spoil their lunch.

'Adjutant 65th RHA.'

'Ah, good morning. This is the Ministry of Defence here,' said the caller, in a chummy voice.

'Ah, good morning,' mirrored the Adjutant, wondering why his voice had decided to pitch itself a little higher than normal. Maybe it was the anticipation of having to break some very bad news. He consciously lowered it again. 'How can I help?'

The caller explained to him, in a rather convoluted way that betrayed the collective embarrassment within the MoD, that they had 'lost' Dr Müller, Mr MacDonald and their Close Protection Team, and that their last known whereabouts had been Windcheater Island for the handover.

'I'm sure there's an innocent explanation,' said the caller, trying to sound jovial, but barely concealing the pressure he was under. 'As you can imagine, there's an extensive operation underway to locate them. Could you confirm what time they left your base yesterday?'

'They didn't leave the base,' said the Adjutant. 'They are still here.'

'Oh, thank God,' replied the caller, who obviously covered his mouthpiece and said something unintelligible to someone nearby. 'So they are okay?' asked the caller, much clearer again.

'Just fine, thank you. They're quite comfortable.'

The Adjutant was not lying. Their rooms in the Officers' Mess were indeed very comfortable, and very secure. They were being well-fed and were unlikely to cause much inconvenience to the guards stationed outside their rooms. The Close Protection Team, being considerably more muscular and more likely to cause trouble, were being held in the rather sparser conditions of the Guardroom cells, under the control of the fearsome Provost Sergeant and his team of Cro-Magnon Men.

'They're quite fine and dandy,' continued the Adjutant. 'Alive and kicking, you could say!'

The caller hesitated for a moment, perplexed by the Adjutant's irreverence. 'Could you pass me over to the Close Protection Team,' he said.

'I'm sorry, but that won't be possible,' said the Adjutant.

'Why on earth not?'

'Well, it's a bit complicated really.'

'Then put me through to Mr MacDonald.'

'That's going to be difficult.'

'What about Dr Müller?' said the caller, now beginning to lose patience.

'Again, a bit tricky.'

'So who the hell *can* I speak to?'

'Me. Or the Commanding Officer.'

'I'm not really following you. Can you tell me *when* they will be leaving Windcheater Island?'

The Adjutant took time to clear his throat, dropping the words in quietly like an afterthought. 'They won't be leaving.'

'What do you mean "won't be leaving"? To whom am I speaking?'

'Still me. Still the Adjutant of the 65th RHA.'

'Put me through to the Commanding Officer. Now!' said the caller, his voice having lost any remaining *bonhomie*.

'Won't keep you a moment.'

The Adjutant opened the door to the Colonel's office. Major Hesketh sat reading a book.

'It's Whitehall on the phone.'

'Excellent,' said Hesketh, as though he had just been served dinner in a restaurant. He picked up the phone by his desk and momentarily steeled himself. During the brief interlude, the caller at the MoD had been replaced by someone with a bit more clout.

Hesketh spoke in his habitual plummy tone.

'Major Hesketh.'

'This is Major General Ogilvy at the Ministry of Defence. I don't want to speak to you, whoever the hell you are. I want to speak to the Commanding Officer.'

'Major General Ogilvy, we meet again,' said Hesketh. 'I do hope you're going to be rather more pleasant than you were the last time we spoke.'

'What did you say? How *dare* you!' said Ogilvy. 'Put me through to the CO this instant.'

'You're speaking to the CO.'

'No, no, no, I want to speak to Colonel Sandford …'

'Colonel Sandford is no longer the Commanding Officer of the 65th,' said Hesketh. 'He has been relieved of his command.'

'Relieved of his command?'

'That is correct.'

'On whose authority?'

'Mine.'

'What? Impossible!' sneered Ogilvy.

'No, this is quite genuine. I am the new Commanding Officer of the 65th.'

'I *beg* your pardon. Just who the hell do you think you are, you insolent little man?' said Ogilvy. 'In fact, hang on a second. Why on earth am I speaking to you? You are supposed to have vacated your base.'

'We decided not to. We've chosen to stay put.'

'This is *preposterous*. Now you look here, you silly little man. I don't know what the hell you think you're up to, but if there's so much as one single British soldier left on Windcheater Island, there really is going to be the most terrible uproar. If necessary, we will have you forcibly evicted and charged with trespass and offences under the Official Secrets Act. Windcheater Island is now European Territory.'

'Really?' said Major Hesketh, with heavy sarcasm.

'I don't particularly like your tone!' said the General. 'I don't know what the hell's going on down there. We'll send in the police if necessary and you'll be arrested.'

'We will not be vacating Windcheater Island. Not on your terms, not on anyone's terms.'

'Oh, this is quite ridiculous. Get me Colonel Sandford now!'

'He's not here.'

'What have you done with him?'

'He's with the others. With Dr Müller and Mr MacDonald.'

'Well, if I can't get any sense out of you then I demand that I speak to them this instant. That is an order!'

'That won't be possible at this moment. They're on fatigues.'

'On fatigues? What the devil do you mean, "on fatigues"?'

'Right at this moment,' said Hesketh, straining his voice slightly to give the impression that he was looking out of a window, 'the European Defence Secretary is cutting the grass outside Regimental Headquarters.'

'Cutting the grass?'

'With some scissors. Under the supervision of the Provost Sergeant. You may be able to speak to him when he's finished, but that won't be until after dinner tonight.'

'Oh dear God.'

'MacDonald is also busy. He's doing some painting.'

'Painting what, dare I ask?'

'Painting the grass.'

'Painting the grass?'

'Painting it green. He's doing a splendid job. It looks lovely.' Hesketh was pleased with his imagery.

'Christ Almighty.'

'In fact, I think it's quite appropriate that someone like MacDonald, as our Defence Secretary, should experience the delights of Basic Training,' said Hesketh. 'I don't recall he's ever served in the Armed Forces, and I doubt he'll take us for granted again, if he survives this. Oh, and by the way, Colonel Sandford, when I last saw him, was polishing coal.'

'Look,' said Ogilvy. 'This is not some sort of dreadful hoax is it? If it's a wind-up then I think it's in very poor taste.'

'If only. No, it's the real thing. The genuine article. If you don't believe me then perhaps I can give you the serial numbers of the Close Protection Team's weapons that we confiscated from them. We also have the serial numbers of the emergency transponders belonging to the politicians. The ones we had to inactivate, you understand. We can give you their credit card numbers, mobile phone numbers, almost anything you ask for, because I have it all here in front of me.'

'I don't believe you.'

'We have even been looking through MacDonald's mobile phone, which has some rather interesting contacts and images stored on it. Clearly, he has a personal life that, how shall I say, extends to very colourful tastes. I wonder what the voters, not to mention his wife and children, would make of it were that to become public knowledge,' hinted Hesketh ominously, before reverting to a more forgiving tone. 'But no, that's not our intention. Not today.'

'This is utterly preposterous, Hesketh. If I understand

correctly, then what you're actually saying, and I can't quite believe this, is that you have actually *kidnapped* them.'

'That, sir, is precisely what we have done.'

'Good God,' said Ogilvy, quietly. 'Good God Almighty. Hesketh, you'll swing for this. I think you'd better stay by the phone.'

'With pleasure.'

Throughout the afternoon, there followed a succession of phone calls from increasingly senior and increasingly irate officers, as the seriousness of the situation became clear. Later, Hesketh sent an electronic communication to the Ministry of Defence, to the Interior Ministry and to all the major news organisations, explaining the reasons for his actions, and the consequences if his demands were not met:

> ... *in order to guarantee the continued well-being of Dr Müller and Mr MacDonald, I suggest that the authorities strongly reconsider their decision to disband the 65th Royal Horse Artillery, to hand over Windcheater Island to a foreign power, and to consign a regiment of highly-trained professional soldiers who have served their country with distinction, to a life of unemployment and poverty.*
>
> *In the meantime I strongly encourage the authorities to stay away from Windcheater Island. Any attempt to evict us from our rightful home, or to forcibly remove our guests, will result in a massive, lethal and overwhelming response.*
>
> *God save the King.*

The last person to phone Hesketh that day was the Chief of Defence Staff; the Admiral of the Fleet. He was the most senior officer in the Armed Forces and the last remaining career serviceman at that level. Their conversation, in contrast to the others Hesketh had that day, was polite and the Admiral seemed remarkably placid, even unconcerned. He listened to Hesketh sympathetically, almost without judgement, like a psychiatrist giving a confidential ear to a patient as he confessed yet more sickening aberrations. Hesketh found it quite therapeutic to pour out his thoughts to someone on the outside, though he was careful not to give too much away.

'I'm duty-bound to ask you to reconsider your actions, Tom,' said the Admiral. 'There are less extreme ways of getting your message across, and you raise some valid points.'

'Sir, I do not intend for our complaints to fall on deaf ears. What we're doing simply shows the depth of feeling over how we've been treated. I want the government's attention.'

'Yes, well, you've certainly achieved that. Now, you're intelligent enough to know that one of the options that will inevitably be discussed here in Whitehall is some sort of operation to rescue the hostages.'

'Quite understandable, sir.'

'In the event of that course of action, have you considered the danger to which you will be exposing your soldiers?'

'They are all volunteers who have elected to stay behind. The fact that they are prepared to put themselves in harm's way surely conveys their anger.'

'Even though this could result in British soldiers deliberately targeting other British soldiers?'

'Sounds like your average Friday night in Aldershot, sir. In any case, ours are not really soldiers any more, insofar as they serve the government. As of midnight, they are redundant.'

'I think you need to dwell on that awful possibility, Tom. I sincerely hope we are able to work together and resolve this situation so that it doesn't come to that.'

'Likewise, sir.'

'The Cabinet is going into an emergency session shortly, and I dare say we'll be in contact with you again soon.'

At the Sentry Post, in front of the rolls of razor wire stretched across the road, the crowd from Holberton, still camped out from the day before, was enjoying a balmy summer's evening as the setting sun cast long shadows on the ground. At the back of the crowd stood the tall, athletic man with blond hair who had orchestrated this show of support. A camera crew from a regional television station had recently arrived after a tip-off earlier in the day.

The 65th was on a war footing. Three heavily-reinforced bunkers had been built further back into the base, and the Sentry Post itself had been enveloped in sandbags. Two small slit trenches had been dug each side of the road. A few soldiers stood behind the wire; armed, helmeted, their faces blackened, and caught a few cans of cold beer thrown to them by the crowd.

Occasionally the crowd attempted to get a few chants going and waved their placards.

'*Suport our boys!*' said one [sic].

'*Gun Control means using both hands,*' said another.

'*I'd rather be drinking in the pub than writing witty slogans.*'

The atmosphere picked up when three logo'd police cars arrived from the South West Crime Reduction Partnership ('*Passionate about delivering Crime Reduction Solutions*'). The crowd welcomed them with jeers. It was rare to see a single police car in Holberton – to see three of them conveyed the magnitude of the situation. From the second car a serious-looking Chief Superintendent got out and strode purposefully up to the razor wire, ignoring the comments from the crowd. Floodlights were switched on as he approached the wire and he had to cup his hands over his eyes, so bright was the light.

'I need to speak to Major Hesketh,' he said to the soldiers, now just dark figures beyond the wire.

Major Hesketh appeared ten minutes later, having been driven up to the Sentry Post. Across the wire he faced the police officer, who held up a sheet of paper.

'This is a statement signed by the Interior Minister. If you release the hostages within the next hour and vacate the base, then your soldiers will face no criminal charges.' The police officer spoke loudly enough for the soldiers to hear, and passed the sheet of paper carefully through the wire to avoid snagging his uniform. Hesketh took it and gave it a cursory glance, before screwing it up into a ball and throwing it back at the police officer.

'Do you have anything else to offer us?' said Hesketh. 'No? Then please don't bother me again.'

The crowd cheered as the police officer trudged back to his car. Ever PR-conscious, he tried to smile for the television camera, but could only produce a rictus grin in light of his humiliation.

A heavily-censored version of the events at the Sentry Post made it onto the television news channels that day. The item was not considered important, tucked away behind the Community Minister's triumphant report on the last three-year plan, and the Diversity Minister's tour of some inner-city schools in the North.

TWENTY-FIVE

In the early hours of next morning, the soldiers of the 65th waited in their accommodation for the order to deploy. In his room, Gunner Moffat lay sprawled on his bed, trumping his way through the torpid hours of waiting. He and his mates were passing the time as soldiers do when there is little to occupy them; gobbing off at each other, smoking heavily and watching hardcore porn.

In contrast, Regimental Headquarters was a hive of activity as the Conference Room was converted to an Operations Room. Down came the regimental pictures and photographs, and up went a series of maps, annotated with arrows and boundaries marked in removable ink. Radios were set up, and lengths of cable snaked over the floor and out through the door to the generators and antennae outside. In the centre of the Ops Room stood a square table with another map – the *Bird Table* – around which all central briefings would take place.

Major Hesketh, accompanied by the Adjutant, walked the short distance from his new office to the Ops Room. Earlier that evening he had humiliated the senior policeman at the Sentry Post, and the authorities in London had clearly got the message by now. A sudden, snap attempt to rescue the hostages was unlikely at this stage, but not out of the question, and he now gave the order for the 65th to deploy.

The Battery Sergeant Major stormed round the accommodation just after two in the morning, throwing doors open and giving the order to move out. For the last time Gunner Moffat checked that he had everything he needed in his Bergan and webbing, and made his way with the others to the Battery building. Each soldier drew his ancient SA–80 rifle from the Armoury and was issued with as much ammunition as he could carry. Their Compo rations would last them for five days and they were issued with a Nuclear, Biological and Chemical Warfare suit and a spare filter for their respirators. They packed their new issues away in whatever space was left in their Bergans, then sat around waiting for the transport to take them to their positions; the air thick with the smell of engine oil and nervous anticipation.

There was no final address or pep-talk or eve-of-battle speech from Major Hesketh. Every soldier knew what he was going to do, and why he was going to do it.

A Bedford truck backed into the garage, enveloping the soldiers seated nearby in clouds of blue diesel smoke. Moffat's Troop was called forward first and they climbed into the back of the truck, passing up Bergans and rifles to those already on board. When the vehicle was loaded, the tailgate was fixed back in place and they set off.

Outside, it was nearly pitch black. A blackout was in force. A few tiny slivers of light escaped from the garages, and the stars seemed much brighter in the night sky. The new buildings formed a skyline of unfamiliar silhouettes and it was difficult to believe, at that moment, that so much activity was going on in the darkness. The driver followed the airfield perimeter road at very low speed, grateful for a little moonlight to guide him, since he could not put his headlights on.

The back of a Bedford truck was a stark and functional place. The slatted seats, merely uncomfortable on short forays, became torturous on longer journeys. Fumes were drawn into the back of the truck, making those sitting near the tailgate nauseous. Fortunately that night there was no need to venture cross-country, which would have turned the ride into one of bouncing, testicle-crushing misery. There was none of the ribald conversation that normally passed the time when being transported around in these cattle trucks; each soldier was alone with his thoughts in the darkness, listening to the gnashing and whining of the gearbox and the flapping of the canvas roof.

Near to their allotted positions, they dismounted from the truck and trudged across the grass to their trenches. Moffat's Troop occupied six small slit trenches to the north of the Sailing Club, dug a month earlier on the exercise, with the front four trenches spaced out in a line about thirty metres back from the seafront, and the other two behind in depth. The Troop Commander, Second Lieutenant Cavendish, took one of the central trenches with his Troop Sergeant and Troop Signaller.

Gunner Moffat was on the far-right of the position, in a trench with three others; Bombardier Podsnap, who was in charge of the trench, Gunner Jones, and a quiet Romany-looking teenager called Gunner Holland, known as 'Dutch'. Bombardier Podsnap fixed up the field telephone, tested it for connectivity, then tuned the radio to the allocated frequency and established contact with the Troop Signaller.

Moffat and Jones repaired the minor damage to the trench that had occurred since it had been dug. Some of the earth had fallen in and several pickets had to be extracted and straightened up. It was a difficult job in the darkness and their clumsy wielding of the sledgehammer in the confines of the trench incurred Bombardier Podsnap's wrath several times. Gunner Holland tidied up the sleeping shelters at either end and laid out the sleeping bags on roll mats. It took them an hour. There was a sense of quiet tension and, despite the late hour, no-one wanted to sleep. This was for real.

If the soldiers found the deployment mildly exciting, then Second Lieutenant Cavendish, who had not yet been on active service, found the whole show positively intoxicating. He was like a Boy Scout on the first night of camp, convinced that the enemy were already out there on the verge of launching an evil and cowardly attack. He spotted some lights on the hills across the other side of the water and speculated loudly while the work went on around him. Was it the enemy? What weapons did they have up there? What was his immediate action in the event of an attack? The rest of his trench ignored him – after all, he was a young officer and so could be forgiven. Unable to read his map in the darkness and no longer able to contain his enthusiasm, he turned on his torch.

'Fookin' hell, sir! They'll see that for miles,' called out a voice from below.

'Oh, terribly sorry,' said Cavendish, turning off the torch.

Soldiers did not order young officers about, but they could advise them in the strongest possible terms. Eventually his Troop Sergeant told him to calm down, and suggested that he might like to visit the rest of the boys in the trenches, as long as he could find his way around in the darkness without the use of aircraft landing lights and without ending up in the sea. Cavendish wandered over to the far right-hand trench, where Gunner Moffat had just made a brew, and climbed down into the trench as a round of cigarettes was lit. The soldiers teased the young officer mercilessly; his plummy accent sounding quite out of place among the colloquial Scouse.

'Do you 'ave a girlfriend, sir?' asked Gunner Moffat.

'Yes. Her name is Madeleine.'

'Madeleine,' repeated Moffat, in a dreamy voice. 'Where did you pull 'er, sir?'

'Oxford. She's at university, reading Politics, Philosophy and Economics.'

'What's she like, sir? Is she fit?'

'Rather! Intelligent, very pretty, well, I like to think so, quite feisty too. I suppose she's a bit clingy, what with me being in the Army.'

'I wish my girlfriend was clingy.'

'What fookin' girlfriend?' said Gunner Jones. 'You don't 'ave a girlfriend. Y'aint been laid since fookin' Christmas.'

'Fookin' have!'

'No,' said Bombardier Podsnap. 'You said that you weren't ever getting laid again after that fookin' bird from Bootle gave you a dose of the clap on Christmas Eve. The only diving you get, Moff', is into that stack of pest you keep hidden under your bed.'

'Fookin' right!' said Gunner Holland, in support. 'The only birds you 'ave anything to do with are Mrs Palmer and 'er five daughters!'

'Pest, Bom' Podsnap?' asked Cavendish.

'Pest. You know, sir. Thrap.'

'Thrap?'

'Thrap. Jesus Christ, sir. You know. Grumble. Razzle. Jazz Mags. Dutch Literature.'

'I'm not sure that I quite follow, Bom' Podsnap.'

'Frankie, sir,' said Jones.

'Frankie?'

'Fookin' 'ell, sir. Frankie Vaughan.'

'Frankie Vaughan?'

'Porn!' said the soldiers, in unison.

'Oh, that.'

'Moff's brought a stash with him,' said Podsnap. 'He nicks everyone else's, the velcro-fingered twat. Go on, lend some to Mr Cavendish.'

Moffat unclipped his Bergan and reached inside.

'No, that's quite alright, thank you,' said Cavendish. 'Hardcore pornography really isn't my scene. In any case, I do have a girlfriend.'

'Yeah, but she can't be with you all the time, sir, can she?' said Moffat.

'No, she can't.'

'It gets lonely, doesn't it, sir, not 'aving your girlfriend around.'

'Well, it sounds like you'd know all about that, Gunner Moffat!' retorted the young officer, to the evident delight of the others.

Moffat retaliated quickly, not to be outdone by an officer.

'So do you bang 'em out when your missus ain't around, sir?'

'Well I …'

'Apparently you're quite good at bangin 'em out, so we've 'eard, sir.'

The soldiers went quiet. Cavendish was not sure, but suspected they were giggling very quietly to themselves in the darkness.

'In fact, we've 'eard that you even bang 'em out ...' Moffat could barely get the words out, '... you even bang 'em out on video in the fookin' Medical Centre.'

They held their composure for a few more seconds before Moffat snorted loudly and they all burst out laughing.

'Oh, you rotten devils,' said Cavendish, realising they were referring to the video played during his dinner-night initiation. 'How did you know? Don't tell me you've all seen it as well?'

'I'm afraid so, sir,' said Gunner Jones. 'It's done the rounds in the accommodation. Moff' likes to watch it when he's locked in his room,' he said, getting a sharp kick to his shin from Moffat.

Cavendish was grateful for the darkness that hid his embarrassment. Contrary to popular belief, what went on in the Officers' Mess was not always destined to stay in the Officers' Mess.

'There's actually a perfectly good explanation for what I was doing,' he offered. 'I was set up.' Cavendish immediately regretted saying that, as the soldiers laughed even harder.

'So what did your bird, the lovely Mada ... fookin'gascar or whatever,' said Moffat.

'Madeleine y'twat,' corrected Jones.

'Madeleine, make of it? I 'eard she was in the fookin' audience, sir.'

'She could see the funny side of it,' said Cavendish.

'She must be quite a small bird, sir?' said Moffat.

'About average height, quite slim, if you must know.'

'Small boned, delicately formed, snake of hip and all that, sir.'

'I guess so,' said Cavendish, perplexed at the soldier's

depth of enquiry and the eloquence of his description.

'Not much to have to fill up.'

'I'm not sure what you ...'

'Must be very tight, sir.'

'Just what are you getting at?'

'Would you say, sir, that you have a happy relationship?'

'Yes, very.'

'Yes, but is she always satisfied, if you know I mean, sir.'

The young officer began to get flustered.

'Yes, if you happen to ask. And why do you?'

The soldiers tried once again to suppress their laughter.

'Well, sir, how can I put this delicately?' said Moffat. 'It's just that we thought Jonesy had the smallest pecker in the world.'

'Eh? Fook off!' said Jones.

'Or we did until the blokes saw yours on the video, sir.'

Again, the soldiers broke into howls of laughter.

'Sorry, sir, with all due respect, it looked like you were trying to strangle a fookin' Arctic prawn,' said Jones.

'Sir, no offence, but I don't think you could even satisfy a fookin' Polo mint!' added Moffat.

The soldiers became hysterical again. Cavendish stayed silent. There was not a hint of malice in their irreverence. The soldiers of the 65th could quickly reduce anyone to the lowest common denominator. No-one, even the officers (especially the officers) was allowed to get above himself or develop an ego that couldn't be pricked in a matter of seconds. Cavendish may have been through Sandhurst and gained his commission, but that meant very little to the soldiers. Young officers had to earn their respect over time. They took pride in their unique training methods and, although he didn't know it, Cavendish was progressing very well indeed.

'A fookin' Polo mint,' said Moffat, as the laughter died away, reminding everyone of his little gem.

'And for being cheeky you can put some scoff on for Mr Cavendish,' ordered Podsnap, suddenly serious again.

Moffat pulled out some Compo rations and another round of cigarettes was lit. In ten minutes the food was ready.

'Are you not eating, Bom' Podsnap?' asked Cavendish.

'No, sir, I'm on a diet.'

'Yeah, the fookin' seafood diet,' said Jones.

'Seafood? How interesting.'

'Yeah. He eats all the food he can see,' said Jones, patting Podsnap's stomach and receiving a dead arm in return.

TWENTY-SIX

Taverner and Hannah spent their last few days together. The presence of the police in Holberton now gave the town a rather sinister air and they did not hang around during the hours of daylight. Instead, they headed to deserted beaches, walked along coastal paths and covered many miles on Exmoor.

Today was their final day. The weather had taken a turn for the worse and they walked from the coastal village of Lee, over the tops of the cliffs, to Ilfracombe; the two of them lashed by the wind and the driving rain, with Flint walking to heel. As they always did on these occasions, they walked hand-in-hand for miles without speaking; a silence that was by no means uncomfortable for either of them. Over the years, they had always gone through this ritual prior to Taverner's six-month operational tours.

This time it was worse.

In the course of his military career, Taverner had been shot at and mortared, he had come under rocket attack and seen a Land Rover, in front of his own, obliterated by a roadside bomb. He had seen soldiers die, sometimes in unspeakable agony, at the hands of the political zealots and the religious fanatics and the juju men who called the shots in the unlovely corners of the world. It was part-and-parcel of taking the King's Shilling. Risk was a part of the job, and while he accepted that risk, he, like so many other soldiers, believed no such horrors would ever befall him personally. It was a state of denial necessary to stay sane on dangerous operations. Each time, all he had to do was to keep his head down for six months, receive his medal at the end of the tour, and then he'd resolve to leave the Army.

Back home on Windcheater Island, Taverner would sometimes lie awake in the small hours as he recalled some of the chances he had taken with his own life and those of his soldiers. Recent tours were far less dangerous, but he'd developed a taste for action and had deliberately gone looking for trouble on such tours to relieve the boredom. He knew that one day, if he kept on like this, he would pay the ultimate price. Spin the wheel enough times and eventually your number comes up.

The risk was relative, of course. Whenever the messy stuff hit the fan, the odds were very much stacked in your favour if you had the British Army on your side, particularly the Scousers of the 65th. They were fearless, quite comfortable in uncomfortable surroundings, and if their enemy was hell-bent on finding Paradise, they were happy to assist him in every way possible.

But Taverner was now involved in something very different. He was on his own, working against the very State he had served over many years. With the attention of the government now focused on Windcheater Island, he knew he could not stay at large for long. The State was paranoid and saw enemies everywhere, and had given its ministries, departments and agencies extraordinary legal powers and the latest surveillance technology to root out subversives and saboteurs.

He did not entertain any illusion about what might happen to him were he to be caught. He would find himself a guest of the Interior Ministry and, if the rumours were true, he would then be turned over to the Special Measures Programme. Taverner had heard the stories about what went on in the discreet camps assigned to the Programme, where a select few involved in the very worst activities against the State were dealt with. If it came down to it, he would choose death over capture and Special Measures, any day. He recalled the old motto of the Gurkhas — *It is better to die than to be a coward* — and wondered, if he found himself cornered, whether he could go through with the unthinkable.

It would not come to that, he told himself. He had an escape plan that could be put into action at a moment's notice, but it was all a question of timing. He had sworn to stay and support the 65th for as long as it needed him, even if things started to become dangerous. Ideally, the 65th would make its point and surrender long before the authorities had started to close in on Taverner. But this was going to be a very high risk venture; he had no idea how it would pan out and, as a former Army officer, he knew only too well that no plan ever survived contact with the enemy.

Taverner looked across at Hannah, who was in a world of her own, staring out over a grey white-capped sea. He could not tell if the water running down her face was rain or tears and wondered, when all this was over, if he would ever see her face again; lit up by a candle over dinner, or asleep on a pillow. He feared that he might not.

They followed the coastal path down into Ilfracombe and found a café on the harbour. Outside the café, fishing nets and lobster pots lay abandoned on the quayside, and in the harbour most of the fishing boats were rotten, listing over or half-submerged. Only one seemed to be remotely seaworthy, Taverner noted. He turned and watched Hannah's face as she stirred her tea.

During their previous separations, it was always Hannah who stayed behind while Taverner went away on his six-month tours. This time however, it was she who was going overseas. She had no family ties, and with some security locked away beyond the reach of the tax gannets that had plundered much of her inheritance, she had little inclination to remain. Her late father's D-type Jaguar and pre-war Bugatti, now far too valuable to race, were in storage in Switzerland; ready to be sold off in a few years' time, as her broker had advised, when the market was expected to peak. The England Hannah had known and loved; the England of a country pub with a wet Labrador drying off in front of an open fire in the snug, of hacking across lush green fields in the early morning mist, was gone. It had been bullied out of existence. With the countryside crumbling, the Vulgaroise catered for by the bland mass media, and the rest of the population kept in line by the sloganeers and the lying thugs in political office, Hannah wanted no more of it. She had sold her little sports car and packed up her belongings, most of which were now in a shipping container out in the North Atlantic, heading for the New World.

Next morning, they set out for London's Heathrow airport before the sun rose. Their last night together had been torrid and lacking in intimacy, and no doubt the Halls were grateful when they eventually vacated the house, having been kept awake for much of the night.

Taverner did not drive directly to the airport, which would have meant passing through a biometric checkpoint. He was keen to leave no trace of himself. They went to the nearby town of Slough, to the coach station, from where an hourly bus service connected to the airport.

Taverner went over the details again.

'The connecting flight goes from Miami to Nassau, and from there you can hire a plane to take you to ...'

'Port Callum. Yes, I do know, Charlie. You've told me a thousand times.'

'It's easy to charter a small plane. Any problems, contact my parents. Their driver will meet you at the airfield. Flint's paperwork is in order, he's micro-chipped and up to date with all his jabs.'

Flint looked up in disappointment at his master's efficiency.

'And when will I have the pleasure of your company out there?' said Hannah. The early hour and lack of sleep had done nothing to affect her looks; indeed, she seemed more vulnerable and more beautiful at that moment than Taverner could ever recall, and he loathed himself for putting her through this.

'You know I don't know the answer to that, sweetheart. It could be weeks, maybe a few months.'

'I won't have a moment's peace.'

'Han', we always went through this before I went away on tour, and those were places where you'd come under fire every time you stepped out the front gate. And I managed to survive that for six months at a go.' Tavener kept his voice low. 'All I'm going to be doing is keeping an eye on things for Tom on the outside. No-one's shooting at me or chucking grenades this time. I don't know how long Tom is going to run with it, but it won't be for long. He'll make his point and then call the whole thing off.'

'But they'll be on to you eventually, Charlie.'

'If they are, I'll be out of there at the speed of a greased cheetah. Woosh! And like *that*, I'll be gone. They'll end up chasing shadows.' He looked at his watch. 'Come on, it's nearly time.'

Taverner spent a few moments with Flint, stroking his head and rubbing his ears. Flint put a paw up on his knee and wagged his tail in anticipation. Taverner led him to a large cage, much to the dog's dismay, and threw in a few of his unwashed T-shirts that Flint loved to snuggle up to. As his dog was taken away for a separate transfer to the airport, he could barely look back at those big brown eyes that bore into him in confusion.

Finally, he embraced Hannah, who was unable to hold back any more and let the tears flow. She made one last attempt to get him to see sense.

'Charlie, for *Christ's sake*, why don't you just get on that coach with me right now? They don't need you! You're going to get yourself killed.'

She could never truly understand Taverner's loyalty to the 65th, to the Army that he hated so much.

'Because I could never live with myself, sweetheart,' he said. 'It's got to be done.'

Hannah knew it was useless. She gripped him harder and dug her fingers hard into his back, and her tears ran onto his shoulder.

'Hannah, six weeks from now, we'll be on a beach somewhere, swimming together in the warmest, clearest water you've ever seen. That's a promise.'

They embraced until the last of the passengers had boarded the coach. He kissed her once more, and hoped he could uphold his promise.

'I love you.'

Hannah took her seat in the coach. When she looked round for him, Taverner had already gone.

TWENTY-SEVEN

The events at Windcheater Island started to creep into the news as the government's spin machine went into action.

People had to sympathise with government ministers, so the editorials ran. They sometimes had to do a very difficult job serving the public, and were quite used to receiving verbal abuse on public duties, or suddenly finding themselves handcuffed to a scruffy prole who'd had the audacity to penetrate the security cordon. If elected politicians found themselves held against their will, then that was simply the nature of political life. An occupational hazard in any liberal democracy. *The government remains committed to peace and stability in the South West Community.*

The newspapers and the television stations played ball at first, ensuring the story was submerged below the latest release of government tittle-tattle, but quietly despatched their newshounds out west to the rural Badlands of North Devon, where the people of the backwater wore clogs and slept with their sisters, or so it was rumoured according to the trendy metropolitan elite.

In Whitehall, much midnight oil was being burned in the buildings of State as the apparatus of government rallied to the cause. The displeasure of the ruling party was tangible and there would be brutal recriminations among those deemed responsible for allowing this to happen. For the time being, the ants laboured away through the fatigue, sustained by strong coffee and fear of the sack.

The rulers in Brussels were particularly irked that this could happen in the new Federal Republic of Britain. Not only had a senior European politician been kidnapped by British soldiers, but the Advance Party of the European Rapid Deployment Force – which was, as they reminded their British lackeys, the new Cornerstone of European Defence Policy – had been attacked by a mob while on their way to occupy their new base on Windcheater Island. The Main Body of the ERDF was waiting on the other side of the English Channel, in temporary accommodation, and they didn't want to wait any longer.

In the Ministry of Defence, red-eyed civil servants produced an assessment of the situation, slogging through the night to slake the incessant thirst for information.

How many soldiers were still on Windcheater Island, under the command of Major Hesketh?

How many officers and senior NCOs were involved?

How many weapons and how much ammunition did they have?

How long could they sustain themselves?

How long had they been planning this?

Finally, and most importantly, would the 65th have the audacity to fight back, in the event of an attempt to rescue the hostages?

The logisticians and accountants delved into MoD records on a vast auditing exercise to trace the activities of the 65th, while grim-faced people from Military Intelligence interrogated former soldiers of the regiment, who'd been arrested and brought to the basements of the Ministry of the Interior. The analysts collated the information and copied their interim report to the various departments. It painted a very bleak picture. The 65th, they suggested, had been planning this stunt for a long time and could occupy its base for many weeks, if not months.

The mood at the Cabinet meeting early next morning was defiant. From a media point of view, the whole affair would be kept very low-key – there were plenty of other initiatives that would make the headlines – although it was out of the question that the situation would be allowed to continue for any length of time. Negotiations would continue with Major Hesketh to reach a peaceful conclusion, but in these times when the State had a much firmer grip of the media, the use of military force to resolve the situation – a decision that in previous years would have made many elected ministers feel distinctly uncomfortable – was authorised with unanimous support. In their dreadlocked youth, these same people had always been the first to protest whenever the government of the day was considering any sort of military action, believing in all sincerity that any conflict could be resolved peacefully through the medium of contemporary dance and the sharing of herbal tea. The metal facial piercings and the red hair dye had long since given way to dark suits and front-page smiles, but under the veneer of respectability the spite and the overwhelming sense of righteousness was still there. As a radical student, the British President had once broken into a military base, sprayed a peace symbol on a tank and handed out flowers to soldiers as he was escorted away. Some thirty years later, he signed the agreement to use military force against his own soldiers without any hesitation at all.

However, the question of exactly *which* military force to deploy against the 65th proved rather more difficult to answer. The Chief of Defence Staff – the same Admiral who had spoken with Major Hesketh a day earlier – told the President, in his typically understated way, that it would be a little unwise to deploy British troops against fellow British troops, even if the 65th were renegades operating outside the chain of command. Privately, the President and his colleagues relished such a possibility of high farce, and the Admiral did not endear himself to the ministers when he went on to suggest that any British troops sent in would have a strong measure of sympathy with the 65th, raising the awful possibility that they might actually go over and join them. The President, so the Admiral explained in a moment that he enjoyed immensely, simply had to understand that soldiers were indeed loyal. But not to him.

By lunchtime, the Admiral had been sacked; the first casualty of the affair and perhaps the most inevitable, to be replaced by a sideways posting from the Interior Ministry. The new Chief of the Defence Staff was a mandarin who had never served in the military, and despite his new rank of Admiral of the Fleet, he would have barely recognised one end of a frigate from the other.

The military strategists went through all possible options. They already knew, like the sacked Admiral, that the rest of the British Army would be of very little use to them. The military were gradually being educated in the correct interpretation of the CODE, though it had yet to permeate through the stubborn rank structure to the required degree and, consequently, using the military in this delicate situation carried an unacceptable risk. There was one unit that might have been sent in; a particularly enlightened battalion that had undergone sufficient re-education, and the only one to date that had been passed by the CODE Inspectorate. But the unit was an Administration battalion, comprised mostly of desk-bound clerks. They would have been annihilated by the toughened combat soldiers of the 65th. Another possibility was to send in armed police in the form of the Special Firearms Group. But the SFG was a shadow of its former self, now seemingly only willing to ventilate innocent civilians. God forbid, the 65th might even fire back at them, and Health and Safety Law was frequently cited by any member of the Group who did not wish to be ordered into action against anyone who might actually return fire.

The solution was forced upon the government by an exasperated Brussels. If the British Army or the police were too spineless to do the job, then there were plenty of units in Europe that were far less squeamish. There was a new force available; adaptable, highly-trained, well-equipped, and manned with numerous individuals with a proven track record of indiscriminate slaughter wherever their political masters had sent them to keep the peace.

Though the 65th might think they were hardened soldiers, they would be no match for the professionalism and fighting spirit of this new force, and there was little doubt it could be deployed effectively against the 65th.

For the despairing British ministers it was a revelation, and the potential to exploit political capital out of the situation was considerable. They could now taste blood in the water, realising the hopelessness of the 65th's situation. Such a famous rout would forever symbolise the ascendancy of the new over the old, the *progressive* over the *anachroniste*, the triumph of the European project over the last vestiges of the Little Englander.

There were still minor details to be worked out, but Brussels finally gave the go-ahead for the European Rapid Deployment Force to be used to evict the illegal occupiers of Windcheater Island and rescue the hostages. And why not? It was supposed to be their base, after all.

TWENTY-EIGHT

Taverner made his way along Holberton High Street towards the Ship and Shovel. The muffled sound of live folk music came from behind its steamed-up windows. The Ship and Shovel was doing good business, even for a sultry summer's evening. Holberton was featuring in the news and its townsfolk were in high spirits now that the boys over on Windcheater Island had done the unthinkable and kidnapped the politicians. People were amazed that this sort of thing could happen in their backyard and they couldn't stop talking about it. Being unwilling to go back to their homes after the shops closed, they all congregated at the pub, filling it to the rafters with lively talk of insurrection and rebellion.

Taverner checked his watch. The meeting was scheduled for ten o'clock. Hannah would be landing in Miami about now. From the pub the music stopped, a drunken cheer went up and the singer said thank you before launching into the next song. Taverner pushed the door open and was hit by a solid wall of sound and acrid body odour. He threaded his way through the sweaty crowd, the size of which the folk band had never played to before, and squeezed past a few couples who were managing to dance in the confined space. A few kids, tipsy after mine-sweeping unattended pints, chased each other excitedly round the dancers' feet, and would no doubt be passing out before long.

Upstairs in the function room, his team was waiting for him. The air was cooler in the room and although the amplified thump of the bass drum shook the floor and made the old window frames rattle, they were able to converse normally. They sat around an old oak table with their beers.

'So, the cat's out the bag, then,' said Terry. 'They've finally gone and done it,'

Everyone murmured in support.

'Sad though,' he continued, 'they reckon it's all going to be over in a few days.'

'Yes, I hears that too,' said Billy. 'They was saying on the news, on the BBC Channel, that they reckon they is going to release the hostages in the next few days. Well, in my book, that's a cop-out. I was well looking forward to a bit more action, I was, me and the boys.'

Taverner raised his hand.

'Gentlemen, please don't believe what they're saying in the news,' he said. 'I can assure you that the 65th will not be releasing the hostages in the next few days, or any time in the next fortnight. They are in this for the long haul, and so are we. What you hear on the news is simply what the government wants us all to hear. Ignore it.'

Billy tamped some tobacco into his Briar. 'Okay, Boss. What do you want us to do?'

'The authorities will be looking to establish some sort of Incident Command Post or Mobile Headquarters in the next twenty-four hours,' said Taverner. 'It could be the police or the Army, even a combination of the two. In fact,

I shouldn't be surprised if they're setting it up somewhere in the town at this very moment. Where are your watchers, Billy?'

'Downstairs,' mumbled Billy, more concerned at that moment with lighting his pipe. He held the lighter flame to the tobacco, sucking on his pipe intermittently, looking like a beached fish on the verge of death. 'Fucking arseholed, too.'

'Well, arseholed or not, you might encourage them to have a quick sweep of the town before they stagger home, with some sober discretion,' said Taverner, 'and first thing tomorrow I want them pushed out along the North Devon Link Road, as far as the M5 motorway. I want to know in plenty of time what they are sending.'

'We'll get on it straight away, Boss, we is going to have the whole place covered,' said Billy.

'And this time they must come in unimpeded. I only want to know where they go.'

There was little else to discuss that evening and the group soon departed.

Next morning, two of Billy's watchers, stationed near the motorway junction at an immobile roadside café with grubby white plastic chairs, were nursing their hangovers with strong coffee and a hefty fry-up. In the still, morning air, they could hear the approaching convoy coming down the M5. They recognised the similar sort of vehicles they had petrol-bombed from the footbridge some days earlier. It was the ERDF again, this time with a substantial police escort. The convoy cleared the roundabout and accelerated past the watchers, heading west towards Holberton; the police outriders pushing on ahead of the convoy, clearing non-existent traffic from its path. The watchers reported up to Billy by phone, speaking in tortured code as they struggled to recall the phrases Billy had given them.

In Holberton the old industrial estate had been cordoned off during the night by the police, who stood guard at the end of the single access road onto the estate. The estate was in a cul–de–sac that backed onto houses on one side, and onto open fields on the other. The industrial estate was a sorry place where rust and weeds spread among the broken windows and graffitied brickwork of old workshops that had once housed successful businesses.

An hour after Billy's watchers had been on the phone from the lay-by, conspiratorially discussing pink squirrels and blue foxes and yellow badgers with a very confused Billy, the ERDF convoy arrived in Holberton and went straight to the industrial estate.

Taverner had been surfing a weakening swell at Saunton Sands. It was locally-generated and the confused peaks came from several directions, rearing up as if to break, then slowly backing off into nothing. The rising tide did little to improve the situation and an annoying onshore wind further ruined what little swell there was. Mother Nature was not up for it today.

In the car park, he found Billy waiting for him. Billy was very excited.

'They're 'ere, Boss! They's gone to the industrial estate!'

'Who?'

''Bout ten vehicles in all.'

'Who?'

'They got 'ere 'bout 'alf 'our ago.'

'Who?'

'Shifty-looking bastards if you ask me, Boss, right shifty they is.'

Taverner waited a moment before asking again quietly. 'Billy, Billy. Who?'

'Who? Oh, fuck knows.'

'That's bloody marvellous. Police? Army?'

'Oh, easy. Army, yes.'

'British?'

'No. They was the same vehicles what we threw the petrol bombs at, only this time they had a load of police on motorbikes with them as well.'

'Ten vehicles, you say. And they've gone to the industrial estate? Well, it's hardly the cavalry. I guess they're just here to have a look round.'

Taverner got out of his wetsuit and put on some dry clothes.

'We need to find a good vantage point overlooking the industrial estate. Those houses in Manley Road that back onto it – we can get a good look from there. Do you know anyone who lives there?'

'Manley Road?' said Billy, sucking thoughtfully on an upper molar. 'Let me see now. Manley Road … Manley Road … Yes, I knows just the place, Boss.'

The view from the small window in the attic was perfect. Billy had chosen well. Taverner had an uninterrupted view of the industrial estate and the officers and soldiers of the ERDF Advance Party. Peering through his binoculars, Taverner examined their uniforms and noted their badge of a yellow eagle on a red background, worn high on the right arm. The same insignia was painted on the sides of their Belgian-registered vehicles. It was the badge of the ERDF with a motto beneath, and although

Taverner couldn't read it at that range, he knew what it would say.

Terra, Mare et Aura

Land, Sea and Air.

'That's definitely the European Rapid Deployment Force,' said Taverner.

'Who are they?' asked Billy.

'They're the unit who were due to occupy Windcheater Island last week after the 65th had left. Here, take a look. No, other way round.'

Taverner was privately elated. Several months earlier, he, Major Hesketh and the Camp Quartermaster had foreseen that a British regiment would never have gone into action against other British soldiers, and that the police were too spineless to intevene. The ERDF was the most likely choice for this operation and it would be the perfect opportunity to baptise it publicly. Hostage-recovery was even one of the Force's stated specialities.

'Pardon me, Boss, but there aint many of the buggers,' said Billy. 'Are they like specialists or something? Crack troops, maybe?'

'No. They're probably just the Advance Party, just checking out the area.'

He took back the binoculars from Billy. A few officers swaggered around looking important and pointing at things, while the soldiers busied themselves setting up radio antennae.

Two floors below the attic, the elderly owner of the house dusted off her fine bone china and brewed up a large pot of tea for her guests. Taverner had recognised her when she'd answered her front door – she was Elsie, the lady who played the organ in the chapel on Windcheater Island. In his scruffy state, she didn't recognise him, although she seemed to know Billy well. In fact, she seemed somewhat indebted to him.

'The old girl downstairs,' said Taverner, 'I take it you know her?'

'Elsie? You don't say,' said Billy. 'Someone nearly diddled with her a few years back. They was going to diddle with her right bad, they was.' He left the words hanging in the air as if he expected Taverner to understand fully.

'Diddled right bad?' repeated Taverner, wondering where this conversation was going.

'Oh yes, and they was going to diddle with quite a few other old people in the town. 'Course, I was never not going to have no-one diddling with my Elsie, I was. No way. She was very grateful for that. She's old. All their functions go when they're that age. Why, she don't even know that she's being diddled with.'

'Good God, there are some sick people out there,' said Taverner, appalled at the thought that anyone might want to diddle with an elderly, arthritic widow.

'Yes, I agree, Boss, definitely I reckon. 'Course, they go for old folk, they like 'em, don't they. All innocent and that, aren't they. Trusting, like. So anyway, this diddler what comes round 'few years back, diddles with Elsie right bad, then, I mean would you believe it, you never guess who he tries to diddle with next?'

'No idea.'

'The old man.'

'The old man?' said Taverner, bewildered.

'Yes, my old man, God rest his soul, for he never would have hurt no-one or nothing, not when it weren't absolutely necessary. He goes to diddle him and you'll never guess what he tries to get his dirty hands on?'

'No idea.'

'The family jewels.'

'Jesus Christ.'

'Wanted to leave a deposit, too,' said Billy. 'Filthy fucker, eh? Nearly went all the way, too. And they're so charming when they come. I mean, my old man was into his eighties. He couldn't see fuck all. He had that eye disease what old people get. Immaculate Conception.'

'There's no accounting for taste,' said Taverner, who thought that failing sight might be something of a relief if one was being interfered with to such an extent.

'Exactly,' said Billy. 'He nearly diddled them out of their homes too, would you believe. I reckon they can't see what they's signing, you know, reading the small print, like. All their life savings and everything.'

The penny teetered on the edge for a moment, then finally dropped.

'Diddlers?' said Taverner. 'You mean con-artists and confidence tricksters.'

'Yes, that's right, Boss, diddlers. Tried to diddle them out of their homes, out of their life savings, out of their pensions. Everything. 'Course, when I found out I went nuts. Tore up the diddler's paperwork and put him in hospital.'

Taverner was genuinely relieved.

'You know, when you said "diddling" with old people, I thought you meant some sort of sexual interfering.'

'Good God, no! Not that, although now I come to think of it there was this bloke 'few years back what ...'

'Stop. That's way too much, Billy. Stop right now.'

'Course. Say, sounds like tea's up, Boss!'

Elsie brought the tea up to her guests; the bone china rattling on the tray as she made her way precariously up the narrow stairs. She called up to the attic. Billy and Taverner dusted themselves off and headed down the ladder. Over the Earl Grey and the Custard Creams, Billy asked her if he could put some trusted friends in the attic for a few days. They would, of course, make themselves scarce. Elsie couldn't have been more willing. She knew something strange was going on in the town and it would be nice for her to have to the company. When Billy and Taverner left, she started spring-cleaning her house in readiness for her visitors.

After leaving Elsie's house, Taverner returned to the beach where the surf had now died off, leaving a confused, wind-blown mess. He had not come back here to surf. From a compartment in the side of the Land Rover he took out his rucksack, hefted it onto his shoulders and headed south along the beach. After a mile he climbed into the sand dunes and lay down in a spiky clump of grass; the fronds swaying in the wind and pricking his skin. Gusts of wind blew sand in his face and he had to shield his eyes. In the distance to the east, he could see Windcheater Island with its new buildings. He could pick out the garages, the Quartermaster's Store and Regimental Headquarters, and standing alone on the eastern side of the Island was the red-brick Edwardian splendour of the Officers' Mess. The island looked idyllic. One would never have guessed that a major international incident was unfolding there. Taverner waited for fifteen minutes, and when he was absolutely certain he was alone he unpacked the radio equipment.

When one transmitted by radio it was presumed there were always three parties involved. The sender and the receiver, obviously, and if one was in a military environment, the enemy as well – listening in to the same frequency and learning about the sort of things the sender and receiver should have been keeping between themselves.

There were ways of ensuring the enemy was unable to intercept radio messages. An encryption device, for example, scrambled a clear message into an unintelligible screech across the airwaves, and only those issued with the appropriate encoding and decoding devices were able to communicate with each other.

In the past, such secure communications were the preserve of high-level formations such as divisions and brigades, though gradual miniaturisation enabled the grunts on the ground to communicate in the same way. But the gruntification of such fragile equipment for the environment of battle was an unreliable process and soldiers knew not to depend on it, and practised transmitting in clear.

The basics of radio security on an insecure net were drummed into everyone. No individuals or units were referred to by name – all had a designated callsign. 'Delta One Zero' might have been a Section of eight soldiers, or an Armoured Division of twenty-two thousand. Grid references were never given in clear, nor was there any mention of future intentions. Codewords were frequently used. In addition, no-one transmitted for more than twenty seconds at a time; it was always wise to assume the enemy had direction-finding equipment, and a continuous transmission would give them enough time to triangulate on the source and plot its precise location, which could then be passed to the artillery.

It was possible to encode messages on an insecure radio net. The system was called Battle Code – BATCO for short. All radio operators were issued with a series of BATCO sheets, each one valid for a twelve-hour period. Locations, units, numbers, intentions, orders and timings were all converted to a series of two-letter codes, which could also be heard by the enemy, who remained ignorant, not having a copy of the relevant sheet.

BATCO sheets for the whole Army were centrally-generated and distributed, but in preparation for this operation the 65th had spent many hours laboriously making its own. Taverner had his own set of sheets and he hoped that the duplicate was at that moment next to a signaller in the 65th's Ops Room on Windcheater Island. He encoded his message, jotted down the letters and double-checked them. When he was ready, he put together the old PRC-351 radio, connected the battery and tuned it to the correct frequency. With a range of six kilometres, it would easily reach the Ops Room of the 65th.

Press, pause, then speak.

'Hello Zero, this is Romeo One Zero. Radio Check. Over.'

He waited.

Nothing.

He repeated the message again.

Still nothing.

He was about to transmit again, when he got a reply.

'Zero. Okay. Over.'

It was the first contact he'd had with the 65th since the operation had started.

He went through the Authentication Procedure, satisfying himself that the person at the other end was genuinely reading from the same BATCO sheet, and he then transmitted his message in short bursts. There was a long pause while the receiving signaller decoded it.

'Message received. Over.'
'Roger. Out'
There was no need for any clarification.

TWENTY-NINE

Taverner spent the next few days hidden away with the watchers in Elsie's attic. Each day, another convoy of vehicles arrived and ERDF Headquarters started to take shape, but from what Taverner could see, there were still no proper combat troops, yet.

Every night he met his team in the pub, and afterwards, if it was necessary, he would send an update by radio to the 65th.

Occasionally, small helicopters flew in and landed in the industrial estate, dispensing senior officers and their entourages. One tried to fly low over Windcheater Island, leading to the first exchange of gunfire, when a machine gun stationed on top of the NAAFI opened fire. The tracer rounds were fired wide deliberately, but it was enough to deter any more probing reconnaissance flights, and helicopters subsequently approached from the safety of the north.

The Press descended on Holberton. The few hotels in the town were quickly booked out, although most of the news organisations were camped out together; their huge array of satellite dishes on their Winnebagos rivalling those of the ERDF. The BBC, in their capacity as the mouthpiece of the government, had set up alongside the ERDF in the industrial estate. The story was featuring in the news, but not yet making the headlines, and would only do so when the government wanted it to. The Press was gearing itself up for that moment.

A new Force Commander of the ERDF had to be appointed as a result of Colonel Sandford's detention, and by the time Headquarters was up and running to his satisfaction, there were about two-hundred soldiers of various nationalities present. Since the Federal British Republic was a fully-integrated member of the European Union, there had to be Brits on the ERDF staff. However, the traditional British officer-class was not liked by the European military hierarchy, who thought them insular and xenophobic. Their tendency to ride roughshod over the intricate rules and restrictions of European military doctrine had not endeared them to their political bosses. In this respect, Colonel Sandford was to have been a much-needed breath of fresh air. Nonetheless, the pan-European credentials of the ERDF still had to be adhered to, so a nominal group of six junior British soldiers had been posted in to do a number of very unimportant jobs at Headquarters. Of the six soldiers, five were present, but one was still missing; Private Morton, from the National Regiment of Signals (formerly the Royal Corps of Signals) who had not yet reported for duty and was therefore Absent Without Leave. Private Morton was a Territorial Army soldier – a part-timer – who was supposed to be taking a sabbatical from his civilian job for six months, when he would be attached to ERDF Headquarters. Enquiries would be made in due course as to his whereabouts, but there were far more pressing matters for the ERDF to deal with at that moment. The job that Morton had been allocated was not exactly mission-critical.

With his Land Rover parked innocuously on a quiet street, his surfboards stored in the Halls' garage and the radio equipment put away in a hide nearby, Taverner had one final meeting with his team, where he left very clear instructions. It was time to enter the next phase.

Taverner, like so many ex-soldiers, had never felt entirely comfortable with his recent beard and long straggly hair. It went against the grain of the indoctrination of Basic Training. After his team had dispersed, Billy's wife, who ran the *Cutie Cuts* hair-dressing salon on the High Street, cut off Taverner's long blond locks and ran a number-two clipper over his scalp. A wet shave completed the transformation.

Negotiations between the 65th and the authorities continued, with very little progress. The government's Chief Negotiator; an infuriatingly patronising woman, had first asked for the release of Dr Müller, in view of his intermittent heart problem. Then, Mr MacDonald's wife had apparently collapsed on being told of his kidnap, and the 65th were invited to make a 'humanitarian gesture'. When that fell on deaf ears, the negotiator assured Major Hesketh that the government would pledge funds for a long-term apprenticeship for any soldier of the 65th. She even mentioned the possibility that former soldiers of the 65th could remain in the military and transfer to the ERDF.

It was all very lame, and Major Hesketh was polite but adamant that all her proposals were unacceptable. He could see they were just playing for time.

Things were stirred up a bit when Hesketh had photographs of the hostages looking haggard and unshaven posted on the 65th's own website. They were also sent directly to the BBC and the major newspapers, but no-one broadcast or printed the images, although there were over twenty-thousand hits on the 65th's website before it was suddenly closed down without warning.

Private Morton, the missing soldier, eventually reported to the ERDF for duty. The policeman manning the checkpoint by the industrial estate inadvertently tried to turn him away, but the soldier was most persistent. An Administration officer from the ERDF, a young French Captain, came down to the police checkpoint and scanned through his paperwork, which correctly identified him as Private Morton, a thirty-four year old part-time soldier from 328 (Volunteer) Signals Squadron, based just outside Poole. His Posting Order confirmed he had been sent to the ERDF on a six-month attachment. Morton explained to the Captain that, although the ERDF was not yet established on Windcheater Island, he felt he should report for duty wherever it was located, though he had hesitated because of the situation.

The Captain thought there was something rather strange about the soldier. Although Morton seemed a little bit slow – he might even have been a little bit simple – his piercing blue eyes made the Captain feel distinctly unsettled. Morton was quite old to still be a Private and should have been at least a Sergeant by his age, but the Captain reminded himself that the soldier was only a part-timer. After all, Territorial volunteers were quite content to stay in the same job at the same rank, weekend in – weekend out.

Morton was escorted to the Administration Cell where the clerks were able to confirm his posting, and poor Morton's face flushed red with shame as he incurred the wrath of a particularly foul-breathed female Sergeant of indeterminate nationality, who tore into him for turning up five days late. The Sergeant was not easy on the eye, being over-generous of saddle, greasy of complexion and cursed with a face like a bag of angry worms. She carried out some more checks – his car details matched those of the Vehicle and Licensing Records Office in Stuttgart, and his Army Identity Card was registered. An impatient Corporal in charge of the accommodation led him away and pointed out the important locations – cookhouse, washhouse and shithouse – and showed him to his bed space, with instructions to report next morning at eight o'clock.

As a lowly Private, Morton was not expecting luxury and he was not disappointed. He was in a long room with about forty other soldiers, with a canvas cot for his bed, onto which he unravelled his sleeping bag and a travel pillow. He took out his wash kit and towel, placed them neatly under his cot with his Bergan and several holdalls, and then went to get a cup of tea.

Before he retired for the night, Morton had a look round ERDF Headquarters. Several days' effort from the engineers had turned one of the deserted buildings into an impressive Operations Room, bristling with radios, speakers, large television screens and a huge electronic map. From there, the Ops Room could control operations out on the ground, and speak to London, Brussels, and a host of intergovernmental agencies. As well as military staff, there were about half as many Public Relations staff, cutting about with far too much confidence in what was supposed to be a very military environment. They appeared to be much busier too; briefing, counter-briefing, always on the go, speaking into their phones or into their microphones, wonderfully adept at holding three or more conversations at once.

Two canteen areas had been fitted out; one for the officers and civilians, and one for the lower ranks. A number of elderly citizens had been recruited from Holberton on weekly contracts to clean the tables, wash the dishes and run the launderette. They were paid a pittance, but they were grateful for any extra cash. A local plumbing firm had reconnected the clean water supply to the industrial estate and fixed some temporary boilers for hot water.

Private Morton had a restless night, interrupted by soldiers going on or coming off duty and by the constant hum of the generators outside. In the morning he rose in good time, showered and shaved, and took a leisurely breakfast. Outside, the sky was a cloudless blue. It was shaping up to be a very hot day and the air conditioning in the Ops Room was already working its magic. A short interview with an officer established the fact that Private Morton was not a particularly versatile soldier; about the only thing he could do was operate a radio. But that was his job, and had been his job for ten years as a signaller in the Territorials, and that was what he had been posted to the ERDF to do. He was assigned to the Logistics Cell located in a corner of the Ops Room. There was little military input required from Private Morton. He was not required to know anything about logistics or tactics or strategy, nor was he required to make any decisions. All he had to do was to pass on or receive messages on the radio, and log the time and content of each transmission – a legal requirement in case of any comeback on incidents, to back up the audio records that were made automatically. Morton's shift would run from eight o'clock to four in the afternoon, and he started straight away.

The Logistics radio net was very quiet. There were a few callsigns out on the ground (being quietly followed at that moment by Taverner's team), but it was a terribly dull way to pass the time. At half past eleven, most staff dispersed for lunch, though Private Morton was not allowed to leave his radio until his shift ended.

Around midday, a small problem developed with Morton's radio and it was apparent to the other signallers in the room that he had lost all contact. A little tinkering with the dials and switches sorted the problem out, and he transmitted a quick burst of messages, no doubt to re-establish contact with the callsigns.

THIRTY

It was a week since the 65th had deployed into the trenches.

Gunner Moffat aimed his rifle over the parapet of his trench with the others, as the sun set behind them. They were 'stood-to', as was everyone else in the 65th at that moment; a procedure carried out in the British Army at dawn and dusk since time immemorial. Only an enemy who wished instantly to attract the entire firepower of a regiment would be foolhardy enough to attack the British at those times of the day. The trenches were well camouflaged and very little movement took place in and around them. At night, the soldiers were careful not to expose any torchlight or naked flames above the parapet; even a cigarette end could be seen over a mile away, in the right conditions.

The soldiers in Moffat's trench were silent during stand-to. The mosquitoes descended in their droves and Moffat regretted that he had forgotten, yet again, to spray himself beforehand with insect repellent. He did not slap his face or his hands as he felt them land, he merely brushed them off slowly. A real enemy was out there somewhere and he did not wish to attract any attention by sudden movement.

Bombardier Podsnap manned the radio. When he received the order, they stood-down and went into their night-time routine.

Gunner Jones was left on 'stag' – sentry duty – and kept his rifle pointing out over the water, while the other three crouched down out of sight. Moffat was cooking tonight and he took out the hexamine burner from his webbing. He folded it out, broke off some chunks of hexamine fuel and lit them with a cigarette lighter. As the flames built up, Moffat half-filled a mess tin with water and placed it on top on the stove. He took out a box of Compo rations. Each box contained enough calories to sustain a soldier in the field for twenty-four hours.

The other soldiers in the trench handed their foil bags containing their meals to Moffat, who placed the first two into the boiling water on the stove. NATO-standard coffee (white, two sugars please) followed the main course, made with the hot water left in the mess tin, and the brew was passed round.

No-one ever made a drink just for himself, or drank more than their fair share. No-one ever kept a chocolate bar from their rations entirely to themselves – you always shared it with your mates. And the more senior your rank, the later you ate, after everyone else had eaten. Through these little conventions, a high level of trust built up in the whole regiment; a cohesion that had served the 65th in the past and would continue to do so in the difficult times that lay ahead.

There was little to do once everyone had finished eating. Moffat was not on stag for another two hours, and with his recent meal repeating on him he manoeuvred into his sleeping bag and fell into a light sleep, thus ending another day as unexciting as all the previous days since they had deployed.

Next day, Major Hesketh summoned the 65th's hierarchy to the Operations Room for a brief, where he updated them in great detail on the preparations of the ERDF. Some of his commanders expressed their concerns about the morale of the troops; they had now been in the field for a week, and with the exception of scaring off the low-flying helicopter, nothing had happened and boredom was setting in.

'Gentleman, it would seem the ERDF is now up and running.' said Hesketh, wrapping up the brief. 'Their Headquarters is set up and functioning, but they are not yet in a position to take any action against us. However, whatever it is they're going to do I believe we'll find out in the next few days. See that the boys have a twelve-hour break back in their accommodation so they can get cleaned up and grab some proper sleep. They are still on one hour's Notice to Move.'

As they departed, one of the Battery Commanders spoke to Hesketh.

'You seem to know an awful lot about the ERDF. If you don't mind me asking, how much of it is fact, and how much is sheer fantasy and supposition?'

Hesketh smiled. 'Oh, it's all fact. How shall I say this?' Hesketh pondered for a while. 'Their communications are far from secure. It's amazing what they are willing to discuss openly on their radio nets. They must really take us for fools if they think we're not listening in to them.'

For the sake of security, Hesketh could not tell the whole truth. Only he, the Quartermaster, and two utterly trustworthy signallers knew that, however talented Private Morton was with a radio, he was proving to be a most indiscreet signaller in ERDF Headquarters.

Private Morton, the short, overweight thirty-four year

old; the supervisor in a Bournemouth superstore, who was, at that very moment, trying to explain to his sceptical fellow workers at the superstore that the sudden cancellation of his six-month posting to the European Rapid Deployment Force was due to 'ultra-top secret classified reasons'. In truth, the letter he'd received cancelling his posting to the ERDF had given no explanation, other than to say he was simply no longer needed. He did not know the letter was a fake. Morton had been looking forward to his six-month attachment to the ERDF and, on learning of its cancellation, had consoled himself with a curry followed by a heavy session in his local pub, adding a few more pounds to his already-ample girth. A far cry from the tall, athletic, blond Private Morton who currently manned the radio in the ERDF's Logistics Cell. The Private Morton with the impeccably-forged paperwork and piercing blue eyes that had unsettled the French Captain on his arrival.

The soldiers in Bombardier Podsnap's trench welcomed the news that they were to be granted twelve hours rest. When they had deployed a week earlier, they had been promised some decent action and the chance, as Second Lieutenant Cavendish had so eloquently put it, to give the enemy a 'damn good biffing', yet in all that time nothing had happened and they were now pissed off, filthy dirty, and worn down by the mindless routine of the trench. They stagged-on, played cards, slept, stagged-on again, ticked and whinged, brewed-up, tried to get comfortable, and stagged-on again. All of them smoked continuously, as if it were a reflex action, like breathing, that they weren't aware of. Their joints ached from the contortions and lack of movement forced upon them in the narrow trench.

Moffat's pornography lay strewn around the trench; the pouting glamour forgotten and trodden into the earth. With so little to do, there was plenty of time for sleep, but it was a double edged-sword; too much sleep was a good thing, for which any soldier was grateful, but *way* too much sleep worked against them, making them even more tired and lethargic. They were in a state of limbo, not really fully awake, and sleeping far too lightly when they nodded off.

Curious behaviour had started to creep into the trench as the days had progressed. They took to bird-spotting, meticulously ticking off each species in a book that Gunner Holland had brought along. Gunner Jones, when he was not on stag, took his rifle apart and polished every single part, every inaccessible port, every square millimetre obsessively, way beyond the standard required to maintain it in good working order.

For their twelve hours off, they were relieved by some administrative staff who were grateful for the chance to pick up a rifle again and get out in the open air. The four replacements also smelt distinctly fresher than the four they were replacing.

Back in the accommodation, Moffat and the others threw their clothes into the washing machine and took long, hot showers, grateful for the chance to feel human again. The effect that some soap, new razor blades and clean towels had on restoring their morale was astonishing.

Of course, the twelve-hour break was too good to be true. Less than an hour after they had gone back to their rooms, they got a 'fastball' and everyone had to deploy immediately back out to the trenches. Within ten minutes they were back in their hole in the ground, decidedly fresher, but complaining more loudly than ever; Moffat loudest of all, uncomfortable with his still-soapy arse-crack. Their clothes had to be taken straight from the washing machine and were still soaking wet. No-one could tell them why they had deployed so suddenly.

Taverner could have kicked himself. Just before one o'clock in the morning he was woken by the hiss of hydraulic brakes, and got up to have a look. Three large articulated flatbed trucks with European number plates were being directed into parking spaces. The tarpaulin covers covering their cargo were removed, revealing the weapons that the ERDF was going to send in against the 65th.

There were six of them. Large, six-wheeled, riot control vehicles known as Civilian Administration Vehicles, or CAVs, which had been used to lethal effect all over Europe. Their commanders and crews had arrived separately by coach.

An awful thought occurred to Taverner. There was a possibility that the ERDF might deploy the CAVs immediately against the 65th, taking advantage of the darkness to launch a snap attack. He needed to warn Major Hesketh straight away. Contacting the 65th from the ERDF Ops Room was out of the question at that moment, so he slipped unseen out the back of the industrial estate. A permanent-patrol around the cordon of the estate was unlikely to run into Taverner, since the patrollers were all drinking coffee in the cookhouse.

In the darkness, he crossed two overgrown fields, keeping to the border where his movement would attract less attention, and came to the corner of a large wood. He proceeded along its edge until he came to a large bush with a small opening, where he slipped inside the wood.

He made slow progress, treading slowly with pointed feet, feeling for the ground so he didn't snap any twigs, and reached a broken elm tree and sat beside it. He took in the smell of earth and vegetation, and occasionally heard the sound of a small woodland creature scampering about in fallen leaves. He waited for his night-vision to optimise. Satisfied that he had not been followed and that no-one was lying in wait, Taverner brushed aside some leaves to reveal a small hide, in which he had previously hidden the radio before infiltrating the ERDF. He carried the radio to a lone copse a few fields away and set it up underneath a poncho, to prevent his torchlight from being seen as he encoded his message and sent it to the 65th.

With his radio safely back in the hide, he was back on his cot in ERDF Headquarters an hour later.

Taverner's fear that the CAVs would be deployed immediately was unfounded. Next morning, as he made his way to the cookhouse, the vehicles were still in the yard being worked on by mechanics. After breakfast, he relieved the off-going signaller on the Logistics radio. Everyone in the Ops Room seemed to be gearing themselves up for something, and he listened with interest to the briefings and conversations going on around him. The CAVs, he learnt, belonged to the Low Countries Battalion of the European Gendarmerie and had been attached to the ERDF for this operation. The ERDF had some intelligence on Windcheater Island and the 65th, but Taverner was pleased to hear that it was not up-to-date. They were going to find out the hard way just how wrong they were.

Just before midday, the Force Commander formally announced to everyone what they had suspected. The offensive operation to rescue the hostages and secure Windcheater Island, he said, would commence at one o'clock that afternoon.

Quietly, Taverner was able to put together a message to this effect, which he then transmitted unnoticed to the 65th from his radio.

THIRTY-ONE

Lieutenant Kiek van Dijk strode confidently out of ERDF Headquarters, securing his helmet as he walked. As commander of the Civilian Administration Platoon of the Low Countries Battalion, he had been given the task of leading the assault-and-rescue mission on Windcheater Island. '*Civilian Administration*' was a comforting euphemism for the unpleasant business of Riot Control, and his six Civilian Administration Vehicles were lined up and waiting on the road outside Headquarters.

The ERDF's Intelligence staff knew that the hostages were being held in the Officers' Mess at the far end of the Island, and once he had penetrated into the base, Lieutenant van Dijk's primary task was to make straight for the Mess and allow his highly-trained snatch squads to recover the hostages to the safety of the CAVs.

His crews had been thoroughly briefed and there were no last-minute changes to the plan. The enemy – the 65th – numbered no more than one-hundred soldiers, equipped with antiquated SA-80 rifles and a few machine guns. They were widely dispersed around the island and concentrated at vulnerable points. Although the 65th's posture and rhetoric had been aggressive, the ERDF

Intelligence staff did not expect them to put up much resistance. They were probably worn down by the lack of action over the past ten days and, now that they had made their point, they were probably looking to surrender. The CAVs were the perfect means to persuade them that such action was in their best interests.

There had also been mandatory briefings from the Legal officers on the Rules of Engagement for this operation, with specific reference to the European Human Rights Act and how it applied to the renegades of the 65th. Their conclusion was perfectly clear. *Get it wrong and we'll hang you out to dry.* Nobody wanted a wounded British squaddie causing trouble in Strasbourg.

Lieutenant van Dijk made three circles with his pointed-up finger, and his soldiers stubbed out their cigarettes and climbed aboard the vehicles. The CAV was a big, heavy, dark, frightening triumph of function over form. It carried a crew of ten soldiers, protected by eight millimetres of armour plating, with six wheels, four-thousand volts of electricity on its outer skin and two water cannon. And one toilet – chemical – just in case they were there for any length of time, or their nerves got the better of them. Primarily, the CAV was a riot control vehicle, but with its ability to plough through immense barricades and withstand tremendous punishment while protecting those inside, it was capable of far more than simply dispersing an agitated crowd of protestors or drunken soccer hooligans. It was the nearest thing to a tank on wheels, and it would take nothing less than some sort of anti-tank weapon to stop it.

Once inside the CAVs, the soldiers pulled down the louvres over the windows and sealed themselves in. When the order was given, the CAVs lurched forward unsteadily out of the industrial estate. Their modified exhausts made them sound like a herd of predators – mildly-wounded predators, and even more threatening for it.

The media prepared themselves for the operation. Though the siege of Windcheater Island had still not featured prominently in the national media, today would be very different. This was going to be a historic occasion. Not only was it a chance to show off the new European Rapid Deployment Force, it would also be the first time since 1066 that foreign ground troops would be going into action against a British force on British soil. Perhaps it would finally convince the heretics and non-believers that England really was no more, and that everyone was now European.

The recapture of Windcheater Island would be broadcast over and over again. Medals and promotion awaited the CAV crews for their courage and daring rescue. The reporters would broadcast their breathless despatches to a nation transfixed, and with luck might even find themselves rewarded with a foreign correspondency or an anchor spot.

There were many in the media who wanted to exploit the build-up to the assault more than they were allowed to. It was like an old tower block about to be demolished; the build-up – so deliciously agonising, the endless parade of experts and bores, the sudden graphic violence, the destruction of a relic and the start of a new future, the advertisers falling over themselves to buy airtime, and the revenue rolling in. The ERDF, however, stressing the need for surprise, told them otherwise. After all, it was enough that they had caved into the Public Relations officers' demand to mount the attack in broad daylight. The assault would be broadcast live, in the manner of the Prince's Gate Siege in 1980, when the SAS stormed the Iranian Embassy in London.

At ERDF Headquarters, all work stopped as attention turned to the large television screen in the Ops Room. The BBC had interrupted a programme to go live to Holberton with a News Flash, and the radio messages from the CAVs were played out over the speakers for everyone to hear.

The soldiers at the 65th's Sentry Post were waiting in their trenches, having donned their respirators.

In the Ops Room, Major Hesketh stirred two sugars into his tea. It was nearly one o'clock and he had raised the alert state ten minutes earlier. The tension in the Ops Room mounted. Hesketh appeared calm and unflappable. A television had been switched on and the soporific chat show was interrupted with the News Flash. The speakers broadcast the radio message from the Sentry Post.

'Mike Two Three Bravo, three CAVs breaking cover in this direction, distance one-thousand metres, wrong, five CAVs, wrong, six, I say again, six CAVs inbound at speed. Wait out.'

The casual tone of the radio operator at the Sentry Post contrasted with the excited commentary that now came from the television. A young BBC correspondent was reporting live, with Windcheater Island clearly visible in the background.

'It looks as though the siege here on Windcheater Island will soon be over,' she shouted, as the six CAVs screamed past her. 'Just over a week ago, a group of renegade soldiers, seeking to protest about the government's policy of re-settlement for former military personnel, kidnapped Dr Ulrich Müller, the European Defence Minister and the British Defence Minister, Geoff MacDonald, and have repeatedly threatened to kill them.

There has been no word about their bodyguards and it is believed they have been tortured. The politicians were visiting the base for a ceremonial function, and for security reasons we have been unable to …'

Major Hesketh turned down the volume and picked up the radio handset. 'Quebec One Zero, this is Zero Alpha. Move now. Over.'

'Quebec One Zero. Roger. Out.'

Quebec One Zero was the callsign for the Quartermaster's Store. The store was about two-hundred metres behind the Sentry Post, just beyond a straight section of road. The store's up-and-over doors were opened to reveal a direct line of sight down the road to the Sentry Post. Inside, the Quartermaster's storemen checked the sights on their equipment.

The convoy of CAVs made a terrifying, high-pitched wail as they screamed down the road towards the Sentry Post. Lieutenant van Dijk was in the lead vehicle, peering through the periscope. He updated his soldiers every few seconds on what he could see; in the back, they could see nothing. As he had been briefed, the road ahead had dykes on either side, and he would be channelled over the bridge and through the Sentry Post. The barricade was a bit amateurish; made from old cars, oil drums and razor wire, and would not present any obstacle to the CAVs. He could not see the enemy soldiers who usually manned the Sentry Post and hoped that he had caught them off-guard, or perhaps they had panicked and run.

Major Hesketh picked up the radio again, watching the live television broadcast.

'All stations, this is Zero Alpha. Clear to go to weapons live. Fire when ready. Out.'

The tension in the Ops Room was close to breaking point. The signallers had mates down at the Sentry Post and any moment now the bullets would start to fly. People were hardly breathing.

Hesketh sipped his tea and waited. With the order now given, there was nothing more he could do. The live news broadcast showed the six CAVs disappearing rapidly into the distance. The Sentry Post updated the Ops Room as they closed in.

'Mike Two Three Bravo, range now five-hundred metres, four-hundred, three-hundred ...'

The leading CAV was about two-hundred metres from the Sentry Post, and Lieutenant van Dijk ordered his driver to accelerate. Suddenly, all hell broke loose. A burst of rifle fire came from up ahead and the noise of the rounds pinging off the armour plating was deafening. Looking towards the Sentry Post, Lieutenant van Dijk could see the helmets of the enemy soldiers poking up from the fire trenches and the gouts of flame from the barrels of their rifles. And although his vehicle was armoured, he wondered how much punishment it could stand, and prayed, as he headed into the maelstrom, that the manufacturers had done their job properly. There was a massive explosion outside.

'Sir?' shouted the driver, above the cacophony.

'Keep going, keep going!' said Lieutenant van Dijk. The rifle fire was simply a nuisance. He looked beyond the barricade to a large building with its garage doors open, and saw a small puff of smoke from inside.

It was the last thing he ever saw.

The lead CAV burst into flame and continued in a perfectly straight line, before rolling to a halt as the fire reached the fuel tank, causing an even bigger secondary explosion.

'Got the bugger!' said the Quartermaster. He sat in a deck chair with an old pair of binoculars, next to the German 88mm anti-tank gun that his storemen were reloading. The second round had found its target. The crack of the 88mm gun reverberated around the whole area, and from inside the Quartermaster's store the sound was truly apocalyptic. All the windows had shattered at the first firing, and a storemen who had refused to wear ear protection was now out of action, staggering around clutching his bleeding ears.

The second CAV in the convoy crashed into the first and stayed tucked up behind it. Though the lead vehicle was burning fiercely, it seemed to offer a degree of protection from the onslaught coming from the Sentry Post.

The third CAV was far more courageous. At high speed it veered round the first two; the driver clearly fighting to prevent the heavy vehicle from fish-tailing. The vehicle commander fired off CS gas grenades in a wide arc towards the Sentry Post. It was no use. The soldiers in the trenches were protected by their respirators.

The 88mm gun picked off the CAV with ease. The shell penetrated through the front armour, and the overpressure inside the vehicle caused a rapid expulsion of smoke from every orifice. The vehicle swerved drunkenly, the flames erupted and were quickly quenched when the vehicle slewed off the road into the dyke, where it sank.

The Quartermaster was in his element, issuing loud and unnecessary instructions to his storemen.

'Left a bit, left a bit ... good shot! Now, watch the bugger coming up from behind ... cheeky sod!'

His storemen ignored him.

The fourth CAV was indecisive. It veered round the burning wreckage and simply stopped on the road and froze, like a rabbit caught in the headlights, seeming to sense what was about to happen. It too went up in a fireball.

The final two CAVs, on seeing the destruction ahead of them, simply turned round and took off at high speed from where they came.

The Sentry Post reported in to the Ops Room.

'Four CAVs destroyed. Two withdrawn out of sight. Out.'

On hearing this, Major Hesketh called for ceasefire.

There were no casualties on the British side, save for the storeman with perforated eardrums. The barricade was still intact. The doors were quickly closed on the Quartermaster's Store and the 88mm gun was left to cool down.

It had taken less than a minute to repel the ERDF.

On the television, the BBC News Flash continued. The camera was some distance away from the Sentry Post and it was difficult to equate the broadcast with the radio messages received in the Ops room.

The reporter kept up a continuous stream of excited ineptitude. 'An incredible amount of noise as the attack goes in,' she said. 'The soldiers of the European Rapid Deployment Force are trained to use the maximum amount of firepower to achieve their mission. I can hear the sound of a lot of firing ... a lot of gunfire ... we can't tell where it is coming from ... oh my goodness, a *huge* explosion, a, er, big ball of flame, it looks like it came from the entrance to the base, where the fugitives have barricaded themselves in ... the Army authorities have told us this would involve minimum firepower and minimum collateral damage, but they are trained to use whatever is necessary, even maximum firepower to minimise collateral damage ...'

The poor girl seemed lost for words. The two surviving CAVs eventually passed behind her at great speed, and the camera panned round to follow their rapid progress back towards the town.

'Two of the vehicles are now returning,' she said, 'we have two vehicles on their way back, just passing us now. This was a rescue mission to free the hostages and there is a strong possibility that they have rescued them and they are in fact on board these two ... coming back now ... this has been a very quick operation ... what, I'm sorry?'

It was just possible to make out some words in the background that sounded like 'retreating, you stupid tart.'

The broadcast cut straight back to the studio, catching the newsreader off-guard before he regained his composure.

'Onto other news, and the Opportunity Ministry has released figures that show unemployment has fallen to its lowest level in history with just over two-hundred thousand people seeking work ...'

Major Hesketh turned off the television. He kept the regiment at a high state of alert for the next thirty minutes, after which he stood them down. He knew there would be no more attacks that day.

THIRTY-TWO

In ERDF Headquarters, the reaction to the rapid destruction of the CAVs was one of silent horror. The supreme confidence that had pervaded Headquarters had evaporated in seconds as, one-by-one, the CAVs started exploding on live television. Something had gone very badly wrong, and the senior officers were going to have some explaining to do to their notoriously unforgiving bosses.

Only the Public Relations staff had any sense of purpose at that moment, and the first CAV had not even rolled to a burning halt before they were drafting their new press releases. As the decisiveness of the defeat became apparent, they set about, in their detached professional manner, weaving their magic to somehow turn what was evidently a dreadful failure into some sort of success.

At the Sentry Post, the soldiers of the 65th removed their respirators, once the CS gas had dispersed. Out in front on the road, thick oily smoke billowed from the two destroyed CAVs. The single surviving vehicle was still tucked up behind the burning vehicle that had led the assault, and from its side-door a makeshift white flag appeared, that might have been a pair of boxer shorts on a stick. A Sergeant at the Sentry Post gave instructions to the crew through a loudhailer, allowing them to leave and make their way on foot back up the road towards Holberton. The 65th did not want to take any more hostages.

After Major Hesketh gave the order for the 65th to stand down, he drove up to the Sentry Post. For some of the soldiers it was their first taste of combat, even though it had been something of a turkey-shoot. They still had the outline of their respirators on their faces and they smoked quickly and nervously. Popping sounds came from the burning CAVs as ammunition detonated from the heat inside.

Hesketh then went to the Quartermaster's Store, where the storemen were sweeping up glass from the shattered windows. Firing the 88mm anti-tank gun in the confines of a building was never going to be terribly sympathetic on glass, and the air was still thick with the sweet, smoky smell of cordite. Hesketh found the Quartermaster reclining on his deck chair.

'What's up with him?' said Hesketh, nodding towards a soldier who was clutching his head and crashing into things.

'Silly bugger. Wasn't wearing his bloody earplugs. My God, that thing makes one *hell* of a bang! How many of the little buggers did we get?'

'Four, we think. There were more, but they cleared off pretty rapidly when you opened fire.'

'Excellent, excellent! I must say, it's good to be back in action again. Just like being back in South Armagh.'

A soldier appeared from a side entrance.

'Major Hesketh, sir, the Ops Room are asking for you. Whitehall's on the phone.'

'Tell them I'll be back in five, thank you.'

He turned to the Quartermaster. 'Perhaps they'll take us more seriously now. Do you think they might want to negotiate properly?' he said, in jest.

'No,' said the Quartermaster. 'Of course, they'll pretend to be humbled, but don't fall for it. They're tricky sods. Professional liars, the lot of them. Don't give the buggers a fucking inch.' The Quartermaster looked round to make sure no-one was listening. 'Though I must say it's jolly useful having young Taverner right in the heart of things. Just hope they don't smoke the poor bugger out too soon. Wouldn't be at all nice for him.'

'Quite. Tell your boys to get some rest, and well-done from me,' said Hesketh, as he departed.

Back in Regimental Headquarters, he went into his office and picked up the phone.

'Major Hesketh.'

'Whitehall here. Chief Negotiator speaking.'

Hesketh slowly tutted down the phone. 'Would you care to explain what the hell that was all about?'

The negotiator had her answer prepared. 'We are most dreadfully sorry. This was a terrible misunderstanding. It seems that some vehicles ...'

'Riot vehicles, by the looks of them.'

'Riot vehicles ... were out on a routine reconnaissance patrol ...'

Major Hesketh laughed heavily down the phone.

'... and got lost,' she said.

'Got lost? My *bottom*, they got lost!' said Hesketh. 'My dear, you are going to have to do a lot better than that.'

The negotiator was undeterred. 'It seems they were a Dutch unit attached to the ERDF and new to the area.'

'One wonders what *riot* vehicles were doing out on

patrol in the first place,' said Hesketh, 'but never mind, do carry on.'

'Please, if you'll just hear me out. It seems as though they got lost and obviously panicked when they realised where they were.'

'*They* panicked? You should have seen the effect on our hostages! They really thought their time was up. We were on the verge of springing a nine-millimetre leak in their heads.'

'Major Hesketh. Look, we want to avoid any more casualties.'

'But we haven't taken any casualties.'

'It was such an awful waste of life.'

'We didn't waste any of our lives.'

'But men are dead!'

'*Your* men are dead. It was you who sent them to their deaths, deliberately or in error as you maintain.'

'You killed them in cold blood, Major Hesketh!'

'This is war! What the hell did you expect? A friendly handshake and a warm welcome? Coffee in the Officers' Mess and a chance to sign the Visitors' Book?'

'We were all rather hoping this could have been resolved without recourse to violence.'

'It can be. You know what our demands are. Perhaps in the light of this afternoon's events you have now changed your position?'

'The Cabinet is working on it as we speak. In the meantime, I am authorised to say that if you release the Close Protection Team we will offer six-month apprenticeships, guaranteed for...'

Major Hesketh put the phone down on her.

Later that day, the staff in the 65th's Ops Room watched the BBC's Six O'Clock News on television. They were disappointed to see that the failed assault was given a cursory mention along with some shaky footage of the CAVs, from which their spectacular destruction had been cut. A junior minister from the Ministry of Defence, who looked like he was not long out of sixth-form college, had been wheeled out for the programme and harped on about some sort of probing reconnaissance mission that had inflicted some heavy casualties on the renegades of the 65th, managing to insert the phrase 'Peace and Stability in the South West Community' several times into his statement.

The Force Commander of the ERDF hastily prepared a report in which he laid the blame for the failure firmly on the Dutch soldiers themselves. They hadn't followed orders, he stated, their planning was insufficient and their intelligence was poor. In short, he blamed everything and everyone except himself. The report was encrypted and transmitted to Brussels, who were by now screaming blue murder at the British government, which they felt was responsible for this whole debacle. That evening's meeting of the government's COBRA Committee (convened in times of emergency) was a heated affair and went on late into the night.

One of the most senior members of the COBRA Committee was the elderly Director-General of Interior Security; a terrifying individual who could strike fear into the heart of any man or woman, including all the other members of the Committee. The Director-General said that he would like to send one of his teams to the area, for reasons that he was not prepared to divulge. The Committee granted him his request, even though, technically, he had no mandate to interfere in what was purely a military matter. He saw no need to inform the

Committee that he had already despatched a team several hours earlier.

Some forty miles from Holberton, the team from Interior Security was heading west along the M5 motorway. Their big 4x4, driven by the team's second-in-command, cruised in the outside lane on the exhilarating side of one-hundred miles per hour, and was followed by a large van with two analyst-technicians. In the passenger seat of the 4x4, Peter Kingston ran through the latest reports as they flashed up on his screen. He'd spent most of the journey bringing himself up to date with the events of that day and the wider picture concerning the 65th, Major Tom Hesketh, the ERDF and the area of Holberton. He watched the footage of the failed attack many times over.

Kingston was a former Special Branch policeman and had done his time in the field. A quiet, intelligent man in his mid-forties, rangy in build, with iron-grey hair cropped close to the scalp, he was an exceptionally determined individual. As his vehicle crossed the county border from Somerset into Devon, he turned off the screen and stared out into the darkness.

Kingston was one of the very best in his particular field of work. He had been ordered to Holberton by the Director-General of Interior Security earlier that day, after some unreleased footage of the attack had been studied in detail by his organisation.

'What do you think, Peter?' asked his deputy. 'Anything for us?'

It was the first exchange of words since they had left London.

'Possibly. There are a few coincidences they want checked out.'

'Such as?'

'Well, the attack went in at one o'clock in the afternoon, in broad bloody daylight for God's sake, but they wanted it broadcast live on the news. Anyway, ten minutes beforehand, the Brit soldiers at the entrance to the base suddenly took up position in their trenches. At all other times they've been stood out in the open and there's no record of them suddenly going to high alert at that time of day. They were also wearing respirators, as though they were anticipating some kind of attempt to incapacitate them. Yet the only vehicles capable of that would have been specialist riot vehicles, such as the Civilian Administration Vehicles used in the assault. They carry CS gas. Why were they expecting riot vehicles, or was it just a coincidence? Or did something spook them?'

'Or they were warned?' said his deputy.

'Personally, I don't think so. I think the ERDF just underestimated the Brits. They were just more switched-on. The Director-General wants it checked out, though. Whitehall won't be happy until we've confirmed there wasn't any more to it.'

His deputy knew what he meant.

With each successive year in power, the government had become increasing paranoid. In the early days, the architects of the administration, having quietly dispensed with the inconvenience of democracy, were excited at the thought that there were members of society who disagreed with their vision and sought to undermine what they were trying to achieve. It made them feel important and it justified the measures that followed. In reality, the threat was far less serious, yet the lethargic, soporific British public had kept quiet, as usual, and had simply taken their medicine without too much grumbling. But whether it was real or imaginary, the menace, in the eyes of the government, justified the need for even more rapid change. In time, the government had started to believe its own fantasies of disorder and insurrection, believing its enemies to be everywhere. Every citizen was a potential suspect unless it could be proved otherwise.

Kingston couldn't have cared less. The State's paranoia kept him in well-paid employment and enabled him and his family to have a standard of living far higher than most of the population. Deep down, he despised the President and his excuse of a government, and part of him hoped the Brits in the 65th would give the ERDF another bloody good kicking in the near future. But he was a consummate professional and would carry out his orders to the letter.

The world of counter-intelligence was a precarious one. Both the rewards and the risks were high. That Kingston had survived for so long was because he had an unmatched record of rooting out subversives. He had seen many others fall by the wayside in his time; in his organisation no-one got a second chance. The Director-General saw to that.

Sometimes, in the small hours, Kingston would see the faces of those he'd handed over to the Interior Ministry and the Special Measures Programme. He knew what went on once these hopeless individuals had become guests of the Ministry, yet it was their own decision to set themselves up against the State that had ultimately got them sent there. He was merely facilitating their inevitable passage, for which he did not feel any remorse. Although he had no immediate suspicion that anything was amiss with Holberton or the ERDF, if there was a leak, he would find it. He always found his man. He never, ever failed.

THIRTY-THREE

Taverner sat at the large table in the function room on the first floor of the Ship and Shovel, polishing off the excellent line-caught sea bass. It tasted wonderful after a week of processed blandishments in the ERDF canteen, and he washed it down with a pint of decent ale. When the last of his team arrived, he began.

'Thank you, gentlemen, for turning up at such short notice. I apologise for being out of contact for so long, but I can assure you I have been fully occupied in the meantime.'

'Nice girl is she, Boss? Keeping you occupied, eh!' said Billy.

'No such luck, I'm afraid. I'm sure you will have seen the news yesterday when the ERDF attempted to storm Windcheater Island. This is being spun in the media as some sort of successful reconnaissance mission, although in truth it was a rout. Four of their vehicles were destroyed and two others withdrew.'

'We went to have a look last night,' said Billy. 'Police turned us away, but you could see them smoking.'

'Any British soldiers killed?' asked Terry.

'Not as far as I am aware,' said Taverner, 'although the

official line is that the 65th have taken some casualties. The ERDF believed this whole operation would be over in days and that the 65th would capitulate at the first show of force. They wanted to extract the maximum amount of propaganda from it, instead they have been given a very bloody nose. Whatever they're going to do next, they won't be so blasé. Anyway, have you got anything to report?'

Billy spoke first. 'Well, me and the missus reckon there're a few strange characters in town. They don't look right.'

There were a few murmurs of agreement around the table.

'Strange characters in town?' asked Taverner.

'Yes, Boss,' said Billy, 'arty types what speak funny. With all due respect, Boss, they speak all posh like you. Bit loud as well. I says to my missus …'

'Almost certainly journalists,' interrupted Taverner. 'Don't worry too much about them, although be careful what you say in public. Anything else?'

'My boys have been scouting the countryside,' said Billy. 'They've got their soldiers hidden in quite a few places, where they can overlook the base. Well, I say hidden. Half of them are sat out in the open with their binoculars without a bleedin' care in the world.'

'Those will be their Observation Posts. Are they moving around?'

'No. They's happy to stay in the same place.'

'Do you have their grid references?' said Taverner, reaching for a map.

'Fuck no. Doubt my boys would know one side of a map from the other. We know exactly where they are, though.'

'Fair enough,' said Taverner. 'Gentlemen, I think it is now time to make our presence felt. I want to make life as difficult as possible for the ERDF. I want to wear them down, and I want some ideas.'

And so the discussion started, and carried on for several hours. No idea was considered too eccentric, and the seeds of those that were clearly unworkable inspired the team and got them thinking, evolving into something that could be put into action. They left the pub with their instructions.

On his way back to ERDF Headquarters, Taverner stopped off at a petrol station and purchased six bottles of mineral water and some ready-meals. In the wood, he changed back into his military uniform and slipped quietly into the industrial estate with his purchases. He hoped that he had brought enough with him and he hid them away in his Bergan.

Over the next few days, a coordinated campaign of vilification against Major Hesketh started in the media. Current affairs programmes on television upped the ante and started to scrutinise him in great detail. As the crescendo built, a steady chain of psychologists, psychiatrists, counsellors, politicians, sociologists, senior police officers and commentators queued to say their bit in front of the cameras, each seemingly qualified to offer an intriguing evaluation of Major Hesketh's psyche and state of mind. He had been elevated from a vaguely mysterious figure to Public Enemy Number One. The nation's favourite bogeyman. A right-wing, port-swilling, fox-hunting, tweed-wearing toff. An eccentric. It was apparent, according to those who now built up his psychological profile, that he had been mentally disturbed by his experiences on operations in the Middle East and the Balkans. His masterminding the kidnapping was the result of his extremely low self-esteem. A classic case of the Napoleon complex. A number of soldiers who had allegedly been under his command were on hand to comment on his exceptionally brutal style of leadership, his condoning of bullying and his open tolerance of racism and sexism.

Hesketh even featured in an episode of *The Codes*, in which the computer-generated depiction of him was uncannily realistic. The producers had clearly used old photos of him to create the image – the same ones that now appeared in every news bulletin – and somehow his voice was spot-on.

Hesketh could do nothing about such slander, as the vitriol poured constantly from the television. The Quartermaster was little help by way of consolation.

'Comes with the territory, old chap. Nature of the Beast.'

'But it's all lies!' protested Hesketh.

'So what did you expect? I shouldn't worry that anyone out there actually believes all that rubbish. In any case, the photos they're using of you are at least ten years old. You looked very beautiful back then. My God, you don't think the buggers will start on me next, do you, Tom? You know, work their way through our hierarchy. Slating us one by one! All I can say is they'd better use a decent picture of me!'

If ERDF Headquarters thought that the failed assault on Windcheater Island marked the low point in the whole operation and that things couldn't get any worse, they were wrong. Fireworks and bangers were now thrown into the industrial estate during the night; probably just local kids having a laugh, but the police failed to catch any of them in the act. The resulting lack of sleep caused people to become rather grouchy.

Two ERDF vehicles had been left unattended for a short time outside a shop when their occupants stopped off to buy cigarettes. When they returned, the tyres of one of the vehicles had been slashed. The other vehicle ground to a halt as it pulled out into the road. ERDF mechanics would later find out that sugar had been poured into the fuel tank, which had turned to toffee in the engine's pistons.

Elsewhere, there were more serious problems. The Observation Posts on the high ground overlooking Windcheater Island were all compromised during the course of a single night. The observers had to withdraw rapidly as several pick-up trucks roared round their locations, headlights blazing, a bunch of rural nutters in the back, holding onto the roll cage and firing off their shotguns into the air, whooping and hollering like Deep South rednecks wasting critters and varmints.

Finally, as the days passed, it became apparent that a severe fever was spreading through ERDF Headquarters. Many of the staff had fallen ill. The Duty Medic, a Corporal armed with nothing more than a large bag of sticking plasters and paracetamol, was overwhelmed by the number reporting sick, and sent most of them back to bed where they lay sweating profusely, clutching their stomachs and frequently dashing to the toilets. Even the Force Commander was affected, and at the daily conference he seemed more concerned with simply staying on his feet.

One day, as the temperature climbed past ninety degrees, and despite the air conditioning, work at

Headquarters ground to a halt. Taverner winced as he watched the ERDF staff attempting to relieve their chronic dehydration by drinking hungrily from the water taps.

THIRTY-FOUR

It was now two weeks since the start of the siege. The ERDF had come to Holberton to evict a relatively small number of soldiers from a base that was meant to be theirs, yet it was they who now felt under siege – from the local population, from the media representatives and the Press, and from their bosses.

In the face of such pressure the sense of common purpose and unity, that had characterised Headquarters from the outset, began to disintegrate. With so many ill, it was under-manned and over-worked, and with recriminations for the initial cock-up looming, national pride that had been simmering away began to rise again, and old rivalries that should have been consigned to history started to resurface.

Although ERDF Headquarters drew on the soldiers of countries from the Mediterranean to the Barents Sea, and from the fringes of the Atlantic Coast to the Bosporus, it was the big-hitters of Western Europe – France, Germany, Italy, Spain and the Low Countries – who held the reins. All other nations were strictly B-list. It was not unusual, for example, to see a Turkish Major doing the same job as a German Corporal. It was quietly resented of course, but it was simply the accepted order of things.

However, these Eastern European serfs had much tougher constitutions and seemed to be relatively immune to the illness that had affected the soft Westerners, who now lay weakened and nauseous on their cots. A Moldovan Captain found himself in charge of the Logistics Cell. A Polish Major oversaw the whole ERDF communications network. Administration and organisation was now, unthinkably, in the hands of the Greeks.

Both the Force Commander and his Chief of Staff were out of action, so the Deputy Chief of Staff – a Greek-Cypriot Major – was now elevated to the position of Force Commander.

And yet, despite the illness and the under-manning and the upheaval caused by the rapid change of command appointments, the barons in Brussels were wholly unsympathetic to their plight and insisted that the ERDF regain the initiative.

Taverner was moved across from Logistics to Operations, where he worked savagely long shifts at the radio, sometimes for eighteen hours at a stretch. He could hardly complain though; it was because of him that Headquarters had fallen sick in the first place.

The Public Relations staff continued to send out their daily releases layered with the silky, reassuring vernacular of their trade, peppering their texts with soothing sound bites; 'Committed to ... forward-looking ... full confidence in ... peaceful resolution of ...'. But everyone knew the ERDF simply could not afford another public humiliation, so as the new, healthier commanders turned their attention once again to the business of evicting the 65th, they planned a rather more stealthy attack, away from the press spotlight. The Cypriot officer who now commanded the ERDF reckoned he had the answer.

Back in the Republic of Cyprus, he had served in a tough Commando unit, tearing about the Mediterranean in fast boats and enjoying the odd nocturnal and very illicit sojourn into the waters and even the beaches of the *de facto* Turkish Republic of Northern Cyprus – the Greek-Cypriots' hated enemy, who had occupied the north of the island since 1974. His unit was, he boasted to the rest of Headquarters, the very best in Europe at landing unseen on a well-defended stretch of coast in order to secure or destroy an objective. After all, they were the only country in Europe able to practise it regularly against a real enemy.

There were many such specialist commando units all over Europe that he might have chosen for the operation he had in mind. Clearly, the search for an available unit, plus the inevitable bureaucracy involved in submitting the request through the Defence Attachés at the various embassies, would take some time to achieve, even with Brussels' clout to back him up. It would take time that he simply didn't have. There were ways of bypassing such inconveniences, and a few phone calls back home to a base near Paphos were all that was needed. Some of the soldiers of the Cypriot Commando Unit were on twenty-four hours' Notice to Move and would be flown over, to be in Holberton by tomorrow evening. In the meantime, small *Rigid Raider* boats were formally commandeered from a former Royal Marines base in Plymouth, where they had been mothballed and left in storage. They were prepped, serviced, tested and then transported north, by road, to Holberton.

A chance to upstage the arrogant European powerhouses was irresistible to the new Cypriot Commander. They had paid the price for their first lily-livered, half-arsed operation, where the planners had become so bogged down in pointless areas such as the legal rights of the enemy soldiers, the overriding need to preserve life, and their obsession with timing to get maximum media coverage that they had, in his opinion, lost sight of what they were there to do in the first place. He knew exactly what was needed on these types of operations. Courage, machismo, daring, *tharros* – guts – and to hell with any of that Health and Safety rubbish. Fuck the human rights of the British soldiers. This was war.

As a good patriotic Cypriot, he was familiar with the history of the EOKA freedom-fighters' struggle against the British occupiers in the 1950s. It filled him with pride to think of his commandos storming Windcheater Island on a daring night-time raid, taking on the former colonial power on its own turf.

Taverner, seated at his radio in the Operations Cell, found himself party to a great deal of information about this coming raid as it started to take shape – details of which he was only too happy to pass on to the 65th from his radio.

Each day, at various different times, the 65th's hostages, Dr Müller, Mr MacDonald and Colonel Sandford, were allowed to exercise independently in the car park in front of the Officers' Mess, guarded at a distance by two impassive soldiers. Denied access to television, radio or newspapers, the hostages were now utterly disorientated and had no idea what was going on outside the regiment. As far as they were concerned, the whole world had forgotten about them. They slept a lot, thumbed through lots of old paperbacks and accepted their three meals each day from the Mess Bombardier. They had come to look forward to their daily exercise in the car park. It was the high spot of their day.

Since the Mess was on the eastern side of the island – away from the main buildings of the regiment and only a short distance from the sea – the hostages were sometimes escorted all the way to the seafront. The tide was always out whenever they were taken there, and the only seawater they saw was a small channel between the mudflats that led south to the estuary. Major Hesketh would not have been pleased if they managed to escape by suddenly jumping in the water at high tide and getting washed away.

Today it was Dr Müller's turn for a coastal stroll. He was grateful for this longer excursion and instinctively thanked his escorts, then wondered why the hell he was thanking them. He was succumbing to the effect known by psychologists as the Stockholm Syndrome, where the captive turns his resentment away from his kidnappers and onto the authorities whose continuing incompetence is responsible for leaving him in the situation. As Dr Müller stood there in his blue coveralls under a clear, azure sky, smoking a meditative cigarette and envying the simple, innocent freedom of the curlews that poked around for worms in the mudflats in front of him, he felt like a condemned man. He looked out to the rolling Devon hills beyond, and wondered if anyone out there was watching.

From a clump of trees on a hillside to the south east of Windcheater Island, Captain Kostas Charalambous watched the forlorn figure of Dr Müller through his binoculars. The stocky, olive-skinned twenty-eight year old was an officer in the Cypriot Commando Unit and had flown in the night before. He had started his detailed reconnaissance of Windcheater Island at first light. Charalambous was a bright and enthusiastic officer, highly regarded by his troops and earmarked for further promotion. It had not taken him long to digest the intelligence reports from the ERDF, giving the estimated strength and dispositions of the occupiers on Windcheater Island, but he wanted to see for himself, and surveyed the whole island from a number of different vantage points. Several young ERDF soldiers were detailed to escort Captain Charalambous on his recce and were visibly anxious as they drove out from Holberton. They told Charalambous of the recent attacks on the ERDF by the locals; how the permanent Observation Posts had all been compromised by civilians hooning around in off-road pick-ups at night, and how ERDF vehicles were likely to get a brick through their windscreen when driving under footbridges. Rural England, they had supposed, was a calm and gentle environment where cheerful, ruddy-faced villagers upheld a slow and peaceful way of life, in contrast to the violent pressure-cooker of the big cities. But the lawlessness in North Devon was like nothing they had ever experienced.

With his binoculars covered with scrim-netting to prevent a tell-tale reflection from the lens that might give his position away, Charalambous switched his attention from Dr Müller to the nearby Officers' Mess. ERDF Intelligence knew that the hostages were being kept there. It was from the Mess that the hostages were seen to emerge whenever they took their exercise, although the 65th did not seem to be making any attempt to be discreet about it. Even the boarded-up windows on the top floor of the Mess indicated the rooms where they might be being held.

Charalambous's primary task was to rescue the hostages from the island and remove them to safety. There were numerous trenches round this part of the island, although not many were actually occupied by troops. The bulk of the 65th's manpower seemed to be deployed elsewhere, mostly on the western and southern edges of the island. Dr Müller stood not far from a white building, marked on Charalambous's map as the Sailing Club. It was undefended, and the nearest occupied trench was at least three-hundred metres away. Some distance north of the Sailing Club was a long concrete ramp that extended out into the water, presumably for launching boats.

The young officer made up his mind. His commandos would go in by the Sailing Club. It was the most vulnerable point in the 65th's defences. Charalambous took photographs to use in later briefings.

There was just one final problem.

Tides.

Coming from the Mediterranean, he was not used to the fact that, for the rest of the world's coastal regions, the sea rushed in and out as near as dammit twice every day. As he looked at the island that morning, the only visible water was a small channel running parallel to the coast, separated by several hundred metres of mud. One of the ERDF escorts explained to him that he was looking at the island at low tide; at high tide the water covered the mud all the way up to the coast.

Back at ERDF Headquarters, Charalambous and his senior NCOs sat down together for some brainstorming. Satisfied that a high tide would give him enough clearance to take the boats right up to the island, he set about planning his mission. He intended to mount the operation in darkness during the early hours, between four and five o'clock in the morning, when the enemy would be at their lowest ebb. The darkness of the hour would not be a problem for his commandos; night-time operations were their speciality. An examination of a tide timetable revealed that high tide on August 12th would be at eleven minutes past four in the morning. That was in three days' time. The weather forecast was looking favourable too, with a light breeze and low cloud cover.

Their mission also had a secondary task. After Charalambous's squad had landed on the east of the island and recovered the hostages back to the boats, a few commandos would stay behind to start a noisy feint attack from the Sailing Club, the intention of which was to draw in enemy troops from elsewhere on the island, leaving certain critical points exposed and allowing the second wave of his commandos to start their attack from the western edge at first light. With the Ops Room, the Quartermaster's Store and the Sentry Post secured, conventional ERDF reinforcements could then be allowed in.

Taverner was impressed with Captain Charalambous's plan. He liked his style. Though it was undoubtedly risky the Cypriots had done their homework. The commandos might have been fewer in number than the 65th, but they knew how to create chaos and confusion, and how to exploit it. If the Cypriots managed to get their boats to the island, the 65th – had they not been forewarned of what was about to happen – might have had a bit of a fight on their hands.

If, indeed, the Cypriots ever managed to get their boats to the island.

For Taverner had noticed, as he innocently flicked

through the tide timetable, that the Cypriots had a problem they had not yet spotted. High tide on August 12th would indeed happen at eleven minutes past four in the morning, but they had not realised that tides were inconsistent in their height. An average tide, Taverner reckoned, would have given them enough depth to get their boats right up to the coast, and a high 'spring' tide would give them more than enough room, with a long enough time-window to land, rescue the hostages and withdraw. But August 12th was in the middle of a 'neap' tide phase – a 'low' high tide – caused by an unfavourable alignment between the sun and the moon. He knew from bitter experience that, during a neap tide, the water would barely be deep enough to get a windsurfing board in, let alone a Rigid Raider.

THIRTY-FIVE

August 12th 3 am

In a small cove north of the coastal village of Mortehoe, twelve Rigid Raiders had been floated into the sea off their trailers. The commandos had been briefed and had memorised the layout of Windcheater Island. They hauled their weapons onto the boats, blackened their faces and put on their lifejackets. Captain Charalambous tested the radios before imposing radio silence for security.

His squad was the first to set off. There were six boats in the squad, each carrying eight commandos. They motored out into the darkness quietly and at low speed, not wishing to draw attention to themselves, and turned south, progressing slowly past the vast expanse of beach on their left at Woolacombe. Since the Americans had corrupted the satellite signal from the Global Positioning System for those outside the US military sphere, Charalambous had to rely on old-fashioned maritime navigation skills to judge his position.

There was a light breeze that night creating a little choppiness, which was no bad thing as the noise of the engines would have carried much further over still water. Charalambous peered aft into the darkness with his night-vision goggles, towards the other boats nearby. They made slow and steady progress, but it was necessary to achieve the element of surprise and to hit Windcheater Island at precisely high tide. The timing was critical. The tide would give them a window of less than half an hour in which to carry out the operation.

They followed the coast round the steep cliffs of Baggy Point, past the beach at Croyde, and around the reef at Downend Point. The second squad of boats would have been launching by now. They passed another long stretch of beach at Saunton Sands, and turned east into the estuary.

There were many inlets on their left, and they continued to progress slowly up the estuary, eventually approaching Windcheater Island. The engine was throttled back almost to idle as they passed the southern tip of the island. They were less than a kilometre from the island — out of effective range of the 65th's weapons, though still uncomfortably close. Charalambous knew that the bulk of the enemy soldiers was concentrated around that point, and his commandos crouched down lower into the boat, hardly daring to breathe, their rifles pointed out in the direction of the enemy, half-expecting the tracer fire to start up immediately.

With agonising slowness they passed safely through the danger area. The boats now made a left turn into the channel and headed north, up the eastern side of the island. They were barely moving, although the small chop began to slap annoyingly against the side of the boats. Their insertion point was the Sailing Club, the silhouette of which could now be made out in the distance. As Charalambous's lead boat drew parallel with the Sailing Club, he ordered the driver to make a left turn. Under such low power the boat took an age to yaw around, and they covered the last few hundred metres to the island. Each commando checked his equipment one last time. They were now out of the channel and riding over shallow water. They would jump out as soon as they hit the coast.

They had less than one-hundred metres to run, when the boat slowed to a halt with a sickening grating noise. The second boat drew up alongside and also ground to a halt, as did the third. They had all run aground. The remaining boats, seeing what was happening, stopped short and slowly reversed back towards the deeper water of the channel behind them. In Charalambous's boat, the driver switched the engine into reverse, gradually increasing the revs to pull them off the bank, to no avail. Charalambous hissed for quiet and checked his watch. High tide had happened about five minutes ago. The water was flowing back out to sea. They were stuck fast.

This was not meant to happen. There was supposed to be plenty of water at high tide. He looked at his watch again. At that moment, he and his team should have been entering the Officers' Mess to recover the hostages. This was meant to have been a very quick operation. Instead he was stuck, and there was now a discernible dark grey creeping into the gloom. The water level had dropped further – there were barely a few inches left – and the boat leaned over noticeably on its keel. They had still not been spotted by the enemy, but they were sitting ducks where they were.

Charalambous was not one to give up easily. They would use the long concrete slipway that extended out into the channel. It was submerged at that moment, but he and the rest of his squad knew where they could find it. They could abandon the boats where they were, get to the shore, carry out their mission and then withdraw to the remaining boats via the slipway, which would soon be visible on the dropping tide. He quickly briefed the other commandos in his boat, then broke radio silence and issued the new instructions over the radio. To the west of Windcheater Island, the second squad of boats was waiting in deeper water, and he ordered them to hold position.

The point man slipped silently over the side, and instead of just getting his boots muddy, as he had expected, he dropped into several feet of wet, sucking mud. He lost his balance, dropped his rifle and floundered noisily as he sank, and had to be hauled back into the boat. Another commando over-reached himself and fell head first into the slime, from where he too had to be recovered.

From their trench, Bombardier Podsnap and his team watched the unfolding events through their night-vision goggles. These idiotic commandos had come armed and ready to fight them – now the only threat to their health was that their sides might split from trying not to laugh out loud.

From the top floor of the Sailing Club, Major Hesketh was also following the proceedings with amusement. Once again, the intelligence from Taverner had been excellent, and he gave the order to proceed with the next phase of the operation.

In the boat, Charalambous and his commandos felt utterly helpless and extremely vulnerable. They were marooned, and hoped the British renegades of the 65th would be merciful when they discovered them, as they surely would as the light improved; the three boats beached guiltily on the mud were not exactly inconspicuous. Charalambous was out of ideas and ordered all the other boats to withdraw. Dejectedly, he radioed back to ERDF Headquarters to tell them of his failure. A white handkerchief was hoisted at the front of his boat.

The water took a long time to go back out. It was now daylight and the commandos could only lay crouched down in the boats with their rifles still trained towards the coast, waiting to be found by the 65th. The gentle background noise of trickling water and swishing rushes was suddenly interrupted by a terrible flapping and cackling. Out of the corner of his eye, Charalambous noticed some movement. Three rotund birds were flying towards them at low level. Though he would not have recognised them as such, they were Red Grouse. Several loud gunshots in quick succession rang out and made everyone jump. Thinking they were coming under attack, the commandos cocked their rifles and aimed them towards the shore. They had no idea where the shots had come from. One of the birds had stopped flapping and curved over in an arc to land in the mud not far away. The remaining two escaped, flying very low over the boat, still cackling loudly, furiously trying to gain some altitude.

'Good shot, Mr Cavendish!' said Major Hesketh.

'Thank you, sir. Beginner's luck, surely,' said the man who had graduated from Sandhurst with one of the worst shooting records in the history of the Academy.

'A crate of champagne to the first gun to land a bird in the boats!' shouted Captain Mellor to the others.

The annual 65th Invitational Shoot was underway. Hesketh saw no reason why it should not go ahead, as it always did on August 12th, but he had adapted the format in view of their current circumstances. Gone were the tweeds and plus-fours, which had been replaced by camouflaged uniform and body armour – a regrettable precaution given the proximity of the Cypriot commandos, however impotent they now were. The lack of any suitable area from which to drive the grouse also necessitated a different approach. They were secured in boxes of three in the back of a Bedford truck and, as each box was brought out and opened on the ground, the birds were gently encouraged to get underway, which they did with some difficulty; the 65th bred an obese strain of bird that could barely generate enough lift to haul itself into the air.

The officers were appalling shots. Skeffington's Purdey was wasted on him and he scored a zero. Cavendish was more of a danger to his fellow guns than the birds. There were quite a few winged, the occasional hit, and at such close range the low-level obliteration was messy and captivating to watch.

The shoot did not take long and most of the birds escaped without harm. In the absence of trained gundogs, the Mess staff scurried round collecting the few kills that would be eaten later that week.

Charalambous and his commandos lay flat in their boat. The water had receded to the narrow channel behind them and they were beached high and almost dry. The firing had stopped and they now heard a voice through a loudspeaker.

'Good morning, gentlemen.'

Charalambous raised his head. Like most Greek-Cypriots, his English was excellent. A line of armed soldiers stood along the coast and a short, fat man wielded the loudspeaker.

'Or should I say *Kali Merasas*? It's a little early for such fun and games, don't you think? Perhaps I can extend an invitation to Windcheater Island. I will personally guarantee your safety. Wave if you agree.'

Charalambous waved his hands. It was over.

'Thank you so much. Please leave your weapons in the boat. You'll find it easier if you crawl.'

Charalambous went over the side and down into the thin, grey mud, trying to spread his weight as wide as possible, scooping up vile worms as he clambered through the filth. It was a long way to crawl and he eventually reached the shore, utterly exhausted, his legs and arms burning from the effort. Major Hesketh introduced himself and helped Charalambous to his feet.

'My dear chap, you must be absolutely shattered.'

One by one, his commandos crawled over, or rather through, the mud, and by the time they had all collected on dry land they looked like survivors pulled from a landslide. Hesketh separated Charalambous from his soldiers and led him away to a large tent from where the delicious smell of bacon and fried eggs emanated. Inside, the officers of the 65th were tucking into a very alcoholic breakfast. Charalambous was hungry, dejected, and covered in so much mud he looked like a molten Terracotta statue. He didn't feel as if he was appropriately dressed for breakfast and scooped off the worst of the slime. If the young lieutenant he now found himself sat next to at the breakfast table was surprised by his appearance, he didn't show it.

'Nice try, old chap,' said the officer. 'How do you do. I'm Skeffington. Won't you have some champagne?'

THIRTY-SIX

'Lovely.'

With a handkerchief pressed to his face, Peter Kingston looked at the floating carcass and wondered if he would ever be able to eat lamb again. In the stifling heat, the stench was overpowering. No wonder sickness was so rife at ERDF Headquarters.

He walked outside into the fresh air, past the Forensic Team who would find out how the small pumping house, that supplied fresh water to the industrial estate, had been broken into. The ERDF engineers would remove the rotting carcass, clean out the affected tanks and return clean water to Headquarters.

Back in his van, Kingston filed a report up to London.

The uncanny preparations of the 65th as the CAVs had attempted to assault the base could have been put down to the professionalism of the Brits and the overconfidence of the ERDF. The disappearance of the Cypriot commandos was just a case of simple, brave stupidity. The sudden compromising of the Observation Posts by armed locals was to be viewed with suspicion, as was their campaign of low-level harassment. But the deliberate poisoning of the

ERDF's water supply confirmed to him that there was a saboteur afoot.

He pondered his options. His team now had a vast amount of work to do, and he initiated the next procedure as a matter of course; an analysis of every resident of Holberton. The process involved electronically interrogating the National Database and would take at least a day, even for a small town like Holberton.

Kingston had to cover every eventuality. For the moment, the computers would crunch on the data regarding the local population. It would also do no harm to have a closer look at the ERDF's staff.

If any saboteurs were uncovered, he would need outside-help in the form of a Field Team from the Security Support Agency. In the past, the SSA had been staffed by calm, professional, intelligent men and women, who could blend into any background without drawing attention to themselves. Not any more. The hardliners in the government, with their disregard of common law, ensured the SSA had since morphed into something very different. There was nothing remotely undercover, as Kingston often said, about a herd of six-foot-plus, dark-suited maniacs, all muscle and attitude and sunglasses and earpieces, fuelled on steroids and amphetamines, tearing about the country in their black 4x4s with all the subtlety of a sow in a kibbutz. As a government agency the SSA was saddled with a Mission Statement – *Engaging Freedom beyond Belief.* Many people suggested *Engaging Fist before Brain* was more appropriate. The comment in some quarters that SSA agents were little better than Neanderthals was, in Kingston's opinion, unfair to Neanderthals. For every genuine suspect the SSA brought in, for every person apprehended who might have been acting against the State, there would be at least ten others perfectly innocent, left to nurse anything from broken noses and the effects of chronic sleep deprivation, to severe head injuries or even disablement. The large numbers arrested by the SSA were trumpeted loudly by the government, justifying its own paranoia and bolstering its argument for more security and further intrusion into people's lives. For the innocent victims, however, there was never any legal redress or compensation, since the SSA operated outside the law.

Kingston sighed wearily at the thought that he'd have to call in the SSA in the near-future. Right now, they would be more of a hindrance, and he had plenty of other things to be getting on with.

Taverner was now back in the Logistics Cell. Whether it was fate or luck or instinct that caused him to glance towards the Administration Cell at the moment he did, the action probably saved his life.

The foul-breathed female Administration Sergeant who had torn a strip off Taverner when he had first arrived, was back at her desk after her illness, guarding the entrance to her lair. She was speaking to a man with close-cropped iron-grey hair who wore a civilian suit. Perhaps the Sergeant looked a little more hideous after her recent vomiting episode, thought Taverner, but all things were relative, in the same way that cholera is a little more hideous than typhoid. He happened to notice that she wore a wedding ring. So, she was actually *married*. Maybe in a Civil Partnership? Taverner was in awe of the man, or woman, or thing, who'd had the nerve to propose to, and then presumably conjugate with, such a creature. Repelled by the imagery of such physical union, he turned his attention to the grey-haired man in the suit. Although Taverner couldn't hear the conversation they were having, the Sergeant was clearly speaking to him in the same bad-tempered manner in which she addressed everyone in Headquarters. Taverner had seen the man round the industrial estate in the last few days. He would not have been immediately noticeable, yet it was his discreet presence that made him stand out, because he did not, like most of the civilian staff, cut about the place with great self-importance while persistently jabbering away into a mobile phone. The man remained unflustered in the face of her tirade, seemingly impervious to insult and halitosis, and then calmly produced an identity card which shut her up. Chastened, the Sergeant sat down at a computer screen and typed in some details. A nearby printer started to dispense reams of paper.

Taverner immediately sensed trouble. Whoever the man was, he obviously had clout, which meant government or police, or possibly the Security Services. Leaving his radio for a moment, Taverner wandered over to the Administration Cell and tried to think of something to say.

The grey-haired man waited for the printing run to finish and stepped back to allow Taverner through to the threshold.

'What do you want?' said the Sergeant, now back to her old ways, fixing Taverner with a stare she probably reserved for cockroaches.

'Ah yes, er ... tubing, Sergeant. We need some tubing please,' said Taverner.

'Tubing?'

'That's right, tubing, Sergeant.'

The Sergeant narrowed her eyes and shook her head

quickly, indicating she did not understand. Next to her, the printer had finished its run.

'It's a very strange type of tubing,' said Taverner, pointing towards the officers in the Logistics Cell. 'They said you'd have some.'

'Wait.'

The Sergeant gathered up the sheets from the printer and handed them to the grey-haired man, along with some sort of memory card. Taverner caught a brief glimpse of the top sheet. It was the entire personnel record of an ERDF soldier. The man randomly checked a few records deeper in the pile. More personnel records, Taverner could see. If the stack of paper contained the records of all ERDF personnel, somewhere within would be the details of Private Morton.

Maybe the authorities were clamping down on the ERDF's lax security. Maybe they were running background checks on all ERDF personnel in the light of recent events. With any luck there was a perfectly innocent explanation? But Taverner could not afford to take that chance.

It was time to get out of there.

He looked at his watch. He still had one hour to go before his duty ended.

Fight or flight? Come on man, think!

'We don't do tubing. Oi, you! We don't do tubing!' The Sergeant brought him back to his senses. 'What the hell are you on about?'

'They said you did,' said Taverner, innocently. 'They said you had loads and loads of it.'

The Sergeant squinted and shook her head.

'It's a very special tubing,' explained Taverner. 'Let me spell it for you. May I?' He reached for a nearby pad and pencil.

The Sergeant had never heard of it before, despite her excellent English. She flicked wearily through her translation dictionary.

The grey-haired man, who was putting the paperwork into a case, smiled when he saw what the British soldier had written down. *Squaddie humour, eh?* The man waited for the reaction.

The stream of invective that was hurled at Taverner when she finally translated was like nothing anyone at Headquarters had ever heard. She could barely get the air into her capacious lungs fast enough to enstench it and ram it back out past her cast-iron vocal chords. Taverner was sent on his way, not so much with a flea in his ear, but more like a hornets' nest stamped vigorously into every opening in his head.

Back in the Logistics Cell, one of the officers asked him what he had just done.

'I just asked her for ten metres of Fallopian tubing, sir,' said Taverner. 'No sense of humour, sir, no sense of humour.'

Taverner looked at his watch again. He needed to get out of ERDF Headquarters as quickly as possible. Assuming the worst – that the grey-haired man was from the Security Services – the data on Private Morton would eventually be processed and the anomalies discovered. With a false identity card, supporting paperwork and even a car that matched that belonging to the real Private Morton, Taverner had covered the basics sufficiently to hoodwink the ERDF, but the Security Services would not be fooled so easily. The temptation to leave at that very moment was overwhelming, yet he knew that his sudden absence while on duty would be noticed. In broad daylight he might not get very far. He was heartened to see the grey-haired man and his team go through to the canteen for dinner. Clearly their analysis hadn't yet started.

Peter Kingston relayed the story of the cheeky British soldier, the angry Sergeant and her Fallopian tubing to his team over their evening meal. They set to work afterwards, downloading the details of all the ERDF soldiers and perusing the supporting paperwork. They had also gathered the details of the Public Relations staff and the locally-recruited pan-bashers and tea ladies.

There was no rush. This was a routine procedure and, in Kingston's experience, one that was very unlikely to throw up anything of interest. Nonetheless, he had to cover all possibilities. His powerful computer system interrogated a vast national network where every single citizen unknowingly left an up-to-the-minute electronic trace.

It did not take them long to discover the inconsistencies with Private Morton. In the last few days, he had apparently been using his credit card on a daily basis in and around Bournemouth. For example, he had withdrawn eighty Euros from a cashpoint machine two nights earlier, and only a few hours ago – at the precise time he was getting a tongue-lashing from the Satan-Breathed One – he had been purchasing twenty-eight litres of biofuel and a packet of twenty cigarettes from a petrol station. There was the possibility that his card might be being used fraudulently, but the spending habits suggested otherwise. Finally, they compared the likeness of Private Morton's driving-licence photograph to the signaller Kingston had seen in the Logistics Cell.

It was not even close.

Kingston contacted his line-manager in Whitehall, and a team from the Security Support Agency was tasked.

THIRTY-SEVEN

The team waited quietly in the shadows as their target lay asleep on his bed. Outside, the black van waited with its engine ticking over, ready to whisk the suspect out of the area to await the persuasive gentlemen from the Interior Ministry.

The team approached the bed silently, several pistols pointing at the target's head. In less than a second, he was shaken awake, turned over onto his front, and his arms were pinned and cuffed behind him. He was then flipped over onto his back, a wedge was inserted into his mouth and a gloved finger was run around his gums to check for suicide pills. They were not taking any chances.

'Clear!'

Suitably restrained, the agents quickly softened him up with a few well-placed blows to his head and crotch, before dragging him out to the van which pulled away in a screech of rubber, waking the residents of the quiet Bournemouth housing estate where Private Morton lived – the real Private Morton.

The arrest of the overweight shop supervisor had gone to plan. He had put up no resistance and the remaining agents sealed off his flat for the Forensic Team.

They were having rather less luck with his impostor.

'Gone?'

It had been a long time since anyone had seen Peter Kingston remotely fazed. His deputy tried to explain.

'He was not in his bunk. The last anyone saw of him was when he went off-duty, just after four o'clock. He didn't go to the cookhouse and the police at the checkpoint said that no-one had left the estate on foot.

'Might he still be here on the estate, hiding?'

'Possibly. He could have got out in the back of a vehicle, or out through the back of the estate. His car's still here.'

'I want a list of all vehicles that left the estate between four and six o'clock this evening,' said Kingston. 'Check with the ERDF that all their vehicles – and their drivers – are accounted for. Did the perimeter patrol see anything?'

'No. They've been in the cookhouse all afternoon.'

'For Christ's sake, what's the point of having them?'

By now, their computer had finished the analysis of the rest of the ERDF staff. Everyone else was clean.

The impostor's car was examined. It was the same as the one registered to Private Morton; the same colour (although badly re-sprayed), same make and model. Even the false number plate was correct. The bomb squad carefully removed some luggage that was still in the vehicle. It was found to contain old cushions and pillows.

Kingston impounded the hand-written radio log and the recordings of transmissions from both the Logistics and Operations Cells, and his technicians started to compare the two. All the messages matched up perfectly – except for an unrecognised combination of letters that was transmitted each day around midday.

Always at midday, thought Kingston. Who was he and

what was he doing? He clearly knew how to operate a military radio.

From the Ministry of Defence, the technicians downloaded identity card photographs of every soldier in the British Army, and into the search parameters they entered a very accurate description of the impostor, which narrowed the number to a dozen images. The piercing blue eyes stood out by a mile.

'Jesus Christ,' said Kingston, when he saw what regiment the impostor had served in.

The senior officers of the ERDF were summoned by Kingston who, after gaining authorisation from Whitehall, briefed them on the serious breach of security that had occurred. They listened in disbelief as Kingston revealed that Private Morton was in fact an officer in the 65th, operating with a false identity, able to gain access to sensitive information and pass it on to the 65th before disappearing into thin air. The security of Headquarters, Kingston told them, was shambolic and needed to be tightened up as a matter of urgency. Damage assessment also started and would tie up staff for days.

ERDF patrols were sent out to search for Taverner. New Observation Posts were set up on high ground and thermal-imaging equipment scoured the darkness. Vehicle checkpoints were set up on all major roads.

Back in the technicians' van, Peter Kingston examined the current file on Captain Charlie Taverner, which had been sent from the Ministry of Defence. Taverner's enlarged Army Identity Card photograph was attached to the front of the file, with its smiling face staring back at him dismissively. Hours earlier, Kingston had actually been standing *next* to the bastard.

Charlie Taverner. Ten years a commissioned officer, unwilling to take promotion to Major, rich background, a public school education, a maverick, intelligent, unconventional, super-fit, and very determined. And seriously courageous. Or mad. Lucky, too. Or very, very good. Kingston could not help but have respect for Taverner. To think he'd had the balls to sit in ERDF Headquarters and transmit on *their* radios to the 65th! How he would like to have got Taverner to work for him one day. There were always means of persuading such people – it was just a shame his myopic superiors would have never entertained such an idea.

If Taverner's aim was to keep the 65th informed of the ERDF's plans, then his task would now be far more difficult, as would sabotaging the ERDF's operations – if that was also his intention. The fact that Taverner had escaped just as they had uncovered him made Kingston wonder if there was not another spy in the ERDF still in place. Maybe Taverner was just the decoy to throw him off the scent. As a precaution, the other British soldiers in the ERDF were quarantined and taken away.

Kingston pondered Taverner's next move.

Would he have gone away for good? Had his fun, then cut-and-run?

He looked long and hard at the photo of Taverner; over-confident, superior, and sneering back at him.

You think everything's beneath you, don't you? This is just a game of cricket to people like you. Of course you're still going to be around to cause trouble.

He telephoned his boss in Whitehall and requested a team from the Security Support Agency to help him in Holberton. The second he got a whiff of Taverner, the team would have to go in.

However, Kingston's boss disagreed with his assessment of the situation, believing that Taverner was almost certainly long gone. Ports and airports would be alerted of course, but he would not release a team of agents. Something had come up elsewhere and all SSA teams were busy. Kingston was told to assist the ERDF with their damage assessment in the meantime.

Kingston did not share his boss's optimism that Taverner was no longer a threat. During the course of his career, Kingston had built up and maintained a number of useful contacts throughout the various branches of government and in a number of corporations and private organisations. Though he did not make a regular habit of calling in favours, he contacted someone who worked in GCHQ – Government Communication Headquarters – and also made calls to several people employed by the main mobile phone networks.

That night on Windcheater Island, the Officers' Mess ate well. Though there was only a little grouse to go around (most of it had escaped to drown in the estuary) the Chateau Margaux '82 was most pleasant. The dusty bottles were placed on the table, their contents having been carefully poured into the crystal decanters by the Mess Manager earlier in the day.

The Cypriot Officer, Captain Charalambous, joined them for dinner. A dinner jacket was procured for him, though it didn't fit quite as well as the tailored jackets of the other officers. The Mess Manager had shown him how to tie a proper bow-tie to avoid the social hand-grenade of sporting a clip-on version at this most prestigious of dinner tables.

To his bewilderment, Charalambous realised the

dinner was in his honour. He was being officially dined into the Officers' Mess, and was required to make a short speech after dinner. It was fitting that he was welcomed into the 65th. After all, Charalambous had led an attack which had seen him beached on treacherous mudflats some distance short of his objective. It had failed, and it had failed wonderfully — very much in the style of the 65th. The fact that it was 65th's base he had intended to attack was considered entirely academic by the rest of the officers and he received huge applause for his speech.

A rather less pleasant experience was the mandatory Yard of Ale in the bar afterwards, where the 65th's record of one minute and twenty-eight seconds was in no danger of being broken. Major Hesketh recorded the time in the Book of the Yard together with a few comments and observations more eloquent than the usual '... blew air and chunks ha ha ha ...', and when he was finished, he drew a line through the remaining blank pages in the book.

Captain Charalambous's Yard would be the last one ever recorded.

THIRTY-EIGHT

Negotiations between the authorities and the 65th had ground to a halt by the end of the following week. The soldiers of the 65th were bored witless in their trenches, and their counterparts in the ERDF, who had been holed up in the industrial estate since the start, were now regretting the day they had ever volunteered for such a wretched organisation. The media lost interest in the story and turned their attention to the riots in Mexico City and the clean-up operation in Bermuda after Hurricane Gregory had stormed through it.

ERDF Headquarters had been devastated by the news that a signaller in the Logistics Cell had been leaking operational information straight to the enemy. With security now tightened up, it became very difficult to carry out even the most basic task at Headquarters. Lack of trust became a problem and, as people sought refuge in their national groups, the cliques became tighter than ever before. Brussels had little sympathy and continued to pile on the pressure, expressing on a daily basis their displeasure with the failure thus far to evict the 65th from Windcheater Island.

Up until now, the ERDF had believed they were

playing fair with the 65th. They certainly did not want to be portrayed in the media as cold-blooded killers and the need to be seen to minimise casualties on both sides was paramount. The same politicians who had talked tough and sent in the military when the situation had flared up, had lost heart once the enormity of what they were doing had hit them and, as a result, the ERDF had been saddled with wholly restrictive rules of engagement.

But the disappearance of the Cypriot commandos was a failure too many, and Brussels and London now steadied their nerves and sanctioned a far more aggressive approach.

Peter Kingston's team continued their search for Charlie Taverner. His decision to get Government Communications Headquarters involved had initially paid dividends. The day after Taverner had eloped from ERDF Headquarters, Kingston had been alerted to a call made from a mobile phone somewhere in Wiltshire. The caller had been speaking to a Chinese takeaway and, by referring to the numbers on a menu, put in a substantial and varied order.

It was innocent enough in the circumstances. But the voice of the person putting in the order was that of Taverner. It had been matched to the recordings of his radio transmissions from the ERDF when he had masqueraded as Private Morton. Taverner's call had been received somewhere on Windcheater Island. Whatever he was doing, Taverner certainly wasn't ordering a Chinese takeaway. The person taking the call had tried to play along with the ridiculous subterfuge by replying in a bizarre accent that sounded like a Scouser doing a terrible impression of an irritable Chinaman. Kingston's technicians established a permanent link through to GCHQ and configured their software so that if Taverner used his or any other mobile phone anywhere in Britain, his voice would be recognised and they could rapidly pinpoint his location.

However, that had been six days ago and there had been no further trace of Taverner. Kingston was beginning to think that maybe his boss had been right; that Taverner, in his presumably-coded message to his mates in the 65th, had simply bid farewell, game over and good luck.

Kingston had taken up smoking again in the last few days. Perhaps it was the stress of leading the search for someone as elusive and potentially dangerous as Taverner, and the knowledge that he would eventually have to explain why Taverner was able to escape in the first place.

It was nearly time for lunch, but Kingston decided to wait a while. Over two-hundred soldiers had arrived at the industrial estate early that morning, ready for the next big operation against the 65th, and the lunch queue now snaked out through the canteen doors. He joined the smokers' union outside Headquarters, from where he regarded these new arrivals. Well-nourished and tanned, physically fit and rather intimidating; these were proper soldiers, not the conscripted dross that made up the bulk of the ERDF. He knew what the ERDF was now planning, and as farcical as some of their previous efforts had been, he was glad they had at last decided to get serious, even if their latest idea was the proverbial sledgehammer cracking a nut. If only they'd had the guts to do this earlier, thought Kingston. The Brits were certainly in for a good kicking from this lot and they'd have no choice but to surrender. With Charlie Taverner out of the way, and nothing but a few pissed-up locals with their fireworks and shotguns to potentially hamper proceedings, this silly little siege would be over in a matter of days.

And yet, the slivers of doubt still persisted in Kingston's mind. He had examined Taverner's military file in great detail and knew how unconventional he was; how he constantly bucked the system and did the unexpected. Every one of Taverner's annual reports had alluded to his leadership and exceptional − if misguided − intelligence. For the sake of his own career, Kingston prayed to God that Taverner, wherever he was, was intelligent enough to have seen sense and gone away for good.

Kingston would have been horrified to learn that his nemesis was, at that very moment, watching him through binoculars from a tiny attic window not more than two-hundred metres away.

'Iberian Peninsula airmobile troops,' said Taverner, aware that he was sounding a bit like a spotter. Their dark-orange berets and insignia on their uniform highlighted their airmobile speciality.

'Sounds tasty,' said Billy, who was crouched next to him, puffing away contentedly on his pipe. 'Who are they, then?'

'Airmobile troops. They're picked up by helicopter then dropped in the combat zone. Think of Vietnam.'

'Don't see many helicopters, Boss. Or any fucking gooks!'

'Good point. They may just be ground troops. On the other hand, why would you want to use specialist airmobile troops for a purely ground operation?' said Taverner, rhetorically. 'There are plenty of other ground troops available.'

He observed the movements in the industrial estate for much of the afternoon. Billy left earlier, with instructions to convene a meeting of the team in the Ship and Shovel.

Two floors below, Elsie was engrossed in an afternoon television quiz show, and when she heard Taverner coming down the ladder to use the bathroom, she made him a cup of tea and took it up to him with some slices of Battenburg cake. She nearly dropped the tray when he came out of the bathroom. Taverner now sported dreadlocks and wore a metal ring through his nose.

'Oooh no, it doesn't suit you, love,' said Elsie, crumpling her face in disapproval when she eventually recognised him.

'I know. It makes me look like I've got cancer of the hair. Don't worry, it's only a wig,' he said, pulling it to one side.

Elsie regarded his filthy clothes. 'Do you want me to do some washing for you, love?' she said.

'That's awfully kind of you. Perhaps tomorrow? That would be lovely.'

They chatted for a while and Taverner listened politely while Elsie told him more than he really wanted to know about poor old Mrs Nicholls next-door-but-one and the problems she was having with her ovaries. As she relayed the unnecessary gynaecological details, he was aware, as he had been in the past few days, of a creeping fatigue in his body. He returned to the attic with his tea and sat on the floor, put his head back on a rafter and closed his eyes for a moment.

It was no use. His mind wouldn't let him rest.

After weeks of living a double-life, living with the fear, the uncertainty and the constant risk of discovery, Taverner was beginning to feel the pressure. Surviving at large as a fugitive, knowing that the authorities were probably out there looking for him, had been invigorating at first. He knew he could rely on his wits and he trusted his instinct.

Holberton was a familiar place and, despite the presence of the ERDF in the industrial estate, he felt he was in friendly territory. However, he had no way of knowing how the hunt for him was progressing, or what organisations were now involved in it. Since he hadn't yet been arrested he could be fairly confident that he wasn't being tracked, although he still took elaborate steps to ensure he would throw a potential trail off the scent. He had only used his mobile phone once from a country lane in Wiltshire – passing a coded message to the 65th to the effect that he was no longer in ERDF Headquarters, although he still intended to assist in whatever way possible. There was a distinct possibility that the call would be traced, so he kept the conversation brief and didn't hang around after he had disconnected.

But the effort of staying one step ahead of the authorities was starting to take its toll. He found himself constantly looking over his shoulder. He checked his rear-view mirror every few seconds when driving. He never met his team in the pub or rendezvoused with anyone without staking out the location for at least half an hour beforehand. He no longer walked down a street, drove down a country lane or entered a building without instinctively looking for an escape route in the event of an ambush. In Holberton, he began to regard people he didn't recognise, not simply as strangers, but as a potential threat. He tried as best he could not to follow any sort of routine. He slept at a number of different locations; in his lodgings at the Halls', at Billy's, sometimes in a sleeping bag in a wood. He was not sleeping well and a degree of paranoia had started to set in. As the days wore on, all he could think about was avoiding arrest, and the temptation to leave Holberton for good became greater.

Taverner still had a job to do though. The 65th remained on Windcheater Island with its hostages, the ERDF was still a threat, and his mission was to harass it in every way possible. He no longer thought of Hannah, or Flint, or the beautiful tropical home where he would go after all this was over; he felt dislocated from that part of his life. His mind was concerned with more pressing matters; constantly active, drawing on some sort of emergency reservoir of chemical stimulant, while physically his body felt drained. Every joint seemed to ache and the dull pain behind his eyes became more persistent.

Back at the Halls' house, Taverner looked over his four false passports. They were beautifully forged – and priced accordingly; the very best the Liverpool underworld could provide.

There was one each for Messrs John Winterbourne of Swindon, Andrew Davies of York, Michael Roos of the Transvaal, South Africa, and James Campbell of Dunedin, New Zealand. They would not attract any attention if presented at any passport control, for these were four *bona fide* gentlemen, going about their day-to-day lives somewhere in the world in ignorance of the fact that their passports had been cloned.

From now on, Taverner would keep them on his possession, in the event he had to leave in a hurry. He also carried a substantial amount of cash on a discreet waistbelt. His escape plan was straightforward, involving a flight from a regional airport in the North East – where there were no biometric scanners – to Norway, from where he would take another flight to the East Coast of the USA, and from there to his final destination in the Bahamas.

He checked these details again on the Internet. He knew which airlines flew where and at what times during the week, and noted there had been no recent changes to their schedules.

There was something else, too.

The surfing websites were going crazy.

The huge hurricane that had lashed Bermuda, Hurricane Gregory, had moved out into the North Atlantic. Tracking into the cooler latitudes, the storm had weakened and lost a little power, but it was now radiating huge pulses of energy across the ocean, which would hit the European coast in about five or six days' time, when a high pressure system was forecast to be sitting over Europe.

Warm, sunny days, thought Taverner. Clear blue skies above huge waves smoothed to glassy perfection by a light offshore wind.

Another epic session was on its way. It was an exact repeat of this time last year. Taverner's stomach tightened a little in reflex; a surfer's natural response to the possibility of dangerous and exhilarating waves.

Of all the bloody times for this swell to arrive, he thought. Whatever the ERDF were planning, he hoped they'd have the courtesy to delay their latest operation until he'd had his fill of these waves. It would be good to surf Saunton one last time.

Taverner turned his thoughts to the impending ERDF operation against the 65th.

All he knew so far was that there were hundreds of airmobile troops in the industrial estate, but there were no troop-carrying helicopters around, so he couldn't even be sure that this was definitely an airmobile operation.

Maybe they would be going in on foot? If so, they

would need a lot of specialist equipment, not just their rifles, if they were going to avoid the mistakes of the first attempt, when the riot vehicles had been destroyed. As far as Taverner could tell, these airmobile troops only had their standard infantry weapons with them.

But what were they doing so close to their intended target? Airmobile troops could be choppered in from hundreds of miles away, thus achieving the element of surprise. Why would you want them any closer?

It was then that Taverner remembered Poland.

Two years earlier, he had been involved in a huge multi-national exercise in Poland. The exercise had been utterly pointless, as all big multi-national exercises were; a rehearsal for the day when some big multi-national force deployed to a Third-World warzone and screwed it up even more, to allay the politicians' consciences. Taverner had spent most of the exercise stuck in a Mobile Command Post at the end of a radio, wishing he was somewhere else. The exercise was cut short after a helicopter crashed some fifty kilometres south of the training area, with an entire company of Portuguese Marines on board. There were no survivors. A simple accident.

In the minds of the safety bureaucrats however, there could never be such a thing as a simple accident, and their subsequent investigation recommended that large numbers of troops should no longer be allowed to travel long distances by helicopter. Helicopters, they decreed, were inherently dangerous. For training, peacekeeping and any minor operation (such as the one at Windcheater Island, where the ERDF was not at war, but officially supporting the civilian authorities), airmobile troops would be picked up as close as possible to the area of operations, to minimise the time exposed to danger – if indeed flying helicopters over friendly territory in friendly airspace could be considered an inherently dangerous activity. The military tacticians hated it, but the edict was not up for negotiation. Parading the Portuguese Marines' relatives on primetime television would always keep the Generals quiet.

In the Ship and Shovel that evening, Taverner gave instructions to his team. If this was going to be an airmobile operation, there would be a large helicopter landing site somewhere not too far away where the troops would embark, probably within a thirty-kilometre radius of Holberton. As an officer in the 65th, he had recce'd such locations, knew what to look for and even how to mark out such an area for the approaching pilots according to international convention. After carefully studying his maps, he suggested certain areas in which his team should focus their search.

THIRTY-NINE

That night, Taverner couldn't sleep again. Each time he drifted off, he started awake. He was agonising over whether to warn Major Hesketh of a possible helicopter assault, but decided against it until he had more evidence.

There was actually very little that Taverner or the 65th could do against a large helicopter assault. The 65th had no anti-aircraft assets. The machine guns might score a few hits and may even bring down a chopper or two with a lucky strike, but with an overwhelming number of enemy troops landing on the island, which may have been softened up by helicopter gunships beforehand, the odds would be firmly stacked against the 65th.

All Taverner could do was to give Hesketh five or ten minutes' notice before the choppers went in so they could surrender before it was too late.

He made himself a cup of tea and put on a movie. *Apocalypse Now* seemed appropriate in the circumstances.

It was one of his favourite films. He especially enjoyed the part where Colonel Kilgore has his squadron of helicopters annihilate a seafront village to the sound of Wagner, risking the lives of his troops and napalming the enemy for a perfectly good reason; he wants to surf the pointbreak in front of the village. Taverner could identify with that.

In an earlier scene, there is a sequence of a cow in a net, underslung below a helicopter, pawing the air and presumably being evacuated. The scene reminded Taverner of the drunken bovine vet in South Molton and his crazy attempts to get his impotent beasts in the mood for passion.

Helicopters.

Cows.

South Molton.

Vets.

An idea began to form in Taverner's head.

Next morning, some of Billy's watchers followed a small convoy from the industrial estate out into the countryside. One of the vehicles contained two Iberian airmobile officers. The convoy spent much of the morning covering the region north of Holberton, stopping every so often to allow the two officers to recce the ground.

Out of sight, the watchers kept an eye on them. They had become very good at their job, and the fact that they knew this stretch of countryside like a black-cab driver knows Central London helped them maintain sufficient discretion. The officers had no idea they were being followed.

Eventually, the convoy returned to a location recce'd earlier. It was a vast field some twenty kilometres north east of Holberton, over forty acres in size and bordered by thick hedgerows. A narrow lane ran along the southern edge of the field and there was a gate for access. To the north of the field there was one of the many derelict farms that could be found throughout the region. From the safety of the farm's outbuildings, the watchers observed the officers in the field.

Later that afternoon, a truck arrived with ten ERDF conscripts, who set up a large tent just inside the entrance to the field.

Taverner had spent most of the day in South Molton with the vet, who had listened in astonishment to his plan. What Taverner was proposing was sheer lunacy; the sort of thing only an unhinged ex-military man could have conceived. Understandably, the vet took a little persuading at first. The plan was not exactly subtle, its effectiveness probably marginal at best, and the potential for it to go badly wrong was considerable. If by some miracle it did work, things would get messy – in every sense of the word – for himself and a lot of other people. He thought briefly of his family, of the children he was no longer allowed to see, of his ex-wife and her comfortable life in the Central London Zone. Here he was; an intelligent and educated man, unpaid for the past six months, eking out a wretched existence working for some long-forgotten government agency in a threadbare and underfunded laboratory with a mildewy, sloping caravan for a home. The chance to exact a little revenge on the system that had reduced him to this was appealing. He might have simply agreed to let Taverner stage a violent break-in to the laboratory to get the specific materials he needed, and pleaded ignorance when the police came knocking. But in order for Taverner's plan to stand any chance of success, he needed to be rather more involved.

The vet came onboard.

Taverner left the vet running some models on an old laptop computer and returned to Holberton to meet his team in the evening. When they told him of the movements of the airmobile officers, he insisted they drive out and take a look.

They parked up some distance away and, in the darkness, approached the derelict farm north of the field, where one of Billy's watchers had hidden away in the loft. Taverner surveyed the scene through night-vision goggles. It was just possible to make out some fluorescent markers on the ground at the south end of the field, where a sentry stood by the gate. The sentry smoked constantly and relieved himself once in the hedge. His rifle, if he had one, was nowhere to be seen. The watcher confirmed that the rest of the guards were in the tent.

Taverner left his team at the farm and drove for several hours. He had seen what he needed to. It was time to warn the 65th.

Peter Kingston, like Taverner, had not been sleeping well either. He was simply not used to such a lengthy investigation as this one. Most of the jobs on which he and his team were sent would be wrapped up in a matter of days – even hours – such were the resources at their disposal.

For a manhunt to last more than a week was rare. The hunt for Taverner was now into its second week, which was unprecedented. They simply had nothing more to go on and Kingston was feeling the pressure. Even bad news would have been better than no news.

His technician roused him from a light sleep in the early hours.

'Charlie Taverner's just been on his mobile phone again. To Windcheater Island. About five minutes ago.'

'Fucking hell,' moaned Kingston, screwing his eyes up tightly.

'He's been making another call to his Chinese takeaway.'

'Where was the call made from?'

'Somerset. About ten kilometres south of Shepton Mallet. His phone has been turned off now. I've already tasked the local police to check out the location. They're going to report back shortly.'

Kingston looked at his watch. 'I'll be over in five minutes. Tell the police to get Forensic involved.'

A bleary-eyed Kingston climbed into the back of the van with a mug of black coffee and spoke over the radio to the policeman now searching an empty lay-by on a minor road south of Shepton Mallet. The target had long since gone.

Over the speakers, the technician replayed the recent conversation between Taverner and the Chinese takeaway. As before, Taverner was speaking to someone who sounded like they came from Merseyside and was doing an appalling imitation of an angry Chinaman.

'Good evening,' said Taverner. 'Is that the Ben Wah Takeaway? I'd like to place an order please.'

'Do you fuh'in know wa' time it is, sir? I mean, mate?'

'I'm so sorry, I thought you were open through the night.'

'Of course we fuh'in open all nigh' no fanks to plicks like you. Now, what you fuh'in wonn?'

Taverner read out an extensive list of numbers.

'Tha' is two-hundred firty free Euros. Fuh' me you sure you can 'ford 'dis? We don' tek card. Cash only.'

'I have the money with me.'

'That's a rot of cash. Leckon you are lich plick then? Ret me check. Number forty one Glilled Chicken Peking Style. Number twenty King Plawns in Satay Mushlooms.

Number sixty eight Kung Po Hot Chirri Vegetabraws. Number erreven Flied Shledded Beef with Callots. Number fifty four Clispy Alomatic Duck. Number eighty one, eighty two, eighty four, Beef Cully, Special Cully and Shlimp Cully …'

'Yes, this phone call *is* costing me money,' interrupted Taverner. 'I have every confidence the numbers are correct. Oh, and I nearly forgot. Number one-hundred and fourteen. Chicken Jalfrezi.'

'Eh? You fink you are crevver git? This is fuh'in Chinese, mate. We don' do Indian shi'. If you take the piss then berieve me you don' wonn to know what we put in your Special Flied Lice. My aged ancestor she clap in it rots.'

'Sorry. I didn't mean any offence. By the way do you deliver?'

'You funny guy. Come and get it your fuh'in sel'. Order ready in half hour.'

'Ah-so,'

'And arsehose to you, you fuh'in git.'

Next morning in the pub, Taverner briefed his team on what was going to happen next. Billy, Terry and the watchers looked on sceptically as he outlined his plan. If this was how Taverner planned to disrupt the ERDF's next operation, then clearly it wasn't the enemy troops that they needed to be worried about.

Gradually, Taverner brought them round with his confidence and his style of delivery. The conviction and faith he had in the plan was contagious. They realised that morning – more so than on previous occasions – that they were in the company of someone who had done this sort of thing many times before.

As their questions turned from the serious to the seriously ribald, Taverner knew he had them in his pocket.

'We need one more vital piece of information,' he said. 'We need to know *when* they are going launch this attack. As I'm sure you can appreciate, this is not something we can put into action at a moment's notice. Keep your ears to the ground.'

'Boss, I reckon you's bloody crazy,' said Billy. 'Still, even if it does go tits-up, it'd be a bloody good laugh. Wouldn't not miss it for the world.'

'Billy, you know I'm not one to pass up the chance to provide good entertainment for the masses. Such a shame, therefore, that we will be the only ones with the ringside seats for this wholly depraved and tasteless event. I'm sure people would pay handsomely to see this. No-one ever lost out underestimating the British public's level of taste, did they?'

FORTY

The media were still camped out in their Winnebagos near the industrial estate. Very little had happened for several weeks and the exclusives were becoming very thin on the ground.

The major news organisation was the BBC; the mouthpiece of the government, and people moved seamlessly between the Corporation and the institutions of State. For the ambitious graduate seeking a glamorous career in the media, the BBC was the diamond-studded option; fiercely competitive to get into, and something of a closed shop, for all sorts of political reasons. Once you were in, you were in for life, barring any careless indiscretions. There were occasional purges at the top as power changed hands and the thrusters higher up realised in horror they had nailed their flag squarely to the wrong mast, but it was, for the correct-minded person, a secure existence in an organisation whose business was essentially that of the government's; to tenderly moralise, to subtly lecture the masses, and in its insipid, chocolaty way, to mould the individual to the approved specification.

Beyond the fringes of the State media were the independent outfits who led a much freer and more precarious existence. Much of what they churned out was tabloid-esque, sensationalist trash, but there were companies who employed some of the better journalists who preferred to retain their editorial independence and work outside the confines of the commissars. These newshounds were usually denied access to official sources, although this mattered not one iota to them. The government tolerated the independent media – keen as they were to portray Britain as a liberal democracy with a free press – but ensured the BBC always had primacy.

From the outset of the operation, the BBC had set itself up inside ERDF Headquarters, where it had up-to-the-minute information on events, and was even allowed to have a say in how and when operations might take place so that events could be politically exploited.

But a few seasoned hacks of the independents had an astonishing ability to find out what was going on as well. On arrival in Holberton they had quickly established some useful sources. They had known, for example, that the ERDF had recruited local civilian labour for menial tasks in Headquarters; a group of sweet old ladies and over-worked single mothers, ignorant and unworldly, who'd all had a cursory background check before being taken on, but had not been judged to be a security risk.

In the first few days, most journalists had latched onto them and pressed them relentlessly for any information – to no avail; the ERDF had chosen them well. Though they gossiped incessantly, their conversation failed to extend beyond the price of tea in the local supermarket, or poor Mrs So-and-so with her painful abscess. They were not much help.

However, not all these workers were cut from the same cloth.

Take dear old Jean, for example. She worked at ERDF Headquarters every day, cleared the plates away in the Officers' canteen and came round on the dot every two hours with the coffee and the tea in the Ops Room. She wore a permanent expression of mild pain, with her mouth agape as if straining for breath. To the casual observer she looked to be several mints short of a full packet.

But dear old Jean could complete *The Times'* crossword in the time it took to boil her little kettle for tea when she got back in the evening. She was sharp and she missed very little. Every other evening, the nice man from the telly visited her with a very generous sum of money. She was grateful for the extra cash to supplement her pension, and with it she would buy her grandchildren something fancy, like, for Christmas.

Jean's ability to recall conversations was phenomenal and, although she had very little idea of what she was relaying to the reporter, she told him everything she heard. It all made sense to the reporter, who had served his time as a war correspondent.

It was a very happy reporter who took his camera crew to the pub that Tuesday lunchtime for a swift half. They avoided the Ship and Shovel, which was always full of swarthy-looking locals, and opted for the much quieter Railway Inn. The lunchtime-half turned unintentionally into a heavy afternoon session – as all good piss-ups do – and the more of the dreadful wine they put away, the louder and more indiscreet they became. They were bored with this assignment and just wanted to get home.

The reporter had got his tip last night from Jean. He had visited her in her tiny flat, drunk her tea, cooed at her

Ginger Tom and put a few more Euros her way. She had told him something very juicy indeed which, if true, would mean this bloody siege would finally be over in a few days. He had already figured out how he would cover the forthcoming operation and, more importantly, how he would outwit the BBC. He could leave the boring coverage of the subsequent clean-up to some up-and-coming young buck, while he would be on his way back home to receive accolades from his bosses and maybe an exciting new assignment. It was in this spirit of eager anticipation that he had brought his crew to the pub in the first place.

The barman kept bringing bottles of wine, which they would taste and then reject, to much laughter and self-congratulation. It was foul stuff and they had expensive palates, but they needn't have been quite so abrupt. The barman was a young lad and not accustomed to such rudeness, especially from townies. From behind the bar, he had been listening with interest to their conversation, and contacted Terry – the pub's owner.

A short time later, a few heavy-looking locals came in and sat at the bar, supping pints and chatting quietly with the barman, ignoring the raucous behaviour of the television crew.

When the reporter staggered off to the gents, Taverner followed after him. The reporter stood at the urinals with his forehead against the wall and did not see Taverner locking the door behind him.

'Looks like you're having a good afternoon, mate,' said Taverner, taking the urinal furthest away from the reporter and staring straight ahead at the wall in accordance with gentlemen's lavatorial etiquette.

'Fucking marvellous!' replied the reporter.

'Ah, a reason to celebrate, then?'

'You bet!'

'I recognise you from the telly,' said Taverner. 'You're down here covering the siege?'

'Yes.'

'And you're out of here soon, by the sound of it?'

'Thank God. No offence, but this place is a fucking hole. I've been in more welcoming warzones.'

Taverner ignored his charm. 'So you've been reassigned? Recalled perhaps?'

'Not quite,' said the reporter, becoming aware that the scruffy, dreadlocked yokel at the other end of the urinals was perhaps a little more intelligent than most of the hicks who lived in the town. His accent certainly wasn't local, come to think of it, and suggested an education at one of the better independent schools.

'You'll be being replaced, then?' said Taverner.

'No,' said the reporter, getting a little irritated.

The two of them zipped up simultaneously and went to the wash basins. Taverner turned to face him.

'Or perhaps,' said Taverner, 'you've recently discovered that there's going to be one big final attack to break the stand-off.'

The reporter stayed silent.

'So big it cannot possibly go wrong this time,' said Taverner, 'using helicopters.'

The reporter looked at him in horror. It was his little exclusive, and he didn't want too many people knowing about it.

'Ah! Your silence tells me everything,' said Taverner. Any friendliness in his voice had evaporated.

'That's none of your fucking business. Anyway, you're

talking crap.' The reporter tried to open the door and became a little agitated when he found it wouldn't move.

Behind him, Taverner continued. 'Well, you seem happy to have discussed it at some length in a rather public place. That wine certainly loosened your tongues. Perhaps you assume that everyone in this town is a web-handed inbred who can't understand the King's English. Well, they're a bit more switched-on than that. Take it from me. Round here, a little knowledge is a dangerous thing.'

A terrible thought dawned on the reporter. The filthy yokel was not some grotty farm labourer – he was an agent working for the Interior Ministry. He had been spouting off in public about things he should have kept quiet about, and the Interior Ministry was not noted for its sympathy in dealing with those who happened to fall out of favour with it. Though he did not work for the State, he was still able to enjoy a comfortable existence inside the Central London Zone, and his job and his livelihood were now at stake. He and his family could be out of their home before the end of the month, and the thought of having to scrape together a living in some outcast hellhole as a hack for some dreadful local tabloid made his stomach churn. His dignity started to fail him and he tried in vain to shake the door open.

'For Christ's sake, you don't think I'm one of *them*?' said Taverner.

The reporter turned round to face him. The flush of the heavy session had drained from his face. 'Then what do you want?' he asked.

'Firstly, I'm concerned for your safety,' said Taverner, insincerely. 'The authorities would be horrified with the extent of your knowledge. There are some suspicious-looking characters hanging around this town at the moment. They look very out of place. One wouldn't like to say who they work for, but I think we both know, eh?'

The reporter supported himself on the wall.

'But I might just have some information someone like you would be most interested in,' said Taverner. 'Who do you work for nowadays?'

The reporter did not protest as Taverner reached into his jacket pocket and pulled out his wallet. Both men were about the same weight, but whereas the reporter's was mostly fat from too many expense-account lunches, Taverner was leaner and considerably more athletic. His dreadlocks and nose-piercing made him look even more malevolent. If things got playful, the reporter would not have stood a chance.

"JKI Television News," read Taverner from his Press card. 'Do you remember the first attack on the base, when the riot vehicles tried to break through the Sentry Post? I daresay you filmed it. The ERDF brushed it off as some sort of probing reconnaissance mission. You didn't buy that, did you? Did you know that those riot vehicles were not destroyed by rifle fire, but by an anti-tank gun that the 65th had hidden out of sight? Look again at your old footage.'

The reporter looked intrigued. He had heard something similar to that from Jean, his informant.

'But I bet you didn't know,' said Taverner, 'that it was a very old anti-tank gun, a German 88mm gun from the Eastern Front, something the 65th recommissioned specially for the occasion.'

'No I didn't. How do you know that?'

Taverner smiled and tapped the side of his nose. 'Did you know that the details of the attack were leaked to the 65th from inside the ERDF? That's not common knowledge either, is it?'

Again, that confirmed something Jean had mentioned. She had also told the reporter that the ERDF suspected that some of the local population were trying to sabotage the operation. He had dismissed the idea; people in Holberton looked to be incapable of tying their shoelaces together without strangling themselves, and the thought of them engaging in some sort of sabotage was risible. Perhaps there was some truth in what Jean had said, after all. The tall dreadlocked local in front of him was somehow involved, and he got the impression that if he was, despite outward appearances, he was high up in the pecking order.

'I would like to further establish your confidence in me,' said Taverner. 'Are you aware that a week ago another attempt was made to rescue the hostages, though rather more stealthily, by commandos in rigid inflatables? Nothing has been heard of them since.'

Once again, this confirmed some snippets of conversation overheard by Jean. Taverner had now got his full attention. The reporter was onto something.

'You see, I think we're both in a position to help each other right now,' said Taverner.

'Go on.'

'You know what the ERDF is going to do next. Frankly, I already knew of their intention to go in by helicopter long before you did. But I would really like to know exactly *when* the attack is due to take place.'

'And what's in it for me? *Quid pro quo,*' said the reporter, his confidence returning.

'An exclusive like you'll never see again. A spectacular to end all spectaculars.'

The reporter was sceptical, but clearly interested.

'You're very vague.'

'I have to be.'

'Why can't you tell me more?'

'Helps me stay alive. No, that's all I'm saying for now. Something very special is being planned by certain people round here. I can assure you that you will not want to miss it.'

The reporter thought for a while.

'If I help you, I want the exclusive. If I don't get it and you renege, the authorities would suddenly become most interested in your activities. That would be a good story as well, and also my exclusive.'

'Please don't insult my intelligence,' said Taverner. 'Unlike most of your lot, I keep to my word.'

'The helicopter assault?'

'Yes. When?'

'Apparently it's going in on ...'

'Uh uh,' interrupted Taverner, wagging his index finger. He gestured to the surroundings. 'The walls have ears. Write it down.'

The reporter took out a notebook and scribbled something down. He tore out the page and handed it to Taverner.

'Thank you,' said Taverner, his mind racing furiously. 'Well, well, well. We had better move quickly on this. You and your crew are to be in this pub tomorrow night, Wednesday. Better make it closing time. So, do we have a deal?'

Taverner shook the reporter's offered hand and didn't let go, holding it in a vice-like grip.

'Good,' said Taverner. 'By the way, if any of our conversation is leaked to anyone else, instead of taking you to our little shindig, my friends, who are at this moment waiting outside this very door, will escort you to a quiet place up on the moor with orders from me to break you down very slowly into your component parts.' He spoke with the steady voice of someone to whom violence is way of life. 'Wherever you are, we will find you.'

Taverner released him and unlocked the door. The reporter washed his hands again and left the gents. He noticed that two large gentlemen had been waiting outside the door and he gestured for his party to leave the pub.

Taverner waited inside the gents for a while. He did not simply want to thwart the helicopter assault. He wanted, above all, to humiliate the ERDF and to do so in a very public way. He wanted to reduce them to a laughing stock. He needed to contact the 65th again.

'It's him! Just outside ... Taunton,' said the technician, plotting the location of the mobile phone's signal on the map.

It was ninety minutes after Taverner had spoken to the reporter.

'Get onto the local police,' ordered Kingston.

The technician tapped away at his keyboard and hit the Enter key.

'Done!'

They listened in real time as Taverner once again read out another lengthy order to the Ben Wah Chinese Takeaway.

The phone was disconnected, and by the time the nearest police had responded, Taverner had long since gone.

Kingston contacted his boss in Whitehall over the secure line.

'Sir, we've now had two coded telephone calls in less than twenty-four hours between Charlie Taverner and the

65th, just as the ERDF are about to mount a very big attack on Windcheater Island. It's too much of a coincidence. I *must* have a Field Team in the next six hours.'

'Charlie Taverner only remains at large because you haven't caught him,' teased his superior. 'It's not like you to let them get away, is it, Peter?'

'Look, it's a critical time now. He might be warning the 65th that something's about to happen, and I wouldn't put it past him to try and somehow sabotage the whole operation.'

His boss laughed heavily down the phone. 'One former Army officer pitting himself heroically against what I understand will be a squadron of helicopters and several-hundred highly-trained troops? Really, Peter! Have you taken leave of your senses?'

Kingston persisted. 'With all due respect, sir, have you actually read his file? Or any of the reports I've sent up to you? This guy is as mad as a fruitcake and as slippery as an eel. He is one seriously unhinged individual. If anything goes wrong with this forthcoming operation because of him, then we, as a department, are going to be well and truly fucked.'

'But you have no proof he's up to anything?'

'I just know he is. You know I'm not one to blow my own trumpet, but I'm never wrong about these things.'

'Just a couple of phone calls?'

'Gut instinct.'

'Peter, Peter,' said his boss, wearily. 'Choose your next words very carefully. In your professional opinion, is there a current threat from this chap Charlie Taverner?'

'Yes. And I am going on record as stating precisely that.'

His boss thought for a while. 'Okay, you've got your Field Team.'

'Thank you, sir.'

'But not until Thursday afternoon.'

'What? No, that's too late! We need to find him before then. The attack is scheduled for Thursday *morning*.'

'Well, if you feel that strongly, get them to postpone it until Friday.'

'I can't do that.'

'*Persuade* them. Look, you know how it is at the moment. The Field Teams have been very busy of late with a big operation in Liverpool, and if I pull a team off the job today, they've got to have one clear day before the next task. You know how it is with the Working Time Directive. If this attack is going to be on the scale they've told me, then I'm sure the ERDF can fend off whatever this Taverner chap has in mind, if indeed he is foolish enough to try and interfere.'

'But the guy is totally fucking crazy! He'll try something, I know it.'

'You used to be a field man too, Peter. Use this whole operation to lure him in. Undertake a little covert surveillance with your team. Then you can give the details to the Field Team when they arrive.'

'But I'm only down here with technicians. They're bloody number-crunchers. They'd stick out like sore thumbs.'

'Then you'll just have to hope the operation is delayed for a day or two. I'm sorry, Peter, but that's final. They'll be down later on Thursday.'

Kingston put down the phone and momentarily lost his self-control in an explosion of frustration.

FORTY-ONE

In the darkness, the sprayers worked quickly through the helicopter landing site. The ERDF soldiers guarding the field had long since retired to their tent.

Four of Billy's watchers had volunteered to do the spraying. Fully donned in their equipment they were a faintly disturbing sight, looking like the sort of gentlemen one might expect to come knocking at the front door to let one know that there had been a nuclear accident nearby. They each wore a thick boiler suit, rubber gloves, boots and gas mask, and carried a heavy tank on their backs. For several hours they sprayed the area with a heavy chemical mist that settled and clung to the grass.

Taverner watched the sprayers through night-vision goggles from the loft in the derelict farm to the north. Short-range radios directed them to certain points in the field and enabled Taverner to alert them if any of the guards came out of their tent. If challenged, their cover story was that they were farm workers innocently spraying insecticide on the land – and yes, Mr Soldierman, round here it's quite normal to do it at this time of night.

On the floor below the loft, the vet finished his calculations and briefed the reporter.

'There's a light north-westerly breeze running tonight, with a small chance that it might pick up later on. We've added a bit more thickening agent so it sticks to the ground better. It will continue to give off vapour for the next twenty-four hours, although the maximum concentration will occur in six hours' time. The compound is quite unstable and denatures gradually over several days after exposure to sunlight. In a week's time, there'll be no trace of it.'

'And this ... stuff. How long has it been around?' asked the reporter.

'Not that long in its present form. It's entirely synthetic. We took four natural pheromones secreted by heifers – they're female cows, by the way – and replicated them, with a few chemical add-ons for greater effect.'

'But if you wanted to build up your cattle stock, why not import virus-free bulls from the Continent and breed from them? What about artificial insemination?'

'It's not allowed. Why not? The usual excuses. Import restrictions, set by Brussels. And the Europeans who are now supplying us with beef and milk want to protect their market. Quite understandable, really. No, the government just doesn't want agriculture in this country. Thinks that farmers are too bloody militant. The whole Bovine Fertility Project is just a sop so they can be seen to show how deeply they care for British farming and agriculture. It's all bullshit. They don't actually want it to succeed.'

'So tell me more about this special chemical.'

'The formula we're using comes in the form of a vapour that has been tested at concentrations between two and ten parts per million. It's very, very strong. The maximum efficacy occurs at eight parts per million.'

'In English, please.'

'That's the point at which the beast reaches the maximum state of sexual arousal and yet still enables us to control him with standard agricultural apparatus. Beyond that, well, to say that things get out of control is an understatement. Two months ago, one of our lab technicians dropped a vial of the pheromone near a bull. He's still in hospital, and if he is ever to walk again he'll need a spinal chord graft. The creature, literally, fell head-over-heels in love with him,' said the vet, wincing at the memory of the whimpering broken-backed technician. 'We calculated the concentration on that occasion reached fifteen parts per million.'

'And how was the creature? Happy, I should imagine.'

'It went completely berserk and had to be destroyed. We were forced to call in police snipers. Their rifles were useless, so they had to use grenade launchers. Best thing for it, really. Its eyeballs had popped out with the excitement and it was so exhausted by the time they blew it up, it could barely stand.'

'May I ask what concentration you're using tonight?' said the reporter.

'Just over sixty parts per million.'

The reporter whistled softly.

The sprayers were finished by two o'clock. They returned to the farm, removed their tanks, and the vet hosed them down with a neutralising solution and sealed their boiler suits in a heavy-duty bag, to be burnt later on. While it was still dark, a camera crew from JKI Television News made their way round the edge of the field and found a spot in a hedge not far from the tent with the sleeping guards. Another camera crew found a similar spot on the opposite side of the field, and a third camera covered the field at longer range from the farm. The Outside Broadcast Unit was tucked away out of sight in an outbuilding on the farm, from where they tested the link to the cameras in the field. In their London studios, the producers at JKI Television News prepared themselves for the broadcast.

Some of Taverner's team quietly fixed barriers in place, creating a channel from the farm courtyard to the entrance to the field. When the last barrier was in position, the connections between the barriers were checked for integrity. A few drops of very dilute pheromone were sprinkled around the courtyard.

When everything was ready, a cattle truck, which had been waiting some distance away, was driven very slowly to the farm and manoeuvred into position with its tailgate backing onto a small gap in the barriers. The truck rocked as the ten large Hereford bulls inside started to get a little agitated.

FORTY-TWO

Just before daybreak, a long convoy of trucks made its way slowly through narrow lanes to the helicopter landing site, trailing a plume of cloying diesel fumes that mixed uneasily with the morning mist. The whining noise of the trucks' gearboxes carried a long way on the still air, waking the ERDF soldier guarding the field, who until then had been dozing in his canvas chair. He called into a very foetid tent to wake the other guards. Beside him, smoke rose slowly from the embers in an old oil drum. The soldier was a conscript; seventeen-years old, tired, utterly indifferent to this whole operation and missing his Mediterranean home. The morning air was chilly. He stomped his feet to get some circulation going and kick-started his lungs with a cigarette, smoking it tactically by instinct, cupping the glowing tip in towards the palm of his glove. He took off his thick woolly hat and picked up his rifle and helmet, brushing wet grass from them.

Better start to look professional, he thought.

The convoy rolled to a halt on the lane and the soldiers jumped out. These soldiers were professional airmobile troops – in a very different league to the conscripted sentries. They were better equipped, better trained, better paid, and they would certainly be able to pull the better-looking *señoritas*. The weapons were passed out the back of the trucks and the soldiers waited by the side of the road, checking their equipment and adjusting their helmets and body armour. The corporals and sergeants did a bit of shouting and swearing – as corporals and sergeants are wont to do in every army – and once they were ready, they made their way through the gate into the field and got into six platoons of thirty, with each platoon spread out along the edge of the field, behind their designated fluorescent marker.

Next to the tent, the sentries looked on and lit another round of cigarettes. Perhaps some of the airmobile boys had overdone the aftershave that morning – in any case, to wear too much was an airmobile soldier's prerogative, they reckoned – but layered above the smell of smoke and damp grass the sentries could detect a distinct odour of something not entirely unpleasant. Slightly sickly, slightly sweet. A dangerous bouquet, both temptingly floral and enticingly musky.

The airmobile troops could smell it too, and put it down to some nearby industrial source, or maybe the conscripts by the gate were just keeping themselves fresh by spraying their uniform with deodorant.

The sun started to burn off the mist. A few crows and jackdaws wheeled overhead, complaining about the early disturbance.

Across the whole country, people were waking up, showering, preparing breakfast, brewing the first coffee of the day and casually flicking between the TV channels. JKI Television News was on standby to go live.

The mist delayed the start of the operation by about

half an hour, but just before half past seven the distinctive sound of helicopters could be heard to the north, where six heavy-lift, twin-rotor Chinooks were approaching. A handful of smaller recce helicopters flew alongside in support.

The Chinooks descended slowly as they neared the field and, one by one, they approached their fluorescent markers. When they were directly above the markers they turned through one-hundred and eighty degrees and settled gently onto the surface, washing hot kerosene exhaust fumes over the troops, and causing the sentries' tent to flap alarmingly.

The pilots kept the engines running and the rotors turning; this was to be a quick pick-up. When all the Chinooks were on the ground, the recce helicopters landed a few hundred yards ahead of them. The platoons waited to be called forward.

Peter Kingston was following events inside ERDF Headquarters. The ERDF had imposed a press blackout, although the BBC had ensured its correspondents were in position near Windcheater Island, ready to film the initial assault. More importantly, they would be the first to broadcast from inside the base, after it had been liberated.

But the BBC was beaten to it. A few of its staff at Headquarters were casually monitoring other TV stations, and watched in horror as JKI Television News – regarded by the BBC as a serious-minded but largely insignificant little organisation – began its own live broadcast direct from the helicopter landing site, as the Chinooks came into land.

That was not meant to happen. The ERDF did not want to give the 65th any warning of the assault and the

BBC was supposed to have the exclusive by right. The JKI Television News broadcast had been on the air for less than ten seconds before telephones started ringing at Headquarters. People in London wanted to know what the hell was going on.

At the derelict farm, Taverner's team gathered around the window in the loft, waiting for him to give the signal. In the courtyard below stood the cattle truck with the waiting bulls. The vet held a control box that was connected to the truck by a long cable. At the press of a button the tailgate would drop down, leaving the bulls free to stampede down the channel.

The noise of the helicopters could only just be heard over the snorting and roaring coming from inside the truck. The vet, whose nerves were already on edge given the pioneering nature of this experiment, not to say its illegality, started to squirm.

'Tav, if we don't let them go soon, they're going to tear each other to shreds!' he shouted. 'They can already smell it!'

The truck bucked and rocked in sympathy with the terrible energy within. Cradling the control box, the vet felt like some sort of demolition engineer.

'Not yet!' barked Taverner. 'Just a few moments.'

The vet moved back as far as the cable would allow, as close as he could to the stairs that led up to the loft. He had seen what these creatures could do when aroused and he had no intention of remaining in the vicinity if the barriers failed under the onslaught.

Upstairs, Taverner fixed his binoculars on the troops.

'Come on you bastards, move.'

The Chinook pilots received clearance from ERDF Headquarters to start loading. They acknowledged and passed the message over the intercom to their Loadmasters. At the helicopters' rear ramps the lights changed from red to green, and the troops started walking towards the ramps, into the noise and the fumes.

JKI Television News now had the nation's attention.

'Now!' shouted Taverner.

The vet pressed the button. The back of the truck dropped down with a deafening crash. The narrow wooden stairs to the loft might have been covered in five hefty bounds by an athlete of Olympic standard, but the vet, who was out of condition, somehow managed to despatch them in three. Below, the herd thundered down off the truck and into the channel.

The barriers initially did their job well, funnelling the bulls into the field where they fanned out in an arc and advanced with tremendous momentum, the scent improving the further they got. The effect of the pheromone was astonishing, and their sexual excitement reached unprecedented levels. Their lust had to be satisfied immediately.

Two bulls couldn't even wait to get into the field and tore into each other as soon as they had exited the truck; rearing up, each trying to scramble over the other. The barriers collapsed under their weight and the intertwined creatures continued their courtship in the yard.

From the safety of the loft, the team watched in a mixture of horror and fascination.

'Jesus, it doesn't make them homosexual, does it?' said Taverner.

Neither of the two creatures was willing to play the

373

female role in the coupling, and their energetic foxtrot degenerated into a frenzy of butting and stamping.

At the other end of the field, the troops were filing towards the Chinooks when the first creature appeared. At first glance it looked like an average docile, grass-munching cow, but it quickly became apparent that it was nothing of the sort. The troops hesitated for a moment, then scattered. A few ran onto the helicopters, while others ran away towards the edge of the field, chased by a couple of bulls desperate to have sex with anything they could.

Suddenly the whole field seemed to be full of cattle, and in an instant the efficient orderliness of the embarkation degenerated into chaos.

The bulls charged at anything that moved, and many things that didn't. A small recce helicopter waited on the ground in front of the Chinooks, with its rotors turning, waiting for the Chinooks to complete loading. The stampede tore past the helicopter and its pilot looked over his shoulder to see soldiers dispersing at speed. Any soldier that tripped or was simply too slow was stamped on, trampled, butted and gored. Nearby, one young soldier ran straight towards the recce helicopter in panic; a vision of bovine insanity had taken a fancy to him and was rapidly closing in. The soldier ran blindly into the back of the helicopter, and the engine revs dropped suddenly as the poor chap was swiftly despatched by the tail rotor.

The recce helicopter, now out of balance, vibrated alarmingly. If the pilot thought he was safe inside his helicopter, then he was about to be proved wrong. The nearby bull – whose desires were dashed by the sudden disappearance of the young soldier, whose legs and lower torso now lay on the floor underneath the tail rotor – stood still for a moment in front of the helicopter. In the throes of such extreme lust the perspex bubble canopy of the helicopter looked as inviting as the curves of a sensuous, naked blonde would look to a sailor after three months at sea. The bull stared at the pilot with its awful come-to-bed eyes, trotted purposefully up to the helicopter and mounted the windscreen. The pilot opened the throttle in the hope of deterring the bull, but it was to no avail. No sooner had the bull mounted the canopy than it climaxed, to its evident enormous pleasure and to the greater disgust of the pilot. It bellowed loudly and arched its head, straight up into the spinning rotors.

Some of the resulting flecks of blood and cranial tissue spattered the lens of the television camera hidden in a nearby hedge. The image went out live to the nation on JKI Television News, causing many viewers, now utterly transfixed to their screens, to vomit in their cornflakes. The programme's producers were delighted.

Sheer good luck had allowed one platoon of soldiers to board their Chinook unimpeded, and they sat inside waiting to take off. The frightening noise and exhaust wash from their helicopter failed to deter one rampant bull who, having failed to find anything terribly receptive outside, cantered towards it, hoping that something beautiful awaited him within. The Loadmaster screamed over the intercom for the pilot to get airborne as the beast came at the loading ramp. He flicked the switch to raise the ramp, desperately trying to shoo the creature away, but it was having none of it and came up the ramp into the aircraft as the helicopter got airborne – the only one to do so that morning – with the pilot quite unaware of his new passenger. The Loadmaster, in a state of hysteria in the back, was now screaming at him over the intercom to land immediately. The pilot, wishing his Loadmaster would make up his mind, looked down at the strange sight in the field below him and searched for a landing spot a little further away. He could hear screaming and crashing in the back of the helicopter and, thinking that he was taking small arms fire from the ground, took evasive action. He dipped the nose to pick up speed and pulled the huge helicopter round to the right in a very low banking turn. The handling of the helicopter had become very cumbersome and it felt as though the centre of gravity was shifting around.

In the back of the helicopter, the bull butted and crushed the soldiers. A group had unbuckled themselves and moved to the front; fighting to get behind everyone else, away from the hideous creature. The bull advanced on them, slipping and sliding over the bloody, metallic floor. Clearly there was nothing for it in here, so it charged back towards the ramp. The helicopter was about four-hundred feet above the ground as the bull trotted off the ramp into thin air; its legs scrabbling for some sort of purchase, and when it hit the ground it exploded in an impressive splash of blood and viscera.

Relieved that the helicopter had suddenly regained more predictable handling, but sensing that all was not well behind him, the pilot set the Chinook down in a field about half a mile away.

Back in the main field the survivors regrouped, and shots rang out as some of the soldiers loaded their weapons and fired on the beasts from the relative safety of the hedge. The 7.62mm rounds were barely making an impact on the enraged creatures, with only the occasional head-shot seeming to have any effect. A few bulls tore round the field oblivious to the noise, humping the carcasses of their fallen brethren. The officer in charge gave the order to the soldiers to load their grenade launchers. One by one, the beasts were taken out in spectacular fashion, and each one that remained alive now drew an increasing amount of fire. The last bull backed towards a helicopter and everyone fired at it at once. The pilot screamed over the radio for them to stop firing as he could hear fragments from the grenades hitting his aircraft. A few splinters penetrated the fuel tank, there was a small lick of flame and then a tremendous explosion as the whole fuel tank went up, setting fire to a neighbouring helicopter.

JKI Television News continued their broadcast. Back at the derelict farm, the reporter continued with his commentary from his Outside Broadcast Unit as his producers in London cut from camera to camera, seeking the best footage and the goriest shot.

Peter Kingston left ERDF Headquarters, where people were burying their heads in their hands, and went to his van. He felt vindicated. His boss was not so supercilious when Kingston phoned him at his home; he had been watching the ensuing chaos on the television over breakfast. Now there would be no question — a team of agents from the Security Support Agency would be in Holberton by ten o'clock that morning.

Taverner's job was done. Thick black smoke billowed into the sky from the wreckage of the two burning Chinooks. As much as the team wanted to hang around to admire their work, they knew it was not safe to do so. They departed in different directions, abandoning the cattle truck and the team from JKI Television News.

They regrouped back at the Ship and Shovel where

they started on the beers, watching wonderful replays of their morning's efforts on the big television screen. Billy and a few of his team joined them an hour later, having taken the vet back to his laboratory at South Molton, where they had left him mildly beaten and tied-up, as he'd requested – the apparent victim of a violent burglary.

Taverner stayed off the beer and told everyone to be back in the pub later that night as usual. He did not intend to be there.

FORTY-THREE

The ERDF received its order to withdraw within the hour. It had failed and it was time to go home.

What was supposed to have been a simple, inaugural operation to evict an outnumbered bunch of renegades had turned into a major international embarrassment. Most of the ERDF's senior officers were already waiting for the transport that would take them back to Brussels, and were thinking through what they were going to say when they eventually tapped the boards in front of their superiors. Meanwhile, the soldiers began the enormous task of dismantling Headquarters.

The Public Relations staff prepared an official release to the effect that the ERDF was 'being re-tasked for operational reasons after a successful operation to provide Military Aid to the Civil Authorities', but it was becoming rather difficult to say anything positive about the situation.

When Peter Kingston's department from the Interior Ministry contacted him later on, he had expected it to be his boss again. Instead, he was surprised to find himself speaking to the man at the very top; the ruthless Director-General of Interior Security.

'Your boss has been removed,' said the Director-

General. The elderly Director-General was a man of immense power and influence in the government, and although his voice had lost much of its timbre with age, the mere sound of it was enough to set a man's nerves on edge. Kingston waited for him to continue. No-one ever interrupted the Director-General or replied to his statements; you only ever responded to his questions. He spoke in his own time and he was a man of few words.

'The 65th will pay a heavy price for their treachery.' His voice quivered very slightly. 'Kingston, bring me Charlie Taverner.'

Kingston's team was already making progress. Every few minutes, more information came in about Taverner's acquaintances and precise whereabouts in the last few hours. The Neanderthals from the Security Support Agency were due to arrive shortly to assist Kingston, and for a number of citizens in Holberton it was not going to be a pleasant day.

Taverner was driving along Holberton High Street in his old Land Rover, still wearing his dreadlock wig and nose-piercing, when several black vehicles passed him in the opposite direction. He did not recognise the make of vehicle, which looked like a cross between a very large estate and a 4x4. The windows were blacked out and Taverner felt, rather than heard, the rumble of a very powerful V8 engine as each one passed by. They might as well have had 'Security Services' written all over them. He half-expected them to turn round and pursue him, but they carried on in the opposite direction, in ignorance of whom they had just passed.

He needed to speak urgently with Major Hesketh to

find out the next move, and drove for about two hours, all the while watching his rear-view mirror. The options open to him were diminishing rapidly and his mind was racing furiously. He had his passports and plenty of cash, and could leave straight away if necessary.

He eventually called Hesketh on his mobile phone, by now aware that his calls were almost certainly being traced.

'Is that the Ben Wah Takeaway?'

'Yes it is,' said Hesketh, 'but we're closed for business. I think we can drop the façade now. They're probably listening in. How lovely to hear from you. Are you well?'

'Couldn't be better. How's the regiment?' asked Taverner.

'We're having an absolute ball here. Wondering when those arses are going to give us something to really get our teeth into. They're not much cop, are they? I could never thank you enough for what you've achieved out there. It's been truly remarkable. The cows and the helicopters. Wonderful! Saw it live on the telly. Quite brilliant and the boys loved it. But it's now time to call it off. Your job is done. Understood?'

'I understand.'

'Good. You might like to know that Colonel Sandford is officially leaving the 65th later today. In the usual way.'

'On the back of a gun?'

'In a manner of speaking.'

Departing Commanding Officers of the 65th were traditionally driven out of the base on the back of an armoured vehicle or self-propelled gun, with the soldiers of the regiment lining the route out, saluting in batches as he passed by, and cheering if he had been any good in command.

'Do give him my love,' said Taverner.

'I will. Anyway, we'll take it from here. You've done more than enough. Above and beyond. Now get off the phone before the buggers trace you. It's been a pleasure. Good luck and Godspeed.'

Hesketh paused for a moment.

'We will go on in the finest traditions of the 65th.'

And with that, Major Hesketh disconnected.

That was it. It was all over, and the time had now come to get out of there for good. Taverner yearned to surf Saunton Sands one last time – to ride the perfect waves that were about to arrive – but this was not the time to get sentimental. Besides, there was sufficient adrenaline flowing through him at that moment to give him enough of a fix.

Taverner's call to Major Hesketh was immediately traced and the details were passed to Peter Kingston, who was at that moment briefing the Team Leader from the Security Support Agency. They all stopped for a moment as the conversation was played over the speakers.

'Same voice,' said the technician, as the speech recognition system flashed green. He pointed to the map with his pen. 'Somewhere round here, just outside Ottery St Mary.'

Kingston thought quickly.

'He knows we're onto him. Give me his number. We've got this bastard over a barrel.'

Taverner looked up and down the road. It was time to head north. He could make the six o'clock flight out of Leeds airport. He was about to turn off his mobile phone when it started to ring. The number was not recognised and he wondered if he should answer it.

'Hallo?'

'Good morning, Private Morton. Or can I call you Captain Charlie Taverner, formerly of the 65th Royal Horse Artillery. My name is … Mr Smith. I work for the government, for the Interior Ministry.'

'Good morning, Mr Smith.'

'You've been a busy man, Mr Taverner, very busy indeed.'

Taverner said nothing.

'We know who you are, and what you've been doing. I must say, you have some serious balls, Mr Taverner.'

'So kind of you to say so.'

'Unfortunately, your little charade has got a lot of people into quite a bit of trouble. We know exactly who you have been working with, and your associates will be helping us with our enquiries over the next few hours. And please do not try to warn them, you will only incriminate them further. Now, you're an intelligent man, Mr Taverner, you will be aware of how we sometimes have to deal with people such as yourself. It isn't very pleasant. So I have an offer. Turn yourself in to me immediately and no harm will come to you or your friends. You know where to find me. We can deal with this in a far more civilised way.'

'I've no idea what you're talking about,' said Taverner, looking into the distance to see if any vehicles were approaching.

'Think about it, Mr Taverner. You'll have access to a lawyer, everything will be above board. If we have to come and get you, then I cannot guarantee that it will be quite so comfortable.'

'Thank you. Go to hell.'

'It would be such a shame, Mr Taverner. So many people are looking for you. Police Service, Customs and

Excise, you name it. There's a general alert out for you. And please don't think that you can escape by using a forged passport belonging to ... let me see ... Mr Davies or Mr Winterbourne or Mr Roos or Mr Campbell.'

Taverner said nothing as his escape plan disintegrated.

'Yes, it's surprising what information a forger from Liverpool will exchange for a shorter jail sentence. He saw sense. It would be so much easier if you could too. Please turn yourself in.'

'I will see you in hell,' said Taverner, disconnecting.

He looked at his road map and, leaving his phone on, started to drive south-east.

Peter Kingston's team picked up the signal from his phone in the moving vehicle.

'He's on the move again, heading south or south-east,' said the technician.

Kingston passed the details to the leader of the Security Support Agency team who sent two of his vehicles out in pursuit. The police were ordered to set up roadblocks in the area.

They tracked the signal from Taverner's phone for three miles before it was turned off. He was still heading south-east.

On Windcheater Island, the soldiers climbed out of their trenches. Above them, the sky was a cloudless, duck-egg blue. They were non-tactical now, ambling along in groups towards the main buildings, chatting and smoking, enjoying the warming sun and swigging intermittently from their water bottles. A few cans of beer were produced; horribly warm in the heat, and they had slung their rifles out of the way behind their backs. It was a relief to remove their heavy body armour and replace the Kevlar helmet with the dark blue beret and bright silver capbadge of the 65th. On reaching the main road that ran through the base, the soldiers lined up either side of it, forming a human corridor that stretched from Regimental Headquarters all the way to the Sentry Post. It was the first time for several weeks that they had seen their mates, and as they waited they passed the time exchanging colourful war stories.

At eleven o'clock, the barricade at the Sentry Post was dismantled. Television crews, waiting on the road north of the base, sensed something was about to happen.

Major Hesketh stepped out of Regimental Headquarters with the Adjutant and the Regimental Sergeant Major to inspect the small group formed up in front of him. Above them, the flag of the 65th flew defiantly in a light breeze. He ignored the two haggard politicians, now wearing the crumpled suits in which they had arrived on that fateful day, and spoke instead to Captain Charalambous, who saluted Major Hesketh on behalf of his commandos, who were lined up behind him. Finally, Hesketh surveyed the highly-polished 17-Pounder gun – the former gate-guardian and an artillery piece from the First World War – to be towed by the waiting Land Rover, driven by one of the Cypriot commandos, in the back of which were the three trussed-up and gagged members of the Close Protection Team.

'Good work,' said Hesketh to the Provost Sergeant.

Tied very securely to the gun as if it were a motorbike with very low handlebars, with his chin resting uncomfortably on the tip of the barrel, Colonel Sandford did not look happy. He was quite naked and a single flower lay between the cheeks of his backside.

'Goodbye, Sandford,' said Hesketh. The duct tape over his mouth prevented Sandford from replying.

The Land Rover drove off slowly from RHQ and turned onto the road, with the two politicians and the commandos walking alongside, as the soldiers applauded the sight of their treacherous former Commanding Officer. They passed the Sentry Post and proceeded slowly out of the base, along the road and into the distance towards the waiting TV cameras.

After driving south-east, Taverner turned his phone off and headed north-west along some quieter roads all the way to the North Somerset coast, in the hope of throwing his pursuers off the scent.

How much longer he could remain a free man he did not know, but it was probably measurable in hours. He did not underestimate the ability of the security services and envisaged pursuing helicopters channelling him into one of the many roadblocks that were almost certainly being set up on every road, where he would face the portable biometric scanners that would never be fooled by his dreadlocks and nose piercing.

He eventually ended up in an internet café in the coastal village of Porlock on the Bristol Channel, drinking strong coffee that did nothing for his nerves. Taverner looked at the latest updates from the surf forecasting websites. It was going to be even better than this time last year. The great storm sat deep in the North Atlantic and the wave buoys south west of Ireland were already registering the swell, now showing ten feet and building.

'Look at that!' said someone watching the large television screen, where the programme had been interrupted to broadcast live scenes from Windcheater

Island. Taverner looked up. A group was walking towards the cameras. As they got closer, the camera focused in on the two politicians and Colonel Sandford's unceremonial parade. The cameras spared Sandford no dignity, especially regarding the intimacy of the flower, and there was pandemonium as the press now jostled for position, pestering the politicians and the Cypriots. Someone eventually untied Sandford and the police escorted them all away.

The events on the television, going on not far from Porlock and probably being broadcast all over the world, improved Taverner's mood somewhat. A few reporters had now driven right up to the Sentry Post and were shouting questions at Major Hesketh, who stood in front of a large crowd of soldiers. They were all smiling for the cameras and looked very pleased with themselves. Just as it seemed they were about to surrender, some soldiers came forward and started to put the barricade back in place. When they had finished, they walked back inside their base and closed the gate behind them.

They were not surrendering. Windcheater Island still belonged to the 65th.

Taverner would have liked to watch more. He did not have the time. He carried on with his internet research, now looking at shipping websites. After leaving the café, he headed west, up the steep hill out of the village and onto Exmoor.

It was only a matter of time before they got to him. The security services might not be subtle in their methods, but they never failed. He wondered what was happening to Terry, to Billy and the watchers, to the Halls.

It was only a matter of time.

It was better to die.

The thing that Taverner had told himself would never occur, might be about to happen. He wondered if he could go through with it. He had nothing to lose by surfing one last time. To be arrested and brutally interrogated without one final ride was an appalling prospect.

Might as well go for it, he thought.

It would not be pleasant, but it would be a hell of a way to go.

Following the winding, undulating road over Exmoor, the paranoia set in again as Taverner started to convince himself that beyond every bend and every brow of a hill would be the flashing blue lights and black vehicles of a security service road block. Birds flying in the distance started to look like police helicopters. Taverner even considered ditching the Land Rover and going on foot. The vehicle wasn't registered to anyone, but they would have almost certainly connected him with it by now. He wondered if he could summon up the courage, if the need arose, to do the unthinkable when a roadblock materialised. Could he put his foot down, unbuckle his seatbelt and pick up speed to ram the vehicles; his head shattered against the steering wheel?

It was at that moment, as he contemplated suicide, that he realised what Major Hesketh had actually meant when he had said 'We will go on in the finest traditions of the 65th.'

He forced himself to get a grip.

Taverner's fears were unfounded. The roadblocks did not materialise and he drove unimpeded into North Devon and stopped in Ilfracombe. He went into a pub by the harbour, where he found the crew of a fishing boat.

For what amounted to about four months' wages, the fishermen were more than willing to assist in Taverner's crazy plan, even if they suspected the dreadlocked surf-bum was out of his mind on some Class-A drug. They spent the afternoon gathering the equipment he requested, and in the evening they set off from the harbour on a small boat with Taverner, heading west, round the headland then south towards Saunton Sands. The sea was quite calm, although it would not be for long, and they were able to get relatively close to the rocks at the north end of the beach. They worked for about three hours and it was dark by the time they returned to Ilfracombe, where their fishing boat waited, fully refuelled.

The swell was starting to build.

Taverner left Ilfracombe and drove cross-country towards Holberton, avoiding the lanes. The moon was low in the sky and it was bright enough to allow him to drive without headlights. He left the vehicle in a copse and covered the last few miles on foot. There was already a hint of blue in the sky to the east.

In the town, he carefully approached the road where the Halls lived. It was not difficult to spot the security service vehicle waiting on the corner, and he wondered if the goons would be catnapping at this hour behind the blackened glass. From the alleyway that ran behind the gardens he slipped unseen into the back garden of the Halls' house. The door to the kitchen lurched at an angle, held on only by the upper hinge. The sliding doors into the back room were wide open and Taverner could see that the place had been ransacked. Books, furniture, paper, the sideboard and the contents of many drawers lay in a heap on the floor. Sparkling in the moonlight was Mrs Hall's prized collection of tiny crystal cats. There was no sign of her or her husband.

Taverner heard a whimpering sound behind him. It was Duke, the Halls' Alsatian, lying on his side at the end of the garden. One of his legs was clearly broken and the creature looked terribly bloated; almost certainly the result of having been kicked violently, thought Taverner. The poor dog was suffering and was close to death.

Moving quietly into the garage, Taverner retrieved what he had come back for – his trusty longboard. He would have been able to borrow other surfboards at the beach, but this was going to be his last ride and only his own board would do. In the garden he heard the whimpering again. He searched the garage once more.

Taverner was not an emotional person – knowing that emotion clouded judgement at critical moments – but at that moment, exhausted and running high on adrenaline, he was as close to losing it as he had ever been in his whole life. He was angry at the thought that anyone associated with him was facing a brutal arrest and interrogation. He was deflated that the siege of Windcheater Island was now effectively over, and furious with himself that he had not escaped while he had the chance. Above all, he was immensely fearful about what he was going to have to do in the next few hours.

All the terrible anger in Taverner was manifested in the sheer violence with which he brought down the side of the spade on Duke's neck. Even though the shaft of the spade broke on impact, it did its job. Duke flinched once, then lay peacefully still.

FORTY-FOUR

Peter Kingston refilled his mug with strong coffee from the percolator, trying to stave off the fatigue. He rubbed his eyes several times with his thumb and forefinger and pinched the bridge of his nose. Throughout the night, the police and the Security Support Agency had kept the roadblocks in place as they continued the search for Charlie Taverner. Several times they had radioed back that they had caught him; each time it was a false alarm or a case of mistaken identity. As it became apparent they weren't going to find him, Kingston ordered the roadblocks to be collapsed and recalled the agents to Holberton.

The bastard had sold them a dummy.

Taverner was still here. He could sense it.

It was half past ten in the morning on another scorching day. The ERDF soldiers were busy packing up Headquarters and were waiting for the first of the transporters to take the equipment back to the European mainland. Above the industrial estate, the seagulls circled, squealing and wailing hysterically at the futile efforts of those on the ground below them. The SSA agents were still on standby, sprawled out in their monstrous vehicles, trying to catch up on some sleep after manning the roadblocks through the night. Kingston started to pore through another interim report that had just been flashed up to him from the interrogators who had been working through the night on Taverner's associates, when his telephone rang.

'Good morning, Mr Smith.'

It was Charlie Taverner. He was calling from his mobile phone again.

Immediately Kingston clicked his fingers at the technician, who flicked a switch on the direction-finding equipment. They would have the grid reference in a few seconds.

'I have been thinking about your offer, Mr Smith,' said Taverner.

The grid reference flashed up. The technician checked his map, then scribbled on a sheet of paper with a marker pen and held it up in front of Kingston.

SAUNTON SANDS BEACH, NORTH END.

It was less than two miles away.

Taverner kept talking, but Kingston wasn't really listening – he was more concerned with waking the agents. Not wanting to scare off Taverner by shouting at them while he was on the phone, he emptied his coffee mug on the ground outside, hurled it at their vehicle, and it shattered against the front wing. The agents woke with a jump and saw Kingston beckoning at them wildly, pointing at his phone. The technician gave them the location, and with their vehicles' tyres squealing, they tore out of the estate.

Kingston and the technician jumped into the back of

the last vehicle. They were both hurled around violently as they tried, unsuccessfully, to find some sort of a seatbelt or panic-handle. In less than three minutes they were at the car park at Saunton Sands. Taverner was still on the phone, talking to him from somewhere in the vicinity.

Why, thought Kingston, had Taverner not disconnected, if he suspected he would be traced? It didn't make any sense.

The SSA agents lived up to their reputation of engaging fist before brain. The first two vehicles had roared into the car park and the agents had simply launched into anyone who happened to be standing around. Most of their victims were surfers, innocently waxing their boards or pulling on wetsuits. Anyone still inside their car or campervan was dragged out and beaten savagely. Teeth were knocked out, noses were broken, and jaws and ribs were fractured in an explosion of violence that took everyone by surprise.

And yet Taverner was still calmly talking away to Kingston on the phone. Kingston looked round the car park, his heart pounding.

Where the fuck was he?

The technician held his monitoring equipment out in front of him, cupping his hands over the screen to block the glare from the sun. 'He's not here,' he said, ignoring a sharp crack as a surfboard was shattered nearby.

Kingston was becoming exasperated. 'What the *fuck* do you mean, he's not here?'

'Not in the car park,' said the technician, pivoting round towards the sea. 'He must be on the beach. There!'

He pointed to a lone figure walking towards the sea, carrying a surfboard under his arm. Kingston got his binoculars out.

The figure in a black wetsuit turned and waved towards the car park. Short blond hair, slim and athletically-built. The figure stopped waving and put his hand to his ear.

'It's been good fun, Mr Smith,' said Taverner. 'Goodbye.'

Kingston roared at the agents, who were still busy kicking and stamping on the prostrate surfers.

'FOR *FUCK'S SAKE* CUT IT OUT! THAT'S HIM DOWN THERE!'

They abandoned their beating and sprinted off down the little slipway to the beach; their suit jackets flailing around them, racing after the figure in the distance. The tide at Saunton Sands was going out and it was a long way to the sea. Their target had a big head-start on them. One of the more switched-on agents jumped in a vehicle and drove it onto the beach, collected the rest of the agents then took off across the sand. By now, the surfer had reached the water and was wading out into the depths with his surfboard. The vehicle ploughed into the sea towards the surfer, stopping only when water came over the windscreen and the engine coughed and cut out. Their target was nearly in reach, not more than twenty metres away, still wading out, now being slowed down by the waves of whitewater coming in the opposite direction. The agents couldn't pile out of the vehicle fast enough and they went after him like men possessed. The surfer saw them coming, lay prone on his board and started paddling out over the waves, arms wind-milling like mad, now getting further away from the agents. Still they did not give up. They waded out until the water was up to their chests, at which point the force of the waves started knocking them off their feet. In front of them the surfer continued to put distance between him and the agents, effortlessly floating over the waves that were knocking them over like ninepins.

Kingston and his technician had sensibly avoided the sea and had started to make their way carefully along the rocky plateau that ran along the north end of the beach below the cliffs. About fifty metres out from the rocks, the lone surfer was still paddling his board out to sea, over bigger swells, paddling up the steep, glassy walls, pivoting over each summit like a see-saw and disappearing down the other side. Still he paddled, further and further out, until he sat up on his board just beyond the point where most of the waves seemed to be breaking. Kingston and the technician continued clambering over the rocks until they were parallel to the surfer. They were close enough to throw stones at him, had they wanted to. Kingston looked at him through his binoculars. It was definitely Charlie Taverner.

Kingston was not used to the ocean. A childhood visit to Cornwall was about all he could remember of the North Atlantic, and it terrified him. He had never seen anything like this before. From the car park, the waves had looked insignificant, but here on the rocks they were huge. He followed a line of swell in fascination. It advanced slowly from the horizon out of the west; steepening gradually, with barely a ripple to spoil the glassy surface. The offshore wind blew against the developing wave, holding it up for a short time, the top of it starting to crackle in warning, then finally it plunged down with such force that Kingston could feel the impact through his feet, a thick spray now blowing back over the wave in the easterly wind.

The energy in front of him was terrifying and the lone

surfer just an insignificant speck among it. Kingston was amazed that human beings would ever want to go out in such conditions. Surfers, he recalled reading once, travelled all over the world in the pursuit of such waves, and if they considered that sort of thing enjoyable, then clearly their brains had been wired together incorrectly. Kingston's idea of physical recreation was a kick–about on a Sunday afternoon on Hampstead Heath with his children. On the rocks he felt relatively safe, but realised that Taverner, despite being no further than the length of a penalty area away from him, might as well have been on another planet. The interface where the sea met the rocks was the line at which his power and jurisdiction stopped; the boundary beyond which the law of the land no longer applied. Where the surfer was, right at that moment, he was immune and quite untouchable, protected by the immense energy around him.

The surfer spun his board round as a bigger wave came through. He paddled hard and the wave lifted him up, maybe ten or fifteen feet, still paddling and gathering speed. The nose of the board dipped and the surfer started to accelerate down the face of the wave, the lip now crackling behind him. He snapped to his feet, crouching to keep his centre of gravity low. He continued dropping down the face with tremendous speed, momentarily driving onto the flat water in front of the wave, and as the lip broke directly behind him he carved the big board around out of its path in a big wide turn that took him high up the face of the wave, where he turned again, the nose of his board pointing up almost vertically for a split second before plummeting down, all the time being chased by the breaking section.

The surfer did not ride the wave for long. As the wave

thundered past Kingston towards the beach, revealing its huge arched back, the surfer disappeared from view, then suddenly appeared flying through the air over the back of the wave, his board spinning in the air behind him, and he cartwheeled into the calm water behind the wave. He resurfaced, punched the air and gave a massive hoot of pleasure that could be heard over the roar of the breaking waves. The surfer pulled on his leash to recover his board and paddled out again to his take-off spot.

By now, Kingston had been joined on the rocks by a few of the agents who were beginning to dry off in the sun. The rest of them waited on the beach. There would be no escape.

Charlie Taverner chose his waves carefully, paddling into each one then popping up to his feet with perfect timing and carving the big board all over the face of the wave, not in a snappy or agitated manner, but with long, powerful turns, as a conductor might wave his baton through the air during an *Adagio* movement. He would turn one way, then another, all the time staying just in front of the lip that threatened to crush him, finishing the ride by using the face as a ramp to launch himself high into the air.

For two hours, the surfer put on a display so exhilarating that Kingston and the agents, watching in awe, almost forgot that they were there to arrest him. During this time the tide had gone out. The surfer was further out to sea and the reception party moved down the beach as the sea level dropped.

Eventually, the surfer began to tire. After each ride, it was clear he was not recovering his board as quickly, nor was he paddling quite so hard back to his take-off spot. Once, on his way back out, he took a fearful hammering from a wave that broke directly on top of him. Two more rides later and he was visibly exhausted.

Kingston turned the binoculars on his target again. Taverner wasn't looking quite as arrogant as he had done in his Army photograph. Instead of sitting upright on his board, he was now leaning forward, supporting his weight with his arms. He looked to be having difficulty breathing. When he looked briefly towards the rocks, Kingston, looking through his binoculars, could see fear in those bright blue eyes.

The sea had gone darker on the horizon as a set of big waves approached. The first of them was building much further out; a wave much bigger than the others. It approached slowly, solid and very dark-blue in colour, and it reared up ominously above the surfer. Instead of peeling gradually, it broke along its entire length and the water came down on the surfer like an avalanche. In the maelstrom of whitewater Kingston could see the board being tossed around. Surfacing after a time behind the wave, the surfer yanked on the leash, pulling the board towards him, but not before the second wave broke directly on top of him. Again the surfer came up behind the wave, and again another big wave smashed down on him from above. Kingston watched carefully through his binoculars, wondering how anyone could take such continuous punishment.

A fourth wave came through and broke on top of the surfer, and this time his board was washed away – the leash had snapped. He was now a tiny lone head in a churning mass of foam, and he started swimming feebly after the board, barely lifting his arms from the water. It was useless. His board had been taken by the wave and was tumbling its way to the beach. The fifth and final wave of the set finished him off. It was massive, the biggest one yet. The surfer had turned round to face the behemoth and tried to dive under it. Kingston watched in disbelief as it plummeted down on him, scanning the point where he had gone under.

This time, Taverner never came back up.

A minute passed. The foam where Taverner had gone under had dissipated and the water was glassy again.

Two minutes. No more big waves came through.

Three minutes.

Kingston looked at the sea in desperation. Surely no-one could hold their breath that long? The agents with him on the rocks eased forward as close to the edge as they dared, to see if he was clinging to the rocks below. He was not. It was now five minutes since he had gone under. Kingston scanned the sea in front of him for a floating body. Again, nothing. He waited for twenty minutes on the rocks, then he sent the agents back to the car park, where they found Taverner's Land Rover with a wig and nose piercing on the front seat. His surfboard was recovered from the shallows, not far from the point where they found his mobile phone half-submerged in the sand.

Charlie Taverner had drowned right in front of him and there was absolutely nothing that Kingston could have done about it. He returned to the industrial estate to start writing his report for the Director-General of Interior Security.

He had failed to apprehend Taverner. He had failed the Director-General. He thought long and hard about how he was going to explain why. The report, he knew, had better be good, and he thought very long and hard about an acceptable conclusion.

FORTY-FIVE

On the eastern edge of Windcheater Island, a very constipated Gunner Jones was in the midst of what soldiers commonly referred to as a *shovel recce*. Though he did not know it, he had only minutes to live. Admittedly, there were better things to be doing at the moment of one's death than trying to curl one out in the less-than-salubrious surroundings of a hawthorn bush, but he was a soldier and he knew the score; he shouldn't have sworn the oath if he wasn't prepared to die halfway through his ablutions.

It was nearly ten pm and Gunner Jones was, like all the soldiers in the 65th, fatigued and slothful, although still modest enough to want some privacy from his colleagues. Colonel Sandford's send-off had been a welcome interlude, but they were now back in their trench and they couldn't give a damn any more. Their kit lay strewn all over the place and no-one was on stag.

The soldiers in the Ops Room led a rather more comfortable, though equally listless, existence in an airless room that now reeked permanently of bad coffee and nicotine. They slept openly at their stations, roused only by the occasional message in their headsets. There were no officers on duty in the Ops Room that night. Some had been strutting round harmlessly after lunch until Major Hesketh summoned them back to the Mess, and they had not been seen since.

Back in the hawthorn bush, Gunner Jones waited. He would have preferred to be sitting on a gleaming example of Armitage Shanks' finest, perusing *Max Power* magazine, debating whether to fork out for a new hotter camshaft for his classic Ford Focus, or a wider, illegal exhaust. Instead, he was here in the darkness, squatting down in a miserable bush; legs aching and thorns pricking his bare arse.

He began to feel a rumbling from within. A rumbling that got deeper. Indeed, so deep was it that he wondered for the state of his insides. The rumble increased to a vibration, then to a distinct throbbing. He thought his insides were about to let go in a most spectacular way, and was half-relieved when he realised the noise, whatever it was, was not coming from inside him. It seemed to be coming from the horizon, from the south-east, and it was getting louder. No, it was coming from due south. Then it came from the north as well. It seemed to be all around. Now the noise was unmistakeable.

Helicopters.

They must have been coming from every direction, thought Gunner Jones, and they sounded like they were converging on him alone. He peered over the top of the bush expecting to see an armada of choppers coming his way; lights flashing, searchlights ablaze, guns and rockets bristling. But he could see nothing whatsoever. The helicopters were invisible in the darkness. Being unable to see what was evidently about to kill him unleashed a wave of horror in the young gunner that loosened his bowels spectacularly. With his trousers still round his ankles, he stumbled and tripped and shat his way back to the trench.

'Shit! It's fookin' choppers 'innit!' he said. 'Fookin' 'ell. Fookin' 'undreds of 'em.'

He tried to get back into the trench, but Bombardier Podsnap was not having an unarmed, panicking young Gunner near him, one who thought that wearing his trousers round his ankles, exposing his tackle and covering his legs in shit was the best posture to adopt against attack helicopters. Podsnap rifle-butted him hard in the shins, and Jones dropped to the ground.

'Fook off!' said Podsnap. 'You're covered in shit! Get the fook away from me! Go and get your fookin' rifle!'

Jones recovered his senses a little and crawled away to the bush to retrieve his weapon.

High above in the darkness, the attack helicopters advanced rapidly on Windcheater Island from several directions. They were each carrying monstrous payloads of missiles, rockets and cannon. Loitering at the back of the formation was a helicopter carrying a load so heavy that it could not carry any additional armaments. This was the Fire Controller, and its sole payload was the very latest targeting system. It scanned the whole island, registering thousands of thermal signatures; soldiers running about, generators, hexamine fuel blocks burning as soldiers brewed up, now quickly extinguished. The eye in the sky saw it all. In a fraction of a second it considered the threats, prioritised them, and allocated specific helicopters to counter them. It had a bewildering array of targets to choose from – even recently-discarded cigarette ends had their place in the rankings. For a reason no-one would ever know, this state-of-the-art, money-no-object system determined that the greatest threat to the fifty or so attack helicopters that screamed in towards the base was ... Gunner Jones's bare arse crawling away from a trench.

The firing restrictions were lifted. The designated missile immediately shot off into the darkness, hellbent on maximum crevice impact. The warhead–camera footage would become the stuff of legend.

In front of the bush, Gunner Jones crawled around feeling for his rifle. He heard a hiss behind him and was lifted quite painlessly into astonishing brightness and beyond, into that which we do not yet know.

Bombardier Podsnap saw the bush explode a split second before his trench was hit by a missile that left little trace of it or the occupants.

Simultaneously, the whole coast of the island erupted in flames. From up above, the helicopter pilots saw the outline of the island marked by a ring of fire.

In the 65th's Ops Room, the messages were coming in thick and fast, as a rapid series of heavy crumps rattled the building. The signallers started to relay the reports to the Watchkeeper.

'Large explosion on the east coast by the Sailing Club.'

'Helicopters reported approaching from the North.'

'B-Troop reported two explosions in their area.'

'Wrong, make that five explosions.'

'Lost contact with B-Troop.'

For about thirty seconds there was a continuous series of explosions before the 65th started returning fire with a few machine guns, firing blindly into the night sky. The flash of an explosion on the ground occasionally lit up a helicopter in close proximity, but the tracer fire from the machine guns was their own undoing – it gave away their position and they were quickly silenced by the all-seeing Fire Controller above.

The 88mm gun still rested in the Quartermaster's Store, where the storemen were in the process of wheeling it out. It was too late – its location was already known, and eight missiles were more than enough to atomise the Store and most of its contents.

In the Ops Room, the Senior Watchkeeper, Staff Sergeant 'Chalky' White, was quite helpess.

'Get your fookin' jackets on, lads!' he said to the signallers, who donned their body armour and helmets.

Gunner Moffat had been in Regimental Headquarters at the time the attack had started, getting a faulty radio repaired by the Signals Sergeant. As the first crump shook the building, the Signals Sergeant abandoned the repair and ran through to the nearby Ops Room, closely followed by Moffat.

'You!' said the Watchkeeper to Moffat. 'Go and get hold of the fookin' CO!'

'Where is he?' asked Moffat.

'In the fookin' Officers' Mess!'

Moffat picked up a telephone and dialled the extension to the Officers' Mess, as the chorus of explosions continued.

'The line's dead,' said Moffat. Another explosion shook the building and dust fell from the ceiling.

'Then fookin' get on your bike and get over there and tell him to get his fat arse up here!'

Moffat dashed down a corridor lit up by yellow flashes, suddenly feeling very alone. When he opened the door at the far end, the noise outside was unbelievable. He jumped into a Land Rover, found the keys still in the ignition and headed out to the Officers' Mess. He could barely hear the noise of the engine. The shockwaves from the explosions seemed to go right through him; each pulse seemed to tickle the back of his throat. No war film he had ever seen could have conveyed the effect of being on the receiving end of so much firepower. The Ops Room was a certain target, he knew, and he was probably better away from it. His mates were out there somewhere and he wondered if Podsnap, Jonesy and Dutch were still alive. He roared past the Sergeants' Mess and the NAAFI, both dark and deserted. Some high-angle tracer started up from the roof of the NAAFI, and he thought of the nights on the piss there, how far this was removed from all that, and whether life would ever be the same again.

He broke from the cover of the buildings and took the bend before the main runway at a speed not designed for a Land Rover. The tall tyres distorted under the load and the vehicle leaned alarmingly, but it made the bend. With the throttle sandwiched between his right foot and the bulkhead, he tore across the width of the runway. He could see the Mess in the distance. It was intact, seemingly untouched and, unbelievably, fully lit up. He fixed his gaze on it and expected it to explode any moment. It seemed crazy to drive towards it.

Somewhere in the darkness above, the Fire Controller's targeting system re-prioritised due to the speeding Land Rover and sent another missile on its way.

Moffat had crossed the runway and was approaching the Mess. He had about three-hundred metres to go when there was a flash and a sharp crack as the back of the vehicle was torn off. Moffat was lucky. Somehow he was thrown out of what remained of the cab, and rolled over and over again in the grass by the side of the road.

Everything was silent.

He lay on his back, winded, not caring what was going on around him, just hoping he would breathe again. A little smoke rose from him. There was hardly any noise to accompany the flashes of explosions. He struggled to his feet and noticed his left arm bent at a funny angle. Strangely enough, it did not hurt – so detached was he from his body – and he found he could still flex his fingers a little. A warm, sticky liquid filling his eyes might have been engine oil, or blood. He wiped it from his eyes and set off towards the Mess, shuffling down the road as if very drunk, admiring in some perverse way the bright lights of the Officers' Mess shining out proudly.

Daylight then seemed to form behind him, and he sensed incredible heat on the back of the head. His shadow was projected far in front of him. He turned round as the sound wave hit him. A truly massive series of fireballs rose above the offices and garages, sending flames and debris hundreds of feet into the air. The air seemed barely able to carry the sound waves effectively and the noise sounded like an apocalyptic, over-distorted crackle. It was too loud. Being downwind, Moffat smelt the sweet aroma of petrol. Windcheater Island had just been napalmed.

He dragged himself across the car park of the Officers' Mess. The rest of the base was burning, and it was surely only a matter of time before this elegant building succumbed as well. Against his better judgement, he went through the revolving doors and stood for a moment in the foyer. The noise of the explosions was dampened considerably and the lights were flickering in sympathy. He was aware that he was wheezing heavily. Blood rolled down his forehead into his eyes and down his face, dripping steadily onto the carpet. Adrenaline had got him here to this sanctuary, but now that he was inside, it drained away rapidly. He looked at his arm, then felt the pain when he saw how distorted it was. A wave of nausea hit Moffat and he was violently sick.

An officer, Lieutenant Skeffington, staggered out of the

gents' lavatory, using the walls to support himself.

'For God's sake, man!' he muttered at the retching Moffat. 'Why can't you use the bloody lavatory like any other human being?'

Skeffington was wearing a dinner jacket and bow tie. The shirt had once been white, but was now covered in about as much blood as Moffat's smock. Even to Moffat's damaged hearing, the sound of a very lively party could be heard, as the doors to the dining room opened and closed behind Skeffington. A loud shot rang out, there was a crash of porcelain and a cheer. Moffat was about to peer inside, when the Mess Manager, Staff Sergeant Lomas, tapped him on the shoulder.

'You shouldn't really be in here, lad,' said the Mess Manager. He helped Moffat to his office and took out a First Aid kit.

Moffat spoke through clenched teeth. 'I came to get Major Hesketh. The shit's hit the fan. I was fookin' blown up on the way here.'

'Bad is it? Sounds nasty,' said the Mess Manager.

'Well, is the CO gonna come and sort this fookin' shit out?'

'Look, I shouldn't worry about all this. You did good to come and tell us, lad. I'll tell Major Hesketh you were here.'

The Mess Manager fixed his arm in a sling, as Moffat spoke quietly in his broad accent. 'Choppers. Millions of the fookers. Didn't stand a fookin' chance. They're all dead. All me mates. All me fookin' mates.'

The Mess Manager mopped up the worst of the blood from the head wound and covered it with a large bandage, as Major Hesketh walked into the office clutching a bottle of port and a large cigar. He was very drunk and spoke too loudly.

'Is this young man alright, Staff?'

'He'll be fine in a minute, sir,' said the Mess Manager.

'What's happened to the back of his head?'

'Looks like it's badly singed, sir.'

'Hell of a lot of smoke coming off the bugger, Staff.'

'Yes, sir.'

'What is he doing here?'

'We couldn't get through to you, sir,' said Moffat. 'I came to tell you that we were under attack, but I was blown up.'

'You thought I needed telling that we were being attacked?' said Hesketh, sarcastically.

'Yes, sir, the Watchkeeper did, sir.'

'And what was I to do then?'

'Come back to the Ops Room, sir.'

'And is the Ops Room still intact?'

'I don't think so, sir.'

'Bit of a wasted trip then, young man!'

'Yes, sir.'

'Helicopters?'

'Yes, sir.'

'Nasty buggers.'

'Yes, sir.'

'Quite a few, by the sound of it.'

'Fookin' millions, sir.'

'Did we get any of the fuckers?'

'I dunno, sir. I didn't see any.'

'Surely we must have brought down a few? This is the 65th Regiment Royal Horse Artillery! Tell the bloody Ops Room from me to bloody well ... bugger, of course, what Ops Room!'

Hesketh turned to the Mess Manager. 'Staff, have we something we can give this young man to ease the pain a little?'

The Mess Manager produced two bottles of port from his desk. Hesketh examined them, as if to ensure that they were not of too expensive a brand to be wasted on the ranks, then led Moffat out to the revolving doors. The head bandage was already failing to contain the bleeding.

'Good hunting, Moffat.' Hesketh turned to face him, gave him the two bottles of port and gripped him firmly by both shoulders, causing Moffat to wince in pain. 'Let me assure you, young man, that you're much safer out there than in here,' said Hesketh, gesturing behind him to the dining room as another shot rang out to more drunken cheering.

'Bugger off, now.'

Moffat went back out through the revolving doors. Someone wedged them shut behind him. He was stood in an oasis of calm, while the island seemed to burn all around him. Round the side of the Mess he found some bicycles, and considered checking up on his mates in the trench. But not one of the bicycles was in working order and, clutching his bottles of port and sporting a broken arm, he was in no fit state to ride. He felt very tired. He went past the windows of the dining room and stopped to look inside.

If the level of violence and horror being inflicted on Windcheater Island by the helicopter assault was the yardstick to go by, then the officers of the 65th were making a fair attempt to surpass it during the course of their Black Tie dinner. The long dinner table glistened with an impressive array of silver and the action was going on all around the room. Only a handful of officers could be seen moving about – the majority were slumped on the floor or at the table, quite unconscious. The others were brandishing shotguns, firing with little success at the plates that Second Lieutenant Cavendish, at the far end of the room, threw high into the air. When he ran out of plates, they started firing directly at Cavendish, winging him badly. They then turned on the chandeliers, merely succeeding in reducing them to bare wire and arcing electrical chord. Someone had a negligent discharge and a nearby window was blown out. Lieutenant Reynolds was evidently trying to get round the walls of the dining room without touching the floor. He was standing on a curtain rail very high up, and apparently stuck. The shotgunners took aim and were threatening to shoot him if he didn't move. Unable to go anywhere, they opened up on him, at which point the curtain rail gave way and he plummeted some twenty feet to a crumpled heap on the floor.

A motorbike engine started up inside the dining room and a door was used to make a ramp at the end of the dinner table. The motorbike, with its elegant and helmetless rider, shot out of the kitchen entrance at surprising speed, up the ramp and launched into the air an impressive distance before coming down hard on the table, scattering the silver and crashing into the heads of some of the unconscious officers. The rider flew off the bike and landed on his head. He lay very still, with his head at an unnatural angle. The other officers fell about laughing, quite unconcerned about the rider, and were far more interested in straightening the bike's handlebars for another attempt.

Someone spotted Moffat and snapped the curtains shut on the window.

His arm started to hurt again. Everywhere he looked there was fire. There was intermittent gunfire and the occasional muffled explosion, probably gas or petrol cylinders going up in sympathy. The helicopters still swarmed overhead, and by the sound of it, higher up there were jet fighters.

This was the moment that heroes live for, thought Moffat. In the movies they would choose moments like this to spring into action, against the odds. True heroes never gave up. But Moffat gave up. Faced with the utter futility of the situation, something died inside him at that moment.

He broke open a bottle of port and swigged heavily. It began to work its magic within minutes. The pain soon began to ease. As he drank more, even the prospect of impending death seemed not to concern him. With the island ablaze, most of his friends probably dead or dying, and the officers next door having the shindig from hell, Moffat felt warm and contented. He was not necessarily trying to kill himself through drink, he told himself, but if he were to die from alcohol poisoning, then so much the better. He finished the first bottle, and as he passed through the latter stages of inebriation he forced down most of the second bottle before he passed out. He slept well, the best he had slept all week.

The inaugural attack of the European Air Assault Brigade had gone well. The 65th had been destroyed. No doubt there would be a few survivors on the ground and it was important that they were taken care of. There could be no witnesses. The second phase of the attack commenced in the dark blue light of dawn. Three helicopters landed on the island and despatched execution squads who worked quickly and efficiently, finding badly burnt survivors crawling blindly across the grass in hideous agony, or hiding under bodies in trenches. A few were simply walking round in a daze. They were all taken care of. The execution squads regrouped before they made their way to the Officers' Mess.

Moffat survived his attempt at suicide by alcohol and woke slumped against the wall of the Mess, on a glorious Indian Summer's day. Smoke lazed its way across the island in the breeze. The intense sunlight hurt one of Moffat's eyes – the other had long since closed over. His uniform no longer resembled anything he had originally been issued with. What was left of it was covered with dried blood and vomit. He lay there for a while, trying to come to his senses. The battering he had taken the previous evening did well to cover the monumental hangover he should have been feeling. He could no longer feel his damaged arm in the sling. His legs still worked though, and with considerable effort he hauled himself to his feet. His head ached and swam like hell.

Moffat had not a clue what he should do. He was too badly hurt to try to escape from the base, and in any case he had no idea how he might do so. He was too weak to fight back against any potential enemy, and just about drunk enough not to feel much fear. Apart from a helicopter taking off about a mile away, there seemed to be no-one about.

The officers! The Mess was still intact. They might have sobered up by now. Perhaps Major Hesketh might let him stay for a few hours to recuperate. He staggered round the building towards the front entrance.

The bodies lay on their fronts in the car park, in a very neat row. Their hands had been tied, and splashmarks of brain and skull panned out in an arc from each head. Each was adorned in a black dinner jacket. From a short distance he was able to recognise some of them. Lieutenant Skeffington was obvious – in any case, his emaciated frame gave him away. Lieutenant Chief Mbotu's dark skin. The Quartermaster, laying effeminately, even in death. The rotund Major Hesketh, his comb-over encrusted and waving in the breeze. The others were a mess of leaking brain, on which the flies were already starting to feast.

A massive searing punch, staggeringly hot, spun Moffat round and threw him to the floor. He barely heard the gunshot that took him in the knee. The pain was excruciating beyond belief and he found himself clutching at his knee with his broken arm. He lay on the ground for a moment, rocking and dry-retching, before a group of soldiers was suddenly upon him, battering him about the head, the stomach, the groin and his strapped arm. They stripped him and tied his arms behind his back, quite oblivious to his screaming as, with much crunching of bone and snapping of tendons, his broken arm was forced to assume a hideous angle. They dragged him by his shoulders along the rough tarmac so his knees grazed down to the bone, and made him kneel down at the end of the row of dead officers.

In this moment of unimaginable agony, Moffat seemed to be outside of himself. He was in hideous pain, yet the worse it got, the more he seemed to have been removed from his body.

His tormentors wore a uniform he didn't recognise and spoke in a harsh, whiny, unfamiliar tongue; definitely European, but not immediately recognisable. Moffat slumped to the floor and was sharply lifted up again. He felt a metallic object pressed into base of his skull. He knew it was a pistol. There was the click of a trigger, but no bang; the hammer had come down on an empty chamber. The soldier above him laughed and kept repeating the action. *Click, click, click.* Moffat looked up to see one of the bastard's mates recording it all on video camera. *Click, click, click.* They were psychopaths – there was no emotion whatsoever in their eyes. The soldier with the pistol pulled a magazine from his jacket and showed it to Moffat. It was loaded with live rounds. Moffat's gaze was drawn to the awful first round in the magazine. The soldier then fitted the magazine to his pistol, cocked it to put a round in its chamber, and put it to Moffat's head. Moffat looked down at the tarmac where his brain was about to be scattered.

Above him, the seagulls suddenly cried out, resurrecting a memory of long ago; of his Mum taking him and his two brothers on a daytrip to Southport; ice cream, amusement arcades, walking along the seafront promenade scoffing fish'n'chips with too much salt and vinegar.

Moffat's spirit had left his body before the bullet was fired.

FORTY-SIX

The mid-afternoon sun was noticeably closer to the horizon and a gentle offshore breeze failed to curb the intense heat. The tanned woman in the white bikini decided she had caught enough sun for the day and retired to the shade of the palm trees lining the back of the beach. She would turn heads wherever she went, but there were no heads to turn on this most private of beaches. A black Labrador woke from his slumber by a palm tree and sauntered down to the water's edge, paddling nonchalantly for a while, sniffing the water and looking out to sea for his master, as he had done many times before. He whimpered a little, then walked back to the tree and lay down again. The woman threw a ball for him, but the dog was not interested. He just peered out to sea towards the waves breaking out on the point. A lone surfer picked off a wave with casual ease, steered the board down the line, only to lose his balance and fall in front of the whitewater. The dog sat up and wagged his tail in approval, then stopped when he saw the surfer paddling back out to sea again to await the next set.

The surfer was at peace. He was not given to karmic philosophy, but this place had energy like he had never known. It was heavenly. The waves seemed to be made not from water, but from intensely clear liquid crystal. As he rode each wave, he felt as though it was gradually slowing down, transferring its life-energy up through the board, up through his feet to fill out his body and radiate out from the extremities. He had never felt so complete, so energised and so spiritual. He let the magnificent light bathe him. The water was so clear he could see fish darting about on the bottom. It was warm too, and there was no need for the heavy, clinging wetsuit he had needed in his previous life. He was free. He peered out to sea for the next set. Although the swell was not big that day, the waves were quite tricky. The sea floor rose out of deep water to form a shallow sandbar, causing waves to appear out of nowhere. He had only been surfing these waves for a few weeks and he had a great deal to learn about them. It would take years to learn how the waves varied with a different swell direction or a veering wind. Time was not a problem here. He had all the time he could ever wish for.

He caught a movement out of the corner of his eye. Lazily, he spun the board round to study the form of the tanned woman in the white bikini as she made her way along the beach to a coolstore. She fetched a drink and returned to her place under the tree. She looked lusty and athletic, yet she was beautifully curvaceous. Her face was both strong-looking and angelic. And despite the privacy of the beach, her bikini was thoroughly decent, but left nothing to the imagination. The surfer liked the woman for her charisma and charm, her elegance and her taste. He admired her *joie de vivre* and her *savoir-faire*, but what he really loved her for was her *derrière*. He heard a rush of water behind him and snapped out of his reverie, just in time to see the wave looming. Before he could react, it had pushed him back, the tail of the board dug in and he was dumped unceremoniously into the water. He pulled himself onto his board and paddled back to the beach, where the dog welcomed him in a frenzy of joy. He lay down on his front next to the woman, facing the sea. She sat up cross-legged and he gazed at her smooth legs and murmured in approval as, unbidden, she rubbed suncream into his back.

This was Nirvana, the place he had dreamt of. A perfect right-hand point break, a nymph on the beach, and the overpowering bouquet of a wet Labrador in close proximity. Maybe this was his reward for good conduct in a past existence. He considered his former life and reflected on its last moments, when the enemy had finally traced him to a car park next to a beach.

He knew his mobile phone would be traced and the Interior Ministry goons were very quick to get a fix on it, as he had anticipated. Sitting deep in the huge surf, he could see them waiting for him on the beach. Two were also making their way along the rocks. He did think that they might try and shoot him, but no; it was clear they wanted him alive. The surf was huge, bigger than last year, and he had to keep paddling to dodge the sledgehammer peaks of the rogue sets. Alone among the heaving slabs of cold Atlantic seawater he felt quite safe. He caught the wave he had come for, and it was an absolute corker. The lip reared up twelve feet above him; crackling, threatening to explode onto him, but he was off, plummeting down the wave's face and carving along its length. The rush was enough to blank out the thoughts of the reception party on the beach.

He took his fill of the waves, keeping an eye on his wristwatch, waiting for the tide to reach the lowest point. Whether it was the near-perfection of the waves, or the knowledge that he couldn't go back to the beach, he surfed better than he had ever done before. He had never before looked at such powerful surf without wondering whether he had any right to be there. That day, he had no choice.

The tide had almost dropped to its lowest point. The moment he had feared was upon him, and he hoped that he could force himself to go through with it, against all his natural instincts. He had no intention of giving himself up to the goons. Surrender was unthinkable. He wanted to be at peace, and there was only one thing to do. He looked around at the North Devon scenery for the last time; at the sand dunes, at the cliffs, and finally at the agents watching him from the rocks. As the next few waves came through he made a half-hearted attempt to ride them, but quickly got trounced. He paddled out beyond a small orange buoy — one of many that lay dotted around the water. He did not have to wait long for the next set of waves to come thundering through. He made no attempt to avoid the first one and was smothered by a pounding, frothing wall. He was under for about ten seconds. When he surfaced, he saw the next wave about to come hammering down on top of him. He had only seconds to spare. He looked round, saw the buoy and swam furiously towards it. He clipped a discreet wrist leash to a line connected to the buoy's anchor, as he was suddenly pounded again. Again he surfaced, after what seemed like an eternity. The wrist leash held. When the turbulence eased, he reached down and undid his ankle leash, disconnecting himself from his surfboard floating nearby. He tried to swim impotently over to his board, but it was clear that he was not going to make it before the next wave reached him. He started to hyperventilate as the wave landed and washed away his board, and with it much chance of survival. He rolled with the wave. There was no point in fighting it, no need to expend unnecessary energy at this difficult moment. The wrist leash still held fast. He waved his free arm in distress at the goons on the rocks. Two more waves rolled over him. He took a deep breath and did not resurface after the last wave. When the turbulence subsided, he kicked out and made for the line under the buoy, pulling himself down into the darkness. He exhaled to help himself sink against the buoyancy of his wetsuit. The effort needed became severe. His heart beat furiously to supply his body's massive demand for oxygen. The urge to breathe was overwhelming, threatening to become an instinctive action. He was beginning to suffer and prayed he didn't have to for much longer. He felt his lungs attempting to inhale by reflex. Even though it was dark, he was aware of tunnel vision as his peripheral view became glittery. His brain was being starved of oxygen.

When he began to see the lights, he knew he was nearly there.

They were quite faint at first and became brighter as he descended further. Furiously, he pulled himself down to the anchor. There were four lights – two blue, one green and one yellow – fluorescent Cylume sticks that he had put in place the previous evening. He coughed once as his lungs finally gave up the fight. At that instant, he reached out to the yellow light and pulled it towards him. He stuck the Demand Valve from the sub aqua equipment into his mouth, pressed the purge-button to clear the water out of it and breathed in beautiful, dry, life-giving air. The vision returned instantly. Pulling on the green light he quickly fitted the weights belt round his waist to prevent him rising. He settled to the floor and cleared his ears. He felt for the mask attached to the air tank, pulled it over his face and, holding his head up, exhaled through his nose, clearing the water from the mask and improving his vision a little in the murky water. When his breathing had settled, he lifted the breathing apparatus onto his shoulders. He had two air tanks, which would give him about forty minutes. He pulled the fins onto his feet and set off to the west, out to sea, following a thin rope with a powerful torch, more by feel than by sight.

He made slow progress, getting deeper as he headed out to sea. After about fifteen minutes of hard finning, he judged himself to be past the headland. The rope turned to the north-west and he kept finning for another twenty minutes, getting deeper all the time. He could hear the throbbing of the fishing boat and saw the silhouette of its hull, with the screws turning slowly as the boat maintained station. The rope stopped by the boat's anchor and he began to rise up the chain, waiting for several minutes at a depth of five metres to avoid decompression sickness. He surfaced on the starboard side of the boat and banged on the hull.

'Bloody hell, you're early, mate,' said the skipper.

The crew hauled Taverner aboard and took him down below to warm up. The vessel set sail to the north, along the coast towards the Bristol Channel. They were in the docks in Bristol by the early afternoon. The freighter departed for Mexico at dusk, carrying among other things, several thousand tonnes of scrap-metal and a renegade former British Army Officer who offered a large sum of money in return for a discreet passage west. He was in the Bahamas just over two weeks later.

'They can't trace you here, can they?' said Hannah.

'No,' said Taverner. 'They think I'm dead.'

A letter had been delivered to his parents' house from the Archipelago Consulate, informing them that their son was 'Missing, presumed drowned'.

'I didn't leave much of a trail,' he told Hannah. 'And even if they did find out the truth, I doubt they'd bother with extradition. We gave them a bloody nose, but they won in the end. They won't want to be reminded of their humiliation.'

Taverner looked out to sea, where some plutocrat's vast gin-palace was anchored. A small launch was making its way from the yacht, carrying a group of fat men and laughing girls, presumably for more tax-free shopping in the boutiques and emporiums of the town that lay further along the coast.

It was highly likely that some smart aleck would figure it out, he thought. They had no body, and the fishing boat's movements around the North Devon coast and the Bristol Channel would have been registered and automatically filed away somewhere. The freighter's departure for Mexico would have been recorded too. Maybe they had already made the connection, and 'Mr Smith' and his goons were, at that very moment, in their bunker deep underneath Whitehall, watching live hi-resolution satellite images of him lying on a tropical beach having suncream rubbed into his back. He waved to an imaginary satellite passing overhead.

'And you should know better, Mr Action Man, putting me through that,' said Hannah, her voice shaking slightly. She went quiet for a while and stroked his hair.

'You're a sod, Charlie. I really thought I'd never see you again. Are they all dead?'

'Probably.'

Taverner had been trying to find out just what had happened to the 65th in its final moments, but details were very sketchy. The 65th had gone the way it had wanted. Heroically. It had refused to cave in to a much bigger and incompetent bully; left it humiliated and provoked it into overkill. The tragedy was perhaps not so much that the regiment was gone, but that the victors would ensure there would be no true historic record of its final valiant hours.

Perhaps a sergeant led his soldiers in a hopeless manoeuvre to out-flank an enemy platoon so that his boys might survive for another few minutes, and a blinded gunner fought on alongside his mates, oblivious to his mortal wounds. Maybe Lieutenant Skeffington barricaded himself in the Mess cellar, desperately quaffing the last of the '82 Chateau Margaux, lest it be captured and wasted on the vulgarians, while upstairs Major Hesketh performed the *coup de grâce* on the Mess silver with his side-arm.

It would be as though none of it had ever happened. The British government would not allow such traitors to have a grave or a memorial.

Taverner did not entertain any illusion that anyone might have escaped from the base, and wondered what had happened to those who had helped him in Holberton. He hoped that they had died. Death was indeed preferable to the living hell of being a permanent guest of the Interior Ministry.

Hannah fell asleep on his chest, and he drifted off too, grateful to be alive and free in such a beautiful place.

When they woke, the sun was lower in the sky and the wind had dropped off. Hannah collected her robe and went back to the house to bathe and change for dinner. Taverner looked at his watch. Daiquiris on the veranda at seven. He had just enough time, and picked up his surfboard.

A rangy, grey-haired man in sunglasses and a linen suit was walking along the beach. The man's face was quite red; a little sunburnt, clearly a recent arrival to these parts, thought Taverner, who ignored him and tied the surfboard's leash to his ankle.

'Good afternoon,' said the man, 'do you know of any good Chinese takeaways round here?'

Taverner spun round. It was 'Mr Smith'. Same voice. The same man he'd stood next to at ERDF Headquarters;

the one who had hunted him down and waited for him on the rocks. Taverner might have dropped him with a sharp blow from the edge of his surfboard, but there was something in the man's voice, something in his posture, that told Taverner he was not in any danger.

'Relax, Charlie,' said the man, showing his empty palms to Taverner. 'You're alright. I'm not here to take you back.' He shook his head. 'I'm out of it now.'

Taverner did not take his eyes off him.

'You see, I caught up with you eventually. I never fail,' said the man. 'You know you lost me my job, don't you?'

'But I'm sure you'll understand if I don't apologise,' said Taverner.

'Of course. Well done, Charlie, you were the first one ever to get away from me.'

'By the looks of things, I'm not so sure that I did.'

'I always get my man. However, with you, I was a bit too late. That not only cost me my job, but for someone in my position, my home and family too.'

'If you don't mind me saying,' said Taverner, 'you don't look like you're doing too badly for it. Your suit is bespoke and I doubt there are many former civil servants who could afford a wristwatch like that. Very nice.'

'I have a new employer.'

'Who?'

The man nodded towards the yacht out at sea.

'Him,' he said. 'Elkhan Khassanov, a Caspian billionaire. He's a moral degenerate, admittedly, but has a damn sight more courage and integrity than my former employers. There are many people who are keen to see Mr Khassanov dead, and he likes to know where they can be found and, occasionally, what they know. The pay's better, the weather's better, and as for the girls …'

'How long have you been following me?' said Taverner.

The man laughed. 'All the way to this very spot! I got back on your trail at the docks at Bristol even before you'd boarded that freighter. Luckily for you, everyone else had their attention focused on Heathrow airport. They practically closed it down. Why they were looking for you there, well, I wouldn't like to say.'

Both of them looked out to sea for a time before Taverner spoke.

'Why did you do it?' he said. 'Why did you let me go?'

'Shall we call it professional courtesy? And the chance to screw those arse-covering tossers in the government. I was their fall-guy from the very first moment we lost you. As we say in my profession, *shit flows downhill*, and my shoulders have been very wide for too long. Perhaps it was time for a change, anyway. Did you know that every piece of national surveillance data for the day you disappeared under the waves was somehow deleted? The fishing boat, your movements at the docks, the freighter. All erased, along with everything else.'

'You did that to cover my tracks?'

'No, Charlie!' said the man, laughing heavily, 'I did that to cover my own!'

Taverner stood there, stunned.

'I was out of the country a few hours after you were,' said the man. 'There was no point in staying behind to face the music and I had no intention of giving them the satisfaction of sending me beyond the wire. Charlie, you're quite safe here, trust me. I'm the one they're now after. They know who it was that pressed the Delete key, and only people like Mr Khassanov can offer the level of protection I need.'

'So why did you *really* come here?'

'I simply came to find you. Like I said, I always find my man, and from now on I shall sleep better at night. Now, if you'd please excuse me I must be getting back. If ever you find yourself getting bored with all this,' he said, gesturing at the scenery, 'give me a call.'

He handed over an embossed business card.

Taverner watched him walk away along the beach and looked at the card.

Pyotr Smith, Security Consultant

Taverner put the card carefully underneath his towel, and paddled out on his surfboard to catch the last of the evening glass-off.

AUTHOR'S NOTES

The locations used in The 65th are genuine, with the exception of Holberton, Windcheater Island and (fleetingly) Chesterford, which are entirely fictional. The military base at Chivenor in North Devon on the Taw Estuary may seem to resemble Windcheater Island in many ways; the layout of Windcheater Island is, in fact, closely modelled on another coastal base elsewhere in England.

The 65th Regiment Royal Horse Artillery has never actually existed.

For more information, or to contact the author, please visit his website: www.the65th.co.uk

ACKNOWLEDGEMENTS

The 65th, thanks largely to my woeful lack of organisation, spent most of its formative years scattered in numerous segments on lost USB sticks, on hard-drives that crashed, and on scraps of paper that inadvertently ended up in the recycling. I even managed to leave some of it behind in New Zealand, and it is probably still there to this day. That The 65th ever made it into print proves the age of miracles is not dead; this was only possible because of the following people, to whom I am indebted: Janet A'Lee, Sophie Anderson, Alistair Deighton-Gibson, Tim Dyke, Rory Findlay, Peter and Jenny Gordon, Jenny Griffiths, John and Tori Griffiths, Trevor Henderson, Sara McGeever, Fiona Mundy, Christine Mundy, Elliot Prior, Lorna Studholme, Ollie Thom, Rob Turner, Emma Webb, Tom Wilks, John Wilson, Yan Yates, my two brothers Andrew and John (thanks for the website!) and, most importantly, my mother, Valerie Chapman, for her love and support.

Peter Chapman
Devon, 2009